Laurie Kingery

and

USA TODAY Bestselling Author

Judy Duarte

The Rancher's Courtship

&

Lone Wolf's Lady

LOVE INSPIRED

INSPIRATIONAL ROMANCE

LOVE INSPIRED®

INSPIRATIONAL ROMANCE

Recycling programs
for this product may
not exist in your area.

ISBN-13: 978-1-335-44875-0

The Rancher's Courtship & Lone Wolf's Lady

Copyright © 2021 by Harlequin Books S.A.

The Rancher's Courtship
First published in 2011. This edition published in 2021.
Copyright © 2011 by Laurie A. Kingery

Lone Wolf's Lady
First published in 2014. This edition published in 2021.
Copyright © 2014 by Judy Duarte

This edition published by arrangement with Harlequin Books S.A.

For questions and comments about the quality of this book,
please contact us at CustomerService@Harlequin.com.

Love Inspired
22 Adelaide St. West, 40th Floor
Toronto, Ontario M5H 4E3, Canada
www.Harlequin.com

Printed in U.S.A.

CONTENTS

Laurie Kingery is a Texas transplant to Ohio who writes romance set in post–Civil War Texas. She was nominated for a Carol Award for her second Love Inspired Historical novel, *The Outlaw's Lady*, and has written a series about mail-order grooms in a small town in the Texas Hill Country.

Visit the Author Profile page
at Harlequin.com for more titles.

THE RANCHER'S
COURTSHIP

Laurie Kingery

And they said, Let us rise up and build. So they strengthened their hands for this good work.
—*Nehemiah* 2:18

To Stephanie, the teacher in our family,
in honor of the teachers who had only
one-room schoolhouses to teach in.

To Susan Alverson, who helped me through the
rough patches and was always there to listen.

And always, to Tom.

Chapter One

Simpson Creek, Texas
October 1868

Jack Collier looked up and down the main street of the little town of Simpson Creek, but try as he might, he didn't see a druggist's store. A hotel, a mercantile, a post office, a combined barbershop-bathhouse, a jail, a bank, a doctor's office and a church, yes, but no druggist's shop. A search of the side streets and Travis Street, which ran parallel to Main Street, netted the same lack of results.

He'd been the recipient of several second looks by the townspeople, as he rode down the streets, his own horse flanked by the dependable old cow pony that didn't mind his twin daughters riding double on it. People tended to stare at twins, and yet it seemed to be his own face they focused on, not Abigail's and Amelia's.

Well, he'd always been told he looked a lot like Pete, so that must be the reason for the stares. He started to ask one or two of them if they knew where to find his brother, but he had wanted his arrival to be a surprise for Pete. He didn't want anyone running ahead of him with the news.

But where was Pete? Had he gone into some other line of work since he'd last written Jack? It was possible, Jack supposed, but it wasn't like Pete to change his mind on such a matter. Pete had always set a course, then held to it. He'd traveled up to the Hill Country town in San Saba County last year with the announced goals of meeting the lady he'd been corresponding with and opening up his own druggist's shop. Around Christmas, Pete had written that he and Miss Caroline Wallace were in love and would be married in early spring. He wanted Jack to be there.

That was the last time he'd heard from Pete—no letter, no wedding invite had followed.

Mail went astray all the time, though. He and his daughters had probably missed the wedding, but Jack had assumed he'd find Collier's Drugs and Patent Medicines prospering, with his happily married brother as the proprietor. Pete and his bride would have a little house on one of these side streets, no doubt with a picket fence around it and the smell of freshly baked bread wafting from the kitchen.

"When are we gonna find Uncle Pete, Papa?" queried his daughter Amelia, clutching a china-headed doll to her chest.

"Yeah, and Aunt Caroline?" her twin sister, Abigail, piped up from behind her. "Did they go someplace else?"

Jack rubbed his chin and considered the matter. "I don't know, girls, but I'm sure enough going to find out."

After riding up Travis Street, they'd passed the

churchyard and headed back onto Main Street, but now he paused by the jail to look around him, wondering where the best place to make inquiries would be.

"Can I help you, mister?"

Jack looked down to see a lanky Mexican youth with black hair and dark eyes looking up at him from beside the open door of the jail. He wore a five-pointed star that had "Deputy" inscribed across its middle.

The sheriff ought to know where to find any of the small town's inhabitants, Jack reckoned. "Is the sheriff in, Deputy?"

"Sheriff Bishop is away for a few days, sir. I'm Deputy Luis Menendez—perhaps I may help you?" The last part was said with courteous pride.

"I hope so. We're looking for Peter Collier and his wife, Caroline. He's my brother. He was supposed to have started a druggist's shop here in Simpson Creek, but I don't see one, so maybe his plans changed. Would you know where they live?"

The young man's brow furrowed, and something troubled shone in the obsidian depths of his eyes. "Miss Caroline is the schoolteacher. Perhaps it is best you speak to her."

"Miss Caroline?" What in thunder? Had Caroline and Pete had a falling-out and never married? Had Pete left Simpson Creek? Why hadn't he written Jack about it? Jack had made plans based on what Pete had told him, and if the marriage was off and Pete had gone elsewhere, Jack was going to find himself in a right pickle.

He was conscious of the youth still studying him, a hand shading his eyes from the bright sun. "May I direct you to the schoolhouse, Mr. Collier?"

Jack shook his head, "No, we passed it a while back, while we were looking for his shop, so I know where it is. Thanks."

The rapping at the door startled Caroline. Who could it be? Her pupils were all present and accounted for—two dozen in number and ranging from first to sixth-graders. Now they all raised their heads from the slates on which they were working sums and looked behind them. No one in Simpson Creek would think of knocking on the door of the one-room schoolhouse. If they had to interrupt the schoolmarm during class, they'd likely just barge right in and explain their business.

When the knock quickly sounded again, as if whoever stood outside had grown impatient, Lizzie raised her hand. "Miss Wallace, do you want me to see who's there?"

"No, thank you, Lizzie. I'll do it. Please continue your work." Rising, Caroline left her desk, walked down the aisle that separated the girls from the boys and went to the door. She hoped whoever it was wouldn't stay long. It was hard enough to keep her students working on arithmetic in the last hour of the school day, even without interruptions. Most of them were fidgeting, staring longingly out the one-room schoolhouse's open window to where fall sunshine beckoned. When would she learn to drill them in mathematics in the morning, when they were still fresh? But she'd only been the schoolteacher for a month, having taken on the job when Miss Phelps left.

She opened the door to see two little girls standing on the uppermost step. They were as alike as two peas in a pod, both dark-haired and blue-eyed, each one's hair done in two thick braids with red bows at the end, their dresses blue gingham with white pinafores. Each clutched a doll with a dress that matched what its owner wore.

Beyond them she could see a man with his back to her, securing the second of two horses to the hitching rail next to the mule a pair of her students rode to school.

"Them girls is *exactly the same*," breathed Lizzie, peeking around her teacher from behind.

"*Those* girls *are* exactly the same," Caroline corrected automatically. "Please go back to your seat, Lizzie."

"Ain't you ever seen twins before, Lizzie Halliday?" one of the boys hooted scornfully.

"*Haven't* you," Caroline corrected again. "Class, be quiet while I speak to their father." She could only guess the man was here to register his daughters, though why he'd come in the afternoon, rather than first thing in the morning, she couldn't imagine—nor why a father would be bringing the children, rather than their mother. A closer look at the girls' dresses revealed a smudge on the hem of one, a rip in the sleeve of the other. Maybe their mother was ill? Or…well. Perhaps there was no mother anymore.

The two girls smiled in unison at her, and Caroline felt an instant liking for them. Already mentally rearranging the seating chart to accommodate two more students while the man was turning from the hitching rail, she now focused on his face.

And blinked. And stared, as he climbed the steps and came closer.

Like his daughters, the man had blue eyes and black hair, but the eyes that studied her were so like Pete's eyes—Peter Collier, her fiancé, who had died in the influenza epidemic last winter, and for whom she still wore mourning black. The mouth that now narrowed reminded her of Pete's mouth, a mouth that had kissed her many times, and would never do so again.

Oh, no, she was doing it again. Right after Pete had died, she had frequently seen his face in that of strangers passing through town, and her heart would give a little happy leap before her brain realized it was not Pete. *Yes, that must be the case. I only think the man looks like Pete. The resemblance will fade in a moment, as it always has before. It isn't real. Pete's brother would have come long ago, if he was going to.*

"You're Miss Caroline Wallace? I was told I would find her here," the man said. Absently she noted that while his voice was similar, it didn't have Pete's exact cadence. Pete always said what he meant right out. This man's voice was deeper and had more of a considering drawl to it.

He continued to study her as if he found her black dress mystifying—had he never seen mourning clothes before?

"Please, come in," she said, gesturing. "You have children to enroll, sir?" she asked, with a meaningful look at them.

They did as she had bidden, stepping into the back of the classroom. The man opened his mouth to say something, but before he could reply to her question, one of his twins asked, "Are you our Aunt Caroline? And where's Uncle Pete?"

Caroline felt her jaw drop and her heart begin to pound as she raised her gaze from the little girl to her father.

"I'm Caroline Wallace," she said slowly, realizing

that she had guessed correctly to begin with. "And you are—?"

The man's gaze narrowed. "Jack Collier, Pete's brother. These are my daughters, Amelia and Abigail. Aren't you supposed to be 'Mrs. Collier' by now? *Where's Pete?*"

She felt the color drain from her face and leave a coating of ice behind. *It couldn't really be happening. Pete's brother couldn't have shown up now, unaware his brother was dead, some seven months after Pete's funeral.*

But thinking it could not be so didn't make it any the less true, and she realized with panic she would have to be the one to break the news to him. She wondered who had told him how to find her, yet had not mentioned his brother was dead.

Determined not to tell him about Pete in front of the two bright-eyed children staring curiously at her—not to mention all the other children eyeing them with avid interest—she forced herself to speak normally.

"Why don't we let your daughters play outside with the other children for a few minutes?" she suggested.

He gave a curt nod by way of permission, his eyes still narrowed, and she bent to speak to Lizzie, whose desk was nearby. "Lizzie, will you take Amelia and Abigail with you and introduce them to the other girls? Let them play with you?"

"Yes, Miss Wallace. Are they gonna come t' school with us?"

"We'll see." In a louder voice she said, "Class, we'll take a fifteen-minute recess." The boys didn't hesitate, scrambling out of their seats and out the door almost before she finished speaking, as if fearing their new schoolmarm would change her mind. The girls were a bit slower but, clustering around the twins, made their way out the door just as happily.

Caroline turned back to the suspicious-eyed man waiting by her desk and took a deep breath.

"Please, Mr. Collier, won't you sit down?" she said and took her place behind the shelter of her desk.

Jack Collier stared at the small desks that sat in neat rows behind him. There were larger desks for the older students, but these were at the back of the room, and his long legs still wouldn't have fit under them. But at last he settled for sitting on top of one of the front desks, though he dwarfed it.

"Where's my brother?" Jack Collier demanded again. "Why are you wearing black?" His questions came like rapidly fired bullets, but his eyes, those eyes so like Pete's, gave away his fear of her answer.

Lord, help me to tell him with compassion, she prayed.

"I'm sorry to tell you this, Mr. Collier, but your brother Peter passed away this last winter—" she paused when she heard his sharp intake of breath "—during an influenza epidemic."

She didn't dare look at him as he absorbed this news and sensed rather than saw him rock back on the small desktop as if he'd been struck a physical blow.

"Pete's...*dead?*" he murmured, his hoarse voice hardly above a whisper. "But...that's impossible. I got his letter...saying he was going to be married to the woman he met from...'the Spinsters' Club,' he called it, this spring. In March. That was you he was marrying, wasn't it? When I didn't hear anything more, the girls and I just came ahead, figuring the invite got lost in the mail or something... I figured we missed the wedding, but we'd find you and Pete all settled in together…. *Why didn't you let me know?*"

The last question was flung at her like a fist, but she heard the piercing loss contained in it.

Caroline had left her hands in her lap below the level of the desk, and now they clutched at one another so he wouldn't see them shake. She let her gaze drop, unable to face the raw grief she'd glimpsed in his face, the mingled astonishment and fury stabbing at her from those too-familiar blue eyes. She felt a tear escape down her cheek, and she swept it away with a trembling hand.

"I—I'm sorry, Mr. Collier. I did try. When it…became apparent that Pete was sinking, I tried to ask him your address… He had it memorized, you see, not written down anywhere. But he was delirious, and… I—I'm afraid I wasn't able to get it from him before…before he d-died." She grabbed the black-edged handkerchief she kept always within reach in her pocket and, after dabbing at her eyes, took a deep breath. "I…tried to write you," she said. "I couldn't remember the name of your ranch, only that it was in Goliad County, so I addressed it General Delivery to Goliad. I… I guess it didn't find you. I'm very sorry about that, but… I didn't know what else to do. Pete said you were his only living relative—relatives," she amended, to include his daughters. Pete had mentioned that his brother was a widower and had a couple of daughters, but after her only attempt to contact them had borne no fruit, she had been too weighed down with sorrow to spare them another thought.

"What am I going to do now?" Jack Collier wondered aloud as if talking to himself, his voice raspy.

She lifted her eyes to his again. "I… I'm sorry you've come all this way, only to hear such awful news… I'm sure Mama and Papa would be glad to put you up until you feel able to return home." Her mind raced ahead. She could dismiss school early and have him follow her to the little house behind the post office where she, her brother and her parents lived. She would explain to them what had happened. Mr. Collier could sleep on the summer porch with his daughters.

"No," he muttered.

She thought he was being polite, not wanting to put them to any inconvenience since his visit had been unexpected. "Oh, it's no trouble," she assured him kindly, "and it's the least we can do for Pete's only family…"

"No, you don't understand," Jack Collier told her, his face haggard. "I can't go back. I—I sold my ranch. I'm on the way to Montana Territory with a herd of cattle, and I thought I could leave the girls here with you and Pete until I got settled up there…." His voice trailed off, and he looked away, but not before she saw the utter misery in his eyes.

She was distracted by it for only a moment until she was able to process what he had said.

"You thought… You were planning…to leave your daughters with us, with Pete and me? *While you went on to Montana with your herd?*" She repeated his words, as if merely asking for clarification, while inside, the effrontery of it took her breath away. He'd thought he could leave two children with his newly wed brother without so much as a word of warning, without writing to ask if it would be all right with Pete and, more importantly, with Pete's bride?

"Yes, I'm going up there to join a couple of partners of mine who bought ranch land. I figured I'd find a nice lady there to marry so the girls could have a new mama, and then I'd send for them…or come back and fetch them." He looked away, focusing on a portrait of Washington that hung on the wall as if George might have the answers.

"But…from what I understand, at least…the snow will be flying before you get halfway there, won't it?" She wasn't a cattleman's daughter, but anyone knew moving a herd of the stubborn, cantankerous critters was no quick proposition—and a potentially dangerous one, at this time of year.

He shrugged, looking uncomfortable—as well he might, she thought, at announcing such a foolhardy notion.

"We got a late start, and that's a fact," he admitted. "I was going to wait to sell the ranch early next year, but… well, let's just say I got an offer that was too good to pass up, so we rounded up the herd and left. Then halfway here my ramrod—my second-in-command, that is—got himself all into some uh…legal trouble, and there was no way I was just going to abandon him and move on. We had to wait till his name was cleared…so we figured we'd winter in Nebraska, then travel on in the spring."

Caroline felt her jaw tightening and the beginnings of a headache throb at her temples. The muddle-headed, half-baked plans men came up with! Now she was angry, and though she was normally a circumspect and thoughtful woman, she was so upset and overwrought over meeting Jack and talking about Pete that her bitter feelings came tumbling out of her mouth.

"You assumed you could dump your children with Pete and me like a couple of sacks of flour, without even writing to ask first? If you had, you would have found out then that Pete had died!"

Chapter Two

His jaw dropped open, and she knew she should have stopped right there, but her emotions were out of control. She'd endured months of well-meaning people saying she had to go on living. "Pete would have wanted you to. After all, you weren't married, only engaged," they'd said. It had stoppered the grief inside her, and now grief, combined with anger and aggravation flooded out like a suddenly unbottled explosive mixture. Tears stung her eyes, but she refused to cry in front of this man.

Instead, she stabbed a finger at him in accusation. "And you assume decent women grow on trees up in that wild country, just waiting for handsome cowboys like yourself to come along and pluck them off the branches?" He *was* handsome, she had to admit, even more so than Pete had been. If she'd never met Pete, she would have found him very attractive indeed. But that didn't mean she wasn't furious at him.

And he with her, apparently. She saw the fire kindle in those blue eyes, those eyes so like Pete's, though she'd never seen Pete's eyes look quite like *that*. She and Pete had never exchanged so much as a cross word.

In fact, she couldn't remember ever yelling at anyone like that in all her life. In her heart, she knew she wasn't being fair to the man who had only learned of his brother's death moments ago, but how good it felt to finally *say* what she was thinking after months of biting her tongue and forcing herself to smile and thank people for their kind words of condolence when all she'd wanted to do was scream that it wasn't fair. It would *never* be fair that she'd had to lose the man she loved. She couldn't yell at Pete for leaving her—he wasn't there to be yelled at. But his brother was. His brother who wasn't even *listening* to her. Instead he stared fixedly at her left hand.

"What—what's wrong?" she asked, mystified.

"Mama's pearl ring," he rasped, pointing at the ring Pete had given her when they'd become engaged, still on her left ring finger.

She followed his gaze, and her anger was doused in shock. "Pete gave it to me when he asked me to marry him." She raised her eyes to his, wondering what he was thinking. *Did he believe she had no right to it anymore because Pete was dead? That must be it.*

"Please…it's all I have left, now that he's gone…"

He said nothing, just stared at her as if trying to think what to say, and she became even more sure she had guessed right. He just didn't know a polite way to ask for it back.

She wrenched it off her finger and held it out to him, feeling the tears escape down her cheeks, but powerless to stop them. "Here…take it. It properly belongs to you now, to keep for your girls…"

* * *

He stared at the gold band with its beautiful pearl while her last words echoed in his ears—*to keep for your girls.*

He was not now and hoped he never would be so low as to take such a thing from a bereaved woman. And Caroline Wallace *was* bereaved, he realized, just as he was. The fact that she was still wearing black and the haunted look in her pretty brown eyes told him this beautiful woman was still grieving for his brother.

He forgot that he was still stinging from her scorn and started to say something, but the realization that they were both sorrowing over Pete tangled the words in his throat. So he shook his head and took a step back.

His tacit refusal, however, seemed to make things worse.

"Take it, I said!" She held out the ring again. "You can keep it for some woman you haven't even met yet!" And then she hurled it at him.

The ring bounced off Jack's chest and fell to the floor with a *clink*. He bent and retrieved it, hesitated for a moment, then pocketed it as he straightened to face her. He'd give it back to her later, when she'd calmed down. Even though the disdainful things she had said to him moments ago still hurt, he should have been quicker to say that she could keep the ring with his blessing. That he understood why she'd want to have this symbol of the love his brother had felt for her.

Shocked by the unexpected news of Pete's death, he had just blurted out his plans, and she had shown him with a few contemptuous words just how ill-considered they appeared. Caroline Wallace's derision made him feel like a silly boy still wet behind the ears. She'd looked at him as if he'd tracked cow manure into her school-room.

It was a cinch she'd never looked at Pete that way. Pete had always been the polished one, the one who'd excelled at book learning. No doubt a lady like Caroline Wallace had valued those qualities.

"We'll be going, ma'am, me and the girls," he said, determined not to say anything else he'd be sorry for later.

"Going? Where?" Caroline asked, sounding dazed.

"On to Montana."

"But…but you can't take those two little girls to that unsettled country up there! Why, there are Indians in Montana, I've heard! And bears, and mountain lions."

"Last *I* heard, you had Comanches around here, too," he retorted. "And cougars. And rattlesnakes."

"And blizzards, and wolves," she went on, as if he hadn't spoken. "You can't possibly be thinking of taking two helpless children into such a situation."

"The girls and I will do just fine, but thanks for your concern, Miss Wallace." He bit out the words. "Sorry to have troubled you." He turned on his heel, hoping he could postpone any explanation to Abigail and Amelia until they were away from her.

He reached the door before she caught up and tugged on his sleeve.

"Please, Mr. Collier, wait a moment."

He turned around and beheld her whitened face, the tears still shining on her cheeks.

"I—I'm sorry. I was unforgivably rude, but I hope you'll reconsider leaving just now. It's already mid-afternoon, and—"

He took out the pocket watch that had been a gift to

him from his mother, who, unlike their father, hadn't played favorites between the two boys. "It's only two o'clock. Plenty of time to make tracks up the road and rid you of our troublesome presence." Then he realized how sarcastic he had been, for he saw pain flash across her face.

"Yes, it's only two o'clock, but if you're heading north, the next town is quite a piece up the road on the other side of the Colorado River."

"Who needs a town? We've been camping out with the herd since we left south Texas. I left the cattle south of town, grazing by the creek. My drovers are there, but we should get back to them." In actuality, his men were not expecting him to return before morning, but Caroline Wallace didn't need to know that.

He could leave the ring at the post office. He remembered Pete telling him her father was postmaster.

"I—I've given you the worst of news. You can't just leave, after that. Please, allow me to apologize, and again, offer you a place for the night at our house. Mama and Papa would want to meet you and your daughters— they would have been their grandnieces..."

If Pete had lived to marry her. "No, thanks," he said and strode out the door. He spotted the twins not far away, each holding one end of a jump rope while a third girl jumped it. It looked as if they'd been readily accepted by the other girls and were having a great time.

He beckoned to them. "Abby, Amelia, come with me." He watched as they bid quick farewells to their new playmates, snatched up their dolls and ran to him. "We'll leave the horses here for now." With any luck, Miss Wallace would be gone by the time they returned for them.

"Are we going to Uncle Pete's house now?" Abby asked.

"Where does he live?" Amelia chimed in, as they fell into step with him.

In Heaven, he thought, but aloud he said, "There's been a change of plans, girls. Let's walk along the creek and I'll tell you about it." He wanted to get away from the schoolyard, in case Caroline Wallace was watching from the schoolhouse window. The girls walked along with him quietly, taking their cue from his solemn demeanor.

The creek for which the town had been named was lined with cottonwood and live oak trees. It wasn't wide—a man on horseback could splash or swim across it in a moment, depending on the time of year, but it was pretty, flowing lazily past them. He saw a fish jump after a dragonfly and regretted for a moment that he wouldn't be here long enough to bring a cane pole and try his luck.

He paused when he found an inviting grassy bank and invited them to sit down with him.

"Miss Wallace told me some bad news, girls," he began, when they were settled on either side of him.

They looked up at him, their faces serious, wary. "You mean Aunt Caroline?" Amelia asked.

He didn't correct her, just nodded. They'd realize Miss Caroline Wallace was never going to be their aunt quickly enough. *Best to get it over with—there was no way to soften the blow.* "Miss Wallace told me that Uncle Pete became very sick this winter, and they couldn't make him well again. He…he passed away, girls. He went to Heaven."

Two identical shocked faces stared up at him, open-mouthed.

"He—he died, Papa? Uncle Pete died? Like Mama?"

Abby asked, her voice breaking as a tear began to slide down her cheek. Beside her, Amelia had closed her eyes and sagged against her twin, whimpering.

He nodded, pulling them both against him, and for a few minutes he just held them while they sobbed. He let a few of his own tears trickle into their soft hair, knowing they would never notice in the midst of their crying, but he was careful not to lose control for fear of frightening them. They had only seen him weep when their mother died, but that had been almost three years ago and he thought they had probably been too young then to remember it.

A man couldn't have asked for a better brother than Pete, Jack thought. He'd been Jack's best friend, his playmate, his confidant—and his defender when Pa had taken out his frustrations on Jack. It hadn't been Pete's fault he was smarter, and he'd never rubbed Jack's nose in it, never flaunted it. He'd thought it only fitting when Jack had inherited the ranch.

"So now where are we going to stay while you go to Montana to find us a new mama?" Amelia asked, knuckling the remains of her tears away. She was always the more direct one of the two.

"I think we should still stay with Aunt Caroline," Abby said. She was the twin who made decisions quickly. Amelia was more wary and liked to consider all sides of a question.

Did her reply mean she'd liked Miss Wallace instantly or only that Abby had gotten used to the idea of staying with her uncle and his bride during the journey from south Texas? When he'd first told them of his plan to move to Montana, and they'd been ignorant of the rigors of a trail drive, they'd been upset that they wouldn't be coming along, but joining him in Montana later. He'd talked up how happy they'd be with their uncle and aunt until the girls had started to sound excited about Simpson Creek and the family they'd find there.

He'd have to tread carefully now so as not to let on that he and Miss Caroline had had sharp words.

"What would you say, Abby, if I told you I've decided to take you two with me after all?" He'd keep them safe, he told himself. Other settlers had taken families with them to Montana Territory. It was a tough, dangerous journey, and even more so with a thousand head of unpredictable longhorns, but what choice did he have now that he couldn't leave them with Pete and his bride? He'd be there to protect them. Surely they'd be all right if they rode in the chuck wagon, even though Cookie was a cranky, irascible old coot given to colorful language.

Identical faces turned identically stormy.

"Do we have to go with those nasty ol' cows?" Abby asked, her voice dangerously close to a whine.

"Well, yes, we—I—have to stay with the herd," he said, dismayed at their reaction, but knowing his daughters couldn't appreciate the profit he'd make by driving cattle to hungry miners yearning for beef.

Abby and Amelia hadn't complained much before this, once they'd gotten used to the ever-present dust and the brutally long days of slow progress northward. But apparently they'd been holding it in since they'd only had to put up with it till they reached Uncle Pete's house.

"I don't like sleeping on the hard ground, Papa," Amelia said, lower lip jutting out.

What kind of father subjected little girls to sleeping outside in all kinds of weather? He could practically hear Caroline—or his father—asking the scornful question.

"But we'll be together—you won't have to wait till I send for you," he said, hoping that would mollify them. After the shock of hearing Pete was dead, Jack didn't have the heart to say he was their papa and they'd do as they were told. Then he remembered he wasn't expected back to the herd till morning. "How about a special treat tonight, girls? We'll stay at the hotel here, then rejoin the herd tomorrow."

Amelia and Abby's faces brightened somewhat. "With real beds and real food, Papa?" Amelia asked.

"Well, don't let Cookie hear you saying that he hasn't been serving you real food, Punkin. But yes, real food—maybe even *fried* chicken." A diet of beans and corn bread and beef got old fast, especially to a child.

Something like a real grin spread across Abby's face. "I *love* fried chicken, Papa."

"All right then, let's go." He rose and gestured for them to follow.

"But…but what about Aunt Caroline, Papa? She's sad, isn't she? And she'll be sadder if we leave," Amelia said as she got to her feet.

She's sad, isn't she? An image of Caroline Wallace's tearful face rose unbidden in his mind. She had wept because she'd thought she had been rude—and her tears had moved him a lot more than he was comfortable with. He had been surprised by his urge to comfort her, in spite of the harsh words they'd just exchanged. He'd wanted to comfort his brother's—what?—almost-widow?

Amelia's question was an awkward one. It would be heartless to tell them she wasn't really their aunt, so they had no reason to ever see her again.

"Yes, she's been sad for a while now, since Uncle

Pete died last winter, but she understands why we have to go on to Montana."

A few paces later, Abby said, "The fellows'll be surprised to see us when we go back in the morning."

Jack tried to suppress a flinch. His drovers wouldn't be surprised in a good way. They'd endured the presence of his girls with good grace, knowing it was temporary, but it had meant they'd had to be ultracareful about their language and their actions. Children had no place on a cattle drive. The men would think their boss had gone loco when he returned with them, but it was his herd, and they were his employees. Knowing he had no choice, they'd have to respect his decision, even though they wouldn't like it—or leave his employ.

"Come on, girls," he said, rising and heading down Main Street toward the hotel.

But the hotel had no rooms available, having rented them out to folks in town for a funeral. The clerk referred him to the boardinghouse behind it.

When they arrived at Mrs. Meyer's establishment, though, the tall, bony proprietress informed him she only had one cot to spare, and it would mean sharing a room with her aged father. Obviously that wouldn't work for the three of them.

It was starting to look as if returning to the herd tonight was their only option. But the day had been overcast, and now the clouds were looking distinctly threatening. Rain was coming. The girls hadn't noticed yet, but they would soon, and Abby was frightened by storms.

"I still think we should stay at Miss Caroline's house," Abby announced.

"Yeah, Papa. After all, we were going to stay with her

and Uncle Pete while you were gone, anyway. I'm sure she wouldn't mind if you stayed there, too."

When pigs fly, he thought. She'd apologized for her heated reaction and politely offered them lodging, but he was sure she was relieved he hadn't taken her up on it. He'd be about as welcome under that woman's roof as fire ants at a picnic.

"Girls, Miss Caroline doesn't have a house of her own, since Uncle Pete died. She lives with her parents. I—I'm not sure there'd be room," he said, feeling guilty because Caroline *had* invited them, so there must be room enough.

Amelia shrugged, as if to say, *So?*

Then thunder rumbled overhead, and Abby cast a fearful eye upward. "Papa, it's going to rain," she said uneasily. "Can we ask her, *please?*"

It was the last word, desperately uttered, as if she was fighting tears again, that did in his resolve. Lucinda, their mother, had died during a thunderstorm, and though his daughter didn't realize that was the source of her fear, Jack knew it, and he knew he was going to have to do the very thing he least wanted to do—swallow his pride, go back and take Caroline up on her offer.

He sighed. "All right, I suppose it wouldn't hurt to ask," he said, and they walked down Simpson Creek's Main Street back toward the school again.

Caroline had just seen her last pupil, Billy Joe Henderson, out the door. She'd had to keep him after class long enough for him to write a list of ten reasons "Why I Should Not Throw Spitballs in Class." After erasing his hurriedly scrawled list on the chalkboard, she was clapping the erasers together outside the window and wishing she'd assigned Billy Joe this chore too when she heard footfalls on the steps outside.

Billy Joe must have returned for his slingshot, which he'd left on top of his desk.

"I thought you might be back," she murmured as she turned around, only to see it wasn't Billy Joe at all.

Jack Collier stood there, and once again, he had a hand on each of his daughters' shoulders. His face was drawn and his blue eyes red-rimmed, and the twins' faces were puffy from recent crying. The girls stared at her, eyes huge in their pale faces.

So he's told them about Pete's death, she thought with a pang, remembering how awful those first few hours of grief had been for her. Their mourning was just beginning.

Caroline's eyes were a bit swollen, Jack noted, and he wondered how hard it had been to carry on with class as if nothing had happened after their emotional confrontation.

"Miss Wallace, I—I wonder if it's too late for me to take you up on your offer of a bed for the night? The hotel doesn't have any rooms available, and the boardinghouse couldn't accommodate all three of us."

She looked at him, then at the girls, then back at him again. "All right. I was just about to go home, so it's good that you came just now." As he watched, she gathered up a handful of slates, tucking them into a poke bag, and took her bonnet and shawl down from hooks by the door.

"I'll take that," he said, indicating her poke, and held the door for her.

She gave him an inscrutable, measuring look. "Thank you, Mr. Collier."

He untied the horses from the hitching post. "Is there a livery where I can board the horses overnight?"

She nodded. "Calhoun's, on Travis Street, near where I live." Then she turned to the girls. "My father is the postmaster," she said as they all walked out of the school-yard and onto the street that led back into town, "so we live right behind the post office. Papa and Mama will sure be happy to have some children to spoil tonight," she told them. "My brother Dan's still at home, but he finished his schooling last year and works at the livery, so he fancies himself a young man now, too old to be cosseted." Jack thought there was something in her gaze that hinted she'd be happy to have the children around, too, if only for one night.

"How old is he?" Abby asked.

"Thirteen," Caroline said. "And how old are you two? I'm guessing six?"

"Right!" Amelia crowed, taking her hand impulsively. "How did you know, Aunt Caroline?"

"*I'm* the oldest," Abby informed Caroline proudly, taking her other hand. "By ten minutes."

"Is that a fact?" Caroline looked suitably impressed.

He was touched by the way she'd taken to his children, even if she'd decided he had about as much sense as last year's bird nest, Jack thought as he followed behind them leading the horses.

He was dreading the meeting with her parents, knowing he'd be unfavorably compared with Pete, who had always been so wise in everything he'd done. Pete would have never been so foolish as to set out for Montana so late in the year with a herd of half-wild cattle. The only remotely impulsive thing Pete had ever done was moving to Simpson Creek to court the very woman Jack now followed.

And yet Jack also looked forward meeting the Wallaces, hoping they would tell him about Pete's life during the months he'd spent in this little town before his death. He'd probably hear more about it from them than he would from Caroline, for she was still a little stiff with him.

He was acutely conscious of the ring that she'd flung at him riding in his pocket. Though it weighed almost nothing, it seemed to burn him like a hot coal—as if he'd stolen it from her.

After leaving the horses at Calhoun's, they reached the Wallaces' small tin-roofed frame house, which was attached to the post office.

"Perhaps I should go ahead into the kitchen and explain," she began, letting go of the twins' hands to open the door. They stepped into a simple room with a stone fireplace, two rocking chairs and a horsehair sofa.

"Papa, Mama—" she began to call and then was clearly startled when an older man rose from one of the rocking chairs, laying aside a book he'd been reading. She apparently hadn't expected him to be there.

"Hello, Caroline," he said. "And who do you have here?"

Before she could answer, however, a woman who had to be Caroline's mother bustled in. She must have come from the kitchen, for she still wore an apron and held a big stirring spoon in one hand. Both of them looked at the girls with obvious delight, but when Mrs. Wallace shifted her eyes from the twins to Jack, she stared at him before her gaze darted uncertainly back to Caroline.

Caroline knew her mother had noticed Jack's striking resemblance to Pete.

Chapter Three

"Mama, Papa, this is Jack, Pete's brother, and his daughters, Amelia and Abigail." Caroline could understand her mother's reaction, for she'd had a similar one herself. Her mother blinked and tried to smile a welcome at Jack and the two girls.

"Jack, h-how nice to meet you," she began in a quavery voice. "And your girls. I…"

"It's all right, Mrs. Wallace. I know I look like my brother," he said, taking the trembling hand the older woman extended to him, before taking Caroline's father's in turn.

"That you do, Jack," her father said, shaking Jack's hand. "Pete told us about you, of course, but you understand that it's still a surprise to…" His voice trailed off and his gaze fell. Then he looked up at Jack again. "We set great store by your brother Pete. He was a good man, and we miss him."

"Yes, he was mighty good to our Caroline," Mama said, her gaze caressing her daughter for a moment. "We were so proud he chose our daughter."

Jack's throat felt tight, but he managed to say, "Thank you, Mr. and Mrs. Wallace."

"Your coming is such a nice surprise," Mrs. Wallace went on, with an attempt at a sociable smile. "Please, won't you sit down?" She gestured to the horsehair couch. "Caroline, why don't you bring in a chair from the kitchen?"

Caroline went to fetch it, wishing as she walked down the hallway that her brother would show up so he could take the twins out of the room to see the kittens in the shed while she explained what had happened—some of it, anyway. She wasn't about to tell her parents about the angry conversation she'd had with Jack before he'd left the schoolhouse the first time. But she *did* want to tell them about Jack's traveling plans, to see if they could help her to change his mind. She didn't want to bring it up with the girls there, yet! Even though it was nearly time for supper, and Dan was always "starving," he hadn't put in an appearance. She hadn't seen him at the livery stable when they'd dropped off Jack's horses, so maybe he was lounging by the creek with the trio of boys he ran around with.

She couldn't send Jack's daughters out to find the kittens by themselves, so she'd have to explain the situation in front of them. By the time she'd brought in the chair for herself, Jack and the girls were settled on the sofa and her parents in their rocking chairs. Caroline took a deep breath and said, "Mama, Papa, Mr. Collier didn't know about his brother's death. He apparently didn't get the letter I sent after Pete passed away."

Her mother gasped and clapped two hands to her cheeks. "Oh, Mr. Collier, I'm so sorry! What a shock that must have been, to come all this way, and... Amos Wallace, I *told* you we should have sent someone down there to find him," she added with a touch of asperity.

"No sense worryin' about that now, dear," her father said, patting his wife's hand soothingly. "What's done is done. Yes, I'm sorry that you got the bad news that way, Mr. Collier—may I call you Jack? Pete was already like a son to us, so I don't feel like we need to stand on ceremony with you."

"Jack is fine," Jack assured them. "Yes, it was a shock, all right. But I reckon I should have suspected something when I never got the wedding invitation. I was busy getting ready to sell the ranch, and—"

Her father interrupted. "You're selling your ranch? Why's that?"

Jack flashed a glance at her. Caroline couldn't tell if he wanted her to tell the rest or if he was merely pleading that she not reveal how little she thought of his scheme. She kept her silence, thinking Jack Collier richly deserved to explain his half-baked plan without her assistance.

"I've sold it, actually," Jack said. "I—we—are on the way to Montana with my herd to join my partners. They bought a big ranch up there, and they asked me to throw in with them."

Caroline saw her mother blink as she came to the same conclusion she had. "But your girls, Mr. Collier—Jack," her mother began. "What were you going to do with them?"

"We're goin' to Montana, too," one of the twins—Abby?—announced. "But I don't like cows and sleeping on the ground."

"And eatin' beans and corn bread," added the other

girl—Amelia? "We were gonna stay with Uncle Pete and Aunt Caroline till Papa found a nice lady to marry and sent for us," she began, "but now we're going with Papa instead of waiting. Right, Papa?"

Caroline was human enough to feel a jolt of satisfaction as her mother's jaw dropped, and her father's jaw set in a hard line.

"Caroline," her father said, "I'll bet those young ladies would like to see the kittens out in the shed, wouldn't you, girls? Why don't you take them out to see them, dear?"

"Sure, Papa, that's a great idea," she said. "And when we come back in, I think Mama's got some lemonade, if Dan hasn't drunk it already." She rose and gestured for Amelia and Abigail to join her, and they seemed happy enough to do so, excitedly asking what color the kittens were, and how many, as they left the room.

She wished she could be a fly on the wall, so she could hear the dressing-down Jack Collier was about to get. Her father wasn't one to suffer fools gladly.

Caroline stayed out in the shed with the girls and played with the kittens as long as she dared, purposely staying away from the parlor. Then they came inside via the kitchen door and found her mother working on supper.

"Jack's agreed to spend the night with us, him and his girls," her mother announced happily and beamed when the girls cheered.

Caroline stifled a snort. He'd "agreed," as if he was bestowing a favor on them? Her mother didn't know she had already invited them. But who was she to complain about something that obviously made her mother so happy? Mama had enjoyed helping Caroline cook special meals for Pete, and now she was clearly overjoyed at the prospect of having girls to spoil, at least for one night.

Caroline had found she was enjoying Abby and Amelia's company, too. Was it because they looked so much like Pete? It was like seeing the children she and Pete might have had together, which made her confusingly happy and sad at the same time.

So she snapped beans and made corn bread while her mother plied the girls with lemonade and got them to talk about themselves.

The rain came at last, pounding on the tin roof with an intensity of a marching army, but neither girl seemed to notice.

Caroline didn't hear any raised voices coming from the parlor, which she thought was a good sign. Of course, it *could* mean the two men had reached a stalemate, with Jack refusing to admit his idea of taking the girls on a trail drive was foolish beyond words, and her father glowering in silent disapproval.

The kitchen door was flung open and Dan burst in, dripping rainwater. "It's comin' a gully washer out there," he announced. "What's for supper? I'm hungry enough to eat an iron skillet." Then he spotted the girls, who smiled at him from over their lemonade, and he headed for the table to meet the newcomers.

Caroline stepped between him and the twins. "A skillet is all you may have to eat unless you take those muddy, smelly boots off, Dan," she told him tartly, pointing at the offending articles. "You can meet our guests after you go take them off outside."

For once, he did as he was bid, without grousing at the sisterly reprimand, and was introduced when he returned. But the twins didn't get much time to talk to him, for as soon as he learned the girls' father planned to drive a herd to Montana, he dashed toward the parlor.

"Montana? Great stars an' garters! Can I go, Ma?"

Caroline caught her brother by his collar. "Dan, you stay out here—Papa and Mr. Collier are talking."

"Oh, let him go, Caroline. They're probably done by now," her mother said calmly, but as Dan wrenched free, she added, "And no, son, you may not go on a trail drive. You're too young yet."

An hour later, when they all sat down to supper together, her father and Jack seemed to be in perfect amity, much to Caroline's mystification. If Jack had received a dressing-down, she couldn't discern it from his relaxed, amiable manner as Dan pestered him with questions about cattle drives. And yet her father had looked so upset when he'd heard Jack's plan…

As it turned out, her father had been biding his time. The twins and Dan ate quickly, then proclaimed themselves full. Once they'd been excused, so Dan could show the girls his collection of arrowheads, Caroline saw her father turn to Jack.

"You know, Jack, late in the year as it is, you won't no more than get to the Panhandle with them beeves before the snow's apt t' start fallin'. And that'll leave you in the *Llano Estacado*—the Staked Plains—right where the Antelope Comanches set up winter camp, so you don't want to be lingerin' around there, no sirree."

He bit off a large chunk of his corn bread, buttered it and sat chewing while he waited for Jack's response.

Jack took a sip of lemonade before he replied, his tone considering. "Oh, I was thinking we could get to Colorado or at least Kansas, depending on the trail we took."

"It's my opinion you wouldn't," her father said. "And you ought not to gamble with those girls of yours along."

Caroline realized Papa and Jack Collier must not have even spoken about Jack's plan when they'd been left alone. Her wily father must have spent the time speaking of some related topic like ranching in general, drawing Jack out, creating a relationship—"softening him up," he'd call it—before broaching this difficult topic now, after Jack and his daughters had been treated to a delicious supper and were about to spend the night.

"Please, won't you leave the girls with us?" her mother pleaded. "You could always send for them once you were settled, as you originally intended."

To Caroline's surprise, Jack's only response was to look at her.

Was he waiting for Caroline to give permission before he agreed, since they'd had a confrontation? She was willing to bend, if it meant the girls would be left in safety with them. She said, "Please, Mr. Collier. We'd be happy to have them for as long as you need them to stay. Let them stay with us."

Jack's eyes were unreadable as he finished chewing before answering, but before he could do so, Caroline's father spoke again.

"I've got a better idea than that. You don't want to lose half your cattle to a pack of hungry Indians, even assuming they'd let you pass safely. Why not spend the winter here in Simpson Creek? You could stay with your girls that way, and set out in the spring, when you'd have the best chance of actually getting to Montana with your herd intact."

That was obviously the last thing Jack Collier expected to hear, for he blinked and set down his fork.

"And where would I keep a thousand head of ornery longhorns around here, Mr. Wallace?"

The fact that Jack hadn't refused to consider her father's suggestion surprised Caroline. Maybe he was beginning to see reason.

"There's a ranch south a' town that's come vacant recently," her father said. "The owner died."

Caroline knew he was referring to the Waters place, next to her friends Nick and Milly Brookfield's ranch. Old Mr. Waters had died in a Comanche attack two years back, while his nephew from the east, who had inherited it, had fallen victim to a murderous bunch of men bent on taking over the area this summer. The Comanches had damaged the ranch house badly, but the conspirators had finished the job, burning it to the ground, along with the Simpson Creek church.

"No buildings on it just now, but you and your men had reckoned on camping out anyway. Seems to me it'd be a perfect place for you to stay the winter, then make a fresh start in the spring," Mr. Wallace went on. "The bank is trustee for the property, since the heir back east wants no part of it."

"And they'd be willing for us to keep the herd there for the winter? How much would they want as rent?"

"Probably not much—maybe even nothing. If you and your cowboys built a cabin there, you'd have a dry, warm roof over your heads, and your cattle would have a place to stay." Her father spread his hands. "Sounds like a perfect solution to me."

Well, it didn't sound perfect to Caroline. She'd liked the idea of keeping Jack's appealing children till he sent for them, but the prospect of having the man himself anywhere near, a man who looked like Pete but could never *be* Pete, rankled. Besides, she hadn't forgotten that Jack had taken back the ring Pete had given her. And there was a disturbing feeling of attraction she'd felt instantly for him, the same attraction that had led her to blurt out during their confrontation at the schoolhouse that he was handsome.

Now as she felt his gaze swing toward her, she turned to stare out the window, lowering her hand below the table so he wouldn't see her touching the empty space on her finger where the ring had been.

Out of the corner of her eye she saw Jack scratch his chin. "I dunno...."

"It wouldn't hurt for you to talk to the bank president, see what the terms would be," her father said reasonably.

None of them had heard the twins creep back into the room until they exploded around their father, jumping and shrieking.

"Papa, do it! Stay on that ranch!"

"Yeah, Papa, then you wouldn't have to travel in cold weather!"

"I don't know, girls...."

It was the most reasonable plan, Caroline thought with irritation. Was Jack too proud, or pigheaded, to see it? Why was he hesitating?

"I'll have to think on it, Punkins," he said, gathering them into his arms and kissing each on the tops of their heads.

Her throat tightened. He was obviously an affectionate father who cared for his children. How could he love them yet be willing to either expose them to danger on the trail or leave them for months on end? They were excited to have him stay nearby now, but wasn't that postponing what would be a painful separation in the spring? Why had he sold the ranch in south Texas?

She burned with questions, but held her tongue. As a result, the evening passed pleasantly enough, with Dan agreeably playing games with the twins while Jack and her father sat reminiscing about the war years, her mother knitting and Caroline sitting silently, listening. As an older man, her father had joined the home guard, rather than the regular army, and had spent the war protecting Texans against the depredations of the Indians. Jack had served with General Hood, rising to the rank of major before the war was over.

When the clock struck nine, her mother rose. "Girls, let's arrange your beds on the summer porch. We can make up your father's bed there, too. I'll put out some quilts, but it's still plenty warm at night, so you'll be comfortable."

Abigail and Amelia followed her eagerly, and Caroline guessed they found it a treat not to be sleeping out in the open for a change. The rain had stopped, but the ground would surely have been muddy.

"I'm tired. Reckon I'll turn in," her father said, yawning as he stood up. "You, too, Dan, since you have to be at the livery at sunrise."

Caroline stared after her father, wishing she could call him back. *What could he be thinking, leaving me alone with this man? Can't he sense the distrust between Jack and me?* She didn't want to admit, even to herself, the feeling of attraction that lay between them, too. She should have gone with her mother and the girls to help make up the beds on the porch, but it was too late. If she left to do that now, she'd obviously be fleeing Jack's presence, and Caroline wasn't about to let it look that way.

Jack watched her father and brother go. Then, when the sound of their doors closing echoed in the parlor, he turned to Caroline.

"Can we call a truce, Miss Caroline?" he asked, the lamplight flickering on his face.

"I… I wasn't aware we were at war," she said stiffly, unable to meet those blue eyes that reminded her so achingly of Pete's.

He uttered a soft sound that might have been a barely stifled snort of disbelief, but he didn't call her a liar, at least. "Please, Miss Caroline, for the sake of the man we both loved?"

Oh, unfair, she thought, *to invoke your brother.* But since he had, how could she disagree?

"Very well, Mr. Collier, in memory of Pete."

"Please call me Jack. Mr. Collier was our father," he said, as if that wasn't a complimentary comparison. "And I have an olive branch of sorts to extend to you." He reached into his shirt pocket, brought out the pearl ring and held it out to her. "Please, take this back and keep it with my blessing. It was wrong of me to take it. Pete would have wanted you to keep it, so…so that's what I want, too."

"But…shouldn't it stay in the family?" she asked, wanting to do the right thing, the self-sacrificing thing. "For your girls?" *For you to give the woman you will marry?*

"I want you to have it."

Something flickered in the depths of those blue eyes, and she wondered what he was thinking. She reached out and took the ring, finding it still warm from his body.

Her hand shook a little as she slipped it back on her finger. "Thank you, M— Jack."

"You're welcome," he said, smiling in approval.

She decided to test this moment of amity. "So…what are you going to do, Jack? About your daughters, and the cattle drive?" she asked, hoping the question wasn't pushing him too hard.

"Said I was going to think about it, didn't I?" he said, but his tone indicated he was amused rather than offended by her persistence.

She refused to be buffaloed by him. "You've already decided, I think."

He rubbed his chin again. "I'm going to leave the girls here, for sure. I reckon it only makes good sense," he admitted. "And I thought I'd talk to the bank president in the morning, and see what the terms would be, if we wintered on that ranch your pa spoke of."

Even though they'd achieved a sort of peace, Caroline knew it wouldn't be easy being around him. But aloud she said, "You're making a wise decision, Jack. Papa wouldn't steer you wrong."

He held up a hand. "Now, hold your horses, Teacher. It's all going to depend on what the banker says. And if I like his terms, I've still got to ride out to where the herd's bedded down and talk that bunch of misfits that call themselves drovers into helping me build a bunkhouse where we can spend the winter. Cowboys are an independent lot, you know. They might not at all be willing to stay, especially if it means doing some hard work between now and cold weather."

She fought to stifle a smile. There was something about the way he called his men misfits that told Caroline the bond between them went deep. And she didn't want to admit, even to herself, how much she'd liked the way he called her "Teacher." Her pupils called her that sometimes, but it felt different, somehow, when this man said it.

As soon as she thought it, she felt guilty, as if she were cheating on Pete. *No. She'd lost the love of her life, and she was done with romance and marriage. And even if she wasn't, she wouldn't give the time of day to a man who would leave for Montana. She wouldn't be left behind again.*

Her mother returned just then, with the twins skipping ahead of her.

"Come see our beds, Papa! They're oh-so-cozy!" one of them—Abby?—called.

"Yeah, we'll be snug as bugs in a rug, Aunt Mary says," the other one added, pulling on her father's hand. "Come see."

Aunt Mary? Caroline darted a glance at Jack, wondering if he would object to the name. After all, there was no real relationship between her mother and these two girls, any more than there was between them and herself.

"I hope you don't mind if they call me that, Jack," her mother said. "Mrs. Wallace just seems so formal."

Jack shook his head. "Not a bit, ma'am. Good night, ladies." His gaze lingered on Caroline, leaving her feeling decidedly unsettled.

Chapter Four

The scent of frying bacon led Jack to the kitchen the next morning where he was surprised to see the twins already freshly scrubbed and sitting at the table, digging into bacon and biscuits.

Caroline sat at the table, too, and raised her head as he entered. She looked clear-eyed and neat as a pin but once again was dressed in black. The hue looked impossibly severe on her, he thought. In spite of the unflattering dress, she was a lovely woman, with her glossy brown hair and large expressive eyes. He had no trouble understanding why his brother had fallen in love with her.

He wondered when she planned to give up wearing mourning. Surely she didn't expect to wear black for Pete forever, even if she grieved inwardly for him? He couldn't help imagining what she'd look like wearing some hue like deep green or gold. But some other man would have the pleasure of seeing her wearing colors again, and that man wouldn't be a rancher with a weathered face and mud, or worse, on his boots. A woman of her education and refinement would pick another safe sort of husband who worked in the town, as Pete had. A shopkeeper or a preacher, perhaps.

"Good morning, Papa," the twins chorused, catching sight of him.

"Morning, girls." They looked neat and tidy, too, he noted. Amelia's hem now was free of stains, and Abigail's sleeve had been mended. Their hair was neatly braided.

He hadn't even heard his daughters get up—which was natural, he supposed, considering how long he'd lain awake last night thinking about Pete. He'd shed some tears, too, but quietly, letting them leak soundlessly out of his eyes and soak into the pillow, lest he wake the girls.

They'd talked about Pete, before falling asleep, and though the girls were sad about the loss of their uncle, they hadn't grown up with Pete as he had. Pete had been working in Houston in a druggist's store by the time they were old enough to remember. He'd made it home to the ranch in Goliad County only a few times a year. In time their uncle would become a distant memory to his daughters, Jack knew. But he would always remember the older brother he'd idolized, the one with all the "book learnin'" their father seemed to prize so much. Jack had always disappointed the old man, even though he, not Pete, had been the one to follow in his father's rancher footsteps.

"Good morning, Jack," Mrs. Wallace said from the stove, where she was turning flapjacks. "I hope you slept well."

"Sure was nicer than sleeping on the hard ground, ma'am," he admitted, not about to let on how long into the night he had lain awake.

Caroline took a sip of coffee, then cleared her throat.

"Why don't you let Abby and Amelia go to school with me today, since you're going to be busy going to the bank and out to talk to your men?"

Abby looked excited at the prospect. "Please, Papa, can we?"

"Yes, please? I love school," Amelia added.

"How do you know, Punkin? So far you've only seen recess," Jack teased. But he felt a surge of guilt, thinking of how slapdash their rearing had been thus far. They were only six, true, but with their mother gone, he'd been too busy around the ranch to teach them the things that children properly learned at their mothers' knees. Things that prepared them to learn in school. He didn't want them growing up ignorant of their letters and sums and history and such. Even wives and mothers needed to know these things. Would there be a school in Montana, when he got there?

"Yes, you can go with Miss Caroline," he told them, and they clapped. "But you mind what she says," he added quickly. "Make me proud."

"We will, Papa," Amelia promised, and Abby nodded. Both girls bounced happily in their chairs. "Hooray! We're goin' to school!"

"Then you'd better finish up," Caroline told them. "The teacher has to be there earlier than anyone to ring the school bell. If you're done with your breakfast in five minutes, you may take turns ringing it."

Immediately they attacked what was left of their meal with enthusiasm.

Evidently done eating, Caroline brought a plate of flapjacks, bacon and biscuits to the table and set it in front of him, then refilled his coffee cup.

"Thank you, Miss Caroline," Jack said. Silence

reigned, broken only by the clink of forks on crockery plates, and he fell to musing about his situation. What would Pete have done, if their situations had been reversed?

Then he realized Mr. Wallace had said something to him while his thoughts wandered. "Pardon me, sir? Guess I'm not fully awake yet."

Mr. Wallace looked faintly amused. "That's all right, Jack. Drink some more of that strong coffee. Caroline makes it so strong a horseshoe will float in it. I was just saying that Caroline tells us you've decided to take my advice and talk to the bank president about the Waters ranch," Mr. Wallace said.

Jack glanced at Caroline, who was smart enough to look down just then—so he couldn't see the satisfaction shining in her eyes, he guessed. "I'll see what the man has to say," Jack said noncommittally. "And whether my men are willing to stay on here."

"You'll find Henry Avery a reasonable soul," Mr. Wallace said. "But it probably wouldn't hurt to tell him I suggested it."

"I will, sir, much obliged." It could only add to his respectability to have the postmaster, a longtime resident, vouch for him. Mr. Wallace had told him yesterday afternoon that the town had held Pete in great esteem, but Jack knew drovers had a reputation everywhere for being wild and irresponsible.

Jack was thankful Mr. Avery wouldn't be aware he'd considered pressing north with his herd and his children even with winter coming soon. The more he thought about it now, the more harebrained the idea seemed. What had he been thinking? It was a good thing Caroline and her parents had talked him out of it.

"Time to go," Caroline announced to the twins. They jumped up, and she scooped up her poke. The slates rattled inside as she did so, and Jack wondered when she'd had time to look at them. Had she sat up, reading her students' work by lamplight, after he and the girls had gone off to bed?

The twins jumped to their feet and dashed over to kiss him. "Bye, Papa," they chorused.

"We'll see you later, Jack," Caroline said. "Good luck with your trip to the bank."

"Bank doesn't open till nine, young man," Mrs. Wallace told him. "You might as well have another round of flapjacks."

"Don't mind if I do, thank you," he said, sure these were better than any flapjacks Cookie had ever made. He thought about asking for the recipe, then realized there'd be no forgiveness from his cook if Jack suggested his pancakes were less than perfect already. Then, to fill the silence, he asked, "Does your daughter like teaching?"

"Seems to," Mr. Wallace said.

"Yes, she needed something to occupy herself," Mrs. Wallace said, as she plunked the coffeepot back on top of the stove. "She was devastated when your brother died during the influenza outbreak, Jack. We were worried she'd—well, we used to call it 'going into a decline,' back before the war. For a while we thought she was going to die of a broken heart."

Jack's own heart ached at the thought of Caroline's grief hitting her so hard that she'd almost died of it. He remembered how he'd felt when his own wife had passed away—bewildered, helpless, but so busy keeping the chores done while trying to console his very young children who had lost their mother that he'd had little time to cry.

It had only been at night, when the ranch house was quiet, that he'd had time to lie awake and mourn for his young wife. He remembered he hadn't slept much for about half a year, until his body eventually tired from sleep deprivation and his sleep became heavy and dreamless.

Was love really worth it if the loss of a mate could wreck a body like that? Yet he missed being married, missed the softness and tenderness of a woman.

Mr. Wallace rose, muttering that it was time to open the post office, and went through the door in the kitchen that connected their house to it. Mrs. Wallace came to the table with a small helping of bacon and eggs, finally sitting down to break her own fast now that everyone else was fed. He hated to leave her at the table by herself, and since his pocket watch indicated it was still only half-past eight, he decided to keep her company.

"When Pete left Houston, he wrote me that he was coming to Simpson Creek to meet the ladies of 'the Spinsters' Club,'" Jack began, thinking he'd satisfy his curiosity and make conversation at the same time.

Mrs. Wallace smiled. "Yes, they started out calling it 'the Simpson Creek Society for the Promotion of Marriage,' but that didn't last too long. They're really something, those girls. When the war ended, and the only men who managed to return home to Simpson Creek were the married men, Milly Matthews decided she didn't want to be an old maid and organized the others who felt likewise into a club. Well, sir, they put an advertisement in the Houston newspaper inviting marriage-minded bachelors to come meet them, and the men began coming, singly and in groups. First one to get married was Milly herself, to a British fellow, Nick Brookfield. In fact, if you do spend the winter on the ranch, they'll be your neighbors. Then her sister Sarah met her match, the new doctor, and Caroline would have been the third, except for the influenza..." Her face sobered, and she looked down.

"I understand quite a few folks died then, not just Pete," Jack put in.

"Yes, too many. People on ranches, people in town. I reckon we might've lost more if Dr. Walker hadn't been here. The mayor's wife died, and her sister, and the livery stable owner, and the proprietor of the mercantile... It was awful, Jack. I don't know why Mr. Wallace and I were spared, but we're thankful."

Jack deliberately changed the subject. "Did your daughter always want to be a teacher?"

Mrs. Wallace wiped her lips with a napkin, then shook her head. "No, she never said anything about it before, though she was always quick to learn. But when the old teacher announced she was leaving to be a missionary this summer, suddenly Caroline decided she was going to take her place and devote herself to the children of the town. Oh, she still helps out with the Spinsters' Club, just because she's friends with those ladies, but she's made it clear she's given up on the idea of marriage."

"Well, hello there, Caroline!" a voice called, and Caroline looked up to see her friend Milly Brookfield just pulling up in her buckboard in front of the doctor's office. No doubt she was here to visit her sister Sarah in the house attached to the back of the clinic. As Caroline approached with the curious girls at her side, the old cowboy who had been holding the reins took the baby Milly had been holding so Milly could descend, then handed him to her on the ground.

"Mornin', Miss Caroline," he called, fingering the brim of his cap. "You got some new students, eh?"

"Morning yourself, Josh. Yes, these are Amelia and Abigail Collier. They're going to be staying with us for a while."

"Nice to meet you, young ladies. Miz Milly, reckon I'll jest mosey over to the mercantile and pick up those things you were wantin'," Josh said. He set the brake, clambered down and walked stiffly down the street. Caroline guessed the old cowboy's rheumatism had gotten worse, along with his hearing.

Milly hadn't missed the significance of the girls' surname, however, and raised her eyebrows, her eyes flashing a question to Caroline.

"Yes, these are Pete's brother Jack's daughters. He arrived yesterday." Caroline stared straight into her old friend's eyes, willing her to understand that there was more to the story that she didn't want to discuss in front of the children. She knew Milly was aware that Caroline had never gotten an answer to the letter she'd sent to Pete's brother informing him of Pete's death.

Milly, God bless her, didn't miss a beat. "Well, isn't that wonderful that you could come for a visit!" she said, bending down to the girls. As she did so, baby Nicholas woke up and cooed, sending the girls into delighted giggles.

"He's darling!" cried Amelia, while Abby asked, "What's his name? How old is he? Can I hold him?"

"Another time, perhaps," Caroline told them. "We have to get to school, remember?"

"I'm sure your mother's thrilled to have two little girls to spoil," Milly said, and then to the girls, she added, "I'm sure you'll have a chance to hold little Nicholas. He's just getting to the age where he likes to flirt with older women."

The girls giggled again.

Milly turned back to Caroline. "I thought I'd drop in on Sarah for coffee, since we came to town to get supplies, but why don't I stop over at the school at morning recess and we can catch up?"

Caroline could see from the avid interest in her friend's eyes that she wanted to hear the full story of Jack Collier's arrival. Which was fine, for Caroline needed to tell someone about it, someone who would understand the feelings that had overwhelmed her yesterday at seeing the man who looked so like his brother. Someone full of common sense, as Milly was, who would understand the contradictory feelings that had warred within Caroline after he had first exasperated her with his foolish plans, then confused her later with his kindness. Suddenly she could hardly wait till recess, when the children would be outside and she and Milly could have a frank talk. It had been too long since Caroline had shared her feelings with her friend.

"That would be wonderful," she said. "I usually have recess at ten. Come on, girls, we'd better hurry, or Billy Joe Henderson will ring that bell before we get there."

Henry Avery studied Jack with a skeptical gaze that told Jack he was drawing conclusions from his bedraggled appearance—Jack's worn denims, down-at-the-heel boots, the shirt and vest he hadn't managed to brush entirely free of trail dust, his battered, broad-brimmed hat. But once Jack told the bank president what he was there for and that Mr. Wallace had sent him, Mr. Avery showed him into his back office with encouraging eagerness.

"That's a capital idea, capital!" he enthused about Jack's proposal to winter at the Waters ranch. "I don't mind telling you it's been difficult to raise any interest in the place after the last two owners were murdered—"

"Yes, Mr. Wallace told me about their deaths," Jack put in quickly, not wanting to hear another long recital of the tale. He didn't want the sun to get too high by the time he made it out to the herd, for he knew his drovers would be wondering about him.

"Yes, folks say the place is cursed, but I know a sensible fellow such as yourself doesn't pay any mind to silly tales like that. Fact is, it's prime ranch land, well-watered. And if you were to build a cabin on it to stay in over the winter, I'd probably have no further difficulty sellin' that place come spring, once you'd gone on to Montana." The bank president spread his hands over a slight potbelly as he leaned back in his chair. "But are you sure you want to do that? Why, you could buy the Waters place, and come spring, you could drive the herd to Kansas and be back by fall with a big profit lining your pockets. You could do worse than this pretty part of Texas."

It *was* lovely, with its rolling blue hills and clear green streams, and so was a certain young woman in black, Jack thought. But she wasn't interested in marriage anymore, certainly not to the likes of him. And he didn't need to spend any more of his life with someone who'd constantly compare him to his brother, against whom he'd always fall short.

"I know. But my mind is made up."

"Once you see the place, you'll change your mind," the banker declared.

Jack shook his head. "I just want to rent it till spring, Mr. Avery. What'll you charge me if my men and I erect some sort of dwelling on it?"

"Mr. Collier, I liked your brother, and I was sorry to hear of his passing. If you'd promise to build at least a cabin there—a decent, sound dwelling, mind you, not some ramshackle hut that falls over when the first bad storm blows by—I won't charge you a penny. But you really ought to buy it."

"What does the heir want for it?" Jack inquired, though more out of courtesy than any real interest.

"Not much *now,*" the bank president said with a wink. "But it'll cost you more once there's a dwelling on it."

Jack couldn't help smiling at the other man's dog-gedness. "I'll think about it, but you better count on us moving on in the spring. There's already a prime piece of ranch land waiting for me up in Montana Territory."

But no prime ranch land in Montana could compare to a woman like Caroline, a voice within him mocked.

Chapter Five

Raleigh Masterson, Jack's ramrod, rose from where he'd been hunkered down by the campfire when he saw Jack approach. He poured coffee into a tin cup, holding it out to Jack as he dismounted. He was the only trail hand by the campfire. Cookie was busy mixing one of his concoctions at the chuck wagon. The rest of the drovers were grooming the remuda horses, mending or cleaning tack, or riding herd. The cattle were clustered on the banks of Simpson Creek, some grazing on the lush grass that grew nearby, while others had waded into the creek flank deep and drank the cool water. It was a peaceful sight, and it gave Jack a sense of contentment, even though he knew those same placid cattle could be off in a flash, spooked by thunder or seemingly nothing, stampeding until the trailhands succeeded in turning them or until they just ran out of the need to run. Impulsive beasts, longhorns, and as dangerous as they were silly. A man never trusted their apparent docility while grazing; he always approached them on horseback because they were so unpredictable.

"You find your brother all right, and settle the girls

with him and his bride?" Raleigh asked, as Jack took the cup.

"No on both counts," Jack said, sitting on a saddle blanket someone had left lying there. Staring into the black Arbuckles' coffee, he told Raleigh about the events of yesterday. "Miss Wallace tried to notify me. Sent it General Delivery. Don't know why I never got that letter," he said with a shrug.

Raleigh whistled. "That's too bad. I'm sorry about your brother, boss."

Jack nodded grimly. "I should have written again," he said, almost to himself. "Pete must not have saved my letters."

"What're you gonna do, then?" Raleigh asked. "Now that you can't leave the girls with your brother and his wife?"

Jack knew his ramrod was too polite to say so, but his mind had already leaped ahead and concluded that Jack would be forced by the unexpected circumstances to take girls along with them.

"Thought I'd talk to you and the rest of the men about that. And I only want to say this once," he said, half turning and raising his voice, "so, Cookie, call the men in." He knew the cook had been listening in on the conversation.

Cookie reached for the iron triangle that hung on the chuck wagon. The carrying jangle of metal on metal yanked cowboy heads up wherever they rode or worked, and they started drifting in toward the campfire.

"Fine, but you tell them yahoos right off that we ain't eatin' early jes' 'cause you're holdin' a palaver," Cookie groused, going back to kneading the biscuit dough. "It'll be ready when it's ready, an' not a moment before."

"So noted," Jack responded, too used to the older man's crotchets to take offense.

When everyone had assembled, he repeated what he'd told his ramrod about Pete's death and let his mind wander as they murmured their shocked condolences.

"Now, we knew we were going to have to winter somewhere along the way," he went on, "and I've been told it'd be smarter to spend the time right here than to head north and pass right by where the Comanches're spendin' the winter."

"Told you that when I got thrown in th' calaboose," Raleigh muttered. "Told you you oughta leave me there and ride on so you'd be past the Staked Plains before the redskins made their winter camp."

"And I told *you* I wasn't leaving you behind," Jack snapped. No one but his ramrod dared talk to him the way Raleigh had, and even he would guess from Jack's curtness that he was treading on thin ice. Jack hadn't heeded his advice, not only because of their friendship, but because he knew none of the other men were seasoned enough to be the new ramrod.

"That's all water under the bridge," Jack went on, and told them about the vacant ranch and the deal the bank was offering if they built a cabin.

Around the circle of men, some faces sparked with interest. In others, eyes narrowed.

"But, boss, it's already October," one of the men pointed out.

"I'm a cowboy, not a carpenter," another groused.

It was what Jack had expected. "I know it would mean getting right to work on building, but I'm told it doesn't get that cold around here until December or so. It wouldn't take that long for us to put up a cabin if we don't dillydally. The bank won't charge me rent if we put up some kind of dwelling, 'cause it'll add to the value of the place. Now, I know you didn't sign on for building anything, so you men are free to stay on or not—no hard feelings if you decide to ride on. But if you stay, I'll expect you to help build."

Two men announced right off they were quitting. Jack wasn't surprised. They were nephews of his stepmother, and he'd judged them as lazy and unreliable from the start, but he'd been nagged into hiring them. With any luck, he could find a pair of hands to replace them come spring.

"All right, you can collect your wages in the morning," he told the two men and studied the rest of them, hoping they would stick. One of the other trail hands rubbed the back of his neck consideringly.

"Simpson Creek got any pretty girls? A saloon? A parlor house? We'd be allowed to ride inta town on Saturday nights, wouldn't we?"

"I sure haven't had time to scout all that out for you, Wes," Jack said evenly, "but I do remember seeing a saloon. You couldn't all go at once, of course—and I'll warn y'all right now I'll tolerate no rowdy behavior in town," he told them, thinking of Caroline and the other ladies of the Spinsters' Club. Trail hands weren't saints, and he didn't want bad behavior to make them unwelcome in town and reflect back on him. "You get thrown in jail, you're fired."

"Aw, boss, you're takin' all the fun out of it," someone grumbled good-naturedly.

"You know where this ranch is, boss?" Raleigh asked. "Why don't a few of us go take a look at it?"

It was a good idea, Jack thought. It was never good

to buy a pig in a poke. Who knew if the banker had exaggerated the quality of the place?

"All right. Raleigh, Quint, Jase, Shep, you're with me. We'll ride over there after we eat. Cookie, any chance you'd have some grub we could take with us and eat in the saddle?" He winked at his ramrod, knowing his request would set Cookie's temper on the boil, but knowing the trail cook wouldn't protest too loudly to his boss.

"I'm a cook, not some kind'a miracle worker!" Cookie groused. "All I got's jerky for ya if you're not gonna wait till dinnertime."

The five men rode up the dirt lane that led to the desolate, charred pile of timbers that was all that remained of the previous house. Jack recounted to his men how the Comanches had committed the initial attack upon the dwelling, but how it been white outlaws working for the so-called Ranchers' Alliance who had finished the destruction just recently, burning down the house old Mr. Waters's nephew had just started rebuilding.

"Those Alliance men are all gone now, right?" Jase asked, a little nervously.

Jack nodded. "I'm told they vamoosed when their bosses were either killed or put in prison, but as for the Comanches…well, this is Texas, boys, and they aren't beaten yet. We ought to be safe enough this winter, though."

"First thing to do would be to clear off the foundation, if you mean to build the bunkhouse in the same place as the old one, boss," Raleigh said, eyeing the ruins.

Jack nodded, already envisioning what he and his men would do. Something about the ruined buildings in this hill country ranch called out to him, as if pleading to be nurtured so it could be reborn. Well, he would do what he could over the winter months, but it would be some future owner who enjoyed the fruits of whatever he and his men would be able to accomplish.

"I'll think about that. Let's ride on and see the rest of the place," Jack said and kneed his roan into a trot past the site.

He liked what he saw of the land. It was good country, with plenty of shady live oak groves, mesquite and a small creek—probably a tributary of Simpson Creek— running onto his land under the western boundary fence. Just beyond the fence, on Brookfield land, the creek was broader and more inviting. He wondered if Brookfield would consider giving him access so his cattle would be able to drink from that broader part, at least on the western side, when summer heat dropped the water level.

But why was he thinking that way? He and the cattle would be long gone, come summer.

Yet he couldn't seem to stop his imaginings. He pictured taking down the faded remains of the sign that read "Waters Ranch" and replacing it with one with his name. A rancher could do much worse than a place like this.

"Looks like a pretty good spot t' spend the winter, boss," Raleigh murmured, and the other men chorused their agreement.

"Yeah, and there's lots of trees we could fell for logs, with plenty left," Shep said.

"Looks like we could salvage a lot of stones from the old fireplace to make a new one," Quint put in.

"Guess we got ourselves a winter camp, then," Jack said, pleased his men agreed with him about the plan. "Mr. Wallace says there's a hardware store in town that can sell us some saws and so forth—reckon I'll stop in there and buy what we'll need first thing tomorrow. We'll have to rent a wagon from the livery for a while, too." Maybe he could make it back to town before the bank closed today and tell Mr. Avery he was going to take him up on the offer. The rest of the men could easily move the herd on down the road to the Waters ranch without his assistance.

He'd told Caroline he'd leave the girls in town with her and her parents, regardless of whether he stayed on the ranch over the winter or not. He wished they could be with him, but leaving them at the Wallaces' was the only practical thing to do. Though they'd slept under the chuck wagon during the journey, the weather would get colder. He didn't want them sleeping in a tent, or later, in the bunkhouse with his men. Staying with the Wallaces, they could go to school, and that would be good for them.

Such an arrangement would mean frequent trips in from the ranch for him to see the girls, at least on Sunday. He pictured treating them to dinners at the hotel and taking them to church. It had been a long time since they'd gone regularly; for a time after Lucinda's death, he hadn't wanted anything to do with God.

But this arrangement would also mean he'd have to keep dealing with Caroline Wallace. He wasn't at all sure exactly how he felt about regular contact with her.

Caroline heard boot heels on the kitchen steps. She forced herself to turn her attention back to where the twins laboriously practiced their letters on borrowed slates at the kitchen table, waiting to rise until he knocked. It wouldn't do to let Jack Collier imagine she'd been watching for his arrival. Then she rose and let him in with a casual "Good afternoon, Jack."

If she was sparing in her welcome, however, the twins had no such reservations. "Papa!" cried one of them—Amelia?—as they exploded away from the table and ran into his waiting arms.

"We're learnin' our ABCs, Papa!" cried the other.

Caroline realized she was going to have to find some foolproof way of telling one twin from the other. Should she have them dress differently?

Bending over, Jack kissed both of them. "That's wonderful, girls. Were you good today?"

"Yes, Papa," they chorused.

He looked over their heads at Caroline. "*Were* they good today?"

His direct gaze did funny things to her equanimity. "Yes, you have every reason to be proud of them. They show a quick aptitude for learning which some of my other students would do well to emulate."

Goodness, did that prim, stuffy speech really come from her? She sounded like—well, a schoolmarm. At least praising the twins gave her a reason for the enthusiasm in her voice and face, so he wouldn't think she was appreciating the way the wind had left color in his cheeks and a sparkle in his blue eyes.

"Look, Papa, see? I can spell my name," Abby said, grabbing her slate off the table and holding it up to him.

He looked at it, and Caroline guessed he was noticing that Abby's b's were backward, written as d's instead.

"We're working on our b's," she said quickly, her eyes warning him not to call attention to his daughter's mistake.

"Yes, I see," he said gravely. "Good job, Abby."

"Me, too, Papa," Amelia said, holding out her slate.

"'Course, mine is harder, 'cause Amelia has more letters than Abby."

"Well, yours will be shorter when she can spell out Abigail," he told her. "Then you'll have the advantage, Punkin."

"Well, hello, Jack," said her mother, returning to the kitchen. She took the lid off a pot and began stirring. Immediately, a savory aroma filled the kitchen, and Caroline saw him lift his head to sniff.

"Mmm, something smells good."

"It's just beef stew," her mother said, but Caroline could see she was pleased by the compliment.

Her father came in from the post office. "Were you able to go out and see the Waters place?"

Jack straightened and nodded. "Yessir. We can stay for free if we build a dwelling. My men were agreeable—all but a couple, anyway."

Abby looked up with a pleased smile curving her lips. "So you're staying the winter, Papa?"

He nodded.

"Hoorah!" the twins yelled in unison, beaming.

Caroline had been watching him as he spoke to her parents, since she could do so without his noticing. When he finished speaking to her father, however, he looked at Caroline, not her father, as if seeking her reaction. She looked down quickly, pretending great interest in the long tail on the y Abby had just scrawled.

"That's good news, Jack," her father said, clapping him on the back. "It's a fine piece of land."

"Yes…shame what happened there," Jack murmured.

Caroline winced inwardly. The stories of Comanches attacking William Waters and outlaws murdering his nephew were not tales fit for little ears.

"What happened there, Papa?" Amelia asked, wrinkling her nose in curiosity.

Realizing his mistake, Jack shot a dismayed look at Caroline.

You'd think the man would have learned by now how little pitchers have big ears. "Oh, the house burned down," she said quickly, "but wait till you see the fine cabin your papa's going to build there to take its place."

The girls' mouths were twin Os. "Why did the—" Abby began.

Before Abby could complete her question, Caroline said, "Girls, why don't you take this pitcher of cream out to the mama cat in the shed? There's a bowl out there for you to pour it in." She handed the little pitcher to Abby. "It's curdled a little, but she won't mind."

The girls scampered for the door, and it banged shut behind them.

"Thanks," Jack said, his eyes grateful. "Sometimes I forget they're listening."

His gaze held hers a moment longer than she was comfortable with, but she couldn't seem to look away.

"So your plan is to let the children live here while you stay on the ranch land this winter, and then leave them with us when you take off with the herd in the spring?" her mother said, then seemed to hold her breath until he nodded.

"When are you going to start building?" her father asked, also looking relieved.

"Tomorrow, after I stop at the bank and tell Mr. Avery. I didn't make it back before the bank closed today. I imagine I'll have to sign some sort of paper," Jack said.

Her father chuckled. "You won't find Mr. Avery at the bank. Tomorrow's Saturday."

Jack's eyes crinkled in the corners just as Pete's had, Caroline thought, as he raked a hand through his hair.

"Guess I've purely lost track while we were traveling."

"I'll be seeing him tomorrow, though," her father said, "so I can let him know for you. I'm sure he won't mind if you go ahead and start working since it's already so late in the year."

"I'll come into town often to see my girls—at least every Sunday, and each time I come into town for supplies. And when the weather isn't too cold, they could come out and spend some time at the ranch," Jack assured them.

"Sounds fine," her mother said. "Why don't you spend another night here and explain the plan to your girls before you start building tomorrow?"

Caroline saw Jack hesitate. Though he hadn't been speaking to her, Caroline sensed he was waiting for her reaction—*why?* It wasn't up to her to approve or disapprove of what he did.

"As Papa said, we'll see the bank president tomorrow," Caroline told him. "The mayor's daughter, Prissy Gilmore, is getting married, and the whole town will be going to the wedding. I thought the girls would enjoy going with us. Did you happen to bring the rest of their clothing with you?"

Jack nodded, a little uneasily. "I left it in my saddlebags on the step," he said.

"Would you go get it, please?" Caroline asked. "I'm thinking we might need to launder what they'll wear to the wedding."

He arose and went to the door, his steps those of a condemned man walking to the gallows. Brushing off the saddlebags as he entered, he crossed the kitchen and laid them on the table.

"Now, you have to remember," he began, his tone apologetic, "they didn't get off the ranch much, and they've been traveling with us drovers and the herd... I—I'm afraid there's not much you'd consider suitable...."

Caroline opened one saddlebag and dumped its contents on the table, then the other. The saddlebags contained boys' shirts and pants—and nothing else.

Chapter Six

"Where…where are the dresses?" Caroline asked, thunderstruck. "This can't be all you packed for those little girls?" Then suddenly she knew it *was* all, and she raised her gaze to Jack's guilty face.

"Their blue pinafore dresses are the only dresses you brought." It was a statement, not a question. She hadn't meant to expose his poor planning again, but it was too late to call back her words. It had just never occurred to her that a father might not see the need for little girls to have more than one dress.

He nodded, then shrugged. "I figured there was no point in dresses on the trail, and they'd been wearing pants around the ranch ever since—well, ever since my wife died," he said. "We only had one Mexican cook who did the laundry, too, and when the girls grew out of their old dresses, I—I didn't see any point in having more than a pair of new ones made as they grew. They used the cook's son's castoffs—he was a little older. Yesterday, I—I wanted them to make a good impression…"

He looked so miserable in his confession. Caroline's heart went out to him. "Well, no matter," she said quickly, "I'm sure they can wear some of my dresses from childhood. Mama never threw anything out, right?" she asked her mother for confirmation.

"Sure, I imagine they're still in that old trunk in the shed. Land sakes, it's not like little girls' fashions change all that much from year to year. They'll do till I have a chance to make up some new dresses," she added, clearly cheered by the prospect. "Maybe I'll pop down to the mercantile first thing tomorrow before the wedding and see what Mrs. Patterson has in the way of pretty fabrics. Caroline, mind that stew. Your father and I can go get those boxes out of the trunk in the shed while it's still light enough to see what we're looking at."

Jack watched as Caroline's parents left the kitchen. Then he turned back to Caroline.

"Reckon you don't think I'm much good as a father, not keeping my girls in proper clothing," he said.

That was exactly what she *had* thought, but Caroline wouldn't have admitted it for the world. "Don't worry, Jack, Mama's been itching to have some little girls to dress ever since I grew up. By Christmas they'll each have such a wardrobe you'll have to address each one as 'Princess.'"

He gave her the ghost of a smile, but she was relieved to see his shoulders slacken their rigid posture.

"Lucinda was a good mother," he said at last. "It's a good thing she doesn't know all I've put them through. If she did, she'd want to come down from Heaven and box my ears."

"No, she wouldn't," she assured him, laying a hand impulsively on his forearm. "Don't be so hard on your-self, Jack. I believe those who've passed on *do* know what their loved ones are going through, and they understand. She knows you've done the best you could. You're trying to build a better life for them and yourself—it's why you're going to Montana, isn't it?"

She hadn't realized she was still touching his forearm till she stopped talking and felt the warmth of his skin penetrating his shirtsleeve. She yanked her hand back, feeling heat flooding her cheeks. She knew her face must have been as red as the bottom stripe on the Texas flag. So much for the prim-and-proper schoolmarm!

"I'm sorry," she muttered. She dashed to the stove as if the world would come to an end if she didn't stir the stew this very minute.

He stayed by the table, but she could feel his gaze on her. "It's all right, Caroline," he said. "I appreciate what you said. It's kind of you."

She didn't deserve the description, Caroline thought, after the way she'd reacted, as if he was a sorry excuse for a father. Caroline sighed.

It was a good thing Jack Collier wouldn't be in town all that much this winter, because so far his presence only confused her, made her forget the clear path she had set her feet on.

She had to get control of herself, to stop letting him affect her so. She was the schoolteacher, and all the town's children were her children. Her life was devoted to their learning, and therefore she had no need for any other relationships outside of her family. She would stay in this house behind the post office and take care of her parents as they grew older, long after her brother Dan married and had a family of his own. Family love and community love would have to be enough—romantic love hurt too much. Especially if she was foolish enough to fall for a man like Jack, who had no intention of staying.

At recess this morning, she'd told Milly all about Jack and the twins' startling, sudden appearance, and since Milly had always been her best friend, she didn't skip the part about the war of words she and Jack had engaged in. Milly's eyes had gotten round as dinner plates when Caroline described the way she had thrown the pearl ring at Jack, then softened as Caroline told her about his returning it to her last evening.

"Oh, Caroline," Milly had said after a gusty sigh. "Men have such foolish notions sometimes. It's up to the womenfolk to keep them sensible. Why, Nick was so proud of his son when he was born, he was all ready to book us passage on a ship so he could show him off to his brothers in England. I had to tell him there was no way I'd let our precious baby be exposed to the dangers of a sea voyage anytime soon—maybe ever." She had chuckled. "But it sounds as if Jack has a good heart underneath his foolishness. You say he looks like Pete?"

"Quite a bit, yes," Caroline had admitted. "But the resemblance is only skin-deep. Inside they're nothing alike. Pete was careful. He planned everything out in his mind, sometimes even on paper. Jack seems much more impulsive, spur-of-the-moment."

"And his wife died? Poor little girls…"

"Yes, three years ago."

Then Caroline had seen the faraway, musing look in Milly's eyes. "Stop right there, Milly Brookfield."

"What?" Milly had asked innocently, but from the guilty look on her face, Caroline had known her guess had hit the bull's-eye.

"You're as transparent as glass, old friend, and I'll tell you right now I am *not interested*."

"But he's a widower with two little girls in need of a mother, and if he looks anything like Pete, he must be at least a little handsome."

Oh, yes, Jack Collier was handsome, all right.

"He's moving to who knows what kind of place in the wilds of Montana, and I'm not leaving Simpson Creek— nor would I marry any man *staying* in Simpson Creek for that matter, as I've said," she had added hastily after noting the speculative gleam in Milly's eye. Reminding herself her friend was "Marrying Milly," the foundress of the Spinsters' Club, Caroline had tried to distract her. "If you want to try to get him interested in a Spinsters' Club match, go right ahead, though I don't know why any of our ladies would want to go up there, either."

"What's that line from Shakespeare—'methinks the lady doth protest too much'?" Milly had quoted coyly.

Caroline didn't realize she'd uttered an exasperated sound until Jack asked, "What's the matter?"

"Oh…oh, nothing," she muttered, aware she'd been woolgathering at the stove for several minutes. "I just think this stew needs a little more salt, that's all…"

The sun was high in the sky the next morning by the time Jack reached the Waters ranch, his horse's reins tied on to the back of a wagon he'd rented to haul the shovels, saws and nails he'd bought at the mercantile before starting out. Jack was pleased to see that his men had already gotten to work clearing the debris and weeds from the charred site of the former bunkhouse and had selected several trees to chop down at some distance away so as not to remove the shade trees from the home site. He hoped whoever bought the place someday would appreciate their thoughtfulness.

They unloaded the tools and set to work cutting down the trees, but they'd only been working an hour when they were interrupted by the arrival of a buckboard driven by a man with a pretty dark-haired woman holding a baby beside him.

Jack laid down his saw and wiped the sweat from his brow, watching as the man jumped down from the wagon and lifted a large covered platter from the back.

"Hullo, might you be Jack Collier?" the man inquired in an English-accented voice as he started toward Jack. Both he and the lady were dressed as if for a special occasion, the man in a frock coat and trousers, the lady in a dress of dark green.

Jack nodded. "What can I do for you, sir?"

"We're your neighbors, Nick and Milly Brookfield," the man said, holding out his free hand as he approached Jack. "I can see you're hard at work and we're on the way to the Gilmore wedding, so we won't hold you up, but my wife thought it would be nice to welcome you with a couple of chocolate cakes." He lifted the covering off of one of them, and murmurs of appreciation erupted from the men gathered around Jack.

"Very nice of you, Mrs. Brookfield," Jack said, grinning. He touched the brim of his hat to her. "I can promise you these won't last long with this bunch, but I'll see you get your platters back safe and sound." He turned back to Brookfield. "You know we're only here for the winter, right? We'll be off for Montana in the spring."

He saw the woman atop the bench seat studying him intently.

"No reason we can't welcome you anyway," she said.

"It's good to have neighbors, if only for a while. I've met your charming daughters, by the way, yesterday. Lovely girls."

"Thank you, ma'am."

"I'd like to invite you and your men to Sunday services," Milly Brookfield went on. "You may have noticed the new church is only half-built, but as long as the weather holds, we've been meeting in the meadow across the creek from the church. The service starts at ten o'clock."

Jack guessed his men were far more interested in what Simpson Creek had to offer on Saturday nights than about church on Sunday, but he didn't say so. "I'm planning to be there, Mrs. Brookfield, with my girls."

"Excellent," she said. "We'll look forward to seeing you there. Nick, we'd better get going. I promised Prissy we wouldn't be late for the wedding, since I'm one of the attendants."

Jack watched as the wagon rolled on toward the main road, touched by the neighborly gesture, while behind him, his men devoured the chocolate cakes. Raleigh made sure they saved a piece for him, but within five minutes, only the tiniest crumbs remained.

"I just *love* weddings!" Amelia cried, spinning around in an effort to get her pinafore to bell out like the skirts of the festively dressed ladies dancing with their partners.

They stood against the wall of the ballroom of Gilmore House, flanking Caroline, who was seated. The floor was filled with celebrating couples dancing to the music of a trio of fiddlers. The after-wedding party was in full swing.

"How do you know if you love *weddings?* This is the first wedding we ever been to, an' you know it," the ever-precise Abby informed her sister, but she swayed in time to the fiddling, her foot tapping.

"*We've* ever been to," Caroline corrected her, out of habit.

"You never been to any weddings before, either, Aunt Caroline?" Abby asked. "I thought grown-up ladies went to lots of weddings."

Caroline said, "Yes, I've been to lots of weddings. I was correcting your grammar, dear."

But Abby apparently had no use for a grammar lesson outside of schoolhouse walls. "Bet this was the first wedding you ever gone to under a tree, Aunt Caroline, ain't it?" she asked, referring to the site where the wedding had taken place, before everyone returned to Gilmore House for the party.

Caroline gave up on grammar lessons, for now, at least. "Yes, it was," she admitted with a smile. "We call the tree the Wedding Oak. Miss Prissy got married there because the church is being rebuilt, and because it's a special place for her and Sheriff Bishop, her new husband." She nodded toward the bride and groom as they waltzed by.

"She's so beautiful," Amelia said, clasping her hands together and sighing. "I wanna be a bride!"

"And so you will be," Caroline told her. "And both of you girls will be lovely brides, when it comes your turn."

"But how do you know, Aunt Caroline? Maybe I'll grow up and be a teacher like you. Then I won't never marry," Abby said. "I'd like to be a teacher, but I'd like to be a bride in a pretty dress like Miss Prissy, too." She looked torn by competing possibilities.

"Then perhaps you'll be a teacher for a while and then marry," Caroline said. She didn't want these girls thinking once one became a teacher, one could never marry, just because that was what she had chosen.

"Don't you want to be a bride, Aunt Caroline?" Abby asked. She lowered her voice to a conspiratorial whisper. "You could marry my papa—he's not married."

"Silly, she can't marry Papa—she's still missing Uncle Pete!" her sister said in a hushed tone.

"But someday?" Abby persisted. "I think you two should—"

"We'll talk about that later, Abby," Caroline interrupted quickly, relieved to see Milly bearing down on them, accompanied by her sister Sarah.

"Are you young ladies having a good time?" Milly said, bending down to them.

"Yes, Miss Milly," they chorused.

"I'll bet you girls would like to dance, wouldn't you? I just happen to know a couple of boys who would like to ask you, but they're shy," Milly said, nodding toward two boys who were eyeing the twins from across the room.

Caroline recognized Billy Joe Henderson and one of the other boys from school. "Why don't you go say hello, and maybe they'll work up the courage?"

Of course, now that they were aware of being looked at, the boys had taken to pushing and shoving each other good-naturedly.

Abby looked at Amelia. By tacit consent, they set off across the floor.

"They understand one another without speaking, don't they?" Sarah commented.

Caroline nodded, fighting the maternal swell of pride

she reminded herself she had no right to. "They're good children."

"I noticed you're not wearing full mourning today, Caroline," Sarah said, with a nod of approval at Caroline's dove-gray dress with black trim at the collar, wrists, waistline and hem. "That's a beautiful dress."

"It's just for the wedding," Caroline insisted, too quickly. She was illogically afraid that the two sisters could guess she had imagined joining in with the dancers, too, with Jack Collier as her partner. "It's a wedding. I didn't want to look so somber." Her mother and father had both looked happy when they'd seen what she'd put on. Caroline knew her mother had made the dress in hopes her daughter would start wearing it months ago.

"I think it's very becoming," Milly said, then added, with the daring only a longtime friend could muster, "Caroline, dear, no one would think less of you if you changed to half-mourning now."

Caroline deliberately let that pass. "And how are you feeling, Sarah?" she asked, for the younger Matthews sister, who had married the town doctor, was with child.

Sarah glanced down at her abdomen, which barely revealed the swell of pregnancy under her dress. "Much better, now that the first few months are over." She glanced meaningfully at the twins, who were in earnest flirtation with the two boys. "Oh, Caroline, what if I have twins, too? Nolan says they run in his family."

"*Now* he tells you! One at a time is enough for me," Milly said, her gaze going to where Mrs. Detwiler, the town matron, was showing off baby Nicholas. "I declare, little Nick keeps me busier than a whole passel of ranch hands. Which reminds me, I met the twins' father this morning, on our way here. Jack Collier is…um, quite the handsome fellow," Milly remarked, as if merely informing her sister.

Caroline shot her a warning look, willing her to remember the conversation they'd had in the schoolhouse the other morning.

"If you're sure you don't mind, Caroline," Milly said, "I think I *will* see if I can tempt him into joining in some of our Spinsters' Club activities while he's here this winter. It's a shame to waste a good bachelor like that."

Sarah giggled, clearly unaware of the undercurrent of challenge in Milly's words.

Caroline knew what Milly was up to—trying to make her jealous. She made her shrug elaborate. "Be my guest. What Jack Collier does or doesn't do is none of my business." She ignored the pang which stabbed her heart at the thought. "And anyway," she added with more sincerity, "the twins need a mother. Who knows what kind of Montana woman Jack would pick?"

I must stick with my purpose. Would it take years before people took her vow of spinsterhood seriously and gave up matchmaking attempts? Surely her resolve would become easier once Jack Collier left. She stifled the thought of how it would feel when he came back to reclaim his children, perhaps with a bride, and Amelia and Abby left, too.

Milly tapped an index finger to her upper lip thoughtfully, staring across the room at a trio of ladies from the Spinsters' Club who had just sat down with cups of punch. "I think Jack just might suit Faith Bennett perfectly."

Caroline followed her gaze, firmly squelching the surge of acid that hit her stomach at the thought of Faith dancing with Jack Collier at an event such as this. Jack probably had two left feet when it came to dancing, anyway. "Oh, I think Faith would die of fright the first time she saw one of those grizzly bears they have up in Montana," she said. "She's sort of the timid type. I think Maude Harkey would suit him better. Her papa used to say she couldn't be stampeded by anything or anyone."

Just then, the music ended. "Oh, look, Prissy and Sam are about to cut the cake," Caroline said, pointing to where the bridal couple had stepped over to the tall confection Sarah had baked. "Let's go watch." She started across the floor, gesturing for Sarah and Milly to follow her.

She missed the wink Milly and Sarah exchanged.

Caroline was conscious of a lump in her throat as she watched Prissy Gilmore, radiant with happiness, feed her handsome groom the first piece of cake. The wedding guests applauded.

That should have been Pete and me, half a year ago. They had been so in love, so sure that nothing would prevent a lifetime of happiness together.

She wasn't conscious of the tear that stole down her cheek, or that Amelia and Abby had rejoined her, until she felt Amelia's hand tugging on the sleeve of her gray, black-trimmed dress. She bent over, and Amelia whispered, "Why are you cryin', Aunt Caroline?"

"Aren't you happy for Miss Prissy?" asked Abby. The twins had met the bride and Sheriff Sam Bishop under the Wedding Oak after the couple had taken their vows.

"Oh, I'm *very* happy for Miss Prissy and Sheriff Sam," Caroline assured them, wishing they hadn't seen the tear. "Lots of ladies cry at weddings…" she began, then stopped.

She wouldn't try to gloss over her honest feelings,

even to the children. "I… I guess I was just missing your Uncle Pete," she told them, and the two regarded her solemnly. Then, spontaneously, each gave her a hug.

When she straightened, Milly was there, too, and placed an arm bracingly around her shoulder. It felt wonderful and reassuring, but she couldn't help missing a different—masculine—shoulder to lean on.

I have to get used to standing on my own, she reminded herself. *I've chosen a different way.*

Chapter Seven

The last notes of "I Love Thy Kingdom, Lord" died away, joined by a rustle of fabric and dried grass as the congregation sat down in the meadow the next morning. The song leader joined them, and Reverend Chadwick strode forward with Bible in hand.

The twins sat with Caroline on a couple of spread-out quilts, with the older Wallaces sitting behind them on cane-backed chairs brought from home. Papa said his rheumatism made it too hard to get up again after the sermon when he sat on the ground.

"I've never been to a church in a meadow, Aunt Caroline," Amelia confided in a whisper, looking up at the overhanging boughs of the cottonwood trees. A mockingbird flitted from branch to branch with a flash of black, gray and white. A grasshopper jumped off her shoe, making her giggle.

"We didn't get to church much at home," Abby whispered. "Papa said we used to go, when Mama was alive."

"Yeah, but he was always too busy around the ranch before we left," Amelia added.

"Well, I hope you like this one," she told the twins.

She felt a surge of love for the motherless girls which surprised her with its strength. In the short time they had been at her house, they had wormed their way into a big portion of her heart.

"The church is coming along quite well, isn't it, congregation?" Reverend Chadwick asked, turning to gesture toward the unpainted frame of the building rising on the site of the old one just beyond the opposite bank of the creek. His white hair gleamed in the gentle fall sunlight. "Lord willing and if the weather cooperates, before you know it, we'll be worshipping inside again, just as the cold weather arrives. Hasn't God been good to Simpson Creek?"

There was a chorus of amens.

"I'm reminded of Ecclesiastes," Chadwick went on, "in which King Solomon writes, 'There is a time to break down, and a time to build up.' We experienced the first time, didn't we? And now we are in the midst of the second, a time to build up."

"Hallelujah!" Mrs. Detwiler exclaimed.

A time to be born, and a time to die... A time to weep, and a time to laugh; a time to mourn, and a time to dance, thought Caroline, remembering about the rest of the passage.

She had dreamed of Pete again last night. She dreamed of him often. When her grief had been new, he'd come to her in dreams every night, and his presence had been so real, she'd hated to wake to the reality that he was gone. The dreams had decreased in frequency, but he always smiled and touched her cheek in that way he had done in life. But last night, after he smiled, he waved and seemed to be walking away from her. *A time to get, and a time to lose...*

At the back of the meadow Caroline heard the sound of creaking axles and the snort of a horse. Some late-comer arriving.

The twins jerked their heads around.

"It's Papa!" Amelia said.

"Here we are, Papa!" Abby said in a stage whisper, waving.

Around them, folks chuckled. Caroline put a finger to her lips, smiling to soften the rebuke, as Jack, hat in hand, made his way across the meadow to where they were sitting.

"And if I may add to Scripture, a time to greet new-comers," Reverend Chadwick said. "You must be the twins' papa. Welcome."

"Sorry I'm late, sir," Jack murmured.

"No problem, young man," Chadwick assured him.

"Here, Papa, sit here!" Amelia said, patting the empty space she had cleared on the blanket.

Reverend Chadwick went on with his sermon, and Caroline did her best to concentrate on the preaching and not on the man sitting with them. It was difficult. Jack shared many of Pete's mannerisms—the way he cocked his head when he was listening intently, the re-laxed way he rested his hands upon his legs, even the way he brushed away a fly—all were the same. If she had been less than the practical, feet-on-the-ground woman that she was, it would have been very tempting to close her eyes and pretend to herself that Pete was once again sitting beside her.

Afterward, of course, everyone in town had to come up to Jack and introduce themselves, for strangers were rare in Simpson Creek—churchgoing strangers, at least. Caroline wanted to go home. After all, her mother could use her help with Sunday dinner, and there were lesson plans to make for the coming week at school. But the real reason was that it made her downright uncomfortable seeing folks who'd known Pete standing in conversational clusters out of earshot, indicating Jack with a nod of their heads and eyeing her in turn. She was fairly certain they were talking about how much Jack resembled his late brother, and speculating how that might make her feel.

Surely no one would assume she would take up with Pete's brother on the shallow basis of that resemblance, would they? Even the remote possibility that anyone could think that made her uneasy.

"How's my Billy Joe doin', Miss Wallace? Behavin' hisself, is he?" Mr. Henderson asked, breaking into her thoughts as his tobacco-scented presence invaded her nostrils. The man stood a few inches closer to her than was comfortable.

Caroline would have liked to have been honest and said that Billy Joe could be the bane of her existence on occasion, but she did not want to be discouraging. "I find him a very high-spirited boy," she said, "but when he applies himself to his lessons, he's very intelligent." She hoped she was being tactful enough but still getting her point across.

But tact was lost on Mr. Henderson, and he hooted with laughter, slapping his leg. "'High-spirited,'" he echoed, hooting again. "Miss Wallace, you said a mouthful! His mama says she has a headache from the time he opens his eyes in the morning till the minute he hops off to th' schoolhouse, and then it's gone right up till th' minute he comes whistlin' home."

Caroline couldn't help but smile. Billy Joe often made her feel like that, too.

"Well, you feel free to paddle him if he deserves it, and I'll take him out to the woodshed when he gets home, too," Mr. Henderson promised. "I heard you kept him after school the other day, but you let him off too light, just havin' to write on the blackboard."

Caroline forced her features to remain pleasant. "In truth, Mr. Henderson, I think he hates having to write on the board a lot worse than he would a paddling." She always thought there were better ways to correct a child's behavior than corporal punishment, anyway.

"Aw, now, don't be goin' too soft on the boy," his father told her. "My paw always took a strap to me when I needed it, and it didn't hurt me none."

Caroline knew his was a popular view, but she hadn't grown up with such a father. Her own papa was firm and could certainly be stern, but he had never found it necessary to get out the strap, even with Dan.

"Excuse me, sir, but I need to speak to Miss Caroline…"

She turned to Jack with a smile, welcoming the interruption. She didn't want to get into a debate with a parent on types of discipline. She was the teacher, and she would decide how to correct her pupils' behavior at school. She had never used the paddle that hung behind her desk and never would. But this was not the place to discuss it.

Henderson gave way affably. "Sure, sure. We were just talkin' about my boy. Remember what I said, Miss Wallace—give 'im a lickin' if he needs it."

"I'll take what you've said into consideration, Mr. Henderson," she said, as the man ambled away.

"I was about to take the girls down to the hotel for dinner," Jack told her, nodding toward the twins, who stood watching them from a few yards away at the roadside. "And then out to see the ranch site so they can see where I'll be staying till spring. We got a fair start on the cabin yesterday, if I do say so myself."

"Of course, Mr. Collier," she said, using the formal address lest anyone overhear them. "I'm sure the twins would enjoy seeing the ranch and your progress on the bunkhouse. And of course the food at the hotel is delicious. Be sure and try the apple pie. We'll be at home, of course, whenever you'd like to bring them back."

He rubbed his jaw. "Well, Miss Caroline, the twins had a good idea and I promised I would ask you. Seems they've taken quite a shine to you, and they'd like you to come along with us for dinner and the ride to the ranch."

Caroline blinked. Of all the things Jack Collier might have said, she wasn't expecting this. She firmly squelched the voice within her that wanted her to smile and accept his invitation eagerly. "I—I wouldn't dream of intruding on your time with your girls, Jack," she said in a low tone, hating the flush she could feel spreading up her cheeks. "You tell them I'll see them whenever you bring them back from the ranch. Oh, and remember tomorrow is a school day, so they'll need to get a good night's rest."

As soon as she said the last sentence, she wanted to call it back. How fussy and proper she sounded again! And it wasn't up to her to dictate how long a father spent with his children in any case, she reprimanded herself.

He smiled. "I don't think they're going to take no for an answer," he said, nodding toward where the girls were hopping from one foot to another now in barely concealed impatience.

"But—"

"You wouldn't want to disappoint them, would you? I'm going to be in a heap of trouble if I have to tell them I couldn't get you to agree." He smiled so winningly that even the hardest-hearted woman couldn't have refused.

"I—I… I'm sorry, Jack, I don't think it's a good idea." She couldn't tell him that she was worried about being too attracted to him. What other excuse would he believe? "It's just that I've made it very plain with everyone in town that teaching is my life, now, and—"

"And two of your students have requested your company," Jack completed her sentence for her, still smiling. "There's no rule against that, is there? Haven't you been invited to a meal with one of your pupils before?"

It was early in the school year, but Caroline had already had Sunday dinner at the Hallidays' a week ago, and other families had spoken of inviting her also. It was an honor to have the schoolteacher eat with a family. But usually there were two parents present, not a handsome widowed father.

He gave her a considering look, as if he guessed the reason for her reluctance. "You'd be making two little girls very happy," he said. "And spending the afternoon with a friend. We *are* friends, aren't we? After our little talk the other night, I thought we were."

She sighed, deciding to give in gracefully, though she squelched the happy feeling accepting gave her. She would have to be on her guard.

"Very well, Jack. On that basis, I will come. But we will have to stop at the house and let Mama know—she and Papa have already headed home."

The pleasure that flashed across his eyes was reward enough. He brushed a hand across his forehead in exaggerated relief. "Whew! I don't know how I would have told them if you hadn't agreed."

She couldn't stop her lips from curving upward. "I certainly wouldn't want to do anything to upset those sweet girls, Jack." And if she enjoyed Jack's pleased grin as much as the thought of the girls' smiles, she kept it to herself.

It only took a few minutes for them to walk down to the hotel. During this time Jack was surprised by an unexpected feeling of completeness. The four of them looked like a family, if one didn't know better. A man and his wife and their two daughters.

It was the first time he had gone anywhere with a female since his wife had died.

Abby and Amelia clearly adored Caroline, and they looked as if they were thriving under the Wallaces' care. They wore two different dresses, one yellow, one pink, which had apparently been retrieved from Caroline's old ones and freshened up. They skipped along the boardwalk just ahead of their father and Caroline, past the post office, the jail and the mercantile.

The restaurant was reached through the hotel lobby. It was obviously a popular place on Sunday afternoons, for most of the tables were full. But one stood empty in the bay window that faced Main Street, so they were shown there by the waitress, a pleasant-faced older woman in an apron.

"Well hello, Miss Caroline," the woman said, while glancing at Jack and the girls with open curiosity. "It's good to see you! It's been a long time since you were in here…"

Her voice trailed off, and she looked flustered.

Perhaps the last time Caroline had dined in the hotel, Pete had been her escort.

"And this must be Mr. Collier and his twins."

Truly, there were no secrets in a small town, Jack thought.

"Well, it's busy as a barefoot boy on a red anthill in here, so I'd best get down to business," the woman said. "Our special today is chicken an' dumplings."

They all chose the special, and the waitress bustled away.

"I see you have new dresses, girls," Jack said. "You both look very nice."

"They were Aunt Caroline's when she was our age," Abby informed him.

"You should see all the clothes Grandma Wallace has in that trunk we can wear," crowed Amelia. "*And* she's makin' us new ones alike. Some in red calico, and some in green gingham."

"Hopefully by the time Mama has the identical dresses made, I'll have learned to tell them apart," Caroline said.

"Oh, that's easy, Aunt Caroline," Amelia said. "Abby has a scar on her forehead from when she fell outa the swing under the tree back home. I don't. I *never* fall out of swings."

Caroline leaned over and peered closely at the spot Amelia indicated. "Why, thank you, Amelia. I never noticed that. That's very helpful."

Jack saw Abby scowl at her sister. "Why'd you tell? Now we can't change places at school."

"You aren't playing the twin games on your teacher, are you, girls?" Jack said, knowing Abby, especially, liked to pass responsibility on to her more compliant twin.

"No, Papa," Amelia said, while Abby had the grace to look a little shamefaced.

"So how do you like being the teacher, Miss Caroline?" Jack asked, after he could think of no more brilliant conversational gambit.

"I enjoy it very much," Caroline said. "Of course, I'm fortunate that I can live at home. Many schoolteachers have to board with one of the students' families, and from the stories Miss Phelps told me—she was the schoolteacher who just left to be a missionary—that wasn't always pleasant. At one of the homes where she boarded, the little boy left a frog in her bed."

The twins squealed in gleeful terror. Jack chuckled.

"Of course, growing up with Dan, I'm used to such pranks, and frogs don't scare me," Caroline said, giving the girls a meaningful look.

"And they pay you fairly?"

"Sixteen dollars a month," Caroline said proudly. "Of course, I give most of it to Mama to help with the household expenses." She shrugged. "My needs are few."

He had no experience with a woman who wanted nothing for herself. Even his Lucinda, who'd been quite content with her lot as a ranch wife, had prized her few knickknacks and the onyx earbobs he'd given her one Christmas. Bringing her a dress-length of calico from the general store had made her whoop and hug him.

But he could not imagine Lucinda working for a living, if something had happened to him, as Caroline was doing.

Caroline held a very honorable position as the town schoolteacher. Even while Jack had been kept busy with introductions after church, he'd noticed a dozen parents coming up to greet her, their children in tow. She'd been the recipient of friendly smiles and nods as they'd entered the restaurant, too. It had made him stand a little taller at her side and realize he'd been more than a little lucky to have placed his children with her family.

He wished he'd been the one to meet her first, not Pete.

The thought made guilt wash over him like a cold, wet blanket. Surely it did not speak well of him that he was envying the love his dead brother had found with this woman. But what if Pete had never met her, and Jack had been the one to find that advertisement the Spinsters' Club had placed? Would he have had the gumption to come up and meet the ladies, as Pete had done?

Their dinners came then, and he stopped speculating, at least for now.

The twins had seized their forks, and Jack was about to dig into the savory-smelling chicken and dumplings when Caroline caught his attention.

"Do you mind if we pray first, Jack?"

He shook his head, wondering if he was automatically expected to give the blessing as the only man at the table. Caroline bowed her head. Quickly, Jack gestured for his daughters to do likewise and bowed his own head.

Then Caroline began to speak. "Heavenly Father, we thank You for this tasty meal and ask that You bless it to the nourishment of our bodies. We thank You for the opportunity to spend some time together, and pray that You give Jack and his men strength and good weather so that they may build their dwelling quickly."

He'd never seen anyone pray so easily outside of a church. If he'd been a good father, grace before meals would have been a rule. He'd grown lax since his wife had died and especially on this trail drive, allowing the girls to adopt the careless manners of his drovers. He'd been brought up better than that by a godly mother, learned Bible stories at her knee and been baptized in the closest creek by the local preacher. It all slipped away so easily, if one didn't pay attention.

He noticed Caroline automatically moved to help the girls tuck their napkins into the neckline of their dresses before they started eating, too. Well, it made good sense and made life easier for whoever did the laundry, didn't it? But it also struck him as such a motherly thing to do.

Perhaps he could learn a few things from Caroline without her knowing he hadn't been doing them, and therefore thinking less of him.

Would he be able to find a lady in Montana who was as good to his children as Caroline was? She was a natural mother, he mused, and didn't even realize it.

Their stomachs filled, they returned to the meadow and boarded the wagon. The twins sat in the bed of the wagon, while Caroline sat next to him on the driver's bench.

"Papa, is it far to your ranch?" Abby asked.

"About five miles, Punkin," he said, guiding the wagon back onto the road. "But remember, it's not *my* ranch. It's just a place where the men and I are keeping the herd until the weather's good enough to drive them to Montana. Then you'll be coming to join me up there." Somehow that no longer felt as exciting as it once had.

He glanced over his shoulder as the horse began to

trot back down Main Street toward the road that led south. Abby looked distinctly mutinous at his words.

"I think we should stay here, Papa. We like Simpson Creek," Abby said, her lower lip jutting out pugnaciously.

"Yeah," Amelia said.

He knew better than to point out they'd only been in Simpson Creek for a few days. "Simpson Creek is nice, but just wait till you see Montana Territory, girls," he said with all the enthusiasm he could muster. "There's big, tall mountains, huge pine forests, snow deeper than you are tall—think of the snowball fights you can have!"

Another glance behind revealed uncomprehending faces. Of course—the girls had never seen snow in south Texas. He hadn't, either, until he'd been on campaign with Hood during the first part of the war, though he hadn't had much time for snowball fights then. Then he'd been furloughed home to recover from a wound, and while he was home his wife died, so he had never returned to the war. There'd been no one else to care for his children.

"There's mountains *here,* Papa," Amelia said, pointing at the distant blue hills.

"Those? Why, those are just anthills compared to the mountains in Montana," he said, then realized his words sounded disparaging. "No offense, Miss Caroline," he said quickly.

"None taken," she said. Her face was serene under her black-trimmed spoon bonnet.

"Those hills *are* nice to look at, right enough," he said, still feeling as if he needed to apologize. "And I like the trees around here." He indicated a stand of liveoaks and pecan trees they were passing. "Why, at home, there's pretty much just scrub mesquite and cactus, and it's so flat. This land kinda rolls," he added. They were going up a gentle grade around a curve now. "Yes, it's pretty country here."

She looked amused, as if she knew full well he was trying to pull his foot out of his mouth. "Just wait till spring, when the fields and roadsides are full of blue-bonnets and all kinds of other flowers—yellow, orange, pink and purple. You'll still be here when it starts."

"You like it here."

She shrugged. "I've never been very far from Simpson Creek in all my life. It's what I know."

"Haven't you ever wanted to see other places?" he asked curiously.

She shrugged. "Maybe I'll travel someday."

She faced straight ahead, so he could see very little of her face because of the scooped sides of the bonnet. Her voice was carefully neutral, as if she didn't mind one way or the other. Could that really be the truth?

He glanced once more into the back. The twins were singing a little song as they played cat's cradle with a bit of string they'd found in the wagon bed.

They were silent for a mile or so. "This must be a very familiar road to you, since your friend lives next to the Waters ranch," he said, trying another conversational gambit.

She nodded. "Yes, I'd borrow Papa's horse and ride out to see Milly and Sarah when we were girls growing up."

They fell silent again after that. The quiet was broken only by the horse's clip-clopping along the dusty road and the screech of a crow commenting on their passing. Jack stole occasional sidelong glances at the self-contained woman in black beside him, but Caroline seemed content to watch the scenery and glance backward once in a while at the twins.

He wondered what she was thinking. Was she glad she had chosen to come with them, or wishing she had stayed home? He wished he was more of a brilliant conversationalist so he could draw her out, win one of her rare smiles. Then when he caught himself thinking such nonsense, he told himself it made no sense. Caroline Wallace wasn't interested in courting—not anyone, but especially not her dead fiancé's brother—or leaving her little town to go to Montana with him and the girls.

Was the woman he would marry already in Montana, waiting for him to come and discover her? Maybe she'd be blonde, with riotously curling golden hair and big blue eyes, or a redhead, whose fiery mane would complement green cats' eyes, completely unlike the woman beside him with her neat brown hair and eyes the color of the Arbuckle's coffee Cookie made. The woman he would meet in Montana would dress in flowery, feminine fabrics, not harsh black.

"When are we going to get there, Papa?" Amelia asked, bringing him back to his present surroundings with a jolt.

"We're almost there, Punkin. That's the neighboring ranch," he said, pointing to the entrance gate of the Brookfield Ranch. "The very next place is the Waters Ranch, where we're staying."

"Perhaps you ought to give the place a new name," Caroline suggested, as they turned off the road and passed the faded "Waters Ranch" sign. "The old owners are gone, after all."

He shrugged. "I would, if I was going to settle there, instead of just roosting there for the winter."

"Colliers' Roost, then?" she suggested, her lips curving upward.

So the woman did have a sense of humor. He tried not to be too pleased at seeing her smile.

By now he could see the men clustered around the beginnings of the bunkhouse. It looked as if they had been hard at work, for the frame was thigh-high with logs that had been trimmed to fit and rounded off on the ends. The mud chinking between the logs would be added last. He was pleased to see they hadn't been idle in his absence.

"Is that your new house, Papa?" Abby asked.

"When will it be finished, Papa? Can we stay there, too?" Amelia chimed in.

"Hopefully it'll be done within a couple of weeks, and no, it won't be nearly nice enough for you girls to stay there, just good enough for a bunch of rowdy cowboys to get in out of the cold," Jack told them with a wink. He wondered if Caroline disapproved of his men laboring on the Sabbath.

She didn't look critical, however, just interested. "They've gotten a good start, haven't they?" she commented. The approving way she said it pleased Jack.

They'd been spotted, and the men were laying down their hammers and saws and waving. Raleigh came forward, shading his eyes against the sun.

"Hi, Mr. Raleigh!" chorused Abby and Amelia.

"Well, howdy, girls, boss. Ma'am," he added, touching the brim of his hat.

"Miss Caroline, this is Raleigh Masterson, my ramrod. Raleigh, Miss Caroline Wallace. She was Pete's fiancée."

Raleigh's face sobered. "I'm right sorry about your loss, Miss Wallace. Nice that the girls could stay with you and your parents."

Not waiting for permission, the girls jumped over the side and went running over to Raleigh. "Well, it's only fair to warn you," he said, grinning as he hugged them, "they're an ornery pair, and that's a fact."

"I'll take your warning very seriously, Mr. Masterson," she said, her face mock-solemn as the girls flung their arms around the young man.

"Don't hurt my right-hand man, girls—I need to get some more work out of him," Jack said with a grin. "The beeves doing all right, Raleigh?"

"Right as rain, boss. They seem to like it here. They're watering at the creek right now."

Cookie was walking toward them, his crabbed, awkward gait making his bowlegs all the more apparent. He'd been quite a cowboy in his heyday, Jack knew, until a horse he was riding fell, then rolled on him, nearly crippling the man.

"Afternoon, boss, ma'am."

Jack made introductions again and made his voice carry loud enough that the men working on the cabin could hear.

"Would you like a bottle of sarsaparilla, Miss Wallace?" Cookie asked. "I know the girls will. Raleigh fetched us some supplies, so I had him get us a few bottles for when the twins visit."

Caroline politely declined, but the girls were happy to take the old cook up on his offer.

"Mind if we go out and check the herd?" Jack asked Caroline.

"Of course not," she said.

"Girls, you stay with Cookie and mind what he says, you hear? It's all right to look at the cabin, but you stay out of the men's way."

"Yes, Papa."

Jack clucked to the horses, steering them onto a dirt track in the scrub that led to the western edge of the ranch's land. He waved to one of his drovers lounging on a limestone boulder over the creek, whittling as he watched over the herd.

The cattle looked good, as Raleigh'd said. Some grazed near the creek's edge, others lay chewing their cuds, their hides twitching, their tails swishing to repel the flies that tormented them.

"That's a funny-looking creature," Caroline said, pointing to a red-spotted steer with crooked horns and a walleye.

"That's the lead steer, Old Red," Jack told her. "He can be cantankerous, but he leads the rest of them right where we need them to go. He's been on the trail before, so he's only one who won't be sold for meat at the end of the trail. We'll keep him for other trail drives, or sell him to another outfit needing a leader."

Caroline asked other questions about trail driving, surprising Jack with her interest and quick grasp of the details. The woman could probably find something to converse about with the President himself.

They returned to the building site, finding Abby and Amelia wrapped up in some yarn Cookie was spinning. Jack saw his men casting speculative glances at Caroline. They were sure to pester him with questions about her later, though they'd be oblique, respectful ones. Cow-hands didn't see many respectable women in their hard-working lives.

Jack was surprised at the regret he felt when it was time to take Caroline and the girls back to town. *Did Caroline feel it, too?*

Chapter Eight

"I think we're ready to go, girls," Caroline said, after sending Billy Joe Henderson on his way home. Once again, she'd been forced by his mischievous behavior to keep him after school to write on the chalkboard.

She was starting to think the boy committed his acts of mischief deliberately, as a way to postpone going home to his chores and his harsh father, even though his actions might result in more punishment for coming home late. She'd have to think of some other way to deal with the boy, she thought—maybe she should pay a call on both parents and tell them she would be giving their son some extra tutoring, so he wouldn't be punished for his lateness, and spend time working with him on his reading and ciphering. The boy wasn't unintelligent, but he wouldn't apply himself. Perhaps he thought acting up was the only way to gain her attention.

Amelia and Abby, who'd been quietly looking at one of the older-grade McGuffey readers while Billy Joe had written on the chalkboard, picked up their lunch pails and came to join her, but just then footfalls sounded on the steps outside. She heard a peremptory knock.

Her first quick thought was that it was Jack, in town for some reason and stopping off to see his girls. She was surprised by the quick lurch of pleasure the idea gave her. But it couldn't be—he'd just seen them yesterday, and he couldn't be leaving the work at the ranch to come see them every day.

Before she could even go to the door, however, a heavyset man with wide muttonchop whiskers and spectacles perched on a bulbous nose entered the room without waiting for an invitation.

"Miss Wallace?"

"Yes?" She tried to place the man, but she didn't think she'd ever met him.

"Everett Thurgood," he said. He didn't offer his hand. "I'm the San Saba school superintendent. I thought it was time I made your acquaintance, young lady."

His tone implied it was somehow her fault that he had not. Miss Phelps had mentioned him before she'd left for India, and the wrinkling of the old spinster's nose had tacitly indicated her opinion of the superintendent.

"And these are—?" he said, indicating the staring, silent twins with a raised brow. "Misbehaving scholars, perhaps?"

"Oh, no, sir, they're very good students," Caroline said, glad she had already sent Billy Joe on his way. "They're Amelia and Abby Collier, and they're staying with my family over the winter."

"I see." Thurgood continued to eye them as if wondering what species they were. "If I might have a moment of your time, Miss Wallace?"

Was he here to assess her work? Why hadn't he come during the school day, if that was the case? It had been a challenging day, and Caroline was eager to get home. But she knew her duty.

"Girls, could you play outside for a few minutes while Mr. Thurgood and I chat? Don't leave the schoolyard."

Mr. Thurgood waited, staring out the window, hands clasped behind him, as the twins scampered out the door.

He turned when the door banged behind them. "Miss Wallace, it's the understanding of every schoolteacher in the county that attendance at the yearly Institute held at the San Saba courthouse is mandatory. At that weeklong meeting, all the teachers in the county are instructed in new aspects of the subjects that they teach. You did not attend."

"No, sir," Caroline said, feeling her hackles rise at the man's sharp tone. "It was held in June, and I did not decide to assume this position until late summer. Miss Phelps, my predecessor, assured me that it would be no problem, providing I attended next summer."

Mr. Thurgood harrumphed. "There wouldn't have been a problem, young lady, had you communicated with me on the matter. Very well, then, you will be present at the next Institute, provided the county keeps you on next term."

Caroline blinked in surprise at the implied threat. "Of course," she murmured. "Would you…would you perhaps like to look over my lesson plans, in the meantime, since you're here?"

She hoped he would decline, but he did not, so she was forced to spend the next hour showing him the outlines of what she had been teaching in every grade. He examined test papers, looked at the McGuffey readers, peered at the slates she was taking home, harrumphing all the while. Every so often she would go to the window to check on the twins, hoping he would get the hint, but he didn't.

When at last he rose—to leave, she thought, stifling a sigh of relief—he peered at her down his nose. "You're in mourning, Miss Wallace?" he asked, as if he had just noticed. "It *is* 'Miss' Wallace, isn't it? Not 'Mrs.'? I don't like my teachers to have been married, even if they are widowed," he told her.

Your *teachers? Why, you pompous old windbag.* She bit her lip to keep back a sharp retort.

"In my day—I was a schoolmaster for many years, you know, before becoming the superintendent—having women teachers who had been married simply was not done."

"No, I was not married, sir," she said. "I wear mourning for my fiancé, who died last winter." *As if it's any of your business.* And then she immediately felt guilty, because the Bible enjoined believers to respect those in authority. *Forgive me, Lord. I'll try harder, though this man makes it difficult.*

He cleared his throat, noisily. "I see. I'll be on my way, Miss Wallace. But expect that I will be calling again, in the course of my duties to this county."

"You're welcome anytime," she forced herself to say. "When you come, why not make it during school hours—so you can observe my teaching, of course," she added, when he looked at her sharply. Did he guess she didn't like being alone with him? "Perhaps you would like to drill the students on their spelling or some other subject."

He harrumphed again. "We shall see, Miss Wallace. Good evening."

The moment he got into his buggy, the twins ran past it back inside.

"Aunt Caroline! Who was that stuffy old man?" Abby asked.

"He stayed forever! Can we go home now?" Amelia added.

She nodded. "You were such good, patient girls to wait so long. That was the school superintendent, Mr. Thurgood."

Amelia's brow wrinkled. "What's a 'sprintenant'?"

Caroline had to smile at the child's attempt to pronounce the big, unfamiliar word. "I suppose you could say the superintendent is my boss, like your papa is the boss of Mr. Masterson and the rest of the drovers."

"Well, our papa is a nicer boss than your boss," Amelia said sympathetically. "All his men like him. Don't you wish Papa was your boss instead?"

Caroline blinked, not knowing quite what to say to that. "Well, I'm sure your papa would say he doesn't know much about being the boss of teachers," she said carefully. "But sometimes, we learn the most from bosses who are tough."

Both girls looked skeptical.

"I hope Aunt Mary will let us have a cookie before supper," Abby said. "I'm famished!"

"I wish Papa could come to supper," Amelia said. "He's probably just having beans and corn bread. Cookie doesn't cook as good as Aunt Mary."

"As *well*," Caroline corrected automatically, her mind summoning a picture of Jack Collier, hunkered down at a campfire with a bowl of beans and corn bread. Her mother had invited him to stay for supper when they'd arrived back from the ranch last evening, but he'd said he had to get back to the ranch before it grew dark. He'd probably had enough of her prim presence by his side. Ah, well, she didn't know how to be anyone but herself.

But she'd been surprised at how disappointed she'd been. There was just something so compelling about the man. He commanded attention without even trying. He drew people to him like iron filings to a magnet.

She must not expect his visits to his children would always include her. After all, she had made her feelings plain, that she had given up the desire for a husband and family and chosen teaching instead. Even if he had feelings for her, she couldn't return them.

Caroline made a change to the twins' school day routine after that, for she decided it wasn't fair for Amelia and Abigail to have to wait at the school when she had to keep a pupil after class. From now on, if she wasn't ready to leave when she dismissed class, the twins would walk home with Lizzie Halliday, since the older girl lived just down the street from the Wallaces.

Today, however, Billy Joe had been uncharacteristically subdued and well-behaved, and none of the other usual mischief makers had given their teacher any reason to keep them after class. Caroline and the twins walked up Fannin Street from the school, but just as they arrived at the intersection with Main Street, a couple of horsemen rode by. They stared at the girls, then their beard-shadowed faces broke into grins of recognition.

Caroline felt Abby and Amelia shrink closer to her.

"Well, if it ain't the twins. Howdy, girls!" said one of them.

"Who's this purty lady with ya?" said the other, looking Caroline up and down.

"It's our teacher, Mr. Shorty," Amelia said.

The other one guffawed. "Tarnation, if teachers had been so purty when I was in school, I might not've been a broke-down outa-work cowboy today."

"Ya would, too. Yore head's too thick for book larnin', Alvin." He fingered the brim of his cap toward Caroline, but the gesture lost its respectful tone when coupled with his frank assessment of her. "Shorty Adams, ma'am. That there's Alvin Sims."

"Mr. Adams. Mr. Sims." Caroline acknowledged them with a brisk nod. She assumed they must be two of Jack's cowhands, yet she didn't remember seeing them at the ranch Sunday. And none of Jack's men had struck her as insolent—quite the opposite. "We must be getting home. Please give our best to Mr. Collier."

"Oh, we don't work for Collier no more," Alvin said with a sneer that wrinkled his mustache, which was uneven due to a scar that bisected it. "We ain't carpenters, we're cowboys."

Caroline remembered now that a pair of Jack's drovers had chosen to quit once he'd announced his plan to winter here. She wondered absently if they'd found other work, but if so, why were they absent from it in mid-afternoon?

"Good day, gentleman," she said, knowing they didn't deserve the term. She gave each girl's arm a meaningful squeeze, then resumed walking toward the post office, flanked on each side by the twins.

She heard snickering as the two rode off.

"I don't like those men," Abby said, once they were out of earshot. "That Mr. Shorty was always spitting tobacco juice anywhere he happened to be. Once it even landed on my boot. Papa made him apologize."

"And rightly so," Caroline said. "Well, you needn't worry about them anymore. No doubt they'll drift on back to south Texas and you'll never see them again."

"I hope so," Amelia said. "Alvin hid my dolly one time. He said he was only teasing, but I don't think Papa thought so, 'cause I heard him giving Alvin a talking-to afterward and he sounded angry."

Caroline could well imagine how much such a prank had upset the child, since Amelia was rarely seen without her doll clutched by one cloth arm. What kind of a man would take a child's doll? Jack was better off without these fellows.

The smell of fresh-baked cookies tickled her nostrils as they entered the kitchen. Molasses, unless she missed her guess.

"There you are," her mother greeted them from the kitchen table, where she was paring apples. "Did you girls have a good day at school? I have cookies and milk waiting for you. Go wash up and you can have a couple. You just missed Faith Bennett," her mother said to Caroline. "She wanted to remind you of the Spinsters' Club meeting tonight at her house."

Caroline groaned. Faith Bennett had become the president of the Spinsters' Club when Prissy had gotten married. "When are they going to understand that I'm not interested anymore? I suppose I should just tell them, flat-out."

Her mother tsked at her. "She said you would say that. She told me to tell you the main purpose of the meeting is to work on the quilt that's to be their contribution for the Christmas raffle for the Deserving Poor of San Saba County."

"Sure, but while we're stitching the quilt, Hannah, Polly and Bess will all be cooing about outings with their *beaux*."

Her mother gave her a look, and Caroline realized how envious her words had sounded. "I'm not jealous, Mama, only disinterested. Besides, with those three matched up this summer, the number of members has to be dwindling. Milly doesn't come much anymore, since she has a baby. Pretty soon everyone will be married and there'll be no more Spinsters' Club," she said with a dismissive gesture.

"No, Faith mentioned there were some new members coming—her cousin, who's come to live with them, for one. She says Louisa loves the theater as you do, and she's even been to plays by that Shakespeare fellow you set such store by."

Caroline sighed. Faith had guessed her Achilles' heel—her love of plays. She hadn't been quite honest when she'd let Jack Collier think she had no interest in traveling. It was true she cared little about journeys in themselves, or sightseeing, but if she could have gone somewhere where theaters were available—ah, that would be Heaven on earth.

"But I have my students' work to look over," she protested, "and what about—" She nodded toward Abby and Amelia, who were back in the kitchen and devouring their cookies like hungry wolf cubs.

"Caroline Wallace, you can look over your students' work right now, while I'm getting supper ready," her mother told her tartly. "And I'm sure the girls can make do with me while you're gone. All work and no play—"

"Makes Caroline Jane Wallace a dull girl," Caroline finished for her, using her mother's usual paraphrase. "All right, I'll go—I *would* like to hear about the plays," she admitted.

Caroline had to admit she was having a good time and was glad she had come to the meeting. The new girls seemed nice enough—Kate Patterson had recently come to live with Mrs. Patterson, her aunt, to help in the store, and Ella Justiss had come to work for the hotel as a waitress and maid-of-all-work. And Caroline liked Faith Bennett's cousin, Louisa Wheeler, immediately. Before she even got a chance to ask her about the plays she'd seen, Louisa peppered her with questions about teaching. She'd inherited a bit of money upon her parents' death, she said, and had no pressing need to work, but she was interested in becoming a teacher. After answering her questions, Caroline finally invited her to observe a class or two to see if she'd like to be a volunteer aide.

When the quilting began, Caroline maneuvered a spot next to Louisa, and maneuvered the talk around to *Romeo and Juliet*, the play she'd seen in Houston put on by a traveling company.

"It was such a tragic story, but so romantic," Louisa said with a sigh of remembrance. "I'm glad I'm unlikely to fall in love with some man whose family and mine are deadly rivals," she said with a wry smile. "If I ever fall in love at all."

"Oh, you will if you want to," Sarah Walker said, overhearing the newcomer's words from across the quilt. "Simpson Creek has seen a lot of matches made since my sister started the Spinsters' Club. It's quite amazing."

"Speaking of matches, Caroline," Polly Shackleford,

seated on Caroline's other side, said in her usual piercing voice, "have you lassoed that trail boss whose girls are staying with you, or is he available?"

Caroline was too shocked by the tactless question to speak, but Faith Bennett had no such difficulty.

"Why, Polly, I thought you and that hardware store man from Austin were keeping company. What happened to that?"

Polly shrugged. "He got homesick and went back to Austin. So I thought I'd ask Caroline about Jack Collier before I started trying to cut him out of the herd." She gave a raucous laugh, while around the quilting circle, the ladies exchanged glances and shot worried looks at Caroline.

Caroline at last found her voice. "I've no claim on the man. I've told everyone who would listen I've given up on such things. But anyone who's interested in the twins' father," she said, "needs to be aware that he's planning on moving on to Montana, come spring, along with his herd." Had she succeeded in sounding disinterested, as she hoped? If only she could convince *herself* completely.

At first there was silence, and then Polly cleared her throat. "Oh. I—I see. I…uh, didn't mean any offense, Caroline. Maybe I ought to become president of the club when Faith's term is up. Seems like they have first pick of the bachelors. Just look at Milly and Sarah and Prissy—all married now."

Faith cleared her throat, clearly embarrassed. She was the hostess, but the red flush on her face betrayed her annoyance. "You can have the presidency now, if you'd like to test that theory, Polly," she said coolly, then glanced meaningfully at the watch pinned to her dress bodice. "My, look how late it's gotten, ladies. Perhaps we'd better adjourn for refreshments, and continue our stitching another time."

Later, Caroline and Sarah left together.

"I'm sorry about Polly's clumsy tongue," Sarah said as they walked.

Caroline waved her concern away. "Polly's always spoken before she thought, but she doesn't mean any harm," Caroline said. "I know everyone thinks I have some sort of claim on Jack, but I don't. I did enjoy meeting Faith's cousin Louisa, though—" She broke off as she saw that Sarah had stopped suddenly, pointing at a wagon which had just pulled up in front of the doctor's office.

"Who can that be?"

Caroline peered through the darkness at a man helping another down from the back of the wagon. The latter cradled an arm in a makeshift sling, and the two women heard a groan and a muttered swear word escape through gritted teeth.

"Easy, Wes," the first man said in a low voice. "You'll feel a lot better once that arm's set…"

Caroline knew that voice. Startled, she nearly stumbled at a dip in the dirt road and couldn't stifle a small cry as she sought to regain her balance. She saw Jack's head jerk in their direction. "Who's there?"

"I'm the doctor's wife," Sarah called out. "Please go on up the steps, gentlemen. I'll summon my husband and we'll meet you at the door."

Was Jack hurt, too, just more able to walk than his trailhand? Worry flooded her soul. She had to know.

Chapter Nine

A second voice came out of the darkness toward Jack and the man he was trying to help. "Jack, it's Caroline. What happened?"

He held up the lantern with his free hand. Caroline's face was pale in the lantern light as she approached, her eyes wide.

"Wes's horse spooked at a jackrabbit and threw him," he said, his eyes drinking in the sight of her. "I think his arm's broken, maybe a rib, too." Her coincidental appearance was oddly comforting.

He transferred his attention to helping Wes up the steps. It was slow going. Wes groaned with every movement, and Jack hoped he wasn't bleeding inside. It was bad enough to be thrown, but did the no-good nag have to pitch the cowboy against a tree? Of all the rotten luck.

By the time they reached the last step, with Caroline following behind them, Dr. Walker had come through from the back of the house, opened the door and was lighting a pair of lamps inside his office. Another already burned in the waiting room, casting the physician's frame into waiting shadow.

"Bring him on in—easy, now," Dr. Walker cautioned in his Down East accent. "What happened?"

As Jack described the accident for the second time in as many minutes, he was aware of Caroline hovering in the background with the doctor's wife.

Wes had been laid gently down on a padded examining table, and now the doctor bent over the injured drover, gently probing his wounds. Each place he touched elicited a groan.

"Cowboy, I'm going to give you a dose of laudanum, and then it won't hurt as bad," Dr. Walker said and turned to a row of amber bottles on a low table behind him. He poured a small amount of brown liquid up to a scored mark on the glass, then looked at Jack and Caroline.

"Miss Caroline, might I ask you to go to the kitchen and make some coffee?" Dr. Walker said, rolling up his shirtsleeves. "We're going to need some when I'm through, I imagine."

"Of course," Caroline said, appearing relieved to have something to do.

"Why don't you go with her, Jack? I'll give this medicine time to take effect, then have a good look at your drover. Once I've done that, I'll come let you know how he is."

"But…won't you need some help?" Jack asked.

"Thanks, but my wife can assist me," Walker murmured, turning back to his patient.

Jack followed Caroline out the door and into the passageway that led to the kitchen and the rest of the living quarters. He lit the lamp on the kitchen table, then watched while Caroline busied herself brewing coffee on the stove, her movements businesslike and economical, yet at the same time, graceful. It was obvious she had been here before.

"How did you happen to be out there just now?" he asked. "Were you and Mrs. Walker out for a stroll? It *is* a fine night, what with the full moon and all."

"We were coming home from a Spinsters' Club meeting."

He must have appeared startled, for she added quickly, "Oh, not because either of us is interested in eligible bachelors, of course. The group is working on a quilt for the annual raffle."

He nodded, amused that she should be defensive with him about going to a meeting with her matchmaking society—and absurdly pleased at the same time she was not looking for a match for herself. If she ever changed her mind about giving up love, he wanted her to love him alone.

"Of course, they're your friends," he murmured, but Caroline Wallace remained flustered for some reason.

"Mama felt I should go…she's watching over the girls, of course."

"I didn't doubt that for a minute, Caroline," he assured her. "When I agreed to leave Abby and Amelia at your house, I didn't expect you to spend every waking minute with them. They seem to have made your parents into substitute grandparents." *The Wallaces were the sort of grandparents they should have had,* Jack thought.

She smiled then, and the effect it had on her face made him wish she would smile more often. She was beautiful when she smiled. It softened features that her black clothing rendered severe.

"When I left she was doing fittings for yet another pair of dresses for them. They're going to be the best-dressed little girls in all of Texas by the time…by the time they leave Simpson Creek." Her last few words seemed to sober her. "I—I should be getting home," she said suddenly. "The coffee will be ready in another few minutes," she said, nodding toward the pot on the stove. "Cups are in that cabinet to the left."

His hand shot out to touch her wrist. "Must you go?" he asked, his action and his words surprising them both.

Her lovely features registered surprise but not annoyance at his touch.

"I mean…if you must go I'll understand, of course, but I was hoping you would keep me company until Dr. Walker is able to tell me how Wes is doing." He was babbling, he thought, and must sound a plumb fool.

She sat down but then neither of them seemed to know what to say.

"Why don't you tell me how my girls are doing at school?" he suggested at last, picking the most obvious thing that came to his head.

She shrugged. "Abby and Amelia are continuing to improve at writing their letters, reciting, and doing their sums accurately. Lizzie Halliday, one of the older girls, has taken them under her wing and walks home with them if I must stay after school. Which can be fairly often, since one of the boys gets in trouble on a regular basis…"

He listened as she told him about Billy Joe Henderson and her suspicions that the boy got into trouble to postpone returning home to fatherly abuse. He remembered Caroline had been conversing with Henderson after church Sunday, and that the red-faced blowhard had been standing a little too close to Caroline.

It was all too easy to imagine a boy in such a situation preferring to spend the rest of his afternoon with a warm friendly teacher such as Caroline rather than go home to such a father.

He'd been that boy once. There had been no teacher for Jack to seek refuge with, however. When they were small, he and his brother had been taught at home, and only Pete had been deemed worthy to go on for more formal education. His mother had been as afraid of her husband as Jack was, and then she had died. Had Pete ever told Caroline about their father? Jack doubted it, for Pete had always preferred to dwell on the positive, and once he'd left the house, their father's tyrannical ways had ceased to impact him very much.

"I think the town is lucky to have you," he said.

She blinked. "Nonsense. I'm just doing my job," she said, as if embarrassed by the compliment, and fled to the stove. The coffee had finished brewing. Caroline poured him a cup, then one for herself, and plopped a couple of lumps from a strawberry-shaped sugar bowl into her cup before pushing the sugar across to him.

They were silent for a few minutes as each sipped their coffee. The only sound was the steady tick-tock of a wall clock by the door. He couldn't hear anything from the doctor's examination room beyond, but that was probably a good thing, for it meant the laudanum had taken hold of Wes and the drover was no longer in agony.

He felt so awkward around Caroline. She was immaculate in her high-necked dress with its attached collar of some sort of gray lacework, not a hair out of place. Jack wished he'd known he was going to see her tonight—he'd have bothered to shave the two-day growth of beard from his cheeks and put on a fresh shirt.

"How is the bunkhouse coming along?" she asked, breaking the silence.

He was glad to have something he could talk about. "We should be putting the roof on about the end of the week, if the weather holds. I imagine some of us will continue to sleep outside, till the cold really sets in, though—"

Dr. Walker entered just then, followed by his wife. Caroline sprang up to pour them coffee.

"Your man's going to be hurting for several weeks, but I've set the fracture to his wrist and put his shoulder back in its socket. Nothing much you can do about those ribs but let them heal. Fortunately, there's no sign of serious internal injuries."

"Can I take him back to the ranch tonight, Doctor?" Jack asked. "Or should I see about getting a room at the hotel?"

"You'll leave him here for the night," Dr. Walker said. "I have a cot and a spare bedroom set up for the purpose. The very last thing he needs is to go bouncing over those roads right now. He's going to be sleeping off that laudanum until morning, anyway. You can come claim him then."

"Then you'll come back to the house with me," Caroline told Jack. "Your daughters will be so happy to wake and find you there."

He smiled his thanks to Caroline, then turned back to the doctor. "Thank you, sir. I'll have to bring your fee next time I'm in town. I leave what cash I have with me with our cook, and in the excitement—"

Nolan Walker held up a hand. "How about we barter instead? I imagine you might be able to find a side of beef somewhere," he said with a wink. "I'm partial to a good steak now and then."

"Sounds like a bargain to me, Doc," Jack said, and the two shook hands.

Caroline told herself she was happy for the girls' sake that Jack had agreed to come back to her family's house for the night. But she couldn't fool herself. The fact was, it felt just purely *good* to be walking through the darkness at Jack Collier's side. It gave her a reason to appreciate the light of a nearly full moon filtering through the leaves of the trees in the churchyard, and a reason not to be frightened as their passage scared a black cat in the alleyway between the post office and the undertaker's and sent it scuttling past her skirts with an unearthly yowl.

"That's probably the tomcat responsible for the litter of kittens in our shed," she commented.

"You're probably right," Jack said. "When the twins showed me the litter, I noticed most of those kittens were black. He's probably hanging about hoping to convince the mama cat to let him come courting all over again."

"Ha! She's a good mama cat, and too smart to fall for his wiles," Caroline retorted. "She knows he'll be charming to her, and then she'll be left alone in the same situation that brought her to our shed. She's learned her lesson."

Suddenly a chilly gust of wind blew up the alley, and she shivered in spite of the shawl she clutched closer around her. For cats and people courting was wonderful while it lasted, but then, all too often, the man left. Either by dying, as Pete had, or by moving on, as Jack would do. No, it didn't do to let a man get too close. It only left a woman with memories, or worse.

But what about her own parents and the happy couples she knew like Sarah and her Nolan, and Milly and her Nick? It didn't do any good to think of them. Their happy endings were not for her to experience.

The best she could hope for was a useful, contented life. And she'd be a fool if she let a walk in the moonlight change her mind.

Jack awoke to joyous shrieks as the twins jumped on his bed out on the summer porch at sunrise. They slept in a spare bedroom now, so his coming hadn't awakened them.

"Papa! Aunt Caroline said you came to surprise us!" Amelia cried, throwing herself against him and hugging his neck.

"Why didn't you tell us when you came last night?" Abby asked, kissing his cheek.

"I didn't want to wake you two up, Punkin. Fact is, I didn't know I was coming myself till I met Miss Caroline at the doctor's office," Jack explained. "Mr. Wes needed some fixing up from Doc Walker, and the doctor said he had to stay all night, so Miss Caroline and her parents were kind enough to give me a bed. We thought it might be nice to surprise you girls by having your papa join you for breakfast."

"I love surprises," Abby said. "But Aunt Caroline told me you hafta get washed up and come to breakfast *pronto*—"

"That means quick, Papa," Amelia added. "'Cause we hafta get to school. Papa, I think you should come to school with us."

"Yeah, Papa, come to school," Abby agreed. "We can show you how good we know our letters."

"I think Miss Caroline would say it's how *well* you

know your letters." There was nothing he'd like better than to watch them being taught by Caroline, Jack thought, but he had to take Wes back to the ranch and probably take over Wes's share of the chores. They were planning to put on the roof today, and they'd already be a man short.

He could hear the sounds of sizzling bacon and the older Wallaces talking in the kitchen. "Y'all go get started on your breakfast, and I'll be along soon as I wash up."

Caroline, he saw when he took his place at the table, had gone back to wearing unrelieved black. Too bad—he thought the gray collar of some sort of handmade lacework she'd worn last night had looked pretty. And there was a troubled look to her eyes this morning that told him she hadn't slept well. *Why?* He'd thought she seemed happy to have him with her last night when they'd left the house, but something along the way had changed her mood. If he could have managed a minute alone with her, he would have asked her about it, but of course he had to be getting over to the doctor's office, and Caroline and the twins needed to leave for school.

"Come, girls, it's time to say goodbye to your papa and get to the schoolhouse," Caroline said, gathering up her things.

"But Papa's coming with us, aren't you, Papa?" Amelia said, coming around the table to stand by his side.

"Yeah, Papa's coming to school," Abby chimed in, tugging on his sleeve.

Caroline raised a brow in inquiry. "Are you coming to school today, Jack? Of course you're welcome, but I thought…"

"I wish I could, Miss Caroline, but I'm afraid that

was wishful thinking on my girls' part. Punkins, I've got to go pick up Mr. Wes and get him back out to the ranch," he said, gathering the hovering twins into his arms. "Maybe another day I can come to school with you, but not today, I'm afraid."

Both his daughters' lips jutted out in mutinous pouts. "But we didn't get to spend much time with you, Papa."

"Yeah, just breakfast. That's not long."

Caroline flashed Jack a sympathetic look over their heads. "Girls, he'll be coming back soon. You'll need to be patient until then."

Abby folded her arms tightly over her chest. "Don't want to wait for 'soon.'"

Her sister mirrored her action. "Yeah. We want you to come with us *now*, Papa."

Jack was all too aware of the silence from the Wallaces as they waited to see what he would do. He was there, so they wouldn't take on the task of disciplining his children.

He made his voice as stern as he could manage. "That's enough sass, girls. You mind Miss Caroline now, you hear me? I'll see you before you know it."

Abby's lip trembled, and he determinedly ignored it and kissed the top of her head, then her sister's.

She looked like her mother when she did that, Jack thought, and later wished that he'd remembered that on rare occasions when Lucinda had worn that expression, trouble had usually followed.

He found Wes, his broken arm splinted, drinking coffee and waiting for him in the Walkers' kitchen. Wes winced when he rose to greet Jack, but all in all, he looked a good deal better than he had last night.

"How're you feeling, cowboy?" Jack said, accepting a cup of coffee from the doctor's wife. "I see Mrs. Walker's been spoiling you, but don't expect Cookie to bring you breakfast in bed."

The drover grinned. "Don't I know it. Yeah, I'm feelin' tolerable, boss. The doc's got my ribs all bound up with strips of old sheets, and it really helps, 'specially if I have to cough. And don't make me laugh—that hurts too much."

Doctor Walker came into the kitchen from his office just then. "Those ribs are going to ache a while," he told Wes, "but I expect the bones in the arm will knit in a few weeks. Leave that splint on for a month, and don't start using the arm to carry anything before then, but be sure to wiggle your fingers. And remember what I told you about taking deep breaths several times a day, Wes, so you don't get lung fever."

"Yes, Doctor," Wes said.

Jack said, "Doctor, I'll bring that beef next time I come to town, or send it with one of the men."

Caroline was pleased to see Louisa Wheeler waiting at the schoolhouse door. "Good morning. I see you were serious about helping out in the classroom."

"No time like the present, I always say," the other woman said with a cheery smile.

"Girls, this is Miss Wheeler, a new friend of mine. She'd like to be a teacher, so she's going to help me here. Miss Wheeler, these are Mr. Collier's daughters, Abby and Amelia. They're six, and they're very smart girls," Caroline said. She was pleased Amelia had stopped sulking about her father's leaving, though Abby still seemed a bit pouty. But surely she'd get over it when class started.

"Pleased to meet you, girls," Louisa said. "Those are the prettiest dresses you're wearing."

"Our Aunt Mary made them," Amelia informed her.

"Perhaps you'd be kind enough to show me where to hang my bonnet?" Louisa asked Abby. Caroline was relieved to see Abby's face relax as she led the way to the cloakroom.

It had to be hard to be with their father for such a brief time and then tell him goodbye again, when they were used to having him around all the time, Caroline thought sympathetically. Maybe it would have been easier if they hadn't seen him at all this morning, but she wouldn't have left Jack sleeping in a chair in the doctor's waiting room last night for the world.

Soon the rest of the children started filing into the schoolhouse. Caroline immersed herself in drilling her pupils in arithmetic and then broke the students up into reading groups according to their grade levels. How wonderful it was to have a helper, she thought, as she directed Louisa to supervise the younger children, while Caroline concentrated on the older ones. She wasn't about to inflict Billy Joe Henderson on Louisa on her first day, for Billy Joe was back to his old tricks.

As soon as Ted began reading, Billy Joe started parroting the other boy's hesitant stammer. The hapless Ted squirmed in embarrassment.

"That's not how we treat our fellow students, is it, Billy Joe? I imagine you don't want to stay in at recess, do you? Now be quiet and let Ted read, and then it will be your turn."

Unlike Ted, Billy Joe was an excellent reader and

liked to show off his proficiency, but when he looked at the page he was to read, he pretended to gag.

"Billy Joe, read it now without making silly rude noises, or you will have to read aloud to me for an hour after school today."

To her relief, Billy Joe complied. Then she went on to the next student.

She was just about to dismiss them all for recess when she glanced over at the younger children and saw Amelia looking worriedly at the door. Abby's chair was empty.

"Miss Wheeler, where is Abby?" she called across the room, interrupting the child who was reading.

Louisa looked confused. "Abby?"

"Amelia's twin," Caroline said, trying to be patient, for Louisa had met two dozen children this morning.

Louisa's face cleared. "Oh, yes, Abby. She raised her hand to go to the…you know…"

"The outhouse? How long ago?"

Louisa looked startled, then flustered. "I—I don't know…it was when we began reading…then little Molly was having trouble, and I forgot all about her."

That had to have been at least thirty minutes ago, maybe longer.

"Amelia, go get your sister and bring her back to class," Caroline told her.

Amelia did as she was bidden, but she ran back inside a minute later. "Miss Caroline, she's not there. She's not anywhere outside. She's *gone*!"

Chapter Ten

Caroline stared at the child. Her words made no sense. How could Abby be gone, if she'd only gone to the outhouse? She flew to the window, expecting to see Abby loitering on the swings or peeking out mischievously from around the trunk of one of the live oaks that lined the perimeter of the schoolyard. She couldn't see so much as a flash of yellow gingham of the dress Abby had worn today.

"She *must* be there! Where could she have gone?" Caroline cried and, gathering her skirts, dashed out the door, down the steps and out into the schoolyard, calling *"Abby! Abby, come out this instant!"* She flung open the outhouse door—Abby wasn't there. Then she dashed around into the bushes beyond the trees, desperate to spot the child. "Abby! It's not funny! Come on out *now!*"

Suddenly she realized that Abby hadn't let go of her disappointment in not getting to see her father longer— *she'd gone to find him.*

She ran to the road and looked in both directions, but saw no one and turned back toward the schoolhouse.

Louisa stood on the steps, looking as worried as Caroline felt. Children peeked around both sides of her, including a wide-eyed Amelia. Others lined the cloakroom window, mouths agape.

"I—I have to go after her," Caroline called. "I think she's gone toward the ranch to find her father. Stay here with the children!"

"She couldn't have gotten very far in that amount of time."

Caroline wanted to laugh hysterically. Louisa didn't know Abby Collier like Caroline did. Abby could be one stubborn and determined child, and what was worse, she knew the road to take. It was a good five miles to the ranch, but in between here and there she could meet up with countless dangers—rattlesnakes, coyotes, outlaws, roaming Indians... Besides, the sun was hot today, and the child didn't have any water with her.

"Maybe you should notify the sheriff and have him look for her," Louisa shouted.

"That'll take too long!" By the time Caroline ran to the jail, Abby would have covered even more ground. And Sheriff Bishop was still on his honeymoon and had left his deputy in charge. She didn't know Menendez well. And what if he wasn't at the jail office, but was making his rounds anywhere in town or its outskirts?

What would Jack say about her failure to keep his daughter safe? Caroline's blood ran cold even as she sprinted down Main Street toward the road that led south out of town, past the doctor's office, the barbershop, the bank, the mercantile and Gilmore House, the mayor's mansion... *What if Abby didn't stay on the road but wandered off into the mesquite-and cactus-strewn brush country? They might never find her...*

Dear Lord, You have to help me! Please let me find

Abby Collier before she runs into danger. Please don't let her come to any harm....

Caroline was already short of breath and sweating, her braid flopping loose from its coil at the back of her head. She was terribly aware that she couldn't even be certain the child had gone this way. *What if she was wrong and the child had gone to play at the creek and had fallen in?* She should have sent Louisa to check at the creek... She should have even looked down into the malodorous depths of the outhouse pit....

And then she saw two figures making their way up the south road, a plump, elderly lady—*and a little girl in a yellow gingham dress, holding the old lady's hand and clutching her doll in her other hand.*

"Abby!" she shrieked and went running toward her with a speed she didn't know she could still manage.

Abby wrenched her hand from the old lady's grasp and rushed toward Caroline, wailing. They met in the middle of the road, and Caroline threw her arms around Abby. She could hardly hear the child's cries over her own sobs.

"Oh, thank God! Oh, Abby, you gave me such a fright!" she said, clutching the girl to her and brushing back her hair with frantic fingers. "What were you thinking, to run off like that? Do you have any idea what could have happened to you?"

"I'm sorry, Miss Caroline! I didn't mean t' scare you! I only wanted to find Papa, and then I got all hot and thirsty, and I didn't find his ranch...."

Caroline looked up through her tears to see Mrs. Detwiler smiling beneficently down at both of them.

"Lose one, did you, dear? I just happened to be out pruning my rosebushes back for fall, and I saw this young'un perambulatin' down the road. I didn't see any-one with her. And I sez to myself, Mrs. D., you'd better check into that because that little child might be lost. And when I got a little closer, I recognized she was one of the twins that came to Prissy's wedding, and I figured we'd better come find you, but I gave her a glass of my lemonade and a cookie first."

"I—I don't know h-how to thank you enough, Mrs. Detwiler," Caroline said, still panting for breath. "Yes, I'm afraid Abby was a naughty girl, but I'm very grate-ful that you found her." She shuddered, remembering all the dire fates she had imagined for Jack's daughter during the last few horrible minutes.

"I—I'm sorrrrrryyyy!" wailed Abby. "I just wanted to see my papa!"

"We'll talk about what you did and why later, Abby," Caroline said, straightening. *After I've had time to get over my terror. Thank You, Lord, for having Mrs. De-twiler find her.* "But now we have to get back to the school. Please thank Mrs. Detwiler for the refresh-ments." She waited as the child meekly obeyed.

"You're very welcome, child," the old woman said, bending over to Abby. "Please come again with Miss Caroline and your sister when you can stay longer. You mind your teacher, now."

"Yes, ma'am."

Mrs. Detwiler winked over the child's head, but Caro-line could only manage a wan, exhausted smile in return.

Feeling like the hot, bedraggled mess she was, Caro-line trudged back down Main Street toward the school, holding tightly to Abby's hand. She was painfully aware of her hair loose on her shoulders and sticking in sweat-plastered clumps to her forehead, and the wetness of cloth clinging to her back. She only encountered a couple of people on the street as they walked, but she imagined what they must have been thinking—*incompetent teacher, can't keep up with the children entrusted to her...*

When she and Abby reached the schoolyard, her heart sank when she saw a black buggy with its horse tied to the hitching rail. It was a common enough sort of buggy, but she recognized the liver chestnut driven by the school superintendent, Mr. Thurgood.

Her heart sank, and she had to fight the urge to send Abby inside, then turn and run away. Of all the times for the superintendent to pay a return visit!

Lord, if You could see Your way clear to helping me one more time this morning... Taking a deep breath, she marched forward with Abby in tow.

Mr. Thurgood stood at the back of the classroom, arms folded over his paunch. Louisa Wheeler stood at the wall map of the United States, using the pointer to indicate New York. Hands were raised at the desks.

Everyone looked around at the sound of Caroline's and Abby's entrance.

"Abby!" Amelia cried and dashed out of her seat to hug her sister.

"Thank God you found her," breathed Louisa, beaming at Caroline and at the sisters who now walked back to their desks together. "Where was she?"

Caroline tried to smile back, but her eyes stung with tears. She hadn't had the courage to look at Mr. Thurgood yet, but she could practically feel his eyes boring into her like hot pokers.

"Perhaps we should talk about it later," she said. *After I've been dismissed from my teaching position by the county superintendent.* "Class, I hope you've been working hard for Miss Wheeler. Have they been well-behaved, Miss Wheeler?" she asked with a brightness she was far from feeling.

"Oh, yes, Miss Wallace, they've worked hard. We've gone through the rest of the reading assignments and have now progressed to geography—"

Mr. Thurgood harrumphed noisily, and Louisa Wheeler froze.

"Miss Wallace," he said, "I would think it painfully obvious you must do more than *hope* your students will be well-behaved."

"Perhaps we should discuss this outside, Mr. Thurgood?" she suggested, nodding toward the door, but he went on as if she had not spoken.

"I was shocked beyond measure to find you absent, with your charges left in the hands of a volunteer—a capable-seeming volunteer, admittedly, but a volunteer whose qualifications were unknown to me. We had not discussed your taking on an aide. Perhaps you feel *inadequate* to handle two dozen children on your own? I assure you, I handled fifty, myself, and I never thought of asking anyone to help. And my pupils were models of correct deportment. Furthermore—"

Caroline waited until his bluster wore itself out, using the time to squelch the angry, defensive replies that sprang to her lips. *Do your worst, Mr. Thurgood, for I am less afraid of losing my position than of Jack's reaction to the news I let his daughter run away from school and did not notice for half an hour. None of the students will respect me now that you are reprimanding me in front of them anyway.*

"Well? Have you nothing to say for yourself?" he

demanded, his eyes raking over her disheveled appearance, his lip curled in scorn.

"I am sorry about what happened, sir," she said, looking straight ahead of her and not at his angry, pink face. "But as Miss Wheeler will have no doubt explained, one of the students went missing, and I believed I knew in which direction she had gone."

"And why didn't you notify the sheriff, and have them look for her?"

"I felt needless delay would have resulted while I did so. As it happens, I guessed right about where she was going, and as you saw, I have brought her back."

"And you will punish her." He stared at Abby, who shrank against her sister as if she thought the superintendent might be about to take on the task himself.

Caroline nodded. "Appropriate consequences will take place." *Lord, don't let him demand I paddle that child here and now. He doesn't need to know I never use that thing.*

"Very well, then. I am placing you on probation, Miss Wallace, and I will be paying follow-up visits. Should there be any repeat of any incidents that would indicate these children are not in capable hands, you will lose your position."

"I understand, sir."

"Good day, Miss Wallace, Miss Wheeler…students."

Caroline hardly dared to move until she heard the creak of buggy wheels, and then she stepped to a window to assure herself he was actually gone.

"Miss Wheeler, did these students miss recess because of the superintendent's visit?" Caroline asked, glancing at the watch which was pinned to her bodice.

Louisa nodded. "It didn't seem wise to dismiss them just as he arrived, under the circumstances."

It was now eleven o'clock. Now that Mr. Thurgood had gone, many of the students were visibly fidgety, especially the boys.

"Well, then, why don't we combine recess with an early lunch, and resume class in an hour?" she said. "Miss Wheeler, would you mind supervising them while I go over the afternoon lesson plans? I'll be out in a few minutes."

"Certainly."

Caroline managed to hold herself together until the children had gathered their lunch pails and thundered outside, and Louisa followed them after a last inquiring glance at Caroline. As soon as the door closed behind them, she collapsed at her desk in tears.

I am the worst teacher who ever lived. What made me think I was capable of teaching? Mr. Thurgood would return, and he would not be satisfied until he found some offense to dismiss her for. By tomorrow the students would have told their parents how their teacher had managed to lose a child right out of the classroom, and they would probably demand her resignation anyway.

But worst of all was the thought of what she was going to say to Jack. Surely it was not right to wait until Sunday, when he would come to see his children—and it would be awkward to tell him about the incident in front of the girls. Should she write him a letter, and have Dan take it out to the ranch? But that was the coward's way....

Later, she waited until Abby and Amelia—who had been perfectly behaved the rest of the day—had gone to bed to tell her mother about what had happened and ask her what she should do.

"Louisa apologized for letting Abby slip away, since she was in her reading group, but it *was* her first day of assisting me. The children are my responsibility in the end," she concluded.

"I thought something was bothering you, dear," her mother said, laying aside the needlework she had been doing by the light of the parlor lamp. "And I knew it was something to do with the twins because they were acting rather subdued, weren't they? Tomorrow's Saturday. Why don't you ride out to Jack's ranch in the morning? I'll keep Abby and Amelia busy—they don't have to know where you're going. I think you'll find Jack more understanding than you think. After all, you kept your head and figured out where Abby was headed, went after her and found her before any harm came to the child. Things could have been a lot worse, couldn't they?"

Caroline's only answer was a shudder, but that said it all.

"*Nothing awful happened.* Don't you think this sort of thing happens to mothers, dear? Dan sneaked away from me once when he had just started walking and fell into a clump of prickly pears. Land sakes, we had to throw out the pants he was wearing, and I thought we'd never get all the spines out of him. Another time I found him sitting on top of a red anthill... Children get into mischief, Caroline. You've had to become a sort of substitute mother all of a sudden as well as being a teacher—it's not easy, I know."

Her understanding did much to smother Caroline's agonizing feeling of incompetence, but she still tossed and turned for hours before finding sleep, rehearsing how she would tell Jack.

Chapter Eleven

Jack was up on the roof with a couple of the other men, hammering the last beams of the roof in place when Raleigh called up to him, "You got company, boss."

He looked around to see Caroline trotting up to the cabin on a yellow dun he'd seen at the livery stable. Even as he raised his hand in greeting, he looked behind her, expecting to see the twins riding double on some other mount, but she was alone.

Alarm shot up his spine. If Amelia and Abby weren't with her, did it mean that one or both of them was ill—or hurt? Had they both come down with lung fever or fallen into the creek? Yet as she drew closer, he could see that she didn't look frantic, as he assumed she would if she were summoning him to a sickbed or worse. But surely *something* had to be amiss for her to visit without them, didn't it?

He sat down on the roof and slid to the roofline, then jumped to the ground.

"Caroline, is anything wrong? Where are the girls? Are they all right?" he asked, searching her face for any hint as to why she had come.

"No, they're fine, Jack," she said. "They're at home with Mother."

The alarm bells stopped clanging, to be replaced immediately by an illogical surging hope—had she come purely to see *him?* She was wearing a charcoal-gray split skirt with a matching spencer and a light gray blouse—was the hue significant?

He moved with instinctive courtesy to the horse's head and made sure the beast stood steady while she dismounted.

"Actually," she said when she stood on the ground, "I needed to talk with you about Abby, and I thought I'd better come alone."

"Oh?" His soaring hope fell like a dove felled by a well-aimed rock. He tried to keep his face expressionless and not reveal his disappointment. "Here, Wes, make yourself useful and take Miss Wallace's horse. Miss Caroline, why don't we walk over there and you can tell me about it," he said, indicating a grove of cottonwoods that hugged the meandering creek.

Caroline was silent as they walked, skirting clumps of prickly pear and mesquite, keeping her eyes on the uneven ground, while he strode alongside her and wondered what his daughter might have done. Of the twins, Abby was the one most inclined to mischief.

Once they reached the creek, Caroline turned and recited the tale of Abby's wandering away from school in search of him, how she'd managed to get as far as Mrs. Detwiler's house on the south road before Caroline had caught up with her and brought her back. Then Caroline stopped and stood still as if she was a condemned criminal waiting to have sentence pronounced.

"Hmm…" he murmured, rubbing his chin and looking down at the autumn-dry grass at his booted feet. "Sounds like I need to have a talk with Abby when I see her tomorrow." He turned back to her. "Sorry she worried you so and disrupted school, Teacher."

She blinked at him, then her eyes widened in astonishment. "*Is that all* you're going to say? Disrupting school is the least of it. Can you imagine what could have happened to the child, walking over this road alone? She'd never have made it here before she collapsed in exhaustion, if some predator didn't get her first!"

"But she didn't. You found her before anything happened, and all's well," he said. He didn't want her to be worried, even if he had to be.

Her mouth tightened, and her fine brown eyes kindled with exasperation. "Yes, that's what my mother said, but I thought you ought to know what happened," she said. "I take full responsibility, Jack. I can't help thinking—"

He didn't want her to heap any more recriminations on her head. "I said I'd speak to her about it tomorrow when I come. I'll let her know there's not to be any repeat of such behavior," he promised. "Afterward, I thought, if you wouldn't mind packing something like a picnic lunch, we might all come out here again so they could see the cabin completed. Cookie's been whittling them some wooden animals as a surprise."

"I—I don't think my coming along would be such a good idea." Now she faced the clear water that meandered merrily over the rocks in the creek bed rather than him. "I think the mischief Abby got into is her way of telling you she and her sister need more time with you, Jack—and not time they have to share with me."

"You…you don't want to come with us?" he asked.

"I don't feel it's best for the girls," she said, avoiding his eyes.

That's not what I asked you, he wanted to protest. *Are you trying to avoid telling me you don't want to spend time with me?* But there was no penetrating her defenses today. She was wearing her prim, schoolmarmish manner like armor.

"I—I'll talk to Abby, and when I bring them back Sunday evening I'll let you know how it went," he said at last.

He would plan to buy supplies in town Monday morning, which would give him a perfect excuse to stay the night at the Wallaces and sit in the parlor with Caroline after the girls were abed. Perhaps it would be a fine night, and he could suggest they could take a stroll....

"Well, that's settled then," she said, with the air of one who's crossing an item off a list. "I've interrupted your work, and now I'd better let you get back to it. I'll see you at church tomorrow, Jack."

"You don't have to rush off," he protested. "Stay and have dinner with the boys and me." Even as he voiced the invitation, he realized it was only mid-morning. What was she to do until the meal, sit on a horse blanket and watch him and the boys hammer on the roof, while listening to Cookie's constant grumbling? But he wanted her to stay.

She looked down at her gloved hands. "Thanks, but I... I thought I'd pay a visit to Milly while I'm out here, and then in the afternoon I promised to gather pecans with the girls and teach them how to make pralines. We'll save some for you."

Then she started back to where Wes had taken her horse, and all he could do was follow her with his eyes.

He watched until she cantered out of sight. Then, uncomfortably aware that Raleigh watched him, he clambered back up onto the roof and went to work.

"Miss Caroline, I apologize for the short notice, but we'd be right proud if you'd come have dinner with us today," the mousy little woman said to her after the church service in the meadow.

If it weren't for Billy Joe hovering at the woman's side, looking hopeful while at the same time affecting disinterest, Caroline would not have recognized Mrs. Henderson, for she never encountered the woman in the shops of Simpson Creek, and Mr. Henderson frequently proclaimed his wife was "too poorly" to come to church.

Caroline struggled to hide her surprise. "Why, I'd be pleased to do that, Mrs. Henderson, thank you." She saw the woman let out a sigh of relief and glance covertly at her husband, who stood nearby opining to Reverend Chadwick about his sermon.

"Well…that's just fine," Mrs. Henderson said, darting a glance at her spouse again. "You kin call me Daisy. When Mr. Henderson is done speaking to the preacher, we'll walk down to our house. I left a roast in the oven, and it'll only take me a little while to get the rest ready."

Caroline nodded understanding, then excused herself to speak to Jack and the twins. She knew Jack had overheard the invitation but was surprised to see Jack eyeing Mr. Henderson with distaste.

She cleared her throat to capture his attention, wondering what had elicited that feeling from him. "Mama and I packed a picnic basket for you and the girls," she told him. "We put it over there in the shade of that cottonwood."

His gaze, as he turned to her, was difficult to read.

"Thanks, Miss Caroline," he said, "but we wish you were coming with us. Don't we, girls?"

Caroline didn't dare tell him how much she wanted to do exactly that. She made herself smile brightly. "Have fun on your picnic." She'd been planning on paying a call on the Hendersons soon to look into Billy's home situation, so the dinner invitation could not have come at a more opportune time. But Caroline couldn't help feeling as wistful as Abby and Amelia looked as she waved goodbye to them and turned back to the Hendersons.

Mr. Henderson was still talking to the preacher. When they were the only people left in the meadow, Mrs. Henderson finally plucked timidly at her husband's sleeve. "Mr. Henderson, we'd better be getting home so I can take the roast from the oven."

I'd never call my husband "Mister" if I was married, Caroline thought. Even if some thought it was the proper, respectful thing to do, she'd never heard her parents address each other in that formal way. Between them it was always "sweetheart" or "dear," if they did not use first names. *But you're not getting married, Caroline, so why are you even thinking about it?*

"Reverend, why don't you come to dinner with us, too?" Caroline heard Mr. Henderson say. "My wife invited the schoolmarm, and if you come we'll have us a regular ol' party."

Caroline could see the quick flash of dismay in Daisy Henderson's eyes and guessed the woman feared she would not have enough to stretch to one more person. Reverend Chadwick must have seen it, too, for he graciously declined, claiming he hadn't slept well the night before and needed to indulge in an afternoon nap.

Too bad, Caroline thought. It would have been nice having Reverend Chadwick with her, if only to keep Mr. Henderson from staring at her in that overbold way he had with every woman but his timid wife. And she might need to consult the preacher about the family if the boy's misbehavior continued.

Billy Joe walked along at her side as if he were a great deal taller than he really was, waving to everyone they passed, clearly not wanting anyone to miss the fact that the teacher was coming to dinner at his house. Caroline could not help but be amused at his pride, since this was the same boy she had kept after school so often.

The Hendersons' house sat at the other end of Travis Street. It had originally been white clapboard, but the paint had deteriorated into a shabby ghost of that hue. Its faded look reminded Caroline of Mrs. Henderson. A ramshackle fence enclosed a half dozen scraggly chickens scratching in a hopeless fashion in the sparse grass. The rickety gate he opened hung from one hinge.

"Here we are, our little bit of Heaven," Mr. Henderson declared with a grand gesture, apparently oblivious to the irony of his statement.

Inside the house, however, the place was neat and tidy, if devoid of much ornamentation, and the delicious smell of roasted chicken filled the air.

"Yippee, chicken! I'm famished! How soon kin we eat, Ma?" Billy Joe cried, as his mother hustled into the kitchen.

His father's hand snaked out and grabbed him by the collarbone. "Billy Joe, mind your manners, boy. Take your teacher's shawl and hang it up. Miss Wallace, why don't we set a spell here while my wife finishes din-

ner?" he said, patting the shabby horsehair couch next
to himself.

She'd seen Billy Joe wince when his father grabbed
him. Flushing dully, he came to her and asked, eyes
downcast, "May I take your wrap, Teacher?"

"Why, thank you, Billy Joe," she said, deliberately
catching the boy's eye and giving him an encouraging
smile. "Mr. Henderson, I think I'll go see if your wife
needs some help."

"Daisy don't need—" he began, but Caroline just
smiled and walked past him into the kitchen.

She found Daisy with her sleeves rolled up, grimly
trying to stir the lumps out of her gravy. She flashed an
alarmed glance at Caroline's entrance and dropped her
spoon in the gravy boat so she could shove down her
sleeves, but she was too late to prevent Caroline from
catching sight of the scattered discolorations of gray,
blue and greenish-brown on both arms. Bruises in various stages of healing—and Caroline could guess who
had given them to her. It made her wonder if Billy Joe
bore similar marks.

Caroline's gaze rose to the woman's frightened eyes.
Mrs. Henderson knew she had seen the bruises and
guessed their origin.

"Can I help you, Daisy?" The question had a double
meaning, and both women knew it. But there was no
door to the kitchen, and it was obvious the man lounging at his ease on the sofa would be able to hear anything that was said.

"No, I—I'm fine, thank you. Sit down, you're our
guest—"

"Nonsense. My mother taught me a trick to get rid
of those lumps in the gravy—may I share it with you?"

Caroline asked and set about showing it to Mrs. Wallace without waiting for an answer. Then she scooped up the stack of dishes and silverware that had obviously been left out for the purpose and set the table. She wouldn't say anything now, when they could easily be overheard, but she would watch for a chance later. Mrs. Henderson needed to know she didn't have to suffer in silence.

When they finally sat down to the table, Mr. Henderson ordered, "Billy Joe, show your teacher how nice you kin say grace." It sounded like a man commanding a dog to perform a parlor trick.

His son dutifully bowed his head and repeated a grace obviously learned by rote.

"Thank you, Billy Joe," Caroline said, trying to catch his eye and failing. Her heart ached for the boy. No wonder he acted up at school, if this was the way he was treated at home. She added a silent prayer of her own, *Lord, please show me how to help this family.*

Mr. Henderson took up the carving tools, then pointed with a thick finger at the roast chicken on its platter. "That there was a speckled broody hen who pecked at me yesterday. I wrung her neck then and there."

Caroline thought she could have done without knowing that. The daring bird must have been the oldest hen they had, too, for in spite of the delicious smell, Caroline found she had to saw at the tough meat to cut it. Or maybe it had just been baked too long. The gravy she had helped with improved the dried-out taste only minimally, but she smiled and praised it and watched Daisy blink back tears. At least the potatoes were tasty and filling.

After the meal, she insisted on helping with the dishes. Mr. Henderson sank into a nap on the sofa before the table was even clear. Billy Joe had slipped off somewhere, too, and Caroline was determined to take advantage of their absence.

"Daisy…" she began.

But the other woman was already speaking. "We're… *I'm* grateful for the attention you're giving our boy," the woman said quickly, looking her in the eyes at last. "I know he's probably not the easiest child to teach…."

"Billy Joe's a very bright boy," Caroline said. "Sometimes the brightest children, especially boys, find it hard to sit still and channel all that energy to learn in a traditional way. With your permission, I'd like to keep him a couple of days a week after school, to work with him individually on those subjects he's finding hard to learn. I hope you'll tell your husband about my plan—" *since he doesn't seem apt to wake up anytime soon* "—so he won't think Billy Joe's been misbehaving and punish him."

She took a deep breath, knowing she'd risked making the other woman defensive.

Mrs. Henderson dabbed at her eyes with the dish towel. "But what about when he acts up at school? You won't let him be a bad boy, will you? Mr. Henderson won't tolerate his boy being bad."

And he can't see how much his son wants to be good. "Oh, no," Caroline assured her. "I'll find other ways to discipline him than keeping him after school, because I don't want learning to be seen as punishment."

"I—I'm grateful to ya, Miss Wallace. Billy Joe…he's all we got. We nearly lost him as a baby, an' after I had him, it don't seem like I could have no more. I know Mr. Henderson's…well, he's bitter about that. Sometimes he's a little hard on him."

And on you?

"Daisy, I'm happy to help. I want Billy Joe to succeed at learning. And I want you to know…" Caroline began carefully, knowing she had to be careful how she said this, for the woman had pride, even if it was a somewhat desperate, threadbare pride, "If there's anything I can do to help *you*, too, you have but to tell me." She glanced meaningfully at the woman's now covered arms and knew she dared not be more specific.

Just then the sofa in the parlor creaked, and the woman's eyes went wide and frightened. Caroline could easily read her thoughts—*Had Mr. Henderson awakened? Had he heard Caroline's last statement? Was he coming out to object?*

But no footsteps sounded on the plank flooring, and then the snoring began again.

The woman stared at her, her eyes wide and frightened. "Just help my boy, Miss Wallace. That's how you can help me."

Then she cleared her throat, as if starting a new paragraph, and hung up her dish towel. "Those two little twin girls stayin' with you are right pretty. Their papa's a right good lookin' fellow, too. You two courtin', by any chance?"

Caroline groaned inwardly. *You too, Brutus?* she wanted to ask, but the woman would not understand the allusion. She opened her mouth to frame a polite reply, but just then Billy Joe dashed into the kitchen.

"Hey, Teacher, you wanna come see my rock collection?"

Relieved at the timely interruption, Caroline followed the boy to his room and saw his rock collection then his bug collection, and finally an assorted collection of treasures—a mule deer antler Billy Joe had found near the

creek, a hawk feather, his slingshot and the slightly malodorous hide of the rabbit he'd brought down with it....

At last it was time to take her leave. Billy Joe insisted
on walking her home, and while she was touched by
the courtly gesture, she suspected the boy also wanted
to go on to play at the creek while his father was still
asleep. She hoped, as she waved goodbye to him from
the kitchen doorstep, that today had been the doorway
to progress in helping him.

Her duty as a teacher done, she could now look forward to Jack returning with the girls. She hoped he
intended to stay for supper, though she was a little surprised at the warm feeling the idea brought her. She
only wanted to tell him about her meal with the Hendersons, she told herself, and see if he had any male in-
sights that would be useful in dealing with Billy Joe.
He'd seemed sympathetic when she'd talked with him
about the boy before.

The knock sounded at the front door as she was helping her mother prepare the meal.

Goodness, why was Jack being formal and coming
to the front door? He'd been to the house often enough
to know that everyone came in via the kitchen.

But it wasn't Jack and the girls.

Chapter Twelve

An overpowering aroma of bay rum assaulted Caroline's nostrils as she opened the door. Superintendent Thurgood stood on the front step clutching a gold-headed cane and wearing a dark frock coat and trousers and a gold brocade vest, his thinning hair pomaded flat to his skull. Beads of perspiration dotted his florid face.

"Mr. Thurgood. What…c-can I do for you?" she stammered, wondering wildly why he'd come. Had it taken him three days to decide to dismiss her after all, and he'd come to her house to humiliate her in front of her family?

A smile turned up both corners of his lips. "Please, Miss Wallace, it's I who hope to do something for you," he said smoothly. "I felt we got off on the wrong foot during our previous meetings—"

"Caroline, dear, who is it?" her mother called from the kitchen. "Tell him to come in."

That was the last thing Caroline wanted to do, but she had no civilized reason to refuse.

"Please, won't you come in, Superintendent?" she managed to say, and stepped back.

Her mother bustled in from the kitchen, wiping her hands on her apron. Caroline spotted Dan lurking in the hallway, too, curious about who had come to call on his sister.

"Mama, this is the county school superintendent, Mr. Thurgood," she said, feeling as if she was in the middle of a dream—no, a nightmare, for she was becoming surer by the second that this was no quick social call. *Oh, don't let Jack and the children come while he's here!*

"Mrs. Wallace, I'm honored to meet the mother of our fine teacher." He extended a hand and shook her mother's a little too heartily.

Caroline stared at the man, certain she'd heard wrong. Her mother, who'd heard the whole story on Friday, blinked in confusion.

"Won't you sit down, sir?" she asked. "Can I get you a cup of coffee?"

Mr. Thurgood looked from Caroline's mother to Caroline and back again. "No, thank you, ma'am. I came to ask your daughter if she'd have supper with me at the hotel—with your permission, of course. Perhaps Miss Wallace has told you about the unfortunate incident the other day. I'm afraid I was a bit harsh with your daughter. I wish to make amends by—ahem!—taking her to supper, so we can start our acquaintance with a clean slate, so to speak—quite an appropriate phrase for two in the profession of education, hmm?" He chuckled at his own joke.

Caroline's jaw fell open. "I—I appreciate your kindness, sir, but th-that's not necessary," she said. "You were entirely correct to upbraid me for what happened, and as I said before, it will not happen again."

"Miss Wallace, it would be *you* who would be doing

me the kindness by accepting my invitation," Mr. Thurgood said, eyes once more goggling dangerously behind his spectacles. "I do not like to think of myself as a harsh man, but I will admit I am a lonely one. My children are grown and gone, and my late wife passed on quite a number of years ago. Please, certainly you could spare an hour or so of your time and allow me to buy you supper, and we could speak of teaching. And I would feel I had made amends. It would make me most happy."

Caroline's gaze darted to her mother in hopes that her mother would find a way to save her, but her mother only gave her a sympathetic smile and murmured, "How nice of you, Mr. Thurgood," before giving Caroline a meaningful look.

"I…uh… I don't know if the hotel restaurant serves supper on Sunday evenings," she said desperately. "After they serve Sunday dinner, I… I believe they close early. At least, they always used to…" Then she worried her mother would feel bound by courtesy to invite the superintendent to supper. The only thing she could imagine worse than dining with the superintendent alone would be dining with him under the watchful eye of Jack Collier, who would almost certainly arrive with the twins in time for the meal.

But Superintendent Thurgood was already smiling in triumph. "I took the liberty of inquiring at the hotel before I came, Miss Wallace. They assure me they will be serving supper for another couple of hours, so I have reserved us a table. I hope you don't find that presumptuous of me."

"No, of course not," she replied with a sinking feeling in the pit of her stomach. There was no graceful way she could refuse to do this. She could not even take refuge and claim she was still in mourning—half-mourning now, to be sure—because he had couched his request as a professional one, a meeting *"between fellow educators."*

Nonsense! As if he'd ask me to supper if I were a man!

Yes, there was no escaping this ordeal. If she refused, it might make the relationship between them even worse—and if he took revenge by dismissing her she could not even cite impropriety on his part. If she accepted, she would have to pray he never asked her out again and hope that her tenure as a teacher would be secure now that she had allowed him to make amends.

"Then you accept?" he asked.

"I… Of course I do." Her voice lacked strength. "Perhaps we'd better be going, then?" she added, hoping she did not sound as if she was trying to hurry him away from the house, even though she was. The sooner they went, the less likely it was that they would encounter Jack and the girls returning from the ranch. She hoped her mother would explain Caroline's absence to Jack so that it sounded like nothing more than what Caroline saw it as, a professional obligation.

But maybe it was presumptuous of her to even think Jack would care.

Caroline breathed a sigh of relief as she closed the door behind her. The last two hours had seemed to take two months. Mr. Thurgood had talked endlessly, telling anecdote after anecdote of his teaching experiences, each one more long-drawn-out than the last. He would ask Caroline her opinion on some point of teaching, pretend to listen to her answer, then go off on a long dissertation about his own experience with that topic. And yet he had managed to put away a prodigious quantity of roast beef, heedless of the gravy that dripped from it and spotted his shirt.

The only thing Caroline could be thankful for was that they'd been the only people, other than a handful of travelers staying in the hotel, dining in the restaurant that night. Ella Justiss, the new Spinsters' Club member, hadn't been waitressing that night, and Caroline and Mr. Thurgood hadn't been close enough to the window to be seen by anyone passing by. The fewer people in Simpson Creek who knew that she had had supper with the school superintendent, the better.

And now it was over, and he was walking away from the house to where he had hitched his buggy.

"Aunt Caroline!" cried Abby, dashing into the hallway where Caroline was hanging up her shawl. "You're back!"

"Yes, dear," she said, hugging the child and then her sister, who came running right behind her twin.

"I don't know why you had to go eat supper with that awful man," Amelia said.

Caroline sighed and knelt so her face was at eye level with the little girl. "Sometimes, when one has a job, one has duties that are not always enjoyable. Mr. Thurgood is my boss, and he wanted to meet with me, so I had an obligation to go—does that make sense?"

Amelia shrugged. "What does 'obulgation' mean?"

"Obligation," Caroline repeated. "It means a duty. Like you have a duty to mind your papa."

"Oh. I see," Amelia said, seemingly reassured that Caroline did not think of her supper with Mr. Thurgood as enjoyable.

Caroline looked over the girls' shoulders. "Is…is your

father here?" she asked, trying not to sound as if it mattered.

Abby shook her head. "No, he went back to the ranch right after supper."

Amelia added, "He said he had to ride herd tonight or something."

By an effort of will, Caroline kept her features blank. Until this moment, she had not realized just how much she had been looking forward to seeing Jack once she escaped Mr. Thurgood. Had Jack left early *because* she had gone out to supper with Mr. Thurgood? Had he misinterpreted the outing as something more than it was, a duty she could not have gracefully avoided? Surely he didn't think Mr. Thurgood was courting her!

And yet, she knew with a sick certainty that the superintendent looked at it that way. Something about the way the man had preened when he'd helped her with her wrap and when other diners had glanced their way told her Mr. Thurgood might well feel it *was* the beginning of a courtship.

Well, she'd have to nip *that* idea in the bud, she thought tartly, straightening. Even if she lost her job as teacher, she was not about to spend another moment in the company of that man, except at the schoolhouse when others were there.

The clock in the hall chimed the hour.

"Girls, it's time for you to go get ready for bed," her mother said, coming into the parlor. "Go wash up and put on your nightgowns."

The twins scampered off.

"I'm afraid your brother's responsible for Jack taking off so early," her mother said with a rueful look. "He's the one who told Jack that Mr. Thurgood had come to take you to supper all gussied up like a prize peacock, and smelling like a rose."

Caroline groaned. She could just imagine the mischievous Dan doing such a thing.

"How did Jack react?" She hated to let her mother see how much she cared, but she had to know.

"He just got quiet," her mother said. "You know how most men are when they're thinking hard about something. He ate supper without hardly saying a word, just thanked me and said he had to be getting back to the ranch."

"And Dan will probably tell everyone he meets about my supper with Mr. Thurgood, too. That's all I don't need, for the whole town thinking he's courting me."

Her mother's smile was full of sympathy. "I don't think you have to worry about that, Caroline. I gave Dan a lecture after Jack left about the virtue of discretion. Dan probably thought he was helping you by making Jack jealous."

So her whole family had guessed she cared about Jack. At least she hadn't had to explain it to her mother—Ma understood how Caroline felt without her saying a word.

"Thanks, Ma." She sighed, then went and hugged her mother. "Do you think Jack *was* jealous? After all, I've told him often enough I wasn't interested."

Still embracing Caroline, her mother's shoulders shook with laughter. "Now, if that isn't a silly question. If he wasn't, why would he have left? And you *are* interested, aren't you?"

Caroline could only nod. Admitting the fact seemed to release a great weight from her shoulders. "So what should I do?"

Her mother let her go so she could look her in the eye. "Sounds like you'd better find a way to show him you care, dear."

Some of Jack's trailhands had been surprised when they'd first joined the drive to see that the trail boss took his turn at night watch just as the rest of them did—often taking the second watch, the time after midnight when it was tough on a man to leave a warm bedroll and ride away from a campfire into the chill of the night.

To Jack it was only common sense to take his turn with the rest, for it was *his herd*. A cattleman who thought he was above taking night watch deserved to lose beeves to predators, both the four-legged and the two-legged kind.

Besides, if he couldn't sleep, between the thoughts that plagued him and the snoring of his men around the campfire—especially old Cookie—he might as well circle the cattle. It was a chance to be alone with his thoughts, which a man didn't often get when he spent his days among other men. Cowboys were usually talk-ative among themselves about other trail drives, other cowboys they had known, girls they had left behind or horses they had been thrown by.

Tonight, he'd ridden out early to meet Raleigh and take over the watch, eager to get away from Caroline's face, which seemed to gaze out at him from the flicker-ing flames of the campfire. He couldn't stop imagining Caroline with the suitor who'd come to call and won-dering how she felt about the man.

Maybe if he immersed himself in the calm of the night he wouldn't think about Caroline stepping out on the arm of an older man, an established man, a man who would have books and learning in common with her. No matter how Mrs. Wallace had tried to downplay Caroline's absence, it was her brother's teasing words that stuck with him— "You shoulda seen that fine gent, Jack, lookin' at my sister like she was a fresh-baked peach pie and he was hungry."

No wonder Caroline had been easing out of strict mourning black. She'd said she wasn't interested in courting—but that must have changed when the right man came to call. Apparently the county school superintendent filled that bill.

Raleigh seemed disinclined to ride back to his bedroll and lingered at Jack's side, even after Jack mentioned leaving a pot of coffee on the fire for him.

"That Miss Wallace, she's a right fine woman, isn't she, boss?" Raleigh said.

Jack had been staring up at the star-studded night sky without really seeing it, but now he looked back at Raleigh sharply. Why was his ramrod mentioning her?

"I reckon she is."

"I mean, takin' the girls in and all. Why, I happened to meet them comin' back from school the other day, when I was in town, and they were each holdin' one a' her hands and lookin' real happy-like."

"Hmm." He wished Raleigh would ride off and leave him to his thoughts, into which Miss Caroline Wallace had intruded far too much as it was.

"It's a shame, your brother dyin' like he did, and her wearin' black for so long."

Raleigh's continuing to talk about Caroline when he should have been back by the fire drinking coffee fanned Jack's spark of irritation into a flame. "Is there a point to your chin-wagging, Raleigh?" Jack demanded, letting the other man hear the edge in his voice. He could feel the other man's surprised gaze on him as he went back to staring at the sinking moon without really seeing it.

"Sorry, boss. It was just that I was wonderin'…"

Jack felt himself tense. Was Raleigh about to ask Jack if he minded him asking Caroline out? He could feel acid churn in his stomach and knew it wasn't just from Cookie's coffee.

"Wondering what?"

"Well, my mama always said a bird in th' hand's worth two in th' bush," Raleigh said. "Mebbe you ought to take notice of what's right under your nose, boss."

"What's that supposed to mean?" Jack snapped, but he was afraid he already knew.

"Well, you've said your plan was to find some nice lady to marry up with in Montana Territory, so the girls would have a mama again. Seems to me like they've found a lady they like plenty well right here in Simpson Creek. Don't you think she'd make a good mama for the twins? Don't you like her yourself?"

Jack's horse shifted restlessly, aware of his rider unconsciously tensing up in the saddle. "I like her just fine, and yes, the twins seem to, too. Only problem with your harebrained scheme, Raleigh, is the lady isn't interested." *Not in me, at least.* He wasn't aware that he'd been gritting his teeth until he felt the pain in his jaw. "Not that it's any of your business."

Raleigh dropped his inquisitive gaze, and his voice was softer now. "Sorry, boss, I didn't mean—"

"But maybe you think *your* charm is just what she needs in her life," Jack went on, temper making him reckless. "Perhaps you think if I say I don't care, you can go court Miss Caroline Wallace and change her mind.

Well, go right ahead. Try your luck." *Wait till Raleigh found out he already had competition.*

Raleigh held up a hand as if to stop the flood of Jack's ire. "Whoa, boss, I didn't say I was thinkin' that. I wasn't, on my honor. I'm too young to get hitched right now, too footloose for some woman to ever want to marry me, I reckon. I was just thinkin' a' you, boss."

"Well, *don't*," Jack snarled. "Go on back and get some shut-eye. Sunrise is still coming when it's coming, and we need to get that potbellied stove put in, unless you want to spend the winter in a cabin without heat."

If he didn't sound like a bear with a backside full of buckshot, Jack thought as he watched Raleigh lope back to the campfire. Sometimes caring for a woman—especially when he wasn't sure she cared back—sure soured a fellow's temper.

Chapter Thirteen

"So, how are things going with the twins now?" Louisa asked after they'd sent the children out for recess. Her manner was casual, but her eyes were bright with curiosity. "Both of them seem back to their cheerful selves."

"They are, I think," Caroline answered, staring out the window to where Abby and Amelia were once again playing jump rope with some of the other girls. "I had a talk with them about running off from school, and I asked their father to do so, too, on Sunday afternoon when he took them out to the ranch. So I don't think it'll happen again."

"I was going to ask you about it at church, but you were talking to Mr. Collier, so I didn't get a chance."

Caroline nodded and decided to steer the conversation away from Jack. She had spent more than enough time already wondering what she ought to do about him, and she had yet to come up with any answers that felt right. She didn't know Louisa well enough yet to want to confide in her, at least about Jack. *If only Milly didn't live so far from town...*

"Then you don't know the Hendersons invited me to

Sunday dinner right after you left," Caroline said. She could share her concerns with Louisa about Billy Joe, since she was a fellow teacher.

"Oh? How did that go? What do you think of Billy Joe's mother? I haven't met her, but my aunt thinks Mrs. Henderson's too meek for her own good," Louisa said.

"Yes…and Mr. Henderson has a rather…um, *forceful* personality, doesn't he?" *Should she tell Louisa about the bruises she'd seen on Mrs. Henderson's arms, bruises she suspected Mr. Henderson had put there?* She hesitated. Perhaps she should just keep her mouth shut and her eyes open right now. Instead, she told Louisa about her plan to tutor Billy Joe after school and the fact that the boy's mother had expressed approval. "I think I'll start today," she concluded, "and do the sessions twice a week."

"That's a great idea," Louisa said. "I think you're right. We could take turns doing it."

Caroline was just about to suggest they join the children and get some fresh air when the other woman murmured, "I happened to be out for a walk last evening and saw you walking into the hotel restaurant with Mr. Thurgood." She said it with the same horror a Southerner would use when uttering the name "Ulysses Grant."

Caroline froze, knowing what was coming.

"Yes, but there was no way I could avoid it, and I beg you not to tell a living soul, Louisa, please."

"Was it *very* awful?"

Louisa's tone of horror had Caroline laughing. "Very," she said and told the other woman all about it.

"So you really had no choice but to accept his invitation," Louisa said, her eyes full of sympathy, as Caroline concluded her story. "And you're afraid he has the impression he is now courting you? Oh, dear."

"Yes…and you can see, can't you, it will be a delicate balancing act to refuse any further invitations without offending him and endangering my job."

"The old goat!" Louisa said, her face indignant. "That isn't fair! He knows you want to keep your teaching job, so he thinks he can take advantage of that! Caroline, you must stand firm."

"I know."

"What if you had another suitor? Then he would have to understand he could not press his attentions."

"*That* would get me dismissed immediately," she said and told Louisa how the superintendent had told her he preferred the county's teachers to have never been married, let alone have gentlemen callers currently. It was comforting to think of encountering Mr. Thurgood while holding Jack's hand, but that was impossible—for so many reasons.

"Hmm…perhaps you could get the preacher to speak to him? Or the mayor? My aunt tells me that one of the Spinsters' Club graduates is the mayor's daughter."

"Yes, Prissy Bishop, the sheriff's wife. And I suppose either of those gentlemen would help." *But how embarrassing, to have to speak to them about such a thing.* Caroline could only hope it wouldn't come to that.

The first tutoring session had been a success. Billy Joe had sulked a bit, when told he would be staying after school an hour, but Caroline suspected this was mostly for show. Once the rest of the children had left, including the twins, he settled right down and applied himself to his arithmetic lesson with a will. It was obvious that mathematics came hard for him. But then, when they progressed to reading, he read a passage from his Mc-Guffey reader so perfectly that Caroline clapped when he finished.

"Billy Joe, you've been hiding your light under a bushel basket," she told him.

Billy Joe wrinkled his nose. "What does that mean, Teacher?"

"It means you've been concealing your ability," she said. "You're supposed to shine like a candle set on top of a basket, not under it."

"Aw, Teacher, then the fellas'll call me a teacher's pet. And what do I need 'rithmetic for, anyway? Soon's I can leave home, I'm gonna go be a cowboy. I won't never use it."

She smiled. "You might need to figure out how much is left of your pay after you spend a few dollars for a Saturday night in town."

He looked dubious. "Reckon I'll have my pay in my pocket, and I can see what's left."

"But what if the rancher makes you foreman, and one of your duties is to figure out each man's pay?"

"Then I guess I ought to know some cipherin'," he admitted with a sheepish grin.

"And what if you'd want to write your sweetheart a letter? We'll work on your handwriting next."

"Aw, Miss Wallace, I don't set much store by girls— 'cept my ma and you, a' course. Oh, and them twins. They're all right."

"*Those* twins. And thank you for including us as exceptions. Now, you go right home and do your chores," Caroline told Billy Joe as she closed the schoolhouse door behind them. "And be sure and tell your papa what we worked on."

"Sure, Miss Wallace," Billy Joe said. "G'night!" Then he ran out of the schoolyard with all the pent-up energy only a boy his age could muster. There was a bit of the show-off in Billy Joe, Caroline thought with amusement, as he looked back to see if she was watching, an action which nearly caused him to trip over the half-buried root of a live oak.

Her tutoring done, she made her way home and, after greeting the twins, joined in supper preparation.

"Going to be a busy week, what with Thanksgiving on Thursday," her mother commented as she sliced corn bread into squares.

Caroline blinked. "Thanksgiving? Goodness, is it time for that already?"

Her mother smiled. "I think you've been too busy to notice."

"Will there be turkey?" Abby asked.

"Can Papa come to dinner?" piped up Amelia.

"Yes, assuming Dan gets one, when he goes hunting on his day off tomorrow," her mother told the girl. "He can stop at the ranch while he's out and invite your papa. Oh, and Caroline, I was talking to Milly at church, and she figured Jack would come here to be with his girls, so she and Nick are going to invite Jack's drovers to have the Thanksgiving meal along with their cowboys at the Brookfields'. I'll have him stop at the Parkers' place and see if he can buy one of their hams, too."

So it was all settled. She wouldn't have to maneuver to see Jack—it would happen quite naturally in just a few days. A vision of Jack sitting down with them at the traditional feast had her quite suddenly giddy with happiness.

Her mother winked, making Caroline think her mother could read her thoughts. "Yes, and now that the new church is done, remember Saturday is the rededication of the church with the carry-in supper in the new social hall afterward. The whole town will be there."

"We'll have to make sure and invite your papa to that, too," Caroline said, speaking to the twins, then added to her mother, "and as many of the drovers as he feels can be spared from their duties."

So there would be not one, but two occasions to see Jack. She felt a stirring of excitement she hadn't felt in a long time.

The bunkhouse was finished. There was no more need to sleep outside—a good thing, now that there was a nip in the air, at least at night. At present, they were still sleeping on bedrolls inside the bunkhouse, since there were no beds. But Jack and some of the men had made their bedding more comfortable by spreading straw underneath their bedrolls, while others were using their newly discovered carpentry skills to construct cots for themselves.

They were a little bored, Jack knew, now that the building was done. There was nothing much to do besides tend the cattle and the remuda. When their chores were done, they played endless rounds of poker—a pastime Jack had always found useless, in addition to the fact his mother had had a rule against it. Their stakes consisted of dried beans donated by Cookie, rather than money, since their wages would be meager until the cattle were sold in Montana. They kept their cash for trips into town. He guessed a few of them were already wishing they had left when the other two drovers had, but winter was no time to be an unemployed cowboy. Still, he'd have to find things to occupy their time, for a restless man was apt to find mischief.

This morning, a little bored and fidgety himself, he stared at the empty scar of land where the ranch house had once sat. What had the house looked like? He knew it had been made mostly of stone, for they had piled up the soot-darkened stones that remained, but he only had his imagination to supply the rest. Almost absently, he picked up a piece of the scrap paper and the stub of a pencil he used to write lists of supplies needed in town, and, using the underside of a clean skillet as a firm backing, he began sketching the house as he envisioned it.

At what point it stopped being the old Waters ranch house and became the house *he* would have built, he wasn't sure. And he couldn't seem to stop himself from picturing what sort of dwelling Caroline would want, if she were living here—a good kitchen, of course, with lots of shelves and hooks for cooking implements and room for a family dining table. What else? A bedroom with an eastern exposure, so she could watch the sun come up? A porch facing west, so she could watch the sun set behind the blue hills? *Several* other bedrooms, for children?

Now where had that idea come from? There was no use planning a house with Caroline in mind, for clearly she preferred an educated, powerful man like that school superintendent, a man she could discuss the classics with, who didn't have to think twice about how to spell a word.

So it was better to think of building the house as

something constructive for himself and his men to do when the cattle-related chores were finished and the weather wasn't bad. Any participation by his men must be strictly voluntary, of course. If one of his men preferred to pass the long days till spring whittling or playing cards, Jack would have no grounds to object, but perhaps he could offer those who participated a greater share of the profits when he sold the herd to motivate them.

He'd reuse as much of the stone as possible and use wood from the ranch land, to keep costs of building this house down...

"What 'cha drawin' there, Mr. Collier?"

He'd been so engrossed in his drawing he hadn't even noticed the horse approaching. He looked up to see Dan Wallace sitting on the horse, peering down at him. A big tom turkey was trussed by his claws to the horn of the saddle, its red wattle hanging limply from its grayish-white head.

"Nothing much, Dan," he said, laying the drawing and skillet down. "Just passing the time. I see you've been hunting. You bagged a big one there."

"Yup, shot us our Thanksgiving turkey. Ma and Caroline asked me to stop and invite you to Thanksgiving dinner."

"I'd be right pleased to attend," he said. The idea was very appealing—until he thought of the possibility of that superintendent fellow at the same table, sitting next to Caroline as her beau.

"Say, that older fellow that took her to supper—is he coming, too, by any chance?" he asked casually.

Dan gave a hoot of laughter. "Shoot, no, Mr. Collier. I don't think Caroline likes Mr. Thurgood much. I think she just had to go to supper with him that one time 'cause he's her boss, an' he got his feathers all ruffled when my sister had to go find Abby."

Jack considered that. Was it possible the boy was right? He felt a stab of guilt that his child had been the cause of the superintendent's disfavor. But he couldn't help being cheered by the idea that Caroline hadn't wanted to go dine with Thurgood. Still, Caroline not liking the paunchy superintendent didn't mean she had any liking for Jack Collier, however—or *any* man, despite the fact she'd started wearing half-mourning rather than austere black.

"Oh, an' you an' all the men're invited to the church Saturday for the rededication service an' carry-in supper, too. You don't hafta worry about bringin' nothin' to that, neither. There'll be enough to feed an army, Ma says."

"That sounds real nice." He couldn't quite imagine his drovers sitting through a church service, but if there was food to be had afterward, he bet they'd be willing to try. They'd have to draw straws to see who got to go, of course, but they'd probably only have to leave two or three here with the cattle. He figured there'd be a way to bring them back some food from the church supper, too.

And he'd get to see Caroline on both occasions.

And perhaps he could show her that, while he was a cattleman, rather than a learned man like the superintendent, he wasn't completely ignorant.

Cookie rang the triangle just then to signal it was time for the noon meal.

"You're welcome to stay and eat with us, Dan," Jack said.

The boy grinned. "Thanks, but I still need to stop by

the Parker ranch and buy a ham for Ma for the Thanksgiving feast. We'll see you Thursday, okay?"

It was just as well. His mind was whirling with thoughts about the ranch house he'd decided to build, and he didn't want Caroline's little brother jumping to the wrong conclusion if he was present while he broached the idea to his men.

He waited till forks were clinking against tin plates before he began. "Men, I've been thinking about a project I'd like to do to pass the time this winter...."

Chapter Fourteen

"Mrs. Wallace, Miss Caroline, that was the mighty-finest Thanksgiving dinner the girls and I have had in years," Jack said, pushing himself back from the table with a barely suppressed groan. He couldn't remember when he'd been this full of good food.

Mrs. Wallace beamed. "You're welcome, Jack. We're mighty glad you could be here with us."

"The pleasure was all ours, ma'am," he said. "Mine and the girls'."

"Papa, mighty-finest isn't a real word," Amelia, sitting next to him, told him primly, then looked to Caroline across the table for confirmation. "It isn't, is it, Teacher?"

"Oh, I think when one is giving a compliment, making up a word that seems to fit is perfectly permissible," Caroline said, giving Jack a quick smile.

"I don't think we *ever* had a real Thanksgiving dinner, Aunt Mary," Abby, sitting on his other side, said, her face wistful. "So of course it's the mighty-finest."

"Punkin, you've had Thanksgiving dinners," Jack said. "You just don't remember. Well…not since your

mama died, true, but we always had them before that."
The old woman who'd cooked and kept house for them
after Lucinda had died hadn't been up to cooking special
meals; in fact, she wasn't even as competent a cook as
Cookie. He'd never pressed her to make a special dinner at Thanksgiving—the holiday had been relegated to
just-another-day status till now.

"I don't remember," Abby said, in her determined
way. "So it doesn't count."

"Then this will be one to remember," Jack said.
"Please tell Aunt Mary and Miss Caroline how much
you appreciate their hard work."

The twins did so with great enthusiasm.

"Would everyone like their pumpkin pie now, or shall
we wait till later?" Caroline asked. She was lovely today,
Jack thought, in a dress of russet brown with black pip-
ing, her dark, glossy brown hair neatly gathered into a
knot at the nape of her neck.

Mr. Wallace rubbed his belly and said, "Believe I'll
wait a spell for mine, wife. I feel as full as a tick that
just fell off an ol' hound dog's back. Girls, why don't
we get out the checkerboard? I'll play a game with one
a' you girls, then Dan can play the other."

"We don't know how to play checkers," Amelia said,
a little uncertainly, as if afraid that the invitation from
Uncle Amos would be withdrawn because of her ad-
mission.

"Then I'll show you how, while Dan shows your sister," her father said, and the four filed away from the
table.

Overhead, the rain drummed on the roof. It was too
bad about the weather, Jack thought. He would have
liked to have suggested to Caroline that they take a walk

while the girls were occupied. But perhaps there was a way to garner some time alone with her after all.

Mrs. Wallace was already up and bustling around the table, gathering up dishes. Jack put out a hand to forestall her.

"Why don't Miss Caroline and I redd up those dishes, while you rest, Mrs. Wallace?"

"Oh, no, I wouldn't dream of letting a guest—" the older woman began.

"Please don't say no, ma'am," he interrupted to plead. "It's the least I can do after such a feast."

"Go ahead, Mama, lie down for a while, or at least put your feet up," Caroline said. "You've been cooking since before first light. Come on, Jack, I'll wash while you dry."

"Why don't I wash and *you* dry?" he teased.

Her mother had put two large kettles of water on the stove to heat for wash water. Jack brought the dirty plates from the table, and she scraped the food from them onto one big platter. Both were quiet at first while they worked.

Jack was thinking about how most of his men had been willing, even enthusiastic, about the project of building the ranch house as he'd proposed it. They'd grinned at his announcement that those who helped would receive a bonus when the cattle were sold, but he'd been encouraged to see they'd seemed agreeable to the project even before he'd mentioned that. They really were a fine bunch of fellows, he thought. They'd listened to ideas and offered up some of their own. Now the winter months wouldn't seem endless anymore.

He'd caught Raleigh eyeing him speculatively again, but he guessed his ramrod wasn't about to ask him any questions after that time Jack had snapped at him for not minding his own business.

And he wasn't about to tell Caroline about it, either, just yet. What if he wasn't capable of translating his ideas into a decent house? After all, he was a rancher, not a builder. Just because they'd managed to put up a bunkhouse that was good enough for a bunch of rough-and-ready drovers didn't mean he could build an entire house a woman would be willing to live in.

Worse yet, what if he told her, and Caroline refused to let him court her? He'd feel like a fool, and the house at Collier's Roost, as she had named the place, might become known as "Collier's Folly." He'd have no choice but to continue on to Montana after that.

He'd have been surprised to know that Caroline was having secret thoughts of her own, too. Now, as Jack poured the steaming water into two wide, shallow buckets, one to wash the dishes in, one to rinse them, she stole a sidelong glance at Jack and wondered how she should make the first move—or if she should leave it up to him.

Then he picked up the dishrag, and she tried to grab it from him. "I'm sure you should let me do the washing," she said, when he jerked his hand upward beyond her grasp. "What will your men say if you show back up at the bunkhouse with dishpan hands?"

Still holding the washrag teasingly out of her reach, he held out his other hand and rotated it for her inspection. "Look at this hand. Do you think they'd even be able to tell I've been washing dishes?"

She studied it. The skin was tanned and creased with a network of small scratches, scrapes and scars. It was a workman's hand, with callused fingertips. Just for a moment she imagined them caressing her cheek.

Where had that thought come from?

Jack dropped the rag into the hot water. "Whereas *your* hands, Teacher," he said, seizing them in his before she knew what he was about, "are not already damaged." She felt him gently assessing the pads of her thumbs with his own for the space of a few heartbeats until she yanked her hands out of his grasp.

Caroline turned startled eyes up to his and was alarmed to see the intensity in the blue eyes that looked back at her. They were Pete's eyes…and yet not.

She felt the heat rise up her neck suffuse her cheeks. "Nonsense. I do dishes every day of the year, J-Jack," she said, stumbling over his name as she tried to adopt her severest tone. Stepping in front of the bucket that held the dishrag, she plunged her hand into the hot water and grabbed a dirty dish from the pile next to her. "Now, since you're dillydallying, I'm going to wash while this water is still hot."

She could feel his amused gaze on her as she started rubbing the wet, soapy rag against the dish as if she was trying to rub the painted-on flowers off.

For a while, they worked in silence, until they had almost entirely gone through the stack of food-stained dishes and silverware.

"Dan tells me you've finished the bunkhouse," she said at last.

"Yes, just the day before he came out. It's nice to be warm and dry at night," he said, "though I'll admit I liked just opening my eyes and looking up at the stars."

"So what will you do to pass the time now?" Caroline asked, "when you're not tending cattle or horses and such?"

"Oh, you know, the usual, I imagine—coming into town to see the twins…hunting game for Cookie's pot… Actually, I was hoping you might be able to help me with that," he said, startling her so badly that she almost dropped the wet cut-crystal jelly dish, her mother's pride and joy, as she was handing it to him to dry.

"*Me?* I'm no hunter! I couldn't hit an elephant if it was standing still in front of me."

His laugh was rich and full and wrapped itself in warm tendrils around her heart. "No, I meant to help me pass the time."

For a moment, she thought perhaps he meant he wanted to spend more time with her, and she felt a little thrill that it had been so easy after all.

Then he said, "I thought I might spend some time reading, and I was going to ask if you might be able to lend me a book off that shelfful out by the fireplace. Your pa tells me they're all yours, except for an almanac of his and the family Bible. I promise I'd take good care of it."

"Oh," she murmured, feeling faintly foolish for misunderstanding. "Well, of course. What sort of thing do you like to read?" She should feel flattered that he wanted to read one of her books.

He shrugged, still holding the dish with one hand, then set it down with the others he'd dried. "I don't know… I haven't had much time for reading, so I couldn't rightly say."

She thought a moment, her hands still in the soapy water. "How about *A Tale of Two Cities,* by Charles Dickens?"

"What's that about?"

"The French Revolution and love that sacrifices for the greater good," she said, imagining him reading Dickens's stirring prose. "It starts out, 'It was the best of times, it was the worst of times,'" she quoted.

He looked quizzical. "I don't know how a time could be both, but I'm willing to try it," he said.

"Or perhaps *Robinson Crusoe* would be more to your taste? It's about a man who's shipwrecked and his life on an island far from civilization."

"I reckon I'll try that Dickens fellow's book first, and then when I finish it, I'll borrow the other one— assuming the French story doesn't take me all winter to read," he said.

She glanced out the window and saw that the rain was still pouring down. "It looks like a good afternoon for reading," she said.

An hour later, he was ensconced in a chair, poring over Dickens's masterpiece, while she graded her pupil's copybook exercises. The twins were still playing checkers with Dan and her father, Amelia crowing as Dan directed her to jump Abby's checker and get herself kinged.

Caroline was aware of a feeling of peace and contentment she had not felt in a long time.

"Jack Collier!" a voice called as he reached the town's main street after picking up his horse at the livery.

Sheriff Bishop beckoned to him from the doorway of the jail. "Wonder if I might have a moment of your time?"

"Of course," Jack said, reining his mount over to the hitching post. A thin snake of apprehension slithered down the back of his neck. Bishop didn't look angry, but he did have his serious face on. Had one of Jack's men sneaked into town last night and, despite warnings on the subject, gotten into a ruckus for which Jack was now going to have to bail him out of jail? Had there been some trouble at the ranch, or worse yet, had one of his drovers been ill-mannered enough to have gotten into a tussle with one of the Brookfield cowboys at the Thanksgiving dinner in the Brookfield bunkhouse?

Jack couldn't believe any of those things could be true, and if they were, Raleigh Masterson would have come and notified him personally, not waited till he returned to the ranch. So what had happened?

"What can I do for you, Sheriff?"

Bishop shrugged. "Maybe nothing. You mentioned two of your men decided to leave your employ when you decided to stay in Simpson Creek over the winter."

"Yes... Shorty Adams and Alvin Sims," Jack said. "They didn't want to turn their hands to building instead of cowboying, when I said we'd be constructing a bunkhouse, so I paid them what I owed them and sent them on their way. No hard feelings. They rode on, far as I know—why?"

"One of 'em a rangy bowlegged fellow and the other short and stocky? Scar on his face?"

Jack nodded, wary, still sitting on his horse. "They in some kind of trouble?" Involuntarily, his gaze lifted past the sheriff to the door of the jail.

Bishop followed the direction of his gaze and shook his head. "No, I don't have 'em in my jail cells, if that's what you're thinkin'. But they've been comin' into town of a night and raising Cain in the saloon, causing trouble for the pair of girls George has working there. Now,

George doesn't keep track of what these ladies do on their own, but they don't have rooms upstairs in the saloon, if you get my meanin'."

Jack did.

"And that isn't all. A couple of ranchers have reported the loss of a steer here or there. The last time whoever butchered the steer didn't trouble to even hide the carcass when he was done with it—just left it on the property. And yesterday, Hal Parker told me one of his horses came up missing, a blaze-faced sorrel gelding."

"What makes you think it was these two?" Jack asked, careful to keep his tone nondefensive. If Adams and Sims were rustling cattle and stealing horses, he didn't want any part of them.

"Some cowhands of a rancher named Beaudine were tryin' to round up a stray and they came upon a couple of fellas they described like I just described 'em to you, roastin' a spit of beef. 'Course, they couldn't prove anything at that point, so they told 'em they were trespassing on Beaudine land and they'd have to leave after they finished their grub. And Parker caught a glimpse of 'em runnin' off with his sorrel, but by the time he'd mounted up, he couldn't catch 'em."

Jack pondered the information. "I haven't seen those two since they left us, though the men have seen them in the saloon a time or two when they've taken turns coming into town. They said Alvin and Shorty told them they were doing odd jobs for ranchers around here."

Bishop looked dubious, but he said nothing.

Then Jack remembered Abby and Amelia reporting their encounter with the two men. "Though now that you mention it, my girls mentioned seeing them in town. I'm afraid they never liked them two much." *Any more than he had.* He wished he'd managed to resist his stepmother's pleas for him to hire them.

"I figured you didn't know what they were up to," Bishop said. "Just thought I'd let you know, in case you see them. You might want to remind them they still hang horse thieves in these parts."

Jack nodded. "Where I come from, too."

"Advise them to be move on, pronto."

"Will do."

The encounter cast a cloud over the buoyant mood he'd had when he left the Wallaces after seeing Caroline and his girls depart for school. It had been too cold and damp to spend the night on the summer porch, and he'd had to bunk with young Dan, who snored as loud as a man four times his age. In spite of that Jack had slept well. When he'd left the house, he'd been looking forward to returning on Saturday for the church rededication supper and seeing Caroline and his girls again. But now it seemed that two of his former drovers were well on their way to becoming outlaws. It made him sick to think that that pair had been around his daughters.

Would they have found their way into trouble if Jack hadn't had to stop and winter in Simpson Creek? There was no way of knowing.

And no use torturing himself wondering, he thought as his horse headed out of Simpson Creek at an easy lope. It was much more enjoyable to contemplate seeing Caroline again and anticipating the hours he'd have tonight to delve back into the exotic world of Paris in the midst of revolution he'd found between the pages of the book Caroline had loaned him. He couldn't wait to discuss it with her.

Halfway between the town and the ranch, he came

upon Masterson headed toward Simpson Creek, driving the wagon they'd rented for the winter.

Raleigh waved as he slowed the wagon horses. "Thought I'd head to the mercantile and the lumberyard and pick up a few things we're gonna need to work on the ranch house, boss. The rest of the boys are cuttin' logs and gatherin' stones from the pastures."

"Good idea." He was pleased his ramrod had taken the initiative, and that the rest of the men were eager to work on the project. "Just don't tell anyone what you're doing with the materials for now, okay? I'd like to keep our little project our secret for the time being, okay?"

Masterson's eyes were shrewd as he studied Jack, and Jack had the feeling his ramrod had already figured out the reason for Jack's request. Which was all right, he supposed, as long as Raleigh didn't say so.

"I'll be quiet as a snowflake fallin' on a feather, boss."

Jack grinned. "You fellows have a good time eating turkey with the Brookfield cowboys yesterday?"

Masterson rubbed his stomach and gave a mock groan. "I'm still so full I could hardly eat more than a dozen of Cookie's flapjacks this mornin'. That Mrs. Brookfield knows how to put on the chow! We ate till we could hardly mount our horses. Ol' Wes, he sure didn't let havin' just one good hand slow him down none. He had to let out his belt three notches."

"Sounds like a fine time was had by all. The girls and I had quite a meal, too."

Raleigh looked as if he wanted to ask more about that, but instead he said, "Boss, you'll never guess who turned up for breakfast this mornin'."

Jack sighed, afraid he already knew the answer.

"Shorty and Alvin. Seems the odd jobs 'round these

parts have run dry, and they want to know if you'd hire 'em on again. I told 'em you were fixin' to rebuild the ranch house, and they'd have to be willin' to pitch in on that before you'd take 'em back. They said they'd help. They're waitin' for your say-so at the bunkhouse, boss."

"Was one of them ridin' a blaze-faced sorrel geld-ing?" Jack asked, feeling a sour taste in his mouth. Surely the pair wasn't loco enough to keep a stolen horse in the same county they stole it in.

"No…" Masterson looked puzzled. "What're you talkin' about, boss?"

Jack told him. "So I won't be rehiring them."

His ramrod whistled. "Can't blame you there. I've gotta admit I never cottoned to either of 'em. Shifty-eyed and lazy."

He left Masterson and traveled the remaining miles to Collier's Roost, dreading the confrontation with Sims and Adams.

It was no more pleasant than he'd expected. He found Shorty Adams and Alvin Sims lounging around the campfire, mugs of coffee and tin plates of beans in their hands. The rest of his drovers hadn't stopped for the noon meal yet and were still hard at work hauling rocks and chopping wood. Cookie looked sourer than ever as he kneaded biscuit dough, most likely because of the two saddle tramps. It had probably been easier to give them food than listen to them jawing.

Alvin Sims got lazily to his feet as Jack rode in, stretched, and scratched the scruff of beard on his face.

"Howdy, Jack. How's those purdy gals of yours?"

Jack had never insisted on formality and didn't mind his men calling him "Jack" or "Boss" instead of "Mr. Collier." But under the circumstances, Sims's familiarity rankled. And he sure didn't like Sims mentioning his children.

Sims didn't seem to notice Jack's lack of response. "Me an' Shorty had a while to think on it," the other man said, "an' we realized we mighta been a mite hasty in leavin' ya like we did. We come back to hire on again." His confident grin was more like a smirk.

Shorty stood, too, but his expression was more ingratiating. "We'll work real hard, boss. You won't have no cause to complain."

"Like you're doing now?" Jack said. If he'd come back to find them working alongside his men, putting in an effort, he might have been able to convince himself the sheriff had been mistaken, but not now.

Both men's smiles faded somewhat, and their faces reddened.

"We was hungry, boss," Alvin said, his tone wheedling now. "Figured we'd get right to work over there," he said, jerking his head in the direction of the other men, "soon's we had our bellies full. We ain't had no regular work, hard as we tried."

"Yeah, Mr. Collier," Shorty put in. "Never shoulda left ya, an' that's a fact."

"You can finish those beans, then ride on. I don't have any work for you." Jack kept his tone matter-of-fact.

"Whaddya mean, no work?" Alvin protested. "Raleigh said you're rebuildin' the ranch house. You sayin' you couldn't use more hands?"

"I could have before I talked to the sheriff this mornin'. I didn't like what I heard. You've been causing trouble at the saloon, and—"

"Last I heard, gettin' familiar with saloon girls ain't

a crime," Alvin said, hands spread wide. He tried to assume an innocent expression and failed.

"If that was all, I still wouldn't take you back," Jack said. "But there's also reports of rustled beef, a stolen horse… No, afraid I can't have you working for me." He kept his hand on his upper leg, as he sat in the saddle, but it was only inches from his pistol.

Alvin's eyes narrowed. "You accusin' us a' *rustlin'*, Jack? An' *horse-stealin'*? On whose say-so?"

"You were seen, Sims. Described. Sheriff told me to remind you that stealing a horse is liable to get you strung up."

Sims's jaw hardened, and he glanced at the gun belt he'd left too far away on his upended saddle. Shorty wasn't armed, either, but Adams wouldn't have had the nerve to draw on him even if he'd been wearing his gun belt. Neither man noticed that Cookie had put down his dough and quietly pulled out a rifle, but Jack appreciated the older man's support. And now he saw Quint and Shep approaching.

"You men go cut your horses out of the remuda, saddle up and ride on. Now."

Sims's eyes blazed. "You're makin' a mistake, Collier. You ain't got no right to accuse us a' anything."

The two drifters hadn't seen Quint and Shep coming toward them, but now they looked to the side and saw that Jack's men held pistols trained on them.

"Keep their pistols, Quint. They can have 'em back when they're mounted and ready to ride out."

"You're gonna wish you'd agreed to take us back, Collier," Sims muttered as he strode off to get his horse.

Chapter Fifteen

"Our text today is taken from the book of Nehemiah," the Reverend Chadwick said, standing in front of his new pulpit in the new Simpson Creek Church. "'And they said, Let us rise up and build. And they strengthened their hands for this good work.' Friends, only a few months ago we stared at the smoking ruins of our beloved church and wondered if we had the strength to build it again. But all of you have 'strengthened your hands,' as the Bible says, and now we sit in our new building."

Caroline looked around her and breathed in the smell of new wood, new paint, new varnish. At the back, over the doorway, a stained glass rose window, one of two that the mayor had contributed, glowed with the late afternoon sunlight, while the other, a simple white cross outlined in royal blue, framed Chadwick's white-topped head.

Amelia and Abby had been wide-eyed as they gazed at all of it, oohing and aahing. "I never seen such pretty windows," Abby breathed.

Amelia nodded. "This must be the prettiest church *ever*."

Thank You, Lord, Caroline thought. *Thank You for this new building, though we need to remember that Your church is not merely a building, but its people. And thank You that Jack and his daughters sit beside me. Show me if it is Your will for Jack and me to build a life together.* Her mother, father and brother sat on her other side, her mother alternately beaming at Reverend Chadwick and her daughter.

All around the sanctuary she saw her students, and one by one, they made eye contact with her, smiling, some giving discreet waves. What a blessing it was to live in a small town, where everyone she knew worshipped in the same church. She didn't see Billy Joe Henderson or his parents, though. She wondered what had kept them from attending. Had Billy Joe's brutish father finally struck his wife or his child somewhere it would show? She'd have to make it a point to check on the Hendersons tomorrow for certain, if they were not at Sunday services.

In the pews behind them sat several of Jack's men, looking a little out of place in these unfamiliar surroundings, their hair slicked down, their faces washed and shaved, and each of them wearing a shirt saved for coming into town. Caroline knew most of them had been lured by the promise of the food the ladies had been carrying into the new social hall since mid-morning, but she hoped perhaps they'd feel welcome enough to want to come back.

Something was eating at Jack, though. He'd smiled when he'd joined her in the pew, while his daughters had arranged themselves between the two of them, but there was an air of distraction about him. She wondered what was amiss. Her father had handed him a letter postmarked "Montana" when he'd taken his seat, so maybe he was eager to read it or feared bad news. *Was he wishing he was already wintering in Montana, his house framed by lodge pole pines and aspens, with massive mountains nearby and snow on the ground?*

When the dedication service was over, everyone filed into the new social hall. Several rows of long, wide planks on sawhorses had been set up, and it seemed every tablecloth in town had been pressed into service on these makeshift tables. Against one wall sat a long, carved rosewood table donated by the mercantile, laden with covered dishes that teased the nose with enticing smells. Pies, cakes and cookies were arranged at one end of the table, sliced hams, roast beef and chicken at the other, and every variety of potatoes, rice, breads and vegetables in between.

Walking behind Caroline, one of Jack's cowboys moan out loud, "I reckon I've died and gone to Heaven."

She couldn't help but smile, and her smile broadened when she heard another cowboy add, "We're gonna get so fat we won't be able to sit our horses. First Missus Brookfield's fed us, and now the whole church is doing the same."

She looked up at Jack to share the amusement, yet he seemed not to have heard his men's remarks.

Everyone found a seat, and the preacher blessed the food. Parents were invited to get food for their children first, and Caroline went with Jack, since he had both Abby and Amelia. Others helped elderly residents.

Once the twins were devouring fried chicken, mashed potatoes and gravy and green beans, Caroline and Jack got back in line behind her mother and father and filled their own plates.

Jack attacked his food with gusto, but every time she looked at him, he seemed to be looking around the room for someone. She saw his gaze land on Sheriff Bishop, eating next to his pretty bride Prissy, and Jack seemed satisfied. *Why was he looking for the sheriff?*

"Papa, I want some apple pie," Abby said,

"Me, too," her sister said. "*And* chocolate cake."

Jack glanced back at his children, then at their plates. "You have to eat all your green beans, and then you can have dessert." Then he glanced around at his cowboys, as if satisfying himself that they were behaving, before going back to his food.

"How are you finding *A Tale of Two Cities*, Jack?" Caroline asked him at last, when he made no attempt at conversation.

The question seemed to recall him to his surroundings, and he met her gaze as if he were really seeing her at last.

"Very absorbing," he said. "A very complicated yarn. First London, then Paris…the French Revolution was certainly a lot more violent than ours."

"Yes…" she agreed, relieved that he seemed to be fully present at last. She thought of the ending, in which Carton goes to the guillotine to save Darnay, but didn't want to speak of guillotines and such in front of the children.

"I've been reading till long after the other fellows are snoring in the bunkhouse," he told her with a chuckle. "I'll be ready for *Robinson Crusoe* soon."

"You can have it whenever you want it," she said, feeling a warm glow of pleasure that he was taking an interest in literature. "I was thinking you might like *Ivanhoe*, too. It's about knights in old England, and jousts and so forth."

"Sounds good. By the time the winter's over, I'll be the best-read trail boss in the West," he said lightly, then began staring toward the sheriff again.

Caroline couldn't help but feel a little disappointed. She'd had such high hopes for furthering her relationship with Jack at this event, yet his mind seemed everywhere but with her. Surely he was planning to spend the night at their house to attend church in the morning with his girls, so she thought about waiting until they got home to ask him. But when he looked in the sheriff's direction again, she decided to go ahead.

She touched his wrist to get his attention. "Jack, is something wrong?" she asked. "Are you worried it's bad news from Montana? Why don't you go ahead and read the letter?"

He shook his head and patted the letter in the pocket of his vest. "I'd forgotten all about that letter. And there's nothing you need to worry about," he said. He seemed to be ready to leave the matter there, but after his eyes met hers again, he must have guessed she wasn't content with his answer. He opened his mouth to speak, but before he could, he was interrupted by Amelia.

"Papa, we cleaned our plates," Amelia announced. "Now can we have dessert?"

"Yeah, Papa, I ate every single bite," Abby added.

Jack looked apologetically at Caroline. "Give me just a minute," he said. "I'll get them their cake and pie, and—"

"Jack, I'll help them get dessert," Caroline's mother said, rising from her seat. "I was going to go get some of

Mrs. Detwiler's chocolate cake myself. Come on, children, let's get a little something for our sweet tooth—or should it be sweet teeth, daughter?"

Caroline shot her mother a grateful look. Had her mother noticed her growing frustration at Jack's distraction?

She turned back to Jack, who was staring down at the remains of his supper. "Well?"

He sighed. "Remember those two fellows that decided to quit when I asked the men to help build the bunkhouse?"

She nodded, remembering the unpleasant encounter when the pair had stopped her and the girls in the street, and what Abby and Amelia had said about them.

"It's probably nothing to worry about," Jack went on, "but the sheriff called out to me when I was leaving the other morning and told me what Sims and Adams had been up to. Seems they've been harassing the girls at the saloon, and some cattle have come up missing, with the leftover carcasses found later, and a couple of men who looked just like those two were seen stealing another rancher's horse."

"But surely he can't hold *you* responsible for what they do," she murmured, "when they're not working for you anymore."

"He doesn't," Jack said. "Just wanted me to be aware, in case they showed up back at the ranch, and a good thing he did. Sure enough, when I got back to Collier's Roost, there they were, bold as brass, sitting around the campfire and waiting for me to hire them again, promising me they'd work as hard as anyone on the—" He stopped himself, as if he'd said too much. "I told them to ride on, that I wasn't taking them back, and gave them the hint that Sheriff Bishop knew they'd been up to mischief and worse."

"Good," she said, remembering the way the twins had shuddered in distaste after their meeting with the men. "And you *don't* have enough work to need to take anyone else on, now that the bunkhouse is built. I mean, that's why you took up reading, isn't it? After the daily chores are done, it sounded to me as if there's not that much to do."

He looked away and seemed to be struggling with how to answer her.

"Well, I reckon the point is," he said, "I wouldn't have a dishonest man working for me no matter how much I had to do. But of course, one of them, Sims, who's mouthier than the other, had to mutter as to how I'd wish later on I'd taken them back."

"He didn't say anything more than that?"

"No."

She nodded, understanding now about Jack's distraction.

"Of course, it wasn't anything but the usual taunt you'd expect when someone like that doesn't get what he wants—in this case, taking the boss for a fool—but all the same I'm feeling a mite uneasy at leaving just three men out there on the ranch with the herd. I think I'm going to ride on back there with the men soon rather than staying tonight—much as I'd like to," he added quickly, for she must have betrayed some sign of dismay.

"I... I understand," she murmured.

"I think I'd better let the sheriff in on what happened out there, too. I didn't want to intrude on the sheriff and his wife's meal, but looks like he's about done eating. I want to catch him before he leaves. Will you excuse me,

Caroline? I'll come back and explain to the girls before I go," he added. The twins were just making their way back to the table.

"Of course." She watched him walk away, telling herself her disappointment was childish and immature, that he had responsibilities as the owner of the herd that were more important than herself. Still, she'd had such high hopes for this event. Was a little gentlemanly attention too much to ask for?

"Who is that lady over there?" the newcomer asked his father, Reverend Chadwick. "The pretty one in the light gray dress with black trim."

The old preacher followed his son's eyes. "Oh, that's Miss Caroline Wallace, the town schoolteacher. Yes, she is very pretty," he agreed.

The younger man's eyes sharpened. "'Miss' Caroline Wallace? Are the twin girls her sisters, then?" He looked at Caroline's mother doubtfully.

"No, not her sisters," Reverend Chadwick said. "They're the daughters of the man who just left the table, Jack Collier. He's a trail boss spending the winter on a ranch near here with his men and his herd before going on to Montana. His daughters are staying with the Wallaces, since Caroline is their teacher and they can hardly stay at the bunkhouse with him and his drovers. The ranch house on the property had burned down, you see."

The other man looked thoughtful. "So there's no other connection between him and Miss Wallace?"

Chadwick recognized the signs of interest in his son's eyes. "Not the kind I think you mean, Gil, as far as I know," he said carefully. "Miss Caroline is just beginning to come out of deep mourning. Her fiancé died in the influenza epidemic I wrote you about last winter, when you were still in seminary. It just so happens he was Jack's brother."

"I see," said Gil, still watching Caroline Wallace, who was bending to hear something one of the twin girls was saying to her, a smile on her lovely face. "You don't sound too certain about Miss Wallace and that Collier fellow."

"You might ask Milly Brookfield," his father said, nodding toward where Milly and her husband sat with her sister Sarah and the doctor. "That lady you met just after you got off the stage? She's sitting over yonder," he said, nodding toward the table. "Anyway, Caroline and Milly are good friends, and they were both in the Spinsters' Club I told you about. If anyone would know about the state of Miss Caroline's heart, she would."

"I think I *will* ask her," he said, rising and brushing a stray crumb from his frock coat.

The old preacher watched his son with pride. A newly minted minister just out of seminary, Gil had not been called to a church yet, but there was no hurry. In the meantime, he'd have a long visit with him, and Gil could help him with his visits to church members. Those trips to far-flung ranches around Simpson Creek tired him so much these days… And he could do the sermon occasionally, Chadwick thought. Let him try out his new preaching skills on the townspeople. Gil hadn't wanted to take part in the service today, saying that was a privilege his father alone had earned after his long service to the town, but he'd introduce him from the pulpit tomorrow.

Oh, wife, we raised such a fine son. I only wish you could be here to see him today.

Gil was obviously already asking about Caroline Wallace, Chadwick thought, judging from the way he nodded toward Caroline while leaning over the table speaking to Milly. Caroline, of course, was oblivious to all of this.

He hoped he'd been right about Caroline and Jack's lack of involvement with each other. Sometimes, when he saw them together in church, it was as if he had just missed a spark flaring between them, but part of the flash remained. It was like lightning a person hadn't turned around in time to see, and which was too far off to hear its accompanying thunder. He didn't want his son's heart to be broken, but one could only protect a grown child from so much, he mused.

Jack had already taken his leave and gone with his men, and Caroline's mother had taken Abby and Amelia home with her. The girls were disappointed that he wasn't staying overnight, of course, but had brightened when he had told them he would come back for church and Sunday dinner with them, assuming everything was all right at Collier's Roost. He hadn't told his children why he was concerned about the ranch, of course, but they had accepted his explanation at face value.

Caroline had stayed behind to help wash dishes with the Spinsters' Club, which had volunteered to do the chore together. Although she was more than ready to leave, it felt good to be part of the group's efforts.

Having set aside the remaining food to take to a couple of the poorer families in town, they washed and rinsed and stacked dishes, whose owners would reclaim them after church tomorrow.

"Who's that tall fellow?" Caroline asked, eyeing the

young man who was standing by the door, chatting with Reverend Chadwick, Nick Brookfield, Nolan Walker and Sheriff Bishop. "He keeps glancing in our direction."

Milly answered, "He's Reverend Chadwick's son, Gilford, just arrived off the noon stage and fresh out of seminary. We arrived in town just about the time the stage did, and his father made the introductions."

"His son, a new minister? Goodness, why didn't Reverend Chadwick introduce him?" Caroline asked.

"I asked him that after the service, and he said Gil said he didn't want to 'steal his papa's thunder' at the service," Milly said. "He met a few folks at the supper, of course, but I expect everyone will meet him tomorrow at the regular service."

"Good-looking fellow," Caroline murmured, noting a long, handsome face, thick chestnut hair, expressive eyes and a tall but sturdy build. It was easy to see their preacher was his father—looking at Gilford Chadwick was like looking at the Reverend as a young man. "Is he a bachelor?"

When Milly nodded, Caroline turned to Faith, the current leader of the group. "Faith, have you invited him to meet the Spinsters yet?"

"Um, no…" Faith said, looking like she knew something Caroline didn't know and found it amusing.

"Actually," Milly said, "he was asking for an introduction to *you*, Caroline."

Chapter Sixteen

Caroline took an involuntary step back, dismay flooding her. Involuntarily, she clapped a dishpan-wet hand to her chest, leaving a damp splotch on her bodice. "Oh, no," she breathed. "Oh, no, you must tell him about my situation, that I'm still in mourning...."

Prissy Bishop glanced meaningfully at Caroline's gray dress. "You're not wearing full mourning anymore," she pointed out.

"But that doesn't mean..." Unaware that her gaze had flown for a moment to the doorway Jack had disappeared through, she now turned to the other ladies. "I—I'm not someone he must think of in that way. You have to tell him."

"Too late," Sarah Walker murmured, drying her hands on a towel. "He's coming this way."

Caroline glanced up, horrified, to see that Sarah was right. Gil Chadwick, the reverend's son, was indeed making his way toward them. If there had been another exit, Caroline would have fled, but going out the doorway that connected the social hall with the church would take her right past the man heading toward them.

No, she mustn't meet him just now, not when she didn't know how Jack felt about her. If she'd never met Jack Collier, perhaps she would find those gentle, scholarly features appealing, but as it was—

"Miss Caroline Wallace, may I present Mr. Gilford Chadwick?" Milly was saying, and Caroline carefully schooled her features to show only a polite interest. There would be a way later to indicate that she wasn't interested in being courted—perhaps a tactful word in his father's ear, or Milly's, and they could let him know he'd better fix his attentions on another of the Spinsters…like Faith Bennett! Faith was a nice, beautiful girl, she thought desperately, a perfect match for a young clergyman.

"How do you do, Mr. Chadwick?" she said. "Welcome to Simpson Creek. And have you met Miss Faith Bennett?" she said, drawing Faith closer.

"Yes, we've met," Faith said, with a pleasant smile in Gil's direction. "Just a few minutes ago."

Caroline glanced at Milly, hoping for some help from her friend, but Milly was watching Caroline with all the concern one might show a lit firecracker due to explode at any moment. *What did she expect her to do, faint?* Why on earth hadn't Milly explained to the young Reverend Chadwick—

Faith was still speaking. "But he asked to meet *you*, and—"

Just then the door slammed open, and a boy propelled himself toward Caroline.

"Teacher!" Billy Joe yelled. "You gotta pertect me— he's right behind me!" He barreled into Caroline, nearly knocking her over in his haste. "Sorry!" he cried, and shifted until he was standing in back of her. As he passed her, she had the quick impression of tears mixed with blood on his pale, frightened face.

"Come back here, you disobedient whelp!" hollered a red-faced William Henderson, lurching into the room, a doubled-up belt clutched in one fist. The group whirled to face him.

Henderson's bleary eyes searched the room and found his son. "Don't you dare think you're gonna hide behind that schoolmarm's skirts, you imp a'—"

Shaking at the suddenness of it, Caroline drew herself up. "Go away, Mr. Henderson! You're obviously drunk. We'll talk again when you've sobered up. Until then, Billy Joe will stay with me."

"Get outa my way, you fussy old maid!" Henderson bellowed. "That's my son, and he's coming with me. Let go a' him or I swear I'll do to you what I did to his ma."

"Stop right there, Henderson!" Sheriff Bishop shouted from across the room, already heading in their direction, but Henderson was oblivious.

"Don't let him catch me, Teacher," cried Billy Joe from behind her. "He's already hit me six times, and my ma…"

Suddenly Gil Chadwick was standing in between Caroline and the mad bull of a man. "In the name of all that's holy, I won't let you hurt this lady, or your son, mister. Do you hear me? You need to leave now."

"Get outa my way, stranger," Henderson shouted, blinking in his attempt to focus on the younger man. Henderson's body stank of sweat and waves of stale whiskey fumes. "Dunno who you are, but in this town, a father's got a right…"

"I'm Gil Chadwick, the preacher's son, and I'm telling you to leave this building immediately."

It was unclear if Chadwick could have stopped Henderson, for the drunken man outweighed him by at least fifty pounds, but Gil Chadwick's willingness to step between Caroline and the raving man gave Sheriff Bishop time to reach them and yank Henderson back by the collar of his shirt. Then, before the drunk could identify the new threat, he laid him out cold on the floor with a well-aimed fist.

"Sorry, ladies," Bishop said, looking down on the unconscious form. "I didn't have my come-alongs with me, so that was the best way I knew to get him under control pronto. Luis, will you run next door to the jail and open up one of the jail cells, and get it ready for Henderson?" he asked the lanky youth who had materialized at his side. "He's going to be spending the night there."

"Of course, Sheriff," Luis said.

Dr. Walker bent to examine Henderson. "He'll be all right after he sleeps it off," he announced, straightening again. "Nick, why don't we help Sam and his deputy take Henderson over to the jail?"

A few minutes later, they had gone, and Caroline was left with Gil, Billy Joe and the other ladies.

"Are you all right, Miss Wallace?" Gil asked, concern lighting his hazel eyes. "I'm sorry if that fellow frightened you. Might I escort you home?"

"I'm fine," she said, touched by his attentiveness. "I believe our concern should be focused on Billy Joe, though," she said, putting an arm around the shaking boy's shoulder, "and his mother. Billy Joe, how are you feeling? Is your mother at home? How is she?"

"I'm all right, Teacher," Billy Joe said, trying to smile with a puffed-up lip. One eye was about to swell shut, while the other was reddened with tears. "Ma's at home. He beat her *bad*...."

"Then we must go check on her immediately," Caroline said.

"I'll go with you," Gil said.

"Thank you. Sarah, will you come, too, just in case she needs medical help?" Sarah was no doctor, but Caroline knew that having worked at her husband's side so much, Sarah Walker was the best one to judge whether or not Mrs. Henderson needed to see a physician.

"Of course," Sarah said.

"I'll go let your mother know where you've gone, on my way home, so she doesn't worry," Prissy said.

Thank God she had already sent Amelia and Abby home with her mother, Caroline thought as they began to gather up their coats. Not for the world would she have wanted those little girls to witness what had just happened.

They found Daisy Henderson shaking and weeping, both eyes blackened and with bruises in various stages of healing all over her. "You and your boy are coming with me," Sarah said in her decisive manner, bundling Mrs. Henderson into her coat and gathering up what they would need overnight. "You can stay the night with us, just to be on the safe side, after my husband examines you and Billy Joe," she said.

"But what about my husband?" whimpered Mrs. Henderson. "What if he comes home and finds us missin'? He won't be happy about that—"

"He won't be coming home tonight, Daisy," Caroline told her gently. "He's intoxicated, and he's spending the night in jail. After that Sheriff Bishop and Reverend

Chadwick can help you sort out what's to be done. But tonight, the main thing is that you and Billy Joe are safe and cared for."

"You were magnificent," Gil told Caroline later, after they'd seen Sarah, Billy Joe and Mrs. Henderson to the doctor's office and he'd escorted her to her door. "Both you ladies, but especially you, Miss Wallace, the way you stood up to that violent, drunken man. You might well have been hurt."

"I think you prevented that from happening, Reverend Chadwick," she said. "Thank you."

"Nonsense. I only gave the sheriff time to cover the distance between where he was standing and us. But please, call me Gil. 'Reverend Chadwick' is my father."

"Gil, then," she said. "And now, I'd best tell you goodnight," she said and put her hand on the doorknob, knowing her mother was undoubtedly anxious to hear what had happened.

"Good night, Miss Wallace. May I be allowed to call you 'Miss Caroline' as everyone else does? And may I call on you sometime?"

Her mind was whirling with too many things. She was too tired to think of whether she should tell Gil straight off that she was not interested in being courted, when at this point she didn't truly know her own mind anymore.

"'Miss Caroline' would be fine, Gil, but as to the other, perhaps you'd give me time to think about—"

"Of course," he said quickly, obviously seeing the fatigue she felt rolling over her in waves now that she was home. "Forgive me for my presumptious haste, but I feel so fortunate to have met you. Good night, Miss Caroline."

* * *

Jack felt faintly foolish when he and his men arrived back at the ranch only to find all was well, the cattle bedded down for the night with one of the men riding herd, while the other two were fast asleep in the bunkhouse. He'd let Sims and Adams render him jumpy as a cat on ice, and for what? He could have stayed overnight at the Wallaces, after all, kissed Abby and Amelia good-night and talked to Caroline—maybe even worked things around so he could have kissed her good-night, too, if all had gone well. At the very least, they could have read books side by side.

Thinking of reading reminded him he had a letter in his vest pocket he hadn't read yet, so after seeing to his horse alongside the other men, he took his letter over by the fire to read.

Howdy Jack,
Hope this letter finds you well. We got yore letter sayin you were going to spend the winter in Simpson Creek Texas and think that is probably the wise thing to do. We are sittin round the fire in the big cabin wishin you was here. There's a foot of snow on the ground & looks to be another foot by mornin so we won't be able to make it into town to have our whiskey at the saloon. The gals there is mighty purdy. We tol them all about you and they cant wait for you to come so they can see if yore as handsome as we built you up to be. Ha. Glad to hear your dotters is gettin some book learnin while yore there—they'll probably be way smarter than you come spring. Ha. Let us know when yore comin and we'll kill the fatted calf for ya. Jake's

already got some Injun squaw to tan you a buffalo
robe to keep ya warm...she wants to know if you
are as pretty as Jake is. Ha.
Yore pards, Jake and Patrick

Well, it didn't sound as if there was anything wrong
there, at least, contrary to Caroline's misgivings. From
the spelling and penmanship of the letter Patrick had
sent, it sounded as if his partners could have used a bit
more time with an exacting schoolmarm such as Caroline Wallace, Jack thought with a grin. What on earth
would they say if they knew he was reading a book in
the evening?

The idea of going to Montana no longer seemed like
journeying to the Promised Land. It sounded like a long
and dangerous trip with only unfamiliarity and an un-
certain happiness at the end. *Would* he go there in the
spring? It all depended on Caroline—

Just then the crack of gunfire made him jump to his
feet. It sounded as if it had come from the far north-
ern border of the ranch, beyond where Simpson Creek
crossed from his land to the Brookfields'. Immediately
he heard cattle bawling and the shouting of men...and
the thundering of hooves—*in their direction*!

"What was that?" cried Masterson, running out of the
bunkhouse, jumping into his boots as he went.

"A stampede, and it's headed this way!" Jack shouted
back, as his other drovers, rubbing their eyes, began to
file out behind Raleigh. "Get to your horses! There's
no time to lose!"

They didn't bother saddling their mounts, just tied
ropes to their halters to use as bridles and trusted in

their animals' training and their own ability to stick like burrs on the horses' bare backs to accomplish the rest.

What followed was a frantic hour of galloping on the fringes of the plunging herd, trying to get ahead of the cattle to turn them. The longhorns had been so frightened by the sudden shots that they had first run headlong into the new barbwire fencing, some lacerating shoulders and forelegs. New shots had rung out, and the beasts had turned in the opposite direction, running headlong toward the bunkhouse. Naturally they ran around it, the herd splitting in the middle as if Moses himself had parted them, but the chuck wagon was not so lucky— the cattle knocked it over and trampled through it until it was no more than a ruin of splintered kindling and scattered supplies.

Spurring their horses with one intent, Jack and his men succeeded in turning the herd just as it seemed it would charge the fencing that bordered the road. At last the herd began to slow and eventually to stop, exhausted.

"Who fired those shots?" Jack demanded when the drovers met back at the campfire.

"Wasn't me, boss," said Ben Compton, the man who had been riding herd. "I was just headin' back to let Shep know it was his turn on watch when someone jes' beyond th' fence started shootin'. I couldn't see nobody in the dark, but I heard 'em laughin' while they galloped off, an' then I was so busy tryin' to turn 'em I didn't have time to think."

"I'll bet it was Sims and Adams, blast their hides," Cookie grumbled, surveying the ruins of his beloved chuck wagon. He'd moved most of his supplies into the bunkhouse, but they'd have to replace the chuck wagon when it came time to hit the trail.

"You can count on that," Jack agreed. "Who else would have a reason?"

"And they're probably clear to the next county by now," added Raleigh. "I hear bawlin' out there," he said, cupping a hand to his ear. "Sounds like a few a' them beeves out there is hurt."

They found a heifer tangled up in barbwire, which had to be cut loose, and a steer that had put a leg in a gopher hole and had to be shot. Another had fallen and been trampled to death. The sudden silence, when they had freed the heifer and put the steer out of his misery, left them staring soberly at one another. Not even the prospect of fresh breakfast steaks was enough to cheer them, because even the greenest of his hands knew that fewer cattle on the trail meant less profit at the end of it for all of them.

"Reckon we'll have some fence to mend in the morning," Jack muttered aloud. "And we'll have to come out and look at that heifer again and make sure those cuts on her leg aren't festering. From now on we'll have two men riding night watch, two in the day.'

"You gonna tell the sheriff about this, boss?" Raleigh asked.

"Yes, I—" he began, then closed his mouth again. It would have to be reported, but if he was the one that did it, his daughters would expect him to come to dinner at the Wallaces', then stay the night and so on. No matter how much he wanted to see them—and Caroline, he realized, just as much—he felt guilty about being in town so often and leaving hard work to the rest of his men while he sat around in comfort with his children. Whoever had attacked—and he was as sure as Cookie that it had been Sims and Adams—may well have known that

Jack and most of his men had gone to town, though they may not have known they'd just returned. That fact had emboldened them to try to stampede the herd.

"No, why don't you ride into Simpson Creek for me, Raleigh, and make the report," Jack said with a sigh. "I'll stay here with the rest and mend fence. Oh, and if you don't mind, stop in and tell my girls I needed to stay out here and get some work done, that I'll see 'em again soon as I can. Don't tell 'em what happened—don't want them to worry about it—though you might mention it to Miss Caroline if you can talk to her apart from the twins. Remember, though, not a word about the house we're building."

He hoped Caroline would understand.

Chapter Seventeen

Masterson had stopped at the house just as the Wallaces, Abby and Amelia had come outside to walk to church, and told the twins their papa wouldn't be able to make it that day. Then he'd asked Caroline if he could speak to her alone.

She sent the rest of them on to church. Masterson told her about the stampede and its probable cause by the drovers Jack hadn't rehired.

Poor Jack! Her disappointment that she wouldn't see him was completely swamped by concern for him and his men.

"Is he all right?" she demanded to know. "Was anyone hurt?"

"He's fine, just mad as a rained-on rooster that we lost two head. But no one else was hurt, thank the good Lord."

"Amen," she said, shaken inside at the thought of the danger Jack and his men had faced last night.

"Well, I've got to be gettin' back. I've notified the sheriff, and he's going to be looking for those two polecats. Jack just didn't want you an' the girls t' worry none when he didn't come."

She made it to church and squeezed into the pew in time to join in singing the last verse of the hymn.

Then Reverend Chadwick introduced his son, who stood at the pulpit next to him. "Gil will be making a long visit with me while he awaits the Lord's direction about his future," the elder Chadwick said. "He'll be helping me by making some of my pastoral calls. I hope you'll all make him welcome, as those who met him last night have already done." He beamed proudly at Gil.

There was a spattering of applause, and Gil smiled back at the congregation, then turned slightly so he seemed to be smiling directly at Caroline.

Oh, dear. Feeling herself flush with embarrassment, she turned and looked around, only to catch Faith Bennett's eye. To her exasperation, the woman winked at her, then glanced meaningfully back at Gil Chadwick, who was now sitting down in the front pew.

"My sermon today concerns…"

Between the incident at Collier's Roost, what had happened to Billy Joe and his mother last night and the normal fidgeting of six-year-old girls, Caroline had no idea what the preacher spoke about. She could hardly wait for the service to be over so she could speak to Prissy Bishop about whether William Henderson had been released from jail this morning. How were they to ensure Billy Joe and his mother's future safety once he was free? Short of a miracle, she didn't expect Mr. Henderson to change.

She wished she could talk to Jack about what had happened. The Walkers weren't there, either, Caroline noticed. Was Daisy Henderson, or her son, in worse condition than they had thought?

After the benediction, Caroline made a beeline for Prissy. She'd told her mother what had happened at the social hall after she'd taken the twins home, so her mother knew Caroline would need to check on Mrs. Henderson and Billy Joe. She'd keep the girls occupied until Caroline returned.

She found Prissy talking to the preacher and his son.

"Ah, there you are, Miss Caroline," Reverend Chadwick said with his benign smile, opening the circle to make room for her. Gil, too, smiled at her, but she kept her gaze directed at his father.

"We were just speaking about the Hendersons, and how to ensure mother and son suffer no further harm," the old preacher said. "Sarah Walker has sent word that they'll be able to return to their home today. But Henderson will pay his fine and be released from jail then, too."

It was precisely what Caroline had been dreading to hear. "But what's to keep Mr. Henderson from going right back to abusing his poor wife and son?"

Prissy looked equally distressed. "My husband can't legally hold him any longer, Caroline. Not if he's able to pay the fine, and he can."

"But we can't just—"

Reverend Chadwick put out a gentle hand to forestall her. "I know you're worried about them, Miss Caroline, but I've met with the man in his cell early this morning, and he's promised to stay away from whiskey and pledged to treat his wife and son better. He seemed most genuinely broken and contrite."

Caroline must have looked as skeptical as she felt, for Prissy jumped in and added, "If I know my husband, after the reverend left, he spent the better part of this morning making Henderson understand if there's any more abuse, the consequences will be severe."

And what would the consequences be for Billy Joe and his mother? But perhaps she shouldn't be so cynical. Surely it was better to believe that with prayer and effort, even a man like Henderson could change.

"I'd like to form a circle of prayer now," Reverend Chadwick said, "then we—and Sheriff Bishop—could personally escort Mrs. Henderson and her son back to their home. Mr. Henderson will already be home by now," he said, checking his pocket watch. "We'll pray with them there, too, then leave them with the understanding that they can call on us anytime."

Caroline hoped with all her heart that those things would work, but doubt remained.

"Let's join hands."

Prissy took one of Caroline's hands, and before she could reach for anyone else's hand, Gil took the other. His big hand felt warm and strong and comforting to her. Yet she longed for it to be Jack's hand she held.

Lord, help them, she prayed, as Chadwick spoke confidently of redemption, forgiveness and Christians supporting one another in trouble. *Help me to help Billy Joe and his mother, and Mr. Henderson, too. Please protect Jack and his men, and let me know if it's Your will that he and I be together.*

She had not imagined, when she had taken on the job of schoolteacher, that she would be drawn into the problems caused by an abusive father and husband, just as the preacher and the sheriff were involved in them. Again, she wished Jack was there to lean on. She'd once thought him impulsive and foolish, but about many things, he was very wise.

The reunion was accomplished. Caroline, the reverend, his son, Prissy and her husband brought a wan-faced Daisy Henderson and Billy Joe to their home, laid hands on the Hendersons and prayed for them. Mr. Henderson, his face swollen and tear-blotched, had stammered his apology to his wife and promised again never to touch liquor or his wife and child in anger. After a final blessing from the preacher, the group left the house.

Once outside, Caroline found herself next to Gil while the others walked ahead of them.

Gil cleared his throat. "Miss Caroline, I want to express my heartfelt admiration of what you did last night, standing up to Henderson. Your devotion to your student and to doing what is right is admirable."

"Please, Gil, I really don't deserve—" she began, only to have him gently interrupt.

"You are too modest, Miss Caroline. And I hope you won't mind if I tell you that in spite of all the unfortunate events last evening, you look fresh as a rose this morning."

She stopped stock-still in the street, staring up at him, while the others strolled on as if unaware she and Gil were no longer right behind them.

"Please, Mr.—I should say, Reverend Chadwick—"

"Gil," he told her, a smile playing about his lips.

"Please," she went on doggedly. "You must not say such things."

"Forgive me for being impulsive on short acquaintance, Miss Caroline," he said, his eyes shining down on her. "It's not normally a failing of mine, as my father can tell you. I—I see by your clothing, and from what my father has told me, that you are still in mourning to some degree."

"There is nothing to apologize for, Gil. Thank you for the kind things you said," she told him and hoped she had said enough that he would not press her again. She could not tell Gil her heart had already begun to belong to another, not when she had no real proof Jack felt the same way about her.

Once home, and feeling guilty she had turned so much of the care for the twins over to her mother lately, she spent the rest of the afternoon playing with Amelia and Abby. Her mother seemed somehow younger and more energetic since the girls had come. But Caroline felt the primary responsibility for them lay with her when their father was not there.

"Will my papa come next Sunday?" Amelia asked wistfully, staring out the window at the cloudy afternoon. They had just had a tea party for the girls' dolls, complete with real tea and cookies and the dolls dressed in their best.

"I imagine so, Punkin," she said, using Jack's pet name for them. "And that reminds me, with Thanksgiving out of the way, Christmas is coming. You said you'd like to learn how to knit, so why don't I teach you both now? You could knit your papa a muffler for a present. I found some blue yarn you could use."

The same blue as his eyes.

"I'll knit half," Abby said excitedly, "and Amelia can knit half, and you can sew them together in the middle, Aunt Caroline."

She would probably have to help them finish it, if it was to be done on time, she thought later, watching with fond amusement when Abby and Amelia bit their lips in concentration as they wielded their knitting needles with great concentration. But the project distracted Amelia from moping about her father's absence, so it had to be a good thing.

She began to wonder what she should give Jack for Christmas, too.

November had turned to December. Jack came to church again the following Sunday and stayed that afternoon and night at the Wallaces. He brought back *A Tale of Two Cities* and began reading *Robinson Crusoe*.

He told Caroline there had been no further depredations by the two rustlers. There was much giggling as the twins hinted at their Christmas knitting projects without actually telling their father they were making him a present.

But, although she treasured every moment of Jack's presence with them, he made no attempt to take his relationship with her any further. On Monday morning she was as confused as ever about how he felt about her.

The rain clouds had finally drifted east, and the sun once again shone over Simpson Creek, so Caroline and Louisa could send their charges out to play at recess time. Billy Joe was back in class, his bruises fading, and when Caroline tutored him, he reported his papa had been "good as gold" lately and had brought home a handful of peppermint sticks for him and a lace handkerchief for his mother from the mercantile. Billy Joe had saved one of the precious candy sticks for her and produced it from his pocket. It was a little the worse for wear for being carried with all his other treasures, but Caroline appreciated the sacrifice nonetheless.

She was less appreciative, when she opened the schoolhouse door for Billy Joe, of the sight of Superintendent Thurgood waiting outside in his buggy for her.

"Go straight home now, Billy Joe," she murmured, as the superintendent made his way toward her. The boy scampered out of the schoolyard.

"Ah, Miss Wallace, there you are. Your mother said you would still be here, but I didn't want to intrude upon your time with your young scholar. I see you had the Henderson boy with you. Causing trouble in class again, was he?"

"No, sir," she said, wishing she had accepted Louisa's offer to tutor Billy Joe this time. But Caroline would not have wanted her assistant to have to face the pompous superintendent alone, either. "Actually, he's been as good as gold," she said, borrowing Billy Joe's phrase. "I'm merely tutoring him in his weaker areas, such as arithmetic, so he can do well at the Christmas recitation. You will be attending it, won't you?"

The students spent extra time during class devising and practicing their parts. With the extra work that such a program entailed, Caroline found herself busier than ever. But the students were excited about the coming program, and she found their enthusiasm catching. Perhaps Jack would come…

"Of course I will attend," Thurgood said, a little huffily. "The December Recitation is a cherished tradition. I know my duty as superintendent to be present."

"Yes, of course. I didn't mean—"

"But I haven't come to discuss the Christmas recitation," he interrupted her to say. "Miss Wallace, I've had a complaint from a parent about you and wanted to speak to you about it. I thought once again we could discuss it over supper—"

Did he really think she would fall for the same ploy as before? "What complaint is that, Superintendent?" she asked, hoping the iciness of her tone made it clear that the only call he had on her time involved her professional responsibilities. "Perhaps it would be better if we discussed it here and now."

His eyes narrowed. "Very well," he said, his tone sharper. "Let us sit down and speak of it, then." Without waiting for permission, he settled himself in her chair, forcing her to sit on one of the closest desks in the front row. She was not about to be left standing like some student who had been called on to recite.

"Mr. Henderson came to see me the other day," he began.

Caroline sat up a little straighter. *"Oh?"*

Thurgood nodded, causing his jowls to waggle comically, an effect she was sure he was unaware of. But any temptation she had to smile was erased by the superintendent's next words. "He's concerned you're attempting to undermine his relationship with his son, and encouraging his wife to lose respect for him. He says you've aligned the sheriff and the preacher against him, too."

Caroline felt a spark of temper. Good as gold, Billy Joe had said? William Henderson had been the model husband and father, yet he'd gone to the superintendent to complain about her? If any undermining had been attempted, surely he was the one attempting it with his lies.

Caroline leaned forward on the desk. "And did he tell

you about the incident in which he chased his terrified, bruised son into the church social hall, and was so drunk he had to spend the night in a jail cell?"

Thurgood looked thoroughly taken aback. "No, he didn't. But perhaps this is all a misunderstanding. We must not be too hasty—"

Any misunderstanding was yours, you fool, she wanted to say. "I think you should speak to Reverend Chadwick and Sheriff Bishop, sir. They'll vouch for what I'm saying." She stood, smoothing her charcoal-gray skirt. "And if that is all—" She was eager to get home and have some supper before joining the other ladies at the Spinsters' Club meeting.

"Perhaps I was being too quick in my judgment. I will consult with the good reverend and the sheriff as you suggested and take anything Mr. Henderson says with a grain of salt hereafter. But I need to be fully informed. The incident sounds…interesting. Would you reconsider my offer, and tell me the full story over some of the hotel's good roast beef?"

He spoke of what happened at the church social hall as if it were merely an entertaining tale! Yet real people had been involved, and real people hurt, people she cared about. And she would not allow him to use the event as an excuse to further his unwanted courtship of her. It was time to make her stand abundantly clear.

She drew herself up to her full height. "Mr. Thurgood, while I appreciate your invitation, I have to tell you that I have no intention of accepting it on this or any other time. I have a duty to you as a teacher, but no obligation to spend any personal time with you."

Thurgood's face went purple, then pale as the chalk writing on the blackboard.

"Miss Wallace," he said, his tone low and threatening as he bowed his head and bent near her. "I would remind you, you serve at my pleasure. Take care, young lady. You can be replaced."

She took up the pointer from her desk, willing to use it as a weapon if she had to. "I do not intend to offend you, sir. But I have spent extra time working with a pupil, and now I am expected at home. Good evening, Mr. Thurgood." With that, she sailed out the door without stopping to pick up her things. She didn't even look back to see if he followed her out the door.

She was going to have to have that meeting with Prissy's father, the mayor. She'd ask Reverend Chadwick to attend as well. She needed someone in authority to help the superintendent understand the limits of her job description.

By the time she reached home, Caroline had such a headache she could only seek her bed. Excusing herself from supper, she told her mother the headache was a result of being overtired, and asked her to have Dan take a message to Faith Bennett that she could not be present at the meeting tonight.

Inevitably, her absence caused some concern to her closest friends, Sarah and Prissy, but they couldn't talk about it in front of the others, so they made sure to walk home together after the meeting.

"What should we do? You know how determined Caroline can be," Prissy asked after Sarah had expressed her worries about Caroline.

"Milly's coming into town to do some Christmas baking with me tomorrow morning. Why don't you come, too, and we can talk about it while we bake?"

Sarah was sure Caroline Wallace was ready for romance again. She just wasn't sure with whom.

Chapter Eighteen

Milly's arms were dusted with flour as she rolled out dough to be cut into shapes. "The problem, as I see it," she began in her usual, forthright manner, "is that we truly don't know Caroline's mind on this matter, or Jack's either, for that matter. Has she really decided to cast aside her mourning and love Jack?"

"I think so," Prissy said. "From what I can see when they're together, and from the way she's starting to wear colors. But *does he love her*?" Prissy had flour on her nose, and a smudge of cookie frosting on her cheek. "I'm sure she must be afraid to commit herself, in case he takes off with his herd for Montana in the spring as he originally planned. That would break her heart. He's given her no real clue of how he feels. When he comes to see his daughters and her, they have an enjoyable time, she tells me. She's been lending her books to him, and they talk of those, and what has gone on since he was last at the Wallaces, but then he never gives her any hint…"

"On the other hand," said Sarah, who was stirring cookie dough, "Gil Chadwick has made it very clear to anyone with eyes that *he* is very taken with Caroline. It wouldn't take much encouragement from her—but she hasn't given him any. He's confided in me that he's willing to merely be Caroline's friend, unless she changes her mind."

"How *interesting*," Milly said, grinning. "What a nice man Gil is."

"Perhaps Jack is just waiting for Christmas to reveal his feelings for Caroline," Milly said thoughtfully. "Perhaps he'll surprise her with a marriage proposal then. That's a romantic time to propose."

"Perhaps," her sister Sarah said, adding sugar to the mixing bowl. "But he's never so much as kissed her! Surely he would give her some idea of his deepening feelings in the meantime? I was never in any doubt of how my Nolan felt."

"Nor I, about Nick," Milly said.

Prissy shrugged. "Who knows how men think? Differently than we ladies, I know that much. I was ready to marry my Sam long before he was willing to fully declare himself. He felt he had to earn the right to court me, the dear man," she said, her eyes dreamy with remembrance. "But perhaps he was right, because we couldn't be happier now."

Milly's lips curved upward in a secret smile. "I know something you ladies don't know, but I won't tell you unless you can keep a secret," she told them.

Immediately Sarah's hand flew to her heart.

"About Caroline and Jack?" Prissy squeaked.

"Maybe... I'm not sure yet. But you must *promise* not to breathe a word of it outside this room," Milly told them. "Just in case I'm wrong."

Prissy's hand touched her heart as well. "I *promise*, on my honor," she said.

"Well… Jack is rebuilding the ranch house," Milly said. "Our cowhands saw it first and told us about it, so Nick went and paid Jack a visit on some pretext, and, sure enough, he and his drovers have been constructing a new house there, right where the old one stood. They're not very far along with it, but…why would they do that if he isn't at least thinking about staying here, rather than going on to Montana? Nick said Jack asked him not to talk about it in town, and he doesn't let his drovers do so, either." She looked from Prissy's face to Sarah's.

"Who knows why men do the things they do?" Prissy said. "They seem to like to do things just to keep busy." She rubbed her cheek, unconsciously spreading the frosting all over that side of her face. "Maybe the bank offered them some money to build a house so they can get more for the property when Jack and his men leave."

"Then *why the secrecy*?" Sarah asked.

"Hmm…" Milly murmured. "It gets curiouser and curiouser, doesn't it?"

Sarah said, "I agree with Milly—I think we ought to wait till after Christmas, and see what happens between the two of them."

"And then what?" Prissy asked. "What if nothing happens then?"

"If nothing happens, we might need to…ah, *encourage* Jack a little. Fight fire with fire, so to speak." Milly's eyes gleamed with purpose.

"What do you mean?" demanded Sarah warily. She'd become a good deal less distrustful of her sister's schemes in the past couple of years—after all, Milly's idea to start the Spinsters' Club had gained the three of them happy marriages—but she didn't have any hint what Milly had up her sleeve now.

"If there's no change after Christmas," Milly said, "we ought to speak to Gil and see if he's willing to make it *appear* that he is seriously courting Caroline,"

"And make Jack jealous," Prissy breathed. "Oh, how delicious!"

"I don't know," Sarah said, twisting the corner of her apron, anxiety clouding her blue eyes. "Couldn't that… um…have unexpected consequences? What if Gil really began to care for her? He already does, to some extent. Can we really ask that of him?"

"Hopefully, it won't be necessary," Milly said. "And it'll only work if Gil is willing, of course. But we want Caroline to be happy, don't we? We'll only take action if we have to, after Christmas," she repeated, and the other two ladies nodded their agreement.

Jack studied the flyspecked calendar Cookie had torn out of his almanac and tacked up on the bunkhouse wall. *Saturday, December 21 already.* The calendar sure seemed to be his enemy these days. He'd wanted to have the house completed, or at least a lot more nearly done than it was, by Christmas. And it just wasn't going to happen. Especially not after Shep had brought the news this afternoon that the mercantile wasn't able to get in the window glass he'd ordered until after New Year's. Apparently there was a lot of snow between here and St. Louis, where he'd ordered it from.

"Of all the luck," he muttered.

He hadn't been aware that he'd said it out loud till Raleigh looked up from the mirror, where he was shaving, and chuckled. "Christmas is right around the corner, boss. Why don't you just get Caroline something special from town for her present and save the surprise of the house for later?"

"Did I ask you?" Jack growled, wondering how his ramrod even knew what he was fretting about. "Why don't you mind your own business?"

"You've been staring at that calendar for half an hour now, and it's gettin' so I can read your mind," Raleigh said, unperturbed at Jack's crossness. "I know you'd've liked to have the house done by Christmas. We've all worked as hard as we could, but we aren't miracle workers."

"I wasn't blaming any of you," Jack murmured, slumping onto his bunk. He hadn't made them feel that way, had he? Maybe he had. "I didn't mean to sound that way, if I did. It was crazy of me to think we could get it done in that space of time. Sorry if I've been hard on you men."

"You haven't been," Raleigh assured him. "If anything, you've mostly been hard on yourself. You've been out there morning, noon and night, and when it rains, you're cranky as a red-eyed cow 'cause you can't work on it. If you're buildin' that place so you can have a life with her, why don't you just go ahead and buy Miss Caroline a ring?"

"'Cause I don't know if she'd accept it," he mumbled, too low for Raleigh to hear.

"What's that?" Raleigh said, shrugging his clean shirt over his head.

"I said, why don't you just go on into town like you were intending to and leave me alone?" Jack snapped. "Just—"

"Don't get yourself into trouble," Raleigh finished for him. "I know, I know. Don't worry, all I'm going to do is go to the saloon. You reckon they got some mistletoe in that place? I reckon there's a pretty girl or two workin' there who wouldn't mind standin' under it with me. Say, why don't you come into town with us? I'm sure Wes an' Cookie an' Shep can handle things by themselves. There's been no trouble lately. Come on, come with us. It'll do you good."

"No thanks," Jack said, pulling off his boots and throwing them into the corner. "Tomorrow's Sunday, so I'll be going into town soon enough for church. You oughta try that sometime. It won't leave you with a sore head."

Raleigh grinned. "If I had a pretty lady like Miss Caroline to sit in a pew with, I just might."

Sunday started out in a promising way—Caroline arrived at church wearing not some version of gray, but a dress of forest green that complemented her dark eyes and hair, and smiled at him in a way that had Jack longing for time alone with her. Amelia and Abby were pretty as a picture in new dresses, too, one in green with a red sash, the other in red with a green sash. They even managed to sit reasonably still, and when the congregation said the Lord's Prayer in unison at the end of the service, his girls joined right in.

Staying with the Wallaces had been good for them, he thought. *Given them the stability they'd been lacking ever since their mother had died.* He silently thanked God they had been led to this family, no matter what happened between himself and Caroline. But having Caroline for their new mother would be even better. If all went well tonight, after the children had gone to bed, he'd start taking steps to make that happen.

Gil Chadwick, the preacher's son and a new preacher himself, was giving the sermon today. Caroline had told him how Gil had intervened to prevent Caroline and young Billy Joe from being harmed by the drunken Mr. Henderson.

Henderson was now sitting in a middle pew with his wife and son as if nothing had happened, Jack noted. He'd like to have been there to give Henderson the drubbing he deserved, but he was glad that in his absence, Reverend Chadwick's son had stepped in.

Gil seemed like a good preacher, too—eloquent without resorting to flowery oratory, persuasive without shaming as he spoke about sin. He seemed like a good man, one Jack would like to get to know better someday.

After the service, while Caroline and the Wallaces were speaking to friends, and his girls chattering to a couple of older girls from their school, Jack caught sight of Sheriff Bishop and ambled over to see if the lawman had anything to report about the drovers-turned-thieves.

"No one's reported seeing them, not hide nor hair, but I heard from Sheriff Teague in Lampasas that a couple of fellows have been up to the same kind of mischief there. They spent some time in jail after shooting up the saloon, then folks started reporting chickens missing, then more cattle rustling... I sure wish those ornery polecats would ride outa Texas, or someone's going to have to put them out of business eventually," he added with a grim look.

"I'm hungry, Papa," Amelia said, coming to grab his hand. Abby seized the other.

"Me too, Punkins. Why don't we find Aunt Caroline and walk back to the house?"

"She's the one who sent us to find you," Abby informed him importantly. "She said the preacher and his son were comin' to dinner with us, and to tell you she'd gone home with Aunt Mary to start cooking. She said to bring the Chadwicks home with us."

"Then that's what we'll do." Looked as though he was going to get his chance to get to know Gil Chadwick better sooner than he'd thought. He was pleased with the prospect.

Pleased, that is, until he was sitting across the table from the younger preacher, and he noticed how Gil Chadwick watched Caroline when he thought no one saw him.

Gil looked like a man who'd caught sight of a priceless jewel sitting just out of his reach. He was always careful not to gaze at her too long or look too deeply into her eyes when she spoke to him, but Jack could still tell. It was too easy when a man loved the same woman.

This was the sort of man Caroline would have much in common with, he thought with a sinking feeling in his heart. An educated man, just as Thurgood was, but young and handsome as the superintendent was not and never had been. A genial, kind man, and good with children, judging by the way he joked with Abby and Amelia and got both the girls giggling.

"More parsnips, Jack?" Mrs. Wallace asked.

"No, thank you, ma'am." He found he'd quite lost his appetite in the past few minutes.

"Miss Caroline tells me you're spending the winter here in Simpson Creek, Jack," Gil said, accepting another helping of parsnips himself.

"That's right," Jack said, wondering what else Caroline had told him. "I've got a herd bedded down at the old Waters Ranch south of town. We were headed to Montana, but it got to be too late in the year to move on."

"Montana, hmm? Beautiful country up there, I'm told. Amazing scenery."

Jack nodded. "So my partners say." *If it's so wonderful why don't you go there? Preferably this very afternoon.*

He was amazed at the ferocity of the thought. Gil Chadwick had never done anything to him—except want the same lady he did.

"When will it be time for you to start out? March or so?"

Why? Are you in a hurry to get me out of the way?

He shrugged. "Probably March is the soonest to start a trail drive in that direction. Winter holds on longer farther north, of course. Why?"

There. It was out in the open, at least between himself and Gil Chadwick. Each man understood it was a direct challenge, even if no one else at the table did.

Gil blinked as if surprised. He shrugged. "Pure curiosity, that's all. Montana sounds wonderful, but from what I've seen of Simpson Creek, a man could do worse than put down roots here."

Caroline looked up then and glanced from one man to the other as if aware of the tense atmosphere that had sprung up between them.

"You're right about that, Gil," Jack said quietly. He looked away from the younger Chadwick to find the older one watching him with perceptive eyes.

"Time for bed, girls," Caroline said. "Don't you have something to tell your papa about before you say goodnight?"

Both girls grinned. Amelia said, "Papa, we got a…a inva-inva—"

"A invitation," Abby said. "We got a invitation for you, Papa."

"Oh? What kind of invitation?" he asked, charmed by the sight of his two girls dressed in their nightgowns, their faces scrubbed, eagerness shining in their eyes.

"To the school Christmas re-reci—" This time Abby looked to Caroline for help with the big word.

"Recitation," she whispered.

"Yeah, recitation!" Abby said. "All us children are gonna recite things we learned, and read things and sing…."

"Will you come, Papa? We worked very hard to learn our parts, an' Aunt Caroline helped us," Amelia told him. "Mr. Raleigh can watch the cows for you, can't he?"

Jack put an arm around each girl and gathered them close. "I wouldn't miss your recitation," he told them solemnly, "for all the cows in Texas." It sent them into gales of giggles. "When is it?"

"Tomorrow, at seven," Caroline said. "I'm sorry, we should have mentioned it earlier, but with all that's been happening, it slipped my mind."

"It's at the school," Amelia added. "And there'll be punch an' cookies!"

"I'll be there." He thought quickly. The shops were closed on Sunday, of course, and Wednesday was Christmas, so he could come into town a little early and visit the mercantile to find Caroline's present. He needed to find gifts for the rest of the Wallaces, too, but he wanted to make Caroline's gift very special.

"We'll have an early supper beforehand, if you want

to join us, Jack," Mrs. Wallace said, as he walked toward the girls' room.

"Thank you, ma'am," Jack said, his throat feeling suddenly tight because of their continuing, generous hospitality. "I hope someday I get a chance to repay y'all for all the kindness you've shown us."

"It's our pleasure, Jack," Amos Wallace said gruffly.

Jack smiled. "Okay, girls, time to scoot off to bed. Come on, I'll tuck you in and hear you say your prayers."

The Wallaces had probably begun doing their kindnesses for his brother's sake, he thought as he pulled the quilt over his children, but it had become something they did for him and the girls.

He hadn't experienced such care once his mother had died. His father had soon become so busy courting a widow named Elnora who lived in town—and keeping her happy once he'd won her and brought her out to the ranch—that he seemed to forget all about his own children. Pete, the favored son, got a little more of their father's attention—but not much. When his father died, he'd left the ranch to Jack—but what little money he had left and everything else of tangible value had gone to Elnora. His stepmother had stripped the ranch house of almost all its furniture, leaving Jack and his girls barely more than their beds when she'd moved back to town.

So when his two friends had moved to Montana and offered to cut him in on their partnership, he'd jumped at the chance to leave his bitterness behind in south Texas.

He didn't want Amelia and Abby to grow up with such a love-poor existence, any more than he wanted to continue without the love of a good woman—*Caroline*. If he could win her, he would never lack for love or have to leave this family who had enveloped him and his daughters with such warmth. *If.*

"God bless Papa and Aunt Caroline—"

"And Aunt Mary and Uncle Amos—"

"And the kitties…"

"Amen," he concluded for them, for he knew from experience that the twins were capable of blessing every one of their fellow students and all his drovers one by one if he let them, just to postpone sleeping.

"And Jesus, please say hello to our Mama in Heaven," Abby added in a determined afterthought. Both of them winked at him, knowing he wouldn't prohibit a prayer postscript like that.

At that moment, both of them reminded him so much of Lucinda—the sweetness of her expression, the way their mouths curved… *Lucinda, they're going to be as beautiful as you were when they're grown—I just hope they marry better men than me.* Could she see them from Heaven? He hoped so. He'd planned to marry again for the sake of the girls, and hadn't expected to love anyone again the way he had Lucinda. But now he did— Caroline.

"Good night, girls," he said, kissing each of them on the forehead, and left the room.

When he returned to the parlor, he was pleased to see that the other Wallaces had gone to bed. Only Caroline remained.

Chapter Nineteen

Caroline saw Jack smile as he reentered the parlor.

"Everyone's gone to bed," he observed. He seemed pleased about that, pleased they were alone, she thought, and her pulse quickened.

She was suddenly nervous about being alone with him—nervous, but excited, too. "Yes…and I probably should go, too…it's been a long day, and tomorrow will be another, what with the recitation and all…." She was babbling, she knew it.

"But?"

She shrugged. "I didn't want you to come back to an empty room, with everyone gone. I… I wanted to say good-night…."

"I'm glad," he said and took a step closer. If Jack took another step he would be close enough to put his arms around her.

All at once he seemed too close. She took a quick breath, struggling not to show her panic. *Stop acting like an old-maid schoolteacher. You've been courted before. You were ready to marry. And now you love Jack.*

"Caroline, what's wrong?" he said. "You can talk to me about anything, you know that."

She seized upon the first subject her brain thought of. "I was just wondering…why don't you like Gil Chadwick?"

He took a step back, paled a little. *"What?"* His jaw tightened, and his blue eyes bored through her. "Why did you ask that, just now?"

She realized immediately that it was the wrong thing to have asked. His reaction told her she'd been right about the way he felt about Gil, but in asking she'd done irreparable harm to the intimate moment between them. Now he was wondering why she'd bring up another man when he was alone with her, and he'd think exactly the wrong thing. But it was too late now to take back the question—now she'd just have to plow her way through it. And maybe, she hoped, she'd learn something about him in the process.

She shrugged. "I… I just noticed there seemed to be some tension between you, that's all. I wondered if he'd somehow done something to offend you?"

He shook his head. "No, of course not. I only met him today. How could he have offended me?" he asked. But there was something about his quick denial that told her he wasn't being entirely honest.

"Because you acted like he had," she insisted. "I've never seen you so quarrelsome with anyone, Jack. Please be honest with me. What has he done?"

He stared at her for a long moment. "This is a mistake," he muttered. "I—I'm going to bed." He turned on his heel and headed for the hallway that led to the bedrooms.

"Jack, please wait. I—"

But he had already entered the room he shared with Dan and shut the door.

He'd been right about Gil Chadwick being attracted to Caroline, he thought as he lay awake, and he'd been *this close* to asking her if the feeling was mutual. But some shred of caution, mixed with hurt that she had brought up another man's name just as he was thinking about how much he wanted to take her into his arms, had shut his mouth before he could say too much. *You've still got your pride left. If a man had no pride, he had nothing,* Pa always said.

This afternoon, he had spent time with his girls until the Chadwicks had left. He knew Caroline had noticed the tension between him and Gil, but he hadn't thought she cared for the young preacher the way Gil did for her.

Until she'd mentioned Gil just as Jack had stepped close to her.

"This is a mistake," he'd said, and he'd been right. He was second best again, just as he'd always been to his father. He'd made a lot of mistakes—was thinking Caroline could love him the biggest one he'd made in a long time? Was he a fool to be building a fine house with her in mind? Should he just stop working on it now— maybe even tear down what they'd built so far?

His men would be sure he was loco if he did such a thing. He couldn't do it, after they'd worked so hard.

And what if he'd jumped to the wrong conclusion about Caroline and Gil? He wasn't wrong about the way Gil thought of Caroline—but was he about to make an even bigger mistake about how she felt about Gil?

Lord, show me the truth, he prayed. *Show me what to do. Show me Caroline's heart.*

But his only answer was silence.

At least she didn't know about the house. He could comfort himself with that. He wasn't a laughingstock— yet.

Perhaps he should just wait and see what developed— how Caroline acted toward him, what she said—or didn't say. Wait for a sign that she wanted a life with him. If there was no sign, he'd have his answer.

But in the meantime, what was he to do about Christmas? He'd wanted to give her something special, maybe something even in the way of a combined Christmas and courtship present, if tonight had gone well. But it hadn't, and now he was left with a quandary.

He needed to give Caroline something—if only to thank her for taking care of his children so well. But it had to be a present that didn't commit him—didn't reveal the full extent of the love that he held for her, until he knew for sure how she felt about him.

If only Christmas wasn't in just a few days. But it was.

He was no clearer about the path he should take when he rode back into town the next afternoon. He'd ridden out to the ranch to check on his herd and explain to the men about the event at the schoolhouse he had to attend that night.

"The herd's doin' fine, boss," Raleigh had told him, as all of them had sat at the bunkhouse table eating some of Cookie's potent chili. "I reckon Sims and Adams skedaddled out of the county and I don't figure they'll be back. And don't worry about us being neglected on Christmas

Day, boss," Raleigh said with a grin. "We knew you'd want to stay with the girls, so we invited the Brookfield fellows here for a little celebratin' in the evening, to return the favor from Thanksgiving. That way we're right here, watching the herd."

"Sounds like a good plan," Jack said, appreciating their thoughtfulness. He glanced at Cookie. "But do they know what they're letting themselves in for?"

It was a subtle dig at Cookie's cooking, but for once, the old chuck wagon cook took no offense. "They're bringin' food, too, boss. So if my trail drive cookin' ain't good enough for 'em, they'll have other vittles, too."

So it was settled. He'd return to town after the meal and do his shopping at the mercantile before having an early supper with the Wallaces, then go to the recitation. It would be too late to return to the ranch after that, so he'd spend the night at the Wallaces, return to the ranch the next morning, then double back to the Wallaces Tuesday night for Christmas Eve. He'd stay through Christmas Day.

He only hoped he would see his way clear by then.

At lunchtime, Caroline left the students in Louisa Wheeler's charge and walked down Main Street for her meeting with the mayor and Reverend Chadwick at the mayor's mansion.

Gilmore House was festive with Christmas decorations. Candles stood in every windowsill, and a holly wreath hung over the brass door knocker. Inside, a wide red satin ribbon was wrapped around the mahogany banister on the stairway inside, interspersed with big red and green bows. A ribbon-topped ball of mistletoe hung from the archway leading into the dining room.

It quite put the humble decorations at her house to shame, Caroline thought. Dan had cut down a juniper bush in the hills, and they'd draped it with strings of popcorn, and Pa had hung a ball of mistletoe in the parlor. After the debacle last evening between Jack and her, Caroline had quietly taken the mistletoe down.

"I appreciate your seeing me, Mayor," Caroline said, "especially this close to Christmas. Under the circumstances, I didn't feel it could wait."

"Nonsense, Miss Caroline," the older man said. "I'm happy to make myself available to our town's schoolteacher at any time. Flora's made some okra gumbo—come in and have some," Mayor Gilmore said, beckoning her into the dining room after the housekeeper had let her in. "Reverend Chadwick's already here. I knew you had to give up your mealtime at the school in order to meet with us, so I don't want you to go hungry."

"Thank you, sir." Once the housekeeper had served her a bowl of the thick soup, Caroline outlined her problem with the school superintendent.

The mayor and the preacher listened carefully, interrupting with a question now and then. Mayor Gilmore *tsk-tsked* when she was through.

"That old goat," he grumbled. "Now that you've taken a stand, however, I doubt if he'll bother you any further."

"I wonder if such behavior played a role in your predecessor's decision to go into missionary work?" Reverend Chadwick mused. "If there's even a hint of similar behavior in the future, Miss Caroline, you just come to me and I'll have a talk with him."

"Yes, if he so much as looks as you cross-eyed, we'll both speak to him. We'll secede from the county school system, if need be."

Gilmore's unexpected fierceness made her want to chuckle. "I hardly think it'll come to that," she told them. "I was just a little apprehensive, given that he plans to attend the Christmas recitation tonight."

"Then so will I," Gilmore boomed. "He needs to see that Simpson Creek supports its schoolteachers, starting with its mayor."

"And I," Chadwick said.

Caroline couldn't help but smile. The schoolhouse was going to be filled to overflowing tonight.

A little while later, as she walked back toward the schoolhouse, she spotted Jack's big chestnut gelding tied up in front of the mercantile.

Was he doing his Christmas shopping? she wondered. Before Sunday night, she might have thought he was buying something that would be a reflection of the growing feelings between them. She had ruined all chance of that, for now, though her heart stubbornly held on to hope things would come right somehow. Surely, in time, Jack would realize she'd shown him no evidence she cared for Gil Chadwick.

Abby and Amelia had finished their scarf for Jack on Saturday, with a little help from Caroline to join the two pieces. She was giving Jack one of her favorite books, *The Last of the Mohicans*, and woolen stockings she'd knitted herself, a real test of her skill with knitting needles. There'd been love in every row she'd completed, but Jack wouldn't realize that. They'd keep his feet warm during those Montana winters, she thought, until eventually he wore them out and he forgot all about the schoolteacher he'd once met in Texas.

Before Sunday, she might have tried to creep up to the window and spy into the mercantile in an attempt to see what Jack was buying. Now, though, she kept her gaze averted and remained on the opposite side of the street as she passed.

Several townspeople were looking around in the mercantile, though Jack was relieved to see none of them belonged to the Spinsters' Club. He certainly didn't want to have any witnesses who would report on his purchases to Caroline or any of the others. He knew Mrs. Patterson, the proprietress, from previous visits, but he could only hope she wouldn't gossip.

He looked around for a while at the well-stocked shelves. The girls were easy to buy for. He picked out a selection of hair ribbons, some candy and a couple of miniature rocking chairs for their dollies that would no doubt delight Amelia and Abby. He selected out ready-made shirts for Mr. Wallace and his son and a red shawl for Mrs. Wallace, and added them to his growing pile on the front counter. But what should he buy Caroline?

His eyes strayed to the velvet-lined box in the glass case that displayed several ladies' rings, some set with garnet, pearl or onyx, some just plain gold or silver bands. She still wore the pearl ring Pete had given her, and which Jack had given back to her, but the ring he'd wanted to give Caroline was a plain gold band—a wedding band. No use thinking of that now.

"Can I help you, Mr. Collier? We do have some lovely rings, as I see you've noticed. Would you like to inspect any more closely?"

The shopkeeper's inquisitive eyes, made larger by spectacles, betrayed her lively interest. She knew his children had been staying with the Wallaces. Did she also suspect the attraction that he felt for the school-teacher?

"Uh…maybe just those silver earbobs," he said. "Something for the twins to give Miss Caroline," he added, lest Mrs. Patterson get the wrong idea.

Just then the bell over the door tinkled, announcing the arrival of another customer.

"Well, good afternoon, Gil," the shopkeeper greeted the newcomer. "Buying your Christmas presents?"

"Yes," the young preacher said. "I need to find something for my father."

"Well, you just look around," Mrs. Patterson said. "Soon as I help Mr. Collier, I'll be available if you need any assistance."

"No problem," the other man said. "How are you, Jack?"

"Just fine," Jack said. He kept his tone cool and polite and didn't look directly at the other man.

He had to get out of here. He didn't want to spend another minute in this store now that Gil Chadwick was in it. Would the presumptuous upstart dare to purchase something for Caroline?

"I'll take the gold shawl, too," Jack said, wrenching his gaze away from the rings in the glass case. It would complement the gold flecks in the depths of Caroline Wallace's fine eyes, he told himself. But a dull ache of disappointment told him it was not what his heart longed for him to buy.

Chapter Twenty

The little schoolhouse was packed to the rafters with people. Mothers and siblings sat at desks, on desks and on borrowed chairs brought in for the occasion. Many fathers stood along the walls.

The entire program had gone well, as far as Jack could tell. Each performer was introduced by Caroline before they began. Abby and Amelia's joint recital of their ABCs and their numbers from one to thirty had been perfect. Lizzie Halliday, the older girl who walked with the twins home from school when Caroline had to stay after school, sang "The First Noel" in a reedy soprano. Another young scholar recited the Christmas story from Luke 2 and only had to be prompted about the name of that Roman king who'd ordered the census; still another recited the Preamble to the Constitution. Billy Joe read the ending passage from *A Christmas Carol* by the same Charles Dickens fellow that had written *A Tale of Two Cities*. Many ladies wiped their eyes when the youth finished Tiny Tim's "God Bless Us Everyone."

Finally, the entire student body gathered at the front to sing "Silent Night."

Throughout the entire performance, even when another little girl had a fit of giggles while reciting the times table, Caroline remained serene and confident. He was as proud of her as he was of Abby and Amelia.

Before the recital had begun, Jack had spotted a red-cheeked middle-aged man who had to be the superintendent sitting by the door, a pompous expression on his face. His arms remained crossed over his paunch as he listened.

That sidewinder better give Caroline credit for her hard work, Jack thought. *Miss Wheeler, too.*

The superintendent happened to be standing by the mayor, an older man who had clapped enthusiastically after every child's performance. Now, as the scholars and their teachers took their bows, the mayor called, "Bravo! Bravo!"

The applause died away and the mayor stepped forward, saying, "On behalf of the residents of Simpson Creek, I'd like to thank Miss Caroline Wallace and her able assistant, Miss Louisa Wheeler, for this excellent exhibition of their teaching. I'm sure Superintendent Thurgood of San Saba County would like to join me in giving his unalloyed approval, wouldn't you, sir?"

All eyes turned to the red-cheeked man sitting by the door. "Of course, of course," the man muttered, but he looked like he'd just tasted something awful.

Jack smothered a grin. How could he have entertained the notion, even for a minute, that Caroline liked Thurgood?

"Thank you, thank you," Caroline was saying. "And now I hope you'll all join us for punch and cookies."

As everyone else surged toward the refreshment table set up in the cloakroom, Jack noticed that Thurgood made a hasty exit, followed by Mr. Henderson.

The air seemed cleaner after their exit.

It was an hour before parents stopped coming to speak to Caroline, and she could finally lock the building. A few other families left at the same time, but Jack was aware of a prickly feeling on his neck. It was the same sensation a fellow got when someone was lining him up in sights.

"What's the matter?" Caroline asked at last, when he stopped and looked behind him a second time, just as they reached the road. "Who are you looking for?"

Abby and Amelia were eyeing him curiously.

"No one, I guess. Thought I heard something."

Caroline was looking at him suspiciously. He knew that prior to the incident between them Sunday night, she might have pressed the matter, but not now.

He'd talk to her after the girls went to bed. But when he left his daughters' room and looked in the parlor for Caroline, he found she had already gone to bed, too.

There was no school the next day, for the students would be on holiday till after New Year's. He'd find a way to talk to her in the morning.

When he arose the next morning, however, she was already out of the house on some errand.

Jack was supposed to have come on Christmas Eve after supper, but he had not arrived when they'd left for the early evening Christmas Eve service.

In a way it had been just as well, Caroline thought, though she'd missed him being with them. But she'd felt she needed the preacher's reminder of what the holiday really meant. She'd realized that in the days leading up to Christmas Eve, she had become so absorbed in the relationship between herself and Jack, as well as in the school program, she had lost touch with the importance of Jesus' coming to the world.

Christmas Day dawned cold and cloudy. She even saw a few snowflakes drifting past the kitchen window as she poured herself a cup of coffee.

"Reckon it'll stick?" Jack asked her, coming into the kitchen, "The girls have never seen snow."

He yawned, so sleep-rumpled she couldn't help but smile. She shrugged. "We rarely get more than an inch or so, some years not even that."

The girls ran into the kitchen just then, and they were wide-eyed with wonder when Jack pointed at the window. Then, heedless of the cold, they raced to the door and threw it open, giggling at the touch of the unfamiliar flakes on their hands and their tongues.

"Can we make a snowman, Papa?" Amelia said. "I always wanted to do that."

Jack chuckled. "I don't think there's enough to do that just yet, and it might quit before there is. Why not go to the parlor and see what Santa Claus left you?"

They rushed back down the hall. Last night they'd each hung up a stocking on the mantel, borrowed from Aunt Mary—their own being too small—and these were now stuffed with apples, nuts, candy sticks and even a couple of precious oranges obtained from the mercantile. Now, too, there were presents wrapped in brown paper or scraps of cloth beneath the juniper Christmas tree. The girls crowed over these until Caroline's mother insisted they have some breakfast.

Later, they all opened the packages. The twins

squealed in delight over the doll chairs from their father, the two new dresses Aunt Mary had made them and the picture books Caroline had bought at the mercantile. They clapped at the jump rope Dan had fashioned out of a discarded length of rope with handles he had carved himself. Her parents seemed pleased about the new dishes Caroline had gotten them, as was her brother with the vest she had made.

Jack opened up the package that Abby and Amelia had clumsily wrapped in a piece of green cloth left over from some sewing project and proclaimed himself the luckiest father in the world to be the recipient of such a muffler knit by not one, but two clever, skillful daughters.

Then the Wallaces opened Jack's presents. Her father and Dan thanked Jack for the shirts, and her mother went pink with pleasure over the red shawl. Caroline gave each of the twins a loud smacking kiss on the cheek for the silver earbobs. At last, only the presents to and from Jack and Caroline remained.

As if by some unseen signal, the rest of the family dispersed, the twins to play with their new toys, Dan and his father to try on their shirts, her mother to start baking the ham for their Christmas dinner.

He opened up her present first and smiled at the pair of stockings she had knit with such care, and the book she had selected from her own.

"Thank you, Caroline," he said, and their gazes locked. There was so much in his blue eyes—but mostly she saw regret. Quickly she looked back at the brown paper-wrapped bundle in her lap.

"Caroline, I—I wish…" he began, and then his voice trailed off as she began to unwrap it.

It was a shawl, just like the one he had given her mother, only gold. Caroline waited for him to tell her something, anything that would tell her how much she meant to him, but apparently he couldn't—or wouldn't. She could appreciate the beauty of the shawl and knew the color would become her, but since it was the same thing he had given her mother, she realized the significance of the gift—or rather, the lack of it. He'd bought it as thanks for caring for his daughters, nothing more.

"Thank you, Jack, it's beautiful," she managed to say and even managed to keep the flatness out of her tone.

He seemed to be struggling for words once again, but she had to hide her disappointment before he saw it.

"I… I should go help Mother," she said, rising and quickly fleeing the room.

New Years' Day had come and gone. In the early days of 1868, the Spinsters' Club had met to plan what had come to be the annual winter taffy pull party. Usually they invited all the cowhands from neighboring ranches, for few bachelor candidates answered their advertisements in the winter. Now, at least, they had an additional male guest, Gil Chadwick. Polly Shackleford was already scheming to make sure she sat by the young minister.

This bachelor invitee and their friend Caroline, who had not attended the Spinsters' Club meeting the previous night, were the subjects of a smaller, secret meeting held the next morning at Prissy Bishop's house on Travis Street.

Milly Brookfield and Sarah Walker were in attendance, and they'd also invited Louisa Wheeler because she worked with Caroline at the school and genuinely cared about her.

Once tea and cookies had been served, Milly got right to the point. "Christmas has come and gone," she said. "And Jack did not declare his feelings for our Caroline."

"I'm worried about her," Sarah said, unconsciously laying a hand over the place where her unborn baby kicked.

"And she's starting to wear gray again," put in Louisa. "I think she's losing weight, too."

"When I saw her at church, she said Jack came on the weekend after Christmas, and after New Year's Day," Milly said. "They talk about books and such after the girls go to bed, but never anything more important."

"Is he still working on the house?" Sarah asked her sister.

Milly nodded. "Our men keep me up on its progress. But as far as I know, he's never told her about it. Do you think the foolish man thinks he has to wait till it's all done, and then make his feelings known?"

"Maybe we should tell her," Prissy said.

The other ladies shook their heads. "What if it has nothing to do with her?" Louisa asked. "What if— Do you ladies suppose he's courting *someone else*? Someone on a neighboring ranch, perhaps? Or in town?"

Prissy actually gasped at the thought. "It's no one in town," she said. Certainty rang in her voice. "I would have seen them, or Sam would have told me. He seems to spot everything that's going on, what with the time he spends patrolling the town, and he knows how worried I am about the two of them."

Milly shook her head, too. "There's no one in our

part of the county he would be courting, at least. And when would he do it, between watching over his herd and building that house for who knows what reason? Caroline told me he seems always to be just on the verge of saying something when they're alone together, but he doesn't."

"Well, I think we have no choice but to put our plan into effect," Prissy said.

Sarah shivered slightly and gathered her shawl more closely about her shoulders. "Are we sure this is a good idea, ladies? Maybe we should pray about it," she said uncertainly.

"I've been praying about it," Milly said.

"So have I," Prissy said. "And I haven't felt any conviction that taking action would be wrong. I vote we pay Gil Chadwick a visit this very morning. Who's with me?"

Within minutes, they had put on their shawls and bonnets and were headed for the rectory.

"Gil's next door in the church," Reverend Chadwick told them, coming to the door. He held a soup spoon in his gnarled hand. "He's doing the sermon next Sunday, so he said he wanted to go over there and work on it. The soup'll be ready in about a half hour, though, and you ladies are welcome to share it."

"Thanks, but we won't keep him that long, Reverend," Milly promised. "We just wanted to talk to him about something, and hand-deliver his invitation to the taffy pull."

They trooped next door to the church and found the young preacher with his shirtsleeves rolled up to his elbows, earnestly discoursing to a brown tabby cat sitting in the front pew.

"Oh, hello, ladies," he said when he noticed them coming up the aisle. "I was just trying my sermon out on Tiger, there." He nodded to the cat, who had hopped down to twine himself around their ankles. "He's not much of a critic, so I don't get discouraged," he added with a chuckle. "What can I do for you?"

"We came to invite you to the taffy pull that the Spinsters' Club is having next Saturday night, Gil," Sarah began.

"Well, I have a bit of a sweet tooth, so I'd be happy to come. Thank you."

"And to speak to you about Caroline Wallace," Milly said.

He'd been leaning on the pulpit, but now he straightened and eyed each of them in turn. "Perhaps we'd better sit down." He gestured to the front pew and brought a chair from behind the pulpit and placed it so he could sit facing them.

"What about Miss Caroline?" he asked warily, once everyone was settled.

Sarah said, glancing at the others for support, "We know you like her…"

Gil nodded slowly. "Yes, I do. I'd like very much like to court her," he admitted, then gave a shrug. "But she made it plain to me that she would not welcome it. I think her heart is given to Mr. Collier."

"But nothing has come of it," Milly said. "I know she was hoping for some sign at Christmas…but nothing happened. We know she loves him. What we would like to know from you, sir, is…" She hesitated and looked to Prissy with a silent plea.

"What we would like to know is if you care enough for Caroline's happiness that you would be willing to

approach her again," Prissy said, "in an effort to force
Jack Collier's hand, so to speak? To get him to see that
he must make an effort, or he will lose her?"

Gil Chadwick's jaw dropped, and for a moment he
seemed incapable of speech.

"Mrs. Bishop, are you suggesting that I try to make
Mr. Collier *jealous*?" he asked at last.

Prissy laughed, but it was an uneasy laugh. She drew
herself up in the pew. "Yes, we are," she said at last.

"Does she know you're here? She didn't put you up
to this, did she?" he asked.

"Oh, no! She has no idea we're here talking to you
like this," Louisa said quickly.

"Is it awful of us to ask?" Prissy asked. "If you find
the suggestion too disturbing, or do not feel you could
participate in such a scheme, please forget we mentioned
it." The other ladies all nodded in agreement.

"We all just want Caroline to be happy," Milly said.
"And we sensed you wanted that, too."

Gil rubbed the back of his neck, and then his chin. "I
do want it, too," he said. "And, no, I don't think you're
awful, ladies. I think you're loyal, caring friends, and
everyone should be so fortunate to have such friends."

A small smile curved the ends of Prissy's lips. "Then
you'll do it?"

It seemed an eternity before Gil made his answer,
and when at last he nodded, the ladies let out their col-
lective breaths.

"I shouldn't agree to do this, in all probability, but
I'm willing to give it a try," Gil said. "Only under cer-
tain conditions, however. You're very sure she loves
Collier?"

All of them nodded and made emphatic murmurs.

Prissy leaned forward. "And your conditions...?"

"I assume you want the lady in question to remain ignorant of this scheme?" Gil asked.

The ladies nodded in unison. "She would never consider such a ploy herself," Milly said. "It's not her way."

"Very well. First of all, Miss Caroline must be willing to spend time with me," Gil said. "I will not press my attentions on an unwilling lady."

"Of course not," Sarah said.

"Second, and perhaps most important, if this tactic doesn't succeed in making Collier jealous after some time has passed, and Miss Caroline seems to like my company, I will consider myself free to court her *for real.*"

There was another long silence as Milly eyed Sarah, then Prissy, then Louisa. Finally Milly swallowed and said, "We agree. As we've said, we seek Caroline's happiness. If Jack Collier sees he could lose her, and he isn't willing to fight for her, then he isn't worthy of her."

"Well said, Milly!" Prissy cried.

Gil looked uneasy. "As long as you don't mean literal fighting," he said. "I'm no coward, but I *am* a preacher, after all."

Milly assured him her meaning had been figurative, not literal.

"So we are all agreed?" Prissy asked the group.

"So say we all," Milly announced, and everyone put in a hand.

"It's like a scene from *The Three Musketeers,*" Louisa breathed. "A book I borrowed from Caroline by some Frenchman. Their motto was 'All for one, and one for all.'"

"Ours should be 'all for Caroline,'" Sarah said.

"Right," Milly said. "Gil, here's how I think you should begin…"

Chapter Twenty-One

As usual after church, everyone milled around and caught up on the news. If it hadn't been for the fact that Milly had engaged her in conversation, however, Caroline would have fled for home long since with the excuse of starting Sunday dinner. Jack could gather up the twins from whatever corner of the church grounds they had disappeared to with Lizzie Halliday, and her parents and Dan would drift home when they were ready.

After dinner they would spend another endless afternoon. She and Jack would read or talk about books when they were not spending time with the children, and she would have to pretend she didn't love him.

At times she positively longed for spring, when he would be gone—and yet as she watched the days of January ticking by, she dreaded the time when he and his men would depart with the herd. Not only would he be leaving, but then it would be just a matter of time before he'd be sending for the girls—or coming for them himself, in the company of some lady he'd made his bride. And then Caroline would lose all three of them forever.

It had been too painful sitting in the same pew with

Jack during the service, after coming so close to a romance with him. So many of the townspeople assumed they were a couple.

"I said, what do you think of Faith Bennett's new kid boots?" Milly said.

Caroline realized Milly had been speaking to her, and she had been looking in Faith's direction—but only because Faith stood near the door Caroline longed to escape through.

She pretended to study them. "Oh, sorry," she said. "Very fetching, I suppose...." It was odd, Caroline thought. Her friend had never seemed overly concerned with footwear before. Since Milly was an excellent seamstress, dresses were much more a subject of fascination to her.

Then suddenly Gil Chadwick joined them. Caroline had the suspicion that Milly had guessed her desire to sneak out and had kept her here with silly chatter until the young preacher could reach them.

"That was an excellent sermon, Reverend," Caroline said, just to make conversation, but it was the truth. Gil Chadwick seemed to have a talent making an old Bible story seem new again. Whatever congregation eventually called him to their pulpit would be lucky to have him.

"Thank you, Miss Caroline," he said, smiling down at her, his hazel eyes twinkling.

Out of the corner of her eye, she saw Jack had collared the twins and that the three of them were making their way toward her.

"I trust you're planning to attend the taffy pull this Saturday night, Miss Caroline?" Gil asked. "I've been invited, but I was hoping you'd be there."

The question, uttered just as Jack drew near, had her blinking with surprise. *Had he heard it?*

It seemed so, for Jack's jaw hardened. "Come on, girls, let's go back to the Wallaces," he said and started past the group.

"You're coming, too, aren't you, Jack?" Milly asked, reaching out a hand to stop him. "To the taffy pull? It's Saturday night at seven, at the church social hall."

"I wanna come!" Abby cried.

"Me, too!" Amelia added. "I love taffy!"

Milly bent down to them and smiled. "Girls, this is a party for grown-ups," she said, "But I promise, your papa and Aunt Caroline will bring lots of taffy home for you, won't you?"

Caroline missed the meaningful look Milly then shot at Jack.

"Oh, I'll probably send Raleigh and a couple other men," Jack muttered. "The ones that like to flirt with the ladies," he said and strode on, pulling the girls with him.

He left a shocked silence in his wake.

"Miss Caroline, I'd be proud to escort you there," Gil said.

Caroline felt tears stinging her eyes, but she raised her chin. His friendly interest was balm to her soul. "That would be very nice, Gil," she said. "Thank you. I accept."

It was all Jack could do to hide his ill humor from his daughters on the short walk between the church and the Wallace home.

So the young preacher had asked Caroline to a social event, right underneath his nose! In fact, it almost seemed as if Gil Chadwick had timed his question and raised the volume of his voice, as if he'd *wanted* Jack to hear him ask it.

He didn't doubt Caroline had accepted Chadwick's invitation. After all, she'd been smiling up at the interloper when he'd approached them.

How ironic that he'd resolved only this morning to start trying to woo Caroline again. Jack had seen the misery she tried to hide every time their eyes met, and it had matched the ache inside his own heart. He had to try again, he *had* to! And when he'd seen the day was going to be sunny and mild for January, it had seemed like a sign.

He'd thought to take Amelia and Abby into his confidence about the house he'd been building and get them to agree not to beg to go along when he asked Caroline to pay a visit to the ranch with him in the afternoon. He'd planned to tell her he wanted her to see a "project" he and the men had been working on. There was still much to be done in the way of finishing the interior, but the outer part of the house was complete—windows from St. Louis, shiny tin roof and all. He'd show her the nearly-done ranch house and tell her he'd built it for her. He'd find a way to put everything right between them and return to Simpson Creek with her promise to marry him.

But his plans had come to nothing. Worse than nothing, because now it seemed the young preacher was dead set on courting Caroline—just as he'd suspected before. Was it extra sinful to want to pummel a man if he was a man of God?

He thought for a few moments, while he changed out of his good Sunday-go-to-meeting clothes, of taking Caroline aside and pouring out his feelings to her and begging her not to go to the taffy pull or anywhere with anyone but him. He could hear her in the kitchen now, talking to her mother, and the metal clank as something was stirred in a pot.

Just as clearly, he could hear his father saying, *"Boy, if a man ain't got his pride, he ain't got nothin'."*

How could he have forgotten he was never the one chosen? It was always Pete, or Elnora, or one of his two disagreeable half sisters. So, too, it was with Caroline. She had picked someone else. First Pete, and now the genial, handsome young preacher.

Suddenly, the idea of spending the afternoon and evening under the same roof as Caroline seemed intolerable. He was almost grateful when he heard hoofbeats, then the sound of a horse skidding to a stop outside the house. A glance outside the window showed it was Raleigh.

That meant trouble. His ramrod would never have come all this way unless something was wrong.

Jack strode quickly to the door and led Masterson in. "Boss, I'm just on the way to notify the sheriff, but I figured I'd better stop here first and let you know. Afternoon, ma'am," he added, with a nod toward Caroline, who'd gotten up from her chair, white-faced.

"Mr. Raleigh!" the twins cried, hearing the familiar voice and running out from the kitchen, where they'd been learning how to make pudding from Caroline's mother.

"Howdy, girls," he said, then turned back to Jack.

"What's happened?"

"Boss, it looks like those no-good sidewinders're back. We found a slaughtered steer out by the creek. Got there just in time to see those two hightailin' off like the—like you-know-who was on their tails," Raleigh said, after glancing at the children.

"They killed a steer in *broad daylight*?" Jack's troubles of the heart were swamped in the anger that surged in the wake of this news.

"Bold as brass, ain't they?"

"You go on to the sheriff, Raleigh, and make your report," Jack said. "I'll head out to the ranch now. Girls, I've got to go." He leaned down and quickly embraced them. He avoided looking at Caroline, but he felt her worried gaze on him.

"Raleigh, I'll take your horse, since he's already saddled," Jack went on, pulling his duster down from the hall peg, "and you get my roan from the livery. Miss Caroline, please make my excuses to your mother—"

"Boss, we might as well go together," Raleigh protested. "Those two are long gone. It won't take long to make my report. Could be they're tryin' to provoke you into coming back in a hurry alone…."

But Jack was already halfway out the door.

He sent a note back later through Cookie, when the older man came to town early the next week to pick up supplies at the mercantile, that they'd found no trace of the two drovers-turned-rustlers. The note was addressed to all of them, not just Caroline. He didn't say when he'd be visiting again, though he did mention that he thought Sims and Adams had become aware of his pattern of visiting on Sundays and taken advantage of it, so in future he would make his visits to the children at less predictable times.

He'd come back to visit the children, not her.

Dan brought the news that a wanted poster had been tacked up on the door of the jail with these two men's likenesses sketched at the top of the sheet, while underneath was listed their names and descriptions, the charges against them and the reward posted for their capture, provided by Mayor Gilmore and the bank.

"I had a lovely time, Gil," Caroline told the young minister as he walked her home from the taffy pull the following Saturday night.

She meant it. She'd made up her mind to enjoy her evening with Gil, since spending time with her clearly wasn't one of Jack's priorities. And it felt good to smile again, to wear a pretty dress and see the fact that she was attractive mirrored in a man's eyes. She hadn't laughed in so long.

"As did I, Caroline," Gil said, smiling down at her.

It seemed as if everyone else had enjoyed themselves, too. As Jack had said, Raleigh Masterson and a couple of other drovers came to the party. Many other cowboys from neighboring ranches, bored with the long winter days and longer nights, had come, too, so every Spinster present could flirt with two or three of them, or pair off with just one if she wanted. Polly Shackleford had held court with four of them hanging on her every word, so she hadn't seemed to notice that the young preacher had eyes only for Caroline. Dr. and Mrs. Walker, and Sheriff and Mrs. Bishop had served as chaperones. Later, after everyone had had their fill of taffy, the tables had been pushed back, and a fiddler had played while everyone danced until they were red-faced and breathless.

They had arrived at her home now. Caroline sent up a brief prayer that Abby and Amelia were asleep and wouldn't wake when she came inside. They'd already plagued her with questions about why their father wasn't coming, and why Aunt Caroline was attending the event with someone else. How could she answer their questions, when she didn't really understand herself what had gone wrong between Jack and herself?

Gil stopped and turned to her on the front step. "I hope I may call on you again, Caroline?"

"I'd like that," Caroline said. "Would you like to come in, Gil?" she asked.

"I would," he said, "but it's late, and I wouldn't want to disturb your family." Perhaps he was also thinking of the inquisitive twins. "But I'll see you tomorrow at church. Papa's giving the sermon, so I'm free to sit where I like. Perhaps we might sit together?"

"Perhaps." Oh dear, thought Caroline, more questions and sad looks from Jack's daughters. And what if Jack came to church? But he'd said he wouldn't be coming to visit at the usual times, so in all likelihood he wouldn't be there. And in any case, he'd given up any right to expect anything of her, she thought, ignoring the echo of sadness that resonated through her soul.

"You never said—did you and Gil have a good time at the taffy pull?" Prissy asked two weeks later, when she and Sarah encountered Caroline in the mercantile on a Saturday morning. "You two seemed to be enjoying yourselves that night."

"Yes, I did," Caroline said, "very much." All too aware that Mrs. Patterson was listening with interest, she raised an eyebrow meaningfully and glanced at the bolts of cloth, lengths of lace trim, cards of buttons and thread piled up on the counter before them.

"Planning to do some sewing, are you?" she asked, deliberately changing the subject.

"Not us," Prissy confessed with a giggle, "we're tak-

ing all this out to Milly's this morning. Dear Sarah's…
ahem, *increasing,* you know—" Prissy nodded toward
Sarah's expanding waistline "—so I thought we'd take
those things out so Milly could start working on some
new clothes for her."

"Isn't that nice of them?" Sarah asked.

Caroline had to agree.

"Well, you never know when *I* might need some new
clothes of the same sort," Prissy said, as Sarah paid for
their purchases. "Sarah's agreed to let me borrow them,
should the need arise."

"Prissy! Are you making an announcement?" Caroline said, amused at the rosy blush that had bloomed on
the other woman's cheeks.

Prissy motioned Caroline away from the counter and
behind a rack of ready-made men's clothes. "Maybe,"
she whispered. "I don't know. I'm not sure yet, so don't
you breathe a word of it."

"I promise," Caroline whispered back.

"Now, don't think you're going to get away with that
short answer about your outing with Gil," Prissy said as
Sarah rejoined them, and Caroline realized too late she
had been lured into a trap. She wasn't at all sure she was
ready to share her feelings, but after another look at the
curious faces of her friends, she sensed how much they
had been worrying about her.

"Have you seen him again? Do you enjoy his company?" Prissy probed.

"Yes and yes," Caroline admitted. "He took me to
supper at the hotel the other night, and we had a very
pleasant time."

"But—?" Sarah asked softly. The question and the perceptive look in her friend's blue eyes startled Caroline.

"But nothing," Caroline said, hearing the trace of defiance in her own voice. "I like his company very much."

"Have you seen Jack lately?" Sarah asked. "I know you said he wasn't going to come on Sundays necessarily, because of the trouble they had out at the ranch. They never did catch those fellows, did they?" She aimed this question at Prissy, since Prissy's husband was the sheriff.

"No, though Sam and his deputy have been scouring the hills for them," Prissy said. "Sneaky and slippery as snakes, he says. They seem to go back and forth from here to Lampasas County and east to San Saba, never in any one place long enough to be caught."

Prissy turned back to Caroline.

"Yes, Jack's come by—he stopped in and took his girls to supper at the hotel, and Tuesday night he spent the night, but other than the usual talking about the weather and the book he'd been reading, we hardly exchanged a word." Caroline shrugged, trying to make it appear it didn't bother her.

Yet suddenly the tears she hadn't known were lurking escaped down her cheeks in a scalding rush.

Sarah gathered her into her arms, while Prissy hunted about in her reticule for a handkerchief and dabbed at Caroline's cheeks as she wept.

"Why sh-shouldn't I enjoy spending time with a man who *wants* to court me?" Caroline demanded, keeping her tear-choked voice down so Mrs. Patterson wouldn't hear her. "Jack will n-never…get off the fence, apparently… And I've found I still want to marry and have children one day, after all. I can tell Gil would love me, if I gave him half a chance—what's wrong with that?"

"Nothing, dear," Sarah told her with a surprising

fierceness, "as long as you're sure Gil's who you want, that you're not merely settling."

Caroline had straightened now and was dabbing at her own eyes when she noticed Prissy and Sarah's locked gazes. What did these two friends know that she didn't?

"Thanks," Caroline said, embarrassed and wondering how she'd escape from the mercantile without the proprietress seeing her tear-swollen eyes.

"Just don't be in a rush to decide," Prissy said putting her arm around Caroline. "Have you prayed about it?"

Caroline couldn't help but smile wryly, and she caught Sarah smothering a grin too. Prissy had always been known for the impulsive way she'd fallen in love time after time, until finally the right man, Sam Bishop, had come along. But she decided not to tease her friend with past habits.

"Oh, Prissy, if you only knew how much I've prayed about this…"

Chapter Twenty-Two

On the same Saturday morning when the three friends met in the Simpson Creek mercantile, two others met in a small cantina west of Simpson Creek. It wasn't a splendid place with a polished mahogany bar with a mirror behind it and brass footrest, just a shack with a few tables and chairs and a plentiful supply of rotgut. Its proprietor was a Mexican, and the place was mostly patronized by *Tejanos*. But it suited the purpose of the two, for one of them couldn't afford to be seen stepping into a saloon in San Saba.

It couldn't be said that the two men were friends— they merely possessed a common cause. Both of them wished for the downfall of Caroline Wallace.

"Life ain't been worth livin' since that woman took over the schoolhouse and started infectin' my son with her notions, and if that wasn't enough, now my woman's got the idea she's got a right to an opinion, too," William Henderson griped over his beer. "It's not like I kin take a strap to 'em like I used to when they got outa line, neither. Ever since them do-gooders put me in jail an' tried to tell me what I could and couldn't do—*in my own house, mind you*—"

"It's not necessary to raise your voice, Mr. Henderson," Mr. Thurgood said. "I'm quite on your side, as I've told you. I don't care for the stubborn and opinionated Miss Wallace, either, and I long for the day I can oust her from her position and put someone more…shall we say *malleable* in place?" He guessed Henderson didn't know what the word meant, but it didn't matter. He just needed to figure out a way to use the man to achieve his goal. "Yet I haven't found a justifiable reason to dismiss her as yet. I thought perhaps the Christmas program might provide some ammunition, but with all the brats perfect in their tedious performances, and that doddering yahoo of a mayor applauding like a fool…" He shrugged. "It didn't seem the right time."

"But then I hid in the bushes afterward like you said, an' I spotted the woman walkin' home with the fellow with the twin girls—cain't you make something a' that?" Henderson asked. "I thought you didn't like your teachers steppin' out with men."

Thurgood disliked the other man's whining tone. It set his teeth on edge.

"I don't," he snapped. "But being escorted to her home with two children along is hardly 'stepping out,' as you call it. It's well known that Collier's brats are staying in her home right now, and you've never seen the two of them anywhere actually *courting*, have you? I told you to tell me of any such event."

The other man shook his head. "Seems like that's over, these days. The young preacher seems to be sparkin' her now."

Thurgood raised a brow and leaned forward. "So she's

fickle, eh?" He rubbed his chin. "Perhaps something can be made of that...." But he didn't know *what*, exactly. He could hardly paint Miss Wallace as a scarlet woman for preferring a civilized minister to an uncouth cattleman.

A pair of drifters sat at the table nearby, one stocky, the other lean and rangy, both bearded and narrow-eyed, the sort of men he wouldn't want to meet on a deserted stretch of road. It was safer not to look such men in the eye. But now one of them spoke. "Sounds like we know some a' the same people, mister. Could be we could join forces."

Thurgood turned and raised his eyebrows as far as they would go. "Whatever do you mean?"

The man at the other table leaned forward, and Thurgood was assailed with the odors of stale whiskey and tobacco. "You mentioned Collier—you're talkin' about Jack Collier, right? The trail boss who's spendin' the winter south a' Simpson Creek?"

Thurgood nodded slowly.

"And you wanna cause trouble for this schoolmarm? We saw her once, with those twins—she's a purty thing, ain't she? What's she ever done to you, mister?"

Thurgood tried to take refuge in hauteur. "It's a long story, but let me summarize it by saying she challenged my authority."

"And mine, too, as head a' my house. She's an uppity, opinionated female," Henderson whined.

The stocky one pulled lips back over yellowed teeth and snickered. "Sounds like it might be fun to put a gal like that in her place, eh, Alvin?"

"It might, at that."

"And what's your problem with Collier?" Thurgood demanded.

The other man's eyes narrowed. "Let's just say he needs to be put in his place, too. And I think if we plan this right, all of us workin' together, we can make it happen all at once."

"I... All right," Thurgood said, wiping sweat from his brow. He felt as if he'd waded into a shallow stream and had suddenly fallen into a deep hole, and the water was closing over his head, icy and dark.

The other smiled. "Won't even ask if you can pay. Seein' Collier ruined's gonna be its own reward."

"Boss, you can dismiss me if you want," Raleigh Masterson said, a few days later, while they pounded wooden pegs into a puncheon floor inside the house. They worked on the first floor, but he could hear the others working upstairs.

"Oh? Are you about to meddle in my business again?" Jack asked, making his voice as forbidding as he could. "I thought sending you and Shep into town last night might give you something else to think about. But evidently you don't mind thinking about having to find another job."

"But I have to tell you you're bein' a—a fool," Raleigh went on stubbornly. "I tried to tell you when it happened, but you wouldn't listen, and now I'm gonna tell you again. I saw Miss Caroline with that young preacher fella at the party a fortnight ago, and last night when we went to the saloon, the two of them were out walkin' together."

Jack favored his ramrod with a basilisk stare. *"It's none of my business,"* he said. "Or yours, for that matter."

"I'll quit, if that's what you want," Raleigh went on.

"But I'm going to speak my piece first. You ain't ever going to find another lady like that, not in Montana, not anywhere. And if you don't stop acting dim-witted, you're going to lose her, and that's a fact."

"I've already lost her," Jack growled.

"Then what're we doin' *this* for?" Raleigh demanded, spreading his arms wide to encompass the house in which they worked.

Jack shrugged. "Just something to do," he said. "I figured we might as well finish what we started. I mentioned to the bank president that we were doing it, and he seemed real pleased. Said he'd give us some traveling money when we left as thanks for making the property more valuable."

Raleigh gave a snort of disgust and refused to be distracted. "That preacher fella would walk through fire for her, you can see it in his eyes. But that night at the party, she kept watching the door each time it opened— for *you,* Collier. Hopin' you'd get down off your high horse and realize the mistake you're makin'."

"You done?" Jack demanded.

"I… I reckon so," Raleigh muttered. He watched his boss warily, probably figuring the next thing he'd see was Jack's fist aimed right at his face.

"Good," Jack said in a dead voice. He got to his feet and walked toward the door.

He knew Raleigh was right, but he also knew that Gil Chadwick was the better man for Caroline. His ramrod would no doubt enjoy a good laugh if he knew Jack had had to defend his actions to Abby and Amelia every time they got him alone. He didn't expect his children to understand now why Caroline couldn't be their new mother, but someday they might, when they were older.

It'd be easier, once they were on the trail, to convince himself.

"Class dismissed. I'll see you again on Monday," Caroline said. Her pronouncement caused a stampede of young scholars down the aisle and, seconds later, a thunder of feet pounding the steps outside.

Louisa bid her goodbye, and in a moment she was gone, too, which left her with just the twins and Billy Joe, who was making his way more slowly to the door, moving stiffly as if he hurt.

"Billy Joe, what's wrong?" she asked him, realizing all at once he'd been uncharacteristically quiet the past few days.

He stopped. "Nothin', Miss Wallace," he said over his shoulder. "I'm fine, I just fell climbin' down from the loft the other day." He quickened his pace.

"Billy Joe, *is your father*—" She hesitated, not wanting to say "beating you again" in front of Abby and Amelia.

But he was gone before she could think of a way to rephrase her question. She'd have to wait till Monday, when he'd once again be staying after class for tutoring, and hope she could wrest the truth from him at that time. She didn't buy his glib explanation for a minute. *Lord, please protect him and his mother until then.*

She knew the girls were watching her. "Come on, girls, let's go home," she said brightly.

"Aunt Caroline, Billy Joe's pa isn't nice to him, is he?" Abby asked as they made their way out of the schoolyard.

She didn't want to talk about it with these innocent

children, but neither could she lie to them. "No, he's not. But don't you worry, there are a lot of folks watching out for Billy Joe, to make sure his papa learns to be kinder. Isn't it wonderful that you girls have such a nice papa?"

Amelia and Abby nodded in unison and were quiet until they reached Fannin Street.

"Aunt Caroline, it's been a lot warmer lately," Amelia said.

"Mmm-hmm. It's February now. Winter's almost over," she murmured. The days were getting milder. Soon green buds would appear on the trees and bluebonnets would spring up in the fields and roadsides, along with red and gold Indian paintbrush, yellow and pink primroses and white prickly poppies. She didn't like to think of what the warmer weather meant—the herd would be leaving Collier's Roost, and Jack Collier with it.

Jack's upcoming departure shouldn't have bothered her. It was very apparent that Gil Chadwick enjoyed spending time with her and that she could have a future with him if she wanted it. But it wasn't Gil she lay awake at night thinking about, and dreamed about when at last she fell asleep.

"Since it's been warmer outside, could we go see Papa, and not wait for him to come see us?"

"Yeah, could we?"

Caroline couldn't deny the little leap of her heart at Amelia's words, but she chewed her lip as she considered the notion. Why shouldn't they go see Jack? Since he'd stopped coming Sundays, his visits seemed shorter, without church and Sunday dinner to prolong them.

Her father would probably object to them going alone, because the two drovers-turned-outlaws were still at large, but Dan could come along, armed with their father's rifle. It wasn't as if they'd have anything the outlaws wanted, anyway.

"All right," she said. "Tomorrow's Saturday. Unless the weather's bad, we'll go," she told them, then smiled as they cheered.

She wondered how he would act around her—would he be stiff, without the buffering presence of her parents? Would he invite them to stay and eat? They could bake a pie, or a cake, she thought, or two, so there'd be plenty to share with Jack's men.

If he didn't seem pleased to see her, she could always leave the twins there and go see Milly for a while. It had been a while since she'd had a cozy chat with her best friend, anyway, and seen baby Nicholas. But she fervently hoped her coming would please him.

Only minutes after his talk with Raleigh, Jack was surprised to see a buggy approach. And the last person Jack expected to emerge from the buggy, once it pulled to a stop between the bunkhouse and the house, was Gil Chadwick. Jack stood blinking in surprise as the young preacher started walking toward him and tried to think why he might be here. *Was something wrong with one of his daughters? With Caroline?* Chadwick did not look alarmed, but he didn't look happy, either.

"Afternoon, Gil," Jack said, with a casualness he did not feel. "Out paying pastoral calls? Is it because I've missed church lately?"

"No, Papa and I heard about your reason for staying out here on Sundays, and of course we understand." He shifted his gaze to indicate the dwelling behind Jack.

"What's this? I heard the house out here had been burned to the ground a while back."

"It was. We got bored over the winter and decided to build a new one," Jack said, shifting the hammer he'd unconsciously carried out of the house from hand to hand. "Just something to pass the time." *So why are you here?* Behind him, he sensed Raleigh, or maybe one of the men upstairs, peering out a window to see who had come.

"What can I do for you, Gil?" he said, choosing to be polite, but he heard the edge in his voice and knew the other man was aware of it, too.

Gil Chadwick took a deep breath. "Thought I might be able to do something for you—or at least try to."

"Oh?"

The other man put a hand on each hip, looked down for a moment, then raised his eyes to Jack. "I've been troubled about something, praying on it. I finally talked to my father—I consider him a man of great wisdom," Gil said. "He made me see I needed to talk to you."

"To me? What about?"

"Caroline."

Jack stiffened. *"What about Caroline?"*

"I think you love her," Gil said, "and she loves you. Your children love her. I don't know what happened that's keeping the two of you apart, but I need to warn you."

"Warn me?" He felt like a fool, repeating what the other man was saying like that stupid parrot his stepmother used to keep in the parlor, but each word from Gil Chadwick's mouth surprised him so much he couldn't seem to get ahead enough to summon his thoughts.

"I love her, too, Collier. And after all this thinking and praying and talking to my father, I decided the only fair, right thing to do was warn you, like I said. Caroline likes me, likes my company, but I can tell it's you she loves. However, I think she's ready to get on with her life, and I don't think she plans to spend it pining for you, if you don't want her."

Chadwick's words were coming thick and fast now, like blows. His earlier hesitation was gone.

"If I don't want her?" Jack echoed. "Chadwick—"

But the other man wasn't waiting for him. "Collier, I came to tell you that if you don't want her, I'm going to court her, and I think I stand a decent chance of winning her. And if I do, I'll thank God every day for it and never make her sorry she chose me."

"I—I do want her," Jack said, his voice hoarse and rusty, like a man who hasn't spoken for a long time. "I love her. But… I'm not the kind of man she needs—educated, well-read. You are."

Chadwick's face was incredulous. "Do you even believe that…those things you're saying? That's a lot of…" he pointed at the distant field where the cattle were grazing. "Well, there's plenty of it lying in clumps out there. All right, I've said my piece. If you don't do anything about it, next week I'm going to start courting Caroline in earnest."

"I'll come right now, with you—just wait while I saddle my horse," Jack said, surprised to hear the words coming from his mouth. But he meant them. If there was even a chance Caroline loved him as the young preacher said, he'd be a fool to let her go.

But the other man shook his head. "No. Don't come now," he said. "If you're smart, you'll take the rest of the day to think and pray about this. Make sure this is what you want to do, because Caroline doesn't need to be hurt anymore. Come tomorrow." He climbed back into the buggy.

"Thank you," Jack muttered, still a little dazed, but the other man showed no sign he heard him as he turned the horse and headed back the way the way he'd come.

He knew the young preacher had given him wise advice but suspected Chadwick also hadn't wanted his company. The other man had some sorrowing to do, knowing his sense of fairness had cost him Caroline, and that was best done alone.

He was going to take Gil Chadwick's advice to the letter. He saddled his horse and rode in the opposite direction of Simpson Creek. He needed to be alone to think and pray.

"I think we have everything we need," Caroline said, covering the chocolate cakes and placing them inside a long rectangular basket so they wouldn't be damaged as the buckboard rolled along the rutted road to the ranch.

"Papa's gonna like the cake," Amelia said.

"And Mr. Raleigh, too," Abby said.

"I'll just see if Dan is ready, and—"

A loud peremptory knock interrupted her.

Could Jack have decided to come see them, just as they were leaving to visit him? It might be Gil, and that would be awkward....

She went to the door, hope lending wings to her feet.

But it was not Jack who stood there, or Gil, but Superintendent Thurgood. She smothered a sigh of irritation.

"Good morning, sir," she said, feeling as grim as his face. *Why had he come now?*

"You look as if you're going somewhere," he said, nodding at her bonneted head and the shawl she wore.

"I— We were, yes, the girls and I…"

"I'm afraid there is something that needs your attention more at the school."

"Is it possible it could wait till Monday?" she asked. "We were just leaving—"

His face darkened like a thundercloud. "No, it can't! Come to the schoolhouse. I must show you the result of your carelessness," he said, his face like thunder.

"My carelessness? Whatever are you talking about?" she asked.

The twins had appeared at her side. "But we were going to see our papa," Abby protested.

"Hush, dear. I have to see what Mr. Thurgood is talking about," Caroline said, leaden with resentment that this man had shown up now. If they'd just left a few minutes earlier… "Very well, then. Lead the way, Mr. Thurgood."

The twins, already dressed for the trip, tagged along at their heels, and she didn't try to stop them, for she didn't fancy being alone with this overbearing man. Perhaps the presence of the children would keep him from the worst of the tirade she sensed he would unleash, though she didn't know what she'd done.

The streets of Simpson Creek were thronged with folks doing their errands, coming into town to stock up on supplies. But once the four left Main Street to turn down Fannin toward the schoolhouse, they were alone with the superintendent.

He stomped up the stairs and shoved the door so hard it slammed against the inside wall. The twins flinched.

"This is what happens when you don't live up to your responsibilities," he said, his face flinty.

Chapter Twenty-Three

He pointed.

"Aunt Caroline!" one of the girls cried.

Her mind couldn't take in the extent of the devastation. Papers littered the floor. Soot and mud blotched the whitewashed walls. Books lay strewn half open, pages ripped out, on desks and in an untidy heap next to the upended bookcase. Her desk had been overturned, too, and scored with deep gouges, as if someone had taken a bowie knife and used it at will. A jagged-edged, fist-size hole was punched through the center of the window. Glass shards glittered on the floor beneath it.

"This is what happens when you're careless about locking the door when you leave, Miss Wallace," Thurgood snarled.

"But I locked it," she said shakily, gazing around her and trying to imagine how this could ever be put right. "I lock the door every time I leave it—or Miss Wheeler does, if she stays longer," she said.

"And Friday? Who was last to leave?" he snapped.

"I was—we were," she amended, indicating the twins.

"The girls and I left together, and Miss Wheeler left only moments before. Do you remember me locking it, girls?"

They nodded in unison.

"Of course they would agree with you," Thurgood said archly. "It means nothing."

Had she locked it? Caroline thought desperately about the routine she always followed when leaving—she took her bonnet from its hook by the door, put it on, picked up her poke, pushed the door open and walked outside, then turned to lock the door. Yes, she was sure she had locked it.

Then who would have done this?

"I don't care what your plans were, Miss Wallace," Thurgood snapped, "but consider them canceled. You will have to work all day today and Sunday, too, if this place is to be fit for the use of your students on Monday, which it must be. Your wages will be docked as well until you have paid for the things damaged beyond repair, which I have yet to assess."

So she would be working for free until the end of the term at least, Caroline guessed. *Was he trying to get her to quit?*

"That's not fair," Abby protested, stomping her foot. "Aunt Caroline didn't do this!"

"Abby, be quiet," Caroline said. She'd talk to them after the superintendent left, but for now, she just wanted to get him out the door. "Have you reported this to the sheriff?"

He nodded, setting his jowls waggling. "Of course, but there's nothing he can do to prove who did this," he said. "You'd best get busy cleaning it up. Perhaps I should escort the children home, so they do not distract you."

"I'm not going anywhere with him," Amelia said, her tone mutinous, her arms crossed. Then she stuck out her tongue at Thurgood.

"Amelia!" Caroline cried, shocked.

"Little brat!" Thurgood shouted, and for a moment Caroline was afraid he might slap the child. Then she would have to resort to violence herself.

But he took a stiff step back. "Very well," he said. "Let them stay and make themselves useful, if you think you can keep them from wreaking any further havoc. It might be a good lesson for them. Wouldn't surprise me a bit if they weren't responsible for all this, anyway."

The utter ridiculousness of his accusation made Caroline's jaw drop. Thurgood left before she could gather her wits enough to respond. Which was just as well, because she might have said something unbecoming to a lady in front of the children.

"I'm sorry, girls," she said, kneeling and pulling them close to her, even as tears of rage and disappointment streamed down her cheeks. "I won't be able to take you out to see your papa today, but maybe if you go back to the house, Dan could take you—"

"No, Aunt Caroline, we're gonna stay and help you," Amelia said, hugging her.

"Yeah, we can go 'nother time. Don't cry, Aunt Caroline." Abby said, hugging her from the other side.

Of course, that had the effect of making her cry harder.

"Girls, I want you to do something for me," Caroline said, when she was finally calm enough to speak. "Go to the house—no, I don't mean you have to stay there—and tell Dan what happened." Her father was on duty at the post office and her mother was visiting Mrs. Detwiler, but her brother could help. "Tell Dan to go tell the sheriff what happened." Caroline wasn't at all sure Thurgood had reported the matter to the sheriff, despite what he'd said. "Then I want him to return home and gather up another bucket, mop and some rags, and bring them here."

Dan wouldn't be too happy about spending his day off from the livery helping her clean, but he'd come to her aid, she was sure. "In the meantime, I'll get started cleaning with the supplies in the cloakroom. Can you remember all that?"

Both girls nodded, their faces solemn, and turned to go.

"And put on your oldest clothes before you come back," she added, for they were wearing their nicest dresses for their papa. "We're going to get very dirty."

She looked down at her own white blouse and wished she had worn something more practical. It was going to be ruined, but she dare not leave to change. Thurgood might be watching. At least her skirt was dark, since she'd planned to take the buckboard.

She watched them go, then headed for the cloakroom. It was the teacher's responsibility to clean the schoolhouse from time to time, so there would already be at least one bucket and mop and some rags to start the project.

"Like shooting fish in a barrel," Sims said to his partner, as they watched the girls marching purposely away from the school. Their path would take them right past the bushes where they waited. He chuckled.

"Yeah, I got a little nervous when Thurgood didn't walk out with the brats," Adams said, "but looks like this'll work out jes' fine." Both men tensed, ready to spring out of hiding.

Caroline opened the cloakroom door and was face to face with William Henderson.

For a moment she could only stare at his leering face. "What are you doing here?" she demanded. Then realization struck her. "*You* did this," she accused. "All that damage out there. But why?"

"Naw, I didn't do it," he said. He seemed amused rather than upset at the charge. "Couple of our partners did. Seems they don't have no respect for education." He guffawed at his own joke.

Our? "Well, I'm going to tell Mr. Thurgood," she said, turning to go, fear rapidly surpassing anger.

"You ain't goin' nowhere," Henderson told her. "That'd mess up our plan." He chuckled, and the sound sent ice sliding down her spine.

"Plan? What plan?" She wanted to run, but her muscles seemed limp.

"Our plan to teach *you* a lesson, Teacher," he said and lunged for her.

Even as his hands closed on her shoulders, she heard a scream. A little girl's scream, suddenly muffled.

Jack's heart was full of joy as he rode into Simpson Creek. After spending the afternoon praying and considering his decision, he had fallen asleep without difficulty and slept the night through.

Why had he ever made things so difficult? He loved Caroline, and if Gil was to be believed, she loved him. All his previous suppositions about Caroline and who she should or should not love didn't matter a hill of beans.

His mistake had been to let what his father thought of him matter more than what the Lord thought of him. His brother had loved him, and his men seemed to like him and certainly respected him—all but those two who had left—and, according to Gil, Caroline loved him. So maybe his father's opinion wasn't accurate. He'd been an idiot to let it affect his decisions all these years.

Well, that was over, starting now. He was going to ride right up to the Wallace house, tell Caroline he loved her and ask her to marry him. Then he'd take her to see her wedding present, the house. It wasn't too late for him to make any changes she deemed necessary.

But Caroline wasn't there when he got to the Wallaces'.

Dan answered his knock. "Hey, Jack, we were just comin' to see *you*," he said, gesturing to a basket which sat upon the kitchen table, "but then that windbag Thurgood showed up, an' I heard him tellin' Caroline she had t'come to the school with him to see something, and then I heard her leavin' with him. The girls must've gone, too, 'cause when I came into the parlor to see what was up, they weren't here."

Jack felt a spark of irritation. If that pompous fool had so much as made Caroline frown, he'd make him pay for it. And if the man had been the least bit unkind to his daughters, he'd bloody his nose. Well, perhaps he'd better trot over to the school and tell that churnhead Caroline didn't need the schoolmarm job because she was going to marry him.

He got back on his roan and was just tying up at the school hitching rail when the sound of a tremendous commotion within reached his ears. He heard a thud, as if something—or *somebody*—was being slammed against a wall. He heard glass shatter.

And then he heard her scream.

He took the steps in one leap.

The schoolroom was empty, but it looked as if a wild bull had charged through it. Then he heard sounds coming from behind the closed cloakroom door—sounds of a man's grunts of pain.

He threw open the door. A wild-eyed Caroline, her breaths coming in heaving gasps, her hair wild, her blouse torn at the neck, wielded a mop like a weapon, bringing it down again and again on the head and shoulders of a big man crouching on all fours who waved his arms above his head in a vain attempt to protect himself.

"Caroline! What's going on?" he shouted.

She whirled around, wild-eyed. "Henderson…" Caroline panted, pointing at the man on the floor. "He tried to…he tried to—" And then she collapsed in tears and ran to him.

"She's crazy…tried to kill me," muttered the man on the floor. "Needs to be locked up…"

"Liar! You attacked me!" Caroline cried, then put out a hand as Jack lunged toward the man on the floor. "Jack, never mind him—someone's taken your girls!"

Jack's blood froze right there in his veins. *"What are you saying?"*

"I—I'd sent the girls home to get Dan…and more cleaning supplies," she said. "I came in here, and found Henderson hiding…. He attacked me, and then I heard one of the girls scream outside…."

Jack was on Henderson in a heartbeat, yanking him to his feet, clutching his shirtfront. *"Where are my daughters? What do you know about them?"*

Henderson, one eye swelling shut, was stupid enough to smirk. "You'll never find 'em till you pay the ransom...."

Jack weighed less than Henderson, but a righteous fury surged through him. He felt angry enough to whip ten Hendersons. He threw him against a wall. *"Who's got them?"* he demanded, twisting the shirt collar as he yanked his Colt from its holster. "Tell me, or I'll shoot you right here and now."

Henderson's eyes crossed as he stared down the barrel of the pistol. Apparently he saw his peril at last, for new beads of sweat broke out on his forehead. "Your d-drovers," he said. "Your former drovers, th-that is."

The idea of his innocent children in the hands of those scoundrels made a red mist swim in front of his eyes. *"Which way were they going?"*

Henderson shrugged. Then, as Jack shoved the pistol into his belly, he began to blubber, "I dunno, I dunno! Don't shoot me. Thurgood said to hide 'em good—"

"Thurgood?" both Jack and Caroline cried at once. "Thurgood's in on this?" Jack rasped, his nose a scant inch from Henderson's.

Henderson nodded, eyes wide. "Don't shoot me...."

"Jack, you've got to go after them! Go! I can manage...." Carolyn cried, wielding the mop threateningly again at Henderson, who actually cringed.

There was no way he was going to leave her to keep Henderson at bay. He brought the butt of his pistol down, and the bigger man collapsed on the floor like a sack of rice with a big hole in it.

Jack turned back to Caroline. "Caroline, sweetheart—run to the sheriff," he said. "Tell him to have his deputy come collect Henderson. Tell Bishop to ride after me—"

"But which way are you going? How do you know which way they'll take?" she demanded.

"There's only two main roads going in and out of Simpson Creek," he said. "The one going south, past the ranch, and the one that heads east past the church and then turns north. They won't chance coming past the ranch. I'm figuring they'll take the east road."

"Okay," she said. She dashed ahead of him toward the door, then turned back. "But how on earth did you happen to come just in time like that? Thank God!"

"Amen to that. I came to tell you I loved you, and to ask you—" He stopped abruptly. He couldn't ask her now, in the shambles of the schoolhouse, when they were both frantic with worry about his girls. She deserved better than that. "I've got a question to be asking you, when I get back," he amended.

She stopped dead in her tracks and stared at him. She gave him the biggest smile he'd ever seen. "Then I'll be waiting."

He took her face quickly in his hands and kissed her. "Now, go, Caroline, hurry!"

"Go with God," she called over her shoulder as they both flew down the steps and into the schoolyard. *"I love you, too!"*

It was several hours later before Jack returned. Sheriff Bishop had galloped out of town heading east, while Deputy Menendez had followed Caroline back to school, handcuffed Henderson, who had just been beginning to come around, and hustled him to one of the jail cells. Then he'd escorted Caroline home, telling her he was going to ask Dr. Walker to come watch over the prisoner so he could ride out, too.

A shaky Caroline had worn out the parlor floor, pacing back and forth, weeping and praying, despite her mother's attempts to calm her. She kept going through the kitchen to the post office, so she could watch out the door for any sign of Jack. He'd be coming from the east....

And finally, just at dusk, she saw him approaching on his horse, flanked by Bishop and the deputy. His gelding moved slowly, and well it should, for he carried his daughters, who were sticking closer to him than two burrs on a saddle blanket. As they drew closer, she could see that Sheriff Bishop and his deputy each led another horse, and each led horse bore a sullen-looking man with his hands bound.

Jack reined in by the post office, and the sheriff and his deputy rode past, each nodding and touching the brim of his hat to her, their faces grim in victory.

The exhausted girls spotted her. "Aunt Caroline! Papa saved us!" Abby cried. And then Caroline waited no longer but went flying off the boardwalk to them, reaching the horse and his rider in time for him to lower first Amelia, then Abby to her. Behind them, Caroline's parents and brother watched, tears of joy in their eyes.

As soon as Jack dismounted, they all embraced together, crying and laughing and murmuring "Thank God!" and "I love you!" at once.

The rest of the Wallace family had gone to bed mysteriously early—right after the twins, in fact. Now Caroline and Jack found themselves alone in the parlor, and they couldn't have been happier about it.

Jack got directly to the point, for once the children

were safe, he'd thought of little else. "We have some unfinished business, Teacher," he began.

She began to smile. "Yes, we do, Jack."

Kneeling in front of her, he took her hand in his, the hand that wore the pearl ring. Gently, he drew it off her finger. "Pete gave you this, and now I'd like to give it to you again, from me."

The hand in his began to tremble, and she gazed into his eyes, her own shining with joy.

"Caroline, will you marry me?" he asked.

"Yes, I will, Jack," she said, her voice tremulous. "I love you so much!"

His own hand shook just a little as he slipped the ring back onto her finger, and then their lips met in a tender kiss full of promise.

"I've been asked to make an announcement before my father begins his sermon," Gil Chadwick announced the next morning at the Simpson Creek church. "In view of what happened yesterday, Caroline and Jack are spending some time together this morning. They have some matters to discuss—" he broke off and looked up, and smiled at the congregation "—regarding a wedding."

Slowly, as people began to grin, Gil smiled, too, and went on. "Today is the Sabbath, and we'll observe that, but tomorrow's been declared a school holiday, because the school needs to be cleaned and repaired. I think we ought to give the couple an early wedding present, don't you? Why don't each of us who are able show up at the school, sleeves rolled up, prepared to help?"

Now the applause was thunderous, with shouts of "I'll be there!" and "You can count on me, Preacher!" added in.

* * *

The sun shone as if winter was already vanquished as the buckboard rolled toward Collier's Roost. Today it seemed as if spring would come early to the Hill Country, and Caroline was more than ready.

"Bishop stopped by this morning to tell me the sheriff of San Saba has Thurgood in his jail," Jack murmured, clearly keeping his voice down so it wouldn't carry back to the bed of the wagon, where Abby and Amelia sat playing "wedding" with their dolls. Children were remarkably resilient, she thought; though they'd been scared out of their wits by their abduction yesterday, they seemed to have survived it with their spirits intact.

"After everything Henderson told him in an effort to save himself," Jack went on, "Bishop says there's more than enough to ensure Thurgood goes to prison right along with Henderson. Your county will be needing a new school superintendent."

"Thank God," Caroline said. She couldn't count the number of times she'd said that phrase since yesterday.

She knew Sheriff Bishop had gone to check on Billy Joe and Henderson's wife yesterday, and that he had taken them to stay with his wife. The mayor was going to give them enough money to resettle elsewhere if Mrs. Henderson wished, so Henderson couldn't find them when he got out from behind bars.

"We are so lucky, you and I…." Caroline murmured and smiled as Jack reached his hand across the seat to clasp hers.

They were nearly at the ranch. "Jack, I—I'll move to Montana, just as soon as you send for us," she said. "It sounds a little scary—the long trip and all, but—"

"You won't have to," he told her, as they pulled off the road and onto the dirt lane.

And then she saw it as they pulled onto the dirt lane of Collier's Roost—a ranch house, where the previous owner's house had once stood. It wasn't completed yet, she could tell, but it would be very fine when it was, with freestone walls and a shiny tin roof, two stories, where the Waters ranch house had been only one.

"Papa! You built a house!" the twins said, and were hopping down from the wagon as soon as it rolled to a stop.

"Why don't you go see it?" Jack told them. "Caroline and I'll be along in a minute."

They did as he had bid, shrieking in excitement, as the drovers emerged from the bunkhouse, grinning. When Jack hadn't returned last night, a couple of them had come into town to check on him, and he'd told them what had happened.

Caroline could only stare at the building, laughing. "When did you do this?"

"While I was trying to think of a way to be worthy of you. It took nearly all winter," he told her with a grin.

"You silly man!" she said and took hold of his face and kissed him. It wasn't the first time they'd kissed since yesterday, and it wouldn't be the last, but each time was wonderful beyond words.

"I'm staying right here, Caroline," he told her. "With you as my wife, and the twins, and as many more children God sees fit to bless us with."

They stopped and kissed again.

"But what about your teaching?" he asked her then, a furrow of concern showing on his brow. "I know it's important to you...."

"It is," she agreed. "But you'll be taking those cattle to Montana, won't you? I can finish the school year, at least, and then Louisa Wheeler can take over as schoolmarm.... Would you even be back before next fall?" Her smile faded somewhat as she thought of the months of waiting for him to return for her and praying he would make the journey safely.

"He's not goin' anywhere, ma'am. *I'm* drivin' those cattle—and to Kansas," Raleigh Masterson called down from an upstairs window of the house, paintbrush in hand. "It's a lot closer'n Montana. Then I'm coming back as Jack's foreman."

She turned from looking up at Raleigh and gazed at Jack. "Sounds as if you have it all figured out."

Jack grinned. "Now why don't we go have a look at the house? It's not done inside, so you have plenty of time to slap your own brand on it...."

Arm in arm, they strolled toward the house he had built for her.

* * * * *

Since 2002, *USA TODAY* bestselling author **Judy Duarte** has written over forty books for Harlequin Special Edition, earned two RITA® Award nominations, won two Maggie Awards and received a National Readers' Choice Award. When she's not cooped up in her writing cave, she enjoys traveling with her husband and spending quality time with her grandchildren. You can learn more about Judy and her books on her website, judyduarte.com, or at Facebook.com/judyduartenovelist.

Books by Judy Duarte

Harlequin Special Edition

Rocking Chair Rodeo

Roping in the Cowgirl
The Bronc Rider's Baby
A Cowboy Family Christmas
The Soldier's Twin Surprise
The Lawman's Convenient Family

The Fortunes of Texas: All Fortune's Children

Wed by Fortune

The Fortunes of Texas: The Secret Fortunes

From Fortune to Family Man

The Fortunes of Texas: The Rulebreakers

No Ordinary Fortune

Visit the Author Profile page
at Harlequin.com for more titles.

LONE WOLF'S LADY

Judy Duarte

Get rid of all bitterness, rage and anger, brawling and slander, along with every form of malice. Be kind and compassionate to one another, forgiving each other, just as in Christ God forgave you.

—*Ephesians* 4:31–32

To my editor, Susan Litman, for going above and beyond. Thank you for believing in me and this book.

Chapter One

Summer, 1884
Pleasant Valley, Texas

"Caroline Graves is dead. And your job is done."

Tom "Lone Wolf" McCain turned in his saddle, the leather creaking with his movement as he faced Trapper Jack, his crotchety old traveling companion. "She left a six-year-old daughter behind."

"And the kid's being raised by a woman who's known her since she was born." Trapper Jack lifted his battered hat and mopped his weathered brow with the dusty red flannel sleeve of the shirt he'd worn for the past several days. "What are you going to do? Uproot her?"

"If I have to." As Tom met the man's glare, he had to admit that when push came to shove, he wasn't sure what he'd do. But he owed it to Caroline to see to it that her daughter was safe and well cared for.

If only Harrison Graves had hired Tom to find his granddaughter six months earlier, Caroline might have been alive when he'd followed her trail to Taylorsville. Then Tom would have had a chance to talk to her. He might have convinced her to go back where she belonged, to her grandfather's ranch in Stillwater.

"You ought to just tell the old man that Caroline died," Trapper added, as he surveyed the typical Texas town that lay nestled in the valley below. "And let that be the end of it."

"Harrison Graves is looking for an heir."

Trapper spit a wad of tobacco to the side. "Seems to me that Graves isn't too fond of *illegitimate* heirs."

Tom knew that better than anyone. And he'd given that some thought, too. After all, when Harrison had learned that his granddaughter was with child, he'd sent her to Mexico to have her baby, instructing her to leave it there. And he'd never mentioned anything to Tom about searching for the baby Caroline was supposed to have left behind in a Mexican orphanage—he'd only wanted his granddaughter back.

So how would the dying cattleman feel when Tom returned with Caroline's illegitimate child in tow? Would that appease him? Would he rewrite his will, leaving everything to the little girl? Or would he insist that Tom leave her where he'd found her?

Maybe Trapper was right. Maybe Caroline's daughter was better off not going back to Stillwater.

But was she better off being raised by a fallen woman?

From what Tom had gathered in Mexico, Caroline had run off with a former prostitute from Pleasant Valley. For the next few years, she'd managed to keep her friend on the straight and narrow—or so it seemed. But after Caroline had died, the woman had returned to the only other life she'd known, taking the child with her.

That might be true, but something didn't sit right. In fact, a lot of things just didn't add up.

"He could have hired any number of bounty hunters to search for his runaway granddaughter," Trapper said. "Why'd it have to be you?"

Tom wasn't sure why Harrison had summoned him, other than his reputation for being good at finding people who didn't want to be found.

"That old man doesn't deserve the time of day from you," Trapper added. "Not after all he did to make your life miserable. I still can't believe you'd even consider working for him."

"I'm not doing this for Harrison Graves." Nor was he doing it for the money. Yet when the wealthy cattleman had handed him the twenty-dollar gold piece, Tom had pocketed the coin rather than explain why he would have agreed to search for Caroline on principle alone.

Trapper chuffed. "I still think you're making a big mistake, kid. And I'm not about to sit around and watch you make a fool of yourself. I'm going back to Hannah's place. We've been away too long as it is."

"No one asked you to come along in the first place, Trapper. In fact, if you recall, I tried to talk you out of it, but you insisted."

"That's only because someone's got to look out for you, because no matter how much book learnin' you've had, you ain't got a thimbleful of common sense."

Tom sighed and squinted into the afternoon sun. He owed a lot to Trapper. That was a fact. But sometimes the old man forced gratitude to the breaking point.

Trapper grumbled under his breath, then said, "You can't blame me for worryin' about you. I've been lookin' after you ever since you was knee-high to a timber wolf."

If truth be told, Tom had no idea where he'd be today if the old man hadn't stumbled upon him about twenty miles outside of Stillwater when he'd been sick, starving and scared.

No, Tom owed his life to the man who hadn't been afraid to take in an orphaned ten-year-old with mixed blood and treat him like the son he'd never had.

"Suit yourself," Trapper said, turning his horse around.

Tom urged his mount forward, onto the road that ran down the hill, through the middle of town and continued along the boardwalk-lined main street, with its typical lineup of businesses—a good-size mercantile, a bank, a small laundry and a saloon.

His plan was to speak to the sheriff first. So he scanned both sides of the street, looking for the jail. He spotted it up ahead, next to the newspaper office, where, just outside the door, an attractive young woman with auburn hair pulled into a topknot studied the open periodical in her hand, her brow furrowed.

She was a pretty one, he noted. And curious, too. Otherwise, she would have waited to take the newspaper home to read it. He wondered what bit of news had caught her eye and held her interest.

Across the street, a group of boys snagged Tom's attention as they gathered around a small girl, taunting her. Most people didn't give much thought to childish squabbles, thinking that kids usually worked things out without adult interference. But Tom wasn't so sure about that. Probably because, more often than not, he'd found himself on the wrong end of a fistfight meant to "teach that half-breed a lesson" when he'd been in school.

And something about this one didn't seem right— or fair.

He pulled back on the reins and slowed his mount,

just as a tall, towheaded kid shoved the little blonde girl into the dusty street.

Before he could turn his horse in the direction of the bullies, the woman on the boardwalk called out, "Silas Codwell! You ought to be ashamed of yourself." Then she tucked the periodical she'd been reading under her arm and marched across the street in a huff.

The other boys froze, both startled and admonished by her arrival, but the ringleader, who was nearly twice the size of the girl, merely crossed his arms and shifted his weight to one hip.

The petite woman glared at the kid she'd called Silas as though she wanted to throttle him, and Tom knew just how she felt. He'd like to put a little fear of God into that one himself.

So he nudged his horse in the direction of the scuffle, ready to step in if the bully gave the redhead any trouble.

As if unfazed by Silas and his bluster, the lady bent to help the tiny heap of blue calico to her feet. "Are you all right, honey?"

The little girl, her bottom lip bloody and quivering, her light blue hair ribbons drooping from where they'd once adorned two blond braids, nodded.

Then the redhead turned to Silas, her eyes narrowed, her finger raised. "You're nearly thirteen years old. Shoving a small girl into the street is brutal and inexcusable. Apologize this instant."

The other boys began to edge away from her, but Silas only shrugged. "I don't know why you're so all fired—"

The redhead grabbed his ear and twisted until he cried out, "Ow! You aren't our teacher anymore. You'd better let go of me or my father will—"

Clearly undeterred by his threat, the redhead twisted

harder until the boy screeched out "I'm...sorry" in a long, drawn-out whine.

The lady, with her cheeks flushed and her eyes sparked with ire, released the boy's ear, just as Tom's shadow eclipsed them both.

Only then did Silas appear the least bit remorseful.

"You owe the lady and the child a real apology," Tom said. "I saw what you did. There was no excuse for it, boy."

Silas opened his mouth, as if he had something to say in his defense. Then, after his gaze locked on Tom's, his stance relaxed and he relented. "I'm sorry, Miss O'Malley. It won't happen again."

The lady, apparently the schoolmarm at one time, stood as tall as her petite stature would allow. "See that it doesn't."

Silas nodded, then, after a quick glance at Tom, took off to join his friends.

Tom's gaze turned to Miss O'Malley, whose rolled newspaper had fallen to the ground.

She glanced at it, but before reaching to pick it up, she said, "Thank you, Mr....?"

"McCain."

She nodded, then released a pent-up sigh. "You'd never know it, but Silas's father is the minister."

"No, ma'am. You're right. I would have expected his father to be the town drunkard. Or maybe to hear that he'd been locked up in jail for the past ten years."

She clucked her tongue. "Silas has a mean, spiteful side to him that his parents refuse to see. I taught school here in Pleasant Valley up until last summer and watched that boy bully the other children many a time." She bit down on her bottom lip, as if she might be wondering if she'd shared too much with a stranger.

Her hands rested on the little girl's shoulders in a loving, protective manner.

Satisfied that the child was in good hands, Tom doffed his hat. "Good day, Miss O'Malley."

Then he urged the gelding across the street and on to the sheriff's office, where he planned to ask a couple of questions and get directions to a place known as the Gardener's House.

He might look like an uneducated half-breed, but he knew better than to ask a lady where he could find the town brothel.

Katie O'Malley held on to Sarah Jane's shoulders as she watched the dark-haired stranger ride away.

The man was frightfully handsome, with eyes the color of fine bourbon, high cheekbones and a square-cut chin. His copper-colored skin suggested he might have a mixed-Indian heritage. And for the first time in her life, she found herself more than a little awestruck by a man's appearance, especially one who spent his days in a saddle.

Mr. McCain wasn't the type of man she usually had reason to talk to—or the type she should find the least bit attractive. Yet she did.

She supposed that was because he'd come to her rescue, even though she hadn't needed him to. She did, however, appreciate the gallant way he'd made the gesture.

He'd studied her in a curious way, which had caused her pause. Then he'd simply said, "Good day," turned his mount and headed down the street.

She wondered what business he had in town. Unable to quell her curiosity, she watched him go until he stopped at the sheriff's office, where he left his big bay gelding tied out in front.

When he was finally out of sight, Katie returned her attention to the disheveled little girl.

"What are you doing in town all by yourself?" Katie asked.

"Blossom gave me a penny, and I wanted to buy a peppermint stick. I was going to wait for someone to take me to the mercantile, but then Sweet Heather told me to go outside and stay out of the way."

"Where's Daisy?"

"She wasn't feeling good, so she went to take a nap. But she's probably in the kitchen now. It's her turn to cook dinner."

Katie pulled a lace-edged handkerchief from her reticule and placed it on the little girl's small, bloodied lip, gently dabbing at the wound. She'd championed many causes in the past, but none had touched her heart as deeply as Sarah Jane Potts.

It was time once again to talk to Daisy and insist that the woman either agree to leave with Katie for Wyoming next week or that she allow Sarah Jane to go without her.

After adjusting the ribbons in the little girl's hair, Katie took her by the hand. "Come on, honey. I'll walk you home."

While they made their way to the brothel at the far edge of town, they talked about important things, like why dogs chased cats and why staring into the sun made a person sneeze.

It hadn't taken many chance visits with Sarah Jane for Katie to realize that she was an absolute delight, and the more time she spent with the charming child, the more she longed to rescue her.

As they stepped off the boardwalk and ventured to the outskirts of town, past several lots that were overgrown with weeds and littered with debris, they made their way to the green-and-white three-story structure that served as a brothel. People referred to it as the Gardener's House, a name that seemed fitting because of its park-like grounds, manicured lawn and rows of marigolds leading to a wraparound porch.

If one didn't know better, one would think that it was a respectable home owned by a wealthy family. But Katie knew better.

Her steps slowed as they neared the ornate wrought-iron gate, and her hold on the child's hand tightened. She took a quick scan of her surroundings, hoping to avoid being seen by a witness prone to gossip. As it was, her welcome in Pleasant Valley had worn thin, thanks in large part to the newspaper articles she wrote in favor of women's rights. And she'd been hard-pressed to find many upstanding citizens willing to write the letters of recommendation she needed to provide the school board in Granville, a growing town in the Wyoming Territory desperate for a schoolteacher.

Sarah Jane tugged at Katie's hand. "Come on. Daisy made a swing for me in the backyard. I want you to see it."

The child led Katie around to the rear of the house and pointed to an elm tree where two lengths of rope and a wooden slat hung from a sturdy branch.

"See?" Sarah Jane said. "Want to watch me swing?"

"Not yet. I'd like to talk to Daisy first."

The sooner she could speak to the fallen dove and get back to a more respectable part of town, the better.

"Let's see if she's in the kitchen," Sarah Jane said.

As they climbed the steps to the rear entrance, Katie's heart began to pound.

Fortunately, after Sarah Jane opened the door and entered the kitchen, they found Daisy seated at the big oak table, snapping green beans.

Daisy, a dark-haired woman with a fair complexion, first glanced at Katie, her big green eyes leery.

When she spotted Sarah Jane's swollen lip, she gasped and scooted back her chair. Then she got to her feet and crossed the kitchen. As she reached the girl, she dropped to her knees. "What in the world happened, sweetie?"

"That big boy named Silas said mean things to me again. And this time he hurt me, but Katie made him stop."

Daisy tensed, then brushed a wisp of hair from the child's face. "Boys can be mean."

They certainly could. While growing up, Katie had suffered a few taunts of her own. She knew what it felt like to be different from the other children, to be singled out in the classroom for not paying attention because she'd had her nose in a book when she was supposed to be drawing a map of Missouri. Or to be teased on the schoolyard because she'd never had a mother to teach her how to properly braid her curly red hair.

But those jeers, while hurtful and humiliating at times, were nothing in comparison to the ones Sarah Jane stood to face if she continued to live in Brighton Valley.

Daisy's gaze lifted and met Katie's. "Thank you for seeing her home."

But her *home* is a *brothel,* Katie wanted to shout. She bit her tongue, instead, unwilling to offend the woman before she could convince her to see reason.

She couldn't hold back her thoughts, though. Couldn't Daisy see the damage she was doing to the little girl by having her live here?

Katie's first impulse was to argue her case, which was a good one. But it wouldn't do her a bit of good to speak her mind if she wanted to convince Daisy to sign over guardianship to her or to leave the brothel behind and move to Granville.

"I don't think Sarah Jane should go outside without an adult present," Katie said, minding her tone and choosing her words carefully.

"She isn't allowed to go out alone." Daisy cupped the child's face. "You know better than that."

"I'm a big girl now." Sarah Jane stood tall, while a swollen, cut lip and traces of blood and dirt on her cheek mocked her self-confidence. "I'm *six.* Remember? I had my birthday when we lived at the other house with Mama."

"You know the rules." Daisy got back on her feet, then made her way to the sink, reached for a cloth and dipped it into a bowl of water. "Come here, sweetie. Let me wash your face."

Katie watched the woman's maternal motions, which demonstrated that she certainly cared about the child. Still, why had they moved into the brothel the very first day they'd arrived in town? Surely Daisy realized that no good could ever come of a decision like that.

"Wyoming is a beautiful territory," Katie said, preparing to state her case one more time. "I'd love to take you and Sarah Jane with me. You could make a new start in a territory where women are treated with dignity and respect, where they're considered equals. In fact, they even have the right to vote."

They'd had this conversation before, with Daisy clearly struggling with the decision.

"A move to a new community is sorely tempting," Daisy said.

"Think of the future Sarah Jane will have if she continues to live in a place like this."

"I have." Daisy bit down on her bottom lip. Then she placed a gentle, loving hand on the child's head. "Sarah Jane, why don't you go into our room and look in the closet. I hid a surprise for you there. It's next to your mama's carpetbag."

When Sarah Jane dashed off to do as she was told, Daisy returned to her seat at the table and pushed the bowl of green beans aside. "Sarah Jane's mother was like a sister to me. I'd be dead if it wasn't for her. And I love Sarah Jane as if she were my own. After the funeral, when she and I left Taylorsville, we didn't have a penny to our names. Please believe me when I say that I don't plan to work here very long. I just need to earn enough money to repay a debt. Then we can make a new start in a town far away from here, where people won't know me."

Now that she knew what had been causing Daisy to hesitate, Katie was finally able to formulate a convincing plan, thanks to the inheritance she'd invested wisely. "If you'll leave with me, I'll help you pay that debt. And I promise that you'll find that new life you're looking for in the Wyoming Territory."

"That sounds promising, Miss O'Malley. But why would you do this for me? You don't even know me.

Pardon me for asking, but what are you? Some kind of church do-gooder, bent on saving my soul? You have no idea how many people have tried that, including Sarah Jane's mother, but I'm afraid my soul is already lost."

A smile tugged at Katie's lips.

Daisy cocked her heard, clearly perplexed. "What's so funny?"

"There are a few church do-gooders in town who think *I'm* the lost soul."

"You?" Daisy's eyes widened, and she all but laughed.

"Actually, some of the townsfolk don't like me speaking my mind about a lot of things, especially women's equality. In fact, I've even had a few run-ins with the minister, who went so far as to complain to the Pleasant Valley school board, which resulted in my being replaced as the schoolteacher last fall."

"They replaced you because you believe women should be allowed to vote?"

"Well, the good reverend also complained that I couldn't control the children, although that wasn't true. It was only his son who gave me trouble. And if I'd had the least bit of paternal support—" Katie bit back the rest of her angry retort and clucked her tongue. "Anyway, needless to say, it's been nearly impossible for me to attend services on Sundays with a joyful heart. So I wouldn't call myself a church do-gooder."

Daisy arched a brow, fresh suspicion etched across her face, which was far prettier today without all the powder and paint she usually wore.

"It's not that I don't read my Bible or believe in God, it's just that I…" Katie blew out a sigh, not sure how to explain herself—or why she even felt the need to. "You see, I've always been a champion of the downtrodden. And when I take up a cause, I'm rather out-spoken about it."

"I see. So Sarah Jane and I have become one of your *causes*."

Katie wished she'd chosen different words. "I wouldn't put it that way. It's just that Sarah Jane is a bright, beautiful child. She deserves a better future. And, Daisy, so do *you*. You must be a smart, resourceful woman to have come so far on your own. But neither of you will get that if you stay in Pleasant Valley, even if you move out of the Gardener's House and try to make it on your own. So I'm offering you both a way out. That is, if you'll take a step of faith and go with me when I leave for Wyoming next week."

Had Katie said too much, pushed too hard? She hoped not, but the words had come straight from her heart.

Daisy seemed to ponder her options for a moment, then said, "The debt is sixty dollars. I've already managed to save twenty-three. If you're willing to pay off the balance for me, as well as provide traveling expenses, I'll go with you to Wyoming. Then, as soon as I'm able to find work, I'll begin to repay you."

"You have yourself a deal." Katie reached out her arm, and the two women shook hands.

Daisy glanced around the kitchen and smiled. "I'm actually a pretty good cook. Maybe I can find work at a restaurant in Wyoming."

Before Katie could respond, a knock sounded at the back door, and her heart lurched, then railed against her chest wall as if trying to break free. The last thing she needed was to be seen by one of Daisy's "callers."

Katie didn't usually put much stock in what others thought of her, but she had reason to be cautious now.

Thanks to Reverend Codwell and a few other more conservative citizens of Pleasant Valley, she was running out of people to approach for those letters she needed for the school board, and she couldn't show up in Granville empty-handed. So the instinct to escape was strong.

But unless she wanted to run through the brothel and go out the front, the only other possibility was the kitchen exit, which was now blocked.

Daisy crossed the room and swung open the door, revealing Mr. McCain, the handsome, dark-haired cowboy Katie and Sarah Jane had met on the street. His dark-eyed gaze snaked around her, nearly squeezing her heart right out of her.

Surely he didn't think she belonged here, did he?

About the time she feared that he did, he turned and gazed at the fallen woman. "I'm looking for Daisy Potts."

Chapter Two

"I'm Daisy. What can I do for you?"

After Tom had talked to Sheriff Droeger and had his suspicions confirmed, he'd learned that a child named Sarah Jane and a woman now going by the name of Daisy Potts had moved into the Gardener's House a few months ago. Because the sheriff said Daisy did most of the cooking and cleaning at the brothel, Tom had decided to bypass the front door and use the rear entrance.

He hadn't been surprised when Daisy answered his knock, but the red-haired schoolmarm standing in the kitchen like she owned the place knocked him completely off stride.

Of course, Miss O'Malley appeared to be more than a little surprised by his arrival, too.

"I'm afraid I need to leave now," she told Daisy. "But I'll be back on Saturday morning. We can talk about our trip to Wyoming then."

Tom had no idea what the two women planned to do in the Wyoming territory, but they wouldn't be taking Sarah Jane with them until he was convinced that she wasn't Caroline's daughter.

If he had reason to believe the girl was Caroline's child, she was going with him to Stillwater, where she belonged.

Of course, that was assuming that Harrison Graves had really softened and would actually claim an illegitimate child as his heir. And, to be honest, Tom had his doubts.

Miss O'Malley glanced his way one more time, her eyes as blue as the Texas sky.

She was a pretty one; that was a fact. And judging by the starched cotton blouse she wore buttoned to her chin, she didn't belong in the same room with one of the women who worked at the Gardener's House and, according to the sheriff, went by flower names.

She watched him doe-eyed, like a fawn sighting a man from across a thicket, curious yet ready to bolt at the slightest movement. Then she seemed to rally her courage.

"Good day," she said, as stiff and proper as the schoolmarm she'd once been.

He gave her a slight nod as she pushed past him, then watched as she let herself out.

When the door snapped shut behind her, he returned his gaze to Daisy.

The fallen woman, who was attractive in her own right, appeared to be in her early twenties and about the same age as the schoolmarm. "How can I help you?" she asked again.

"I was sent by Harrison Graves to find his granddaughter, Caroline. And my search led me here."

Daisy stiffened. "I don't know what you're talking about."

"I've been to Casa de Los Angelitos," Tom said,

"where you and Caroline met. And I followed her trail to several different towns in Texas, ending up in Taylorsville, where you both lived for the past year. You went by the name of Erin Kelly back then and worked as a cook at the restaurant until the owner went out of business. Caroline was a clerk at the hotel."

Daisy drew back but didn't deny it. Finally, she said, "If you're looking for Caroline, she's not here. She died a few months back."

"I know. And she's survived by a daughter, a girl who'd be about six years old now."

Before he decided how much to divulge of what he already knew, the child who'd been bullied on the town street entered the kitchen, carrying a handmade rag doll, and approached Daisy.

Tom hadn't noticed a resemblance to Caroline before, although he hadn't thought to even look for one. But he studied her carefully now.

Her blond hair was a bit darker than her mother's, more the color of sunflowers than fresh-churned butter. Yet there were other similarities—green eyes, a turned-up nose.

The fairness of her skin, too, which had made young Caroline appear to be angelic to a boy with mixed blood.

Had she also inherited her mother's kind heart, the inner beauty that had allowed Caroline to befriend the boy known as Tom Lone Wolf when so many others in Stillwater had turned their backs on him?

Daisy reached for Sarah Jane and drew her close. "I'm afraid I'm not able to talk to you now, so you'll have to leave."

Tom wasn't about to get into specifics in front of the child. Nor did he want to tip his hand about a possible inheritance at this point, especially with a woman who clearly could be purchased.

"I brought the child a gift," he said. "May I give it to her?"

Sarah Jane looked up at Daisy, her eyes wide, seeking approval. Finally, it came with a nod.

Tom reached inside his vest pocket and pulled a pair of beaded moccasins, as well as a small medicine bag he'd made for her when he'd learned Caroline had not only borne a daughter but kept her.

"When I was a boy," he said, "I knew a little girl who looked a lot like you. Her name was Caroline Graves. And one day, she did something very brave. As a reward for her bravery, my mother made her a pair of moccasins just like these."

"Thank you," Sarah Jane said, as she reached for the soft deerskin gifts. "That was my mama's name."

"I thought that it might be."

The girl studied the handmade shoes and the medicine bag, then gazed at Tom. "What did she do that was brave?"

"She saw a grown man being mean to an Indian boy, and she told him to get off her ranch and to never come back."

Sarah Jane's eyes grew wide. "What did the man do to her?"

"He was afraid that she'd tell her grandfather, Harrison Graves, who was a very powerful man. So he left the boy alone."

Daisy glanced down at the child, then at a bowl of green beans that sat on the kitchen table and back to Tom. "Thank you for your gifts, Mr. McCain. And for sharing the story. But I meant what I said. Now isn't a good time to talk."

"It won't take long. I just want to ask you a few questions and get some honest answers." Tom reached into his pocket and pulled out the twenty-dollar gold piece Harrison had given him. "Would this be enough to tempt you to find the time?"

Daisy's eyes, while wary, studied the coin for only a moment. "Come back Thursday morning. Most of the girls sleep in. If you come around eight, I'll be in the kitchen. And I'll have a pot of coffee on the stove."

"Fair enough."

Again his gaze settled on little Sarah Jane. Would Harrison see a resemblance to her mother? If so, would he take that into consideration?

Would he be pleased to learn that Tom had found Caroline's daughter? Or would he cast out the illegitimate child, just as he'd done to Caroline when he'd learned she was pregnant without a husband in sight?

Time would tell, he supposed, but first things first. In two days, he'd have to convince Daisy to let Sarah Jane go with him back to the Lazy G.

And if Daisy didn't agree?

He'd take her anyway. Caroline's daughter didn't belong in a place like this. And Tom wasn't about to leave her here.

On Friday morning, Katie hurried down the boardwalk to the newspaper office, her skirts swishing with each brisk step she took. She intended to pick up her copy of the *Pleasant Valley Journal* fresh off the press, just as she always did.

As she opened the front door, a bell tinkled to let the clerk know she'd arrived.

The bespectacled young man glanced up from his desk. When he spotted Katie, he smiled. "Here to read the latest rebuttal to your last article, Miss O'Malley?"

"Yes, Harold." Katie slipped off her gloves and tucked them into her reticule. "What does Reverend Codwell have to say this time?"

"He doesn't mention any new arguments, if that's what you mean." Harold adjusted his eyeglasses, pushed his swivel chair away from the desk and got to his feet.

While he went for her copy, Katie scanned the small office, breathing in the scent of ink and admiring the intricate machinery that worked the printing press. She'd actually considered the idea of becoming a reporter or even an editor herself. Edward Townsend, Harold's boss, had once offered her a job, but he'd told her she'd have to temper some of her outspoken comments if she wanted to work for him.

Katie, of course, had refused to do that.

Noticing the publisher wasn't around, she asked about him. "Where's Edward?"

"He went to visit…" Harold flushed a brilliant shade of scarlet, then adjusted his shirt collar. "Um… I'm not sure where he is."

Katie placed her hands on the countertop and leaned forward. "Harold Decker, you're holding something back. Why is that? What don't you want to tell me?"

"I'm sorry, Miss O'Malley. I shouldn't have mentioned it. It just isn't proper."

Katie arched a brow. "Where is this improper visit taking place?"

Harold ran a hand over his slicked-down hair, then

looked at Katie as though he wanted her either to ask someone else or to forget the question completely, but she wasn't about to do that.

She crossed her arms like a parent scolding an errant child. *"Harold?"*

"Oh, for goodness' sake. Edward went to see…one of the women from…um…the Gardener's House. She was assaulted and nearly killed yesterday."

Katie's hands unfolded and slipped to her sides. "What happened?"

Harold's ruddy cheeks grew a deeper shade of red with each tick of the clock. "Why don't you ask Edward when he gets back? I don't feel right talking to you about it."

"You might as well tell me. There will be an article in the paper, and we both know that Reverend Codwell will be proclaiming it from the pulpit. You heard him bring up Miss Potts and Sarah Jane last week, which caused a rash of public outrage against the woman and the child."

"You're right, I suppose." He ambled toward the counter and sighed. "And I certainly hope that didn't have anything to do with the assault."

"Why would it?"

"Because Daisy was the one who was attacked."

The unexpected news slammed into Katie like a hammer on a blacksmith's anvil. "Oh, no. At the brothel?"

"No, while she was coming to town to do some shopping at the mercantile."

"Who attacked her?"

"No one knows. The little girl was the only witness, but she's not talking. Doc Hennessy says the child is in shock."

"Dear Lord," Katie whispered out loud, as she launched

into a silent prayer. *Please look after Sarah Jane until I can get to her.*

"Don't worry," Harold added. "There's a group of concerned citizens who plan to take the child away from there and put her in an orphanage. Anything would be better than being where she is right now."

A thousand thoughts swirled in Katie's head, the foremost being the need to protect little Sarah Jane. She eyed Harold carefully. "What time do you expect Edward to return?"

"I'm not sure. After checking on Daisy, he was going over to the saloon to take up a collection for her. She's a nice woman." Harold stiffened. "I mean, she's nice for a…" He cleared his throat, then chuffed. "Oh, never mind."

Katie ignored the man's discomfort. Her only concern was for Sarah Jane. Daisy had already agreed to go to Wyoming. After all, she couldn't very well change her mind about leaving now.

Either way, Sarah Jane needed a champion, someone who would take her far away from this unforgiving town, someone who wouldn't allow her to be placed in an orphanage.

And Katie was just the one to do it.

As she turned on her heel and strode for the door, Harold called out, "Miss O'Malley, you forgot your newspaper."

"I'll get it later." Katie slammed the door behind her, nearly jarring the little bell off its perch.

She wasn't sure what the townspeople would say when she announced that she would be the one adopting Sarah Jane, particularly if the Reverend Codwell stepped in to raise a fuss, but she was taking Sarah Jane and Daisy to Wyoming.

And she was prepared to fight anyone who stood in her way.

Tom nursed a cup of coffee while he sat in the red-and-gold parlor of the Gardener's House, waiting for a chance to see Daisy again. The doctor was with her now, and as soon as he was finished with his exam, Tom planned to take her and Sarah Jane to a place they'd be safe.

The attack had been brutal. And there'd been no reason for it. Daisy had been on her way to the mercantile. Sarah Jane had been with her. At some point, she'd screamed. Blossom, one of the other women at the brothel, had heard her and come running. She'd fired a shot at the man, and he'd fled before anyone could get a good look at him.

Daisy, who'd been battered senseless, had no recollection of the assault. When Sarah Jane was asked if she could describe the man who'd attacked them, she'd shaken her head no. One day later, and she still hadn't uttered a single word.

The doctor said the little girl, who bore bruises along one of her arms, had been traumatized. Poor little thing. Tom had no idea what her life had been like so far, but losing her mother so young…and now this.

He reached into his pocket and pulled out his gold watch. What was taking the doctor so long? He was hoping to get out of town as soon as Daisy was able to travel. Unfortunately, Daisy couldn't mount a horse in her condition, even if she'd wanted to. And since Tom couldn't rid himself of the suspicion that the attacker had intended to kill Daisy for some reason and might want to follow them so he could finish what he'd started, it would be difficult to hide their wagon tracks.

Something else niggled at him, too. Something that could be a coincidence. But why had the two women moved so many times since meeting in Mexico? Had they been running from someone?

Too bad Trapper Jack had already gone home. Tom could have used the man's help today, even if he would have had to listen to his infernal jabbering and advice.

To make matters worse, Tom also had to look after Sarah Jane. And as much as he wanted to do right by Caroline's daughter, he didn't know squat about kids—especially little girls. And Daisy wasn't going to be much help since she couldn't even see to her own needs right now.

The doctor didn't think her skull had been fractured by the blows to her head, but she'd suffered a serious concussion.

If that weren't enough, that safe place he had in mind was a three-day ride from here.

Needless to say, Tom was growing too antsy to sit any longer. So he stuffed his father's gold watch back into his pocket and got to his feet. He might as well do something useful, like head to the livery and get that wagon. But before he could cross the room, a sharp rap sounded at the door.

Sweet Heather, a plump blonde wearing a black, low-cut gown, sashayed toward the entry. "I'm comin', sugar."

As she swung open the door and a familiar redhead strode into the parlor with a determined step, her smile drooped to a frown and her hand fisted against her hip.

This ought to be interesting, Tom thought, as he studied the lady who was clearly out of place.

Afternoon sunlight peered through the front window and glistened upon her red hair, highlighting shades of fire and autumn. Expressive blue eyes blazed in a passionate array of emotions—worry, concern, nervous indignation, he guessed.

In spite of the modest apparel, he had to admit that she intrigued him far more than any of the women who lived and worked at the Gardener's House.

As she scanned the parlor, the room grew still and intense with silent fury, like the air before a Texas twister.

"You again?" Sweet Heather asked. "What do you want this time?"

The redhead swept past her. "I just heard what happened. I came to see Sarah Jane and to talk to Daisy."

Sweet Heather crossed her arms under her ample bust. "I told you before. You aren't welcome here, so you'd better skedaddle."

"I'm not leaving until I see them."

Sweet Heather laughed heartily, her bosom bouncing like a bowl of calf's-foot jelly. "Then I guess you'll be here for a long, long time."

"I can wait." The redhead surveyed the room. When her gaze moved to Tom and recognition sparked, her breath caught.

Tom had to admit she had guts. Most decent women would rather drop dead than walk into a place like this.

"I told you to *go*," Sweet Heather bellowed, her face reddening, her mouth set in grim determination. "We lost two customers the last time you came here."

Sweet Heather looked like a ruckus ready to happen, and if the lady knew what was best for her she'd leave now.

Miss O'Malley didn't flinch. Instead, she strode deeper into the parlor, her head still held high. "Then I'll wait for someone to tell me where to find Sarah Jane."

Sweet Heather closed the gap between them. "You'll get out even if I have to pick you up and throw you out myself."

About that time, the women who'd gathered at the top of the stairs began to file down the steps.

Realizing things could get out of hand, Tom made his way to the lady. "Miss O'Malley, I think you'd better leave. Sweet Heather would actually favor a fight."

Miss O'Malley stood a bit taller, if that was possible. "I appreciate your concern, Mr. McCain, but I'm not going to leave until I'm ready to do so. And that's not going to happen unless someone tells me where I can find Sarah Jane."

Tom scanned the length of her. He could throw her over his shoulder and force her to leave, but it really wasn't any of his business.

How involved did he want to get?

He figured he might as well head to the livery stable.

As he made his way to the door, Sweet Heather called out to him. "Where are you going, handsome?"

Tom stopped long enough to turn and say, "I'll be back."

But that didn't seem to appease Sweet Heather, because she grabbed a vase and threw it at Miss O'Malley, who ducked just in the nick of time.

As the glass shattered on the floor, Sweet Heather looked as smug as a fat cat with its paw pressed down on a mouse's tail. "The next thing I break will be your teeth."

Tom sighed heavily. He sensed a real fight coming, and, in spite of his better judgment, he sauntered toward the redhead, lifted her feet off the floor and threw her across his shoulder like a sack of grain.

He'd been prepared for the weight of her—but not the delicate scent of lilac on her clothes and hair.

"Put me down this instant," she cried, her words coming out in raspy shrieks. She kicked her feet and pounded her fists on his back like an ornery cougar kit that had been caught and placed in an empty feed sack.

As feisty as the former schoolmarm was, she might actually hold her own in a tussle with Sweet Heather.

He wrapped one arm around her knees and tried to still her flailing legs as he carried her outside and down the porch steps to the lawn in front of the brothel.

"I said, put me down!" she shrieked.

"Stop fighting me and I will."

She took a deep breath, then groaned in exasperation before ceasing her struggle. He took in one last whiff of lilac, then lowered her to the ground. As he did so, she slid down the front of him, leaving them both standing in awkward silence.

Their eyes locked, and for one brief moment, something passed between them, something that stirred the senses. But Tom didn't have time to lose his focus.

He cleared his throat. "I'm sorry, ma'am, but your presence was creating more trouble than either of us need. Now get out of here before the sheriff is called and your reputation is in shreds."

"I don't give a fig about my reputation right now. I'm

going back in there, even if I have to climb in a window or slip down the chimney."

If that were the case, Tom would either have to let her go—or wrestle her himself. And right now, tangling with her any more than he already had didn't seem to be a wise option. Still, maybe he could ease her mind and send her on her way.

"Don't worry about Sarah Jane," he said. "I'm taking her someplace safe."

"That's not necessary. I already have plans to take her and Daisy to Wyoming just as soon as Daisy has recovered enough to travel. They'll both be able to make a fresh start there. Daisy will find respectable work, and Sarah Jane will have…well, rest assured that I'll provide her with opportunities she'd never have otherwise."

Tom lifted his hat, then readjusted it on his head. "First off, I don't think it's in either of their best interests to remain in town long enough for Daisy to recover fully. And, secondly, while I appreciate your concern for the child, I have reason to believe that she has family in Stillwater."

That gave Miss O'Malley pause. "You have *reason* to believe? You're not sure?"

Actually, he knew that she had a great-grandfather. But he wasn't convinced the dying old man would welcome her with open arms. "Let's just say that I'm sure enough."

The schoolmarm seemed to think on that, and as she did, she worried her lip. All the while, the sun continued to shine on her hair, dancing upon the glossy strands.

The autumn color was remarkable. Tom wondered what it looked like when she removed the pins, brushed out the tresses and let them hang long.

When she finally glanced up, her expressive eyes, the shade of bluebonnets, caught his. "But if she has a family, where have they been all her life? Why is she living in a place like this?"

"I'm still trying to figure out how that might have come about." He'd tried to talk to Daisy earlier, but her throat had been badly bruised by the near strangling. The doctor had given her something for pain and to help her rest, and she'd dozed off before he could get anything out of her.

"What if that family Sarah Jane supposedly has doesn't want her?" Miss O'Malley asked.

He'd thought of that possibility more than he dared to admit. "I don't know. I'll think of something."

Apparently, that wasn't enough to appease her, because she crossed her arms and lifted her chin in defiance. "I won't let you take Sarah Jane anywhere."

Tom snorted at her hollow challenge. "I wouldn't recommend fighting with me, Miss O'Malley."

She studied him a moment, as if calculating the odds, then softened her stance. "Daisy is Sarah Jane's guardian. And the two of us have reached an agreement. We're taking Sarah Jane to Wyoming."

"Daisy also goes by the name of Erin Kelly," he said. "Did you know that?"

A twitch at the corner of a single blue eye suggested that she didn't, yet she brushed off his comment. "I'm not surprised. I didn't think her name was actually Daisy Potts."

"There's a lot you don't know."

She stiffened. "I'm sure that's true. Nevertheless, Daisy—or whatever name she'd prefer to go by—has agreed to go with me to Wyoming. And I plan to leave town just as soon as Dr. Hennessy says she can travel."

"I'm afraid her plans changed when she was attacked and nearly killed."

"It seems to me that would be all the more reason for her to want a new life. And I can help her attain that dream—in Wyoming."

"And just whose dream is that, Miss O'Malley? Yours or Daisy's?"

She seemed to ponder that a moment, as if he'd finally tossed something her way that she hadn't expected. Then she seemed to shrug it off. "Does it matter? Some people become so downtrodden that they forget how to dream."

The fool woman had an answer for everything.

"At this point," he said, "the only thing that matters is getting Erin and Sarah Jane out of town before that man comes back and tries to finish what he started."

Her lips parted, and the color in her cheeks drained. "Do you think the man will come back and try to kill her?"

"Come now. You're a bright woman. Think about it. The man attacked a woman and child in broad daylight. He certainly wasn't a drunken, unhappy customer. And when another woman interrupted the attack, he ran off before she could get a good look at him. But as far as the attacker knows, there are still two witnesses."

She bit down on her bottom lip again as she considered what he was suggesting, so he continued to make himself clear. "From what I've been told, Erin has no memory of the attack—at least, not now. And Sarah Jane hasn't uttered a word since that morning. The doctor thinks she's traumatized by what she saw, and who knows if or when she'll speak again. But the attacker doesn't know that."

Tom didn't see any point in telling Miss O'Malley that he'd been following Caroline's trail for the past three weeks, from Casa de Los Angelitos in Mexico, where Sarah Jane was born, to the town of Taylorsville, where Caroline had died after a fall down a flight of stairs.

And that was another thing that just didn't sit right with him. Caroline had been a healthy and vivacious twenty-four-year-old. How had she managed to take a fatal tumble like that? And why had Erin left right after the funeral?

Something about that just didn't make sense. The women had put down roots several different times in the past six years. And then all of a sudden, they would up and move again.

Had one or the other been running from something? Or from someone?

If so, Tom didn't like the idea of Sarah Jane being caught up in the backlash of whatever the adults in her life had been involved in—or running from.

He hoped he was wrong, but the only one who could answer his questions was Erin, and she was in no condition to talk yet.

"How do you plan to travel with a child and an injured woman?" Miss O'Malley asked.

That wasn't going to be easy. And Tom didn't expect to do much sleeping on the three-day ride to Hannah's house, where he intended to leave Daisy to heal.

"I can see that you haven't thought that through," Miss O'Malley said, her tone and stance a little too smug for her bustle.

"Actually," Tom said, "I've done a lot of thinking."

More than she would ever know—and not just while he'd been on the trail looking for Caroline.

"Perhaps we should compromise," she said.

"About what? The way I see it, Miss O'Malley, you don't have a dog in this fight."

As though his words had fallen on deaf ears, she continued to speak her mind. "Erin and Sarah Jane need to get out of town fast, correct?"

"That's the way I see it." What was her point?

"And Sarah Jane might or might not have a family who might—or might not—want her. Is that a safe assumption?"

"I suppose so." Where was she going with this?

"If she has no family—or if they don't want her— she'll need another home."

He didn't dispute that.

"And if they want her, we'll need to determine whether they deserve her. And if they don't, then we'll still need to find her another home."

We? Who included Miss O'Malley in any of this?

"So you see, it's all very simple." Miss O'Malley crossed her arms and smiled. "I'll go with you. And if Sarah Jane needs a home for any reason, I'll be prepared to take her and Erin with me to Wyoming as planned."

She couldn't be suggesting that he travel for three days with her, an outspoken, headstrong schoolmarm. He'd be a fool to even consider such a notion. A woman like Miss O'Malley, no matter how pretty she was, would make the trip as unbearable as a throbbing ingrown toenail.

"Miss O'Malley, thank you for the kind offer, but I'm afraid that won't work."

"Why not?"

"To be honest, I'd run naked through a briar patch before I'd travel with you any longer than necessary."

Up went that pretty little chin again. "Traveling with you wouldn't be a picnic, Mr. McCain."

"It certainly won't. I'm not packing silver tea service or linen napkins."

"How dare you accuse me of being prissy. I've made it a point to not be cast in that mold."

"The mold of a lady?" He asked, awaiting a slap—or a sharp retort.

Instead, she uncrossed her arms and tossed him a pretty smile. "I don't really care what others think of me, Mr. McCain—you included. But that's beside the point right now. You're going to need help traveling with an injured woman and a traumatized child. And it looks as though I'm the only one willing to go with you. So the way I see it, you don't have much choice."

Trouble was, as much as he hated to admit it, she was right.

Chapter Three

McCain glared at Katie as though she'd gone daft, then he shook his head. "Be ready in an hour—and not one minute more. We'll leave from here."

Before she could object to the unreasonable time limit, the man left her standing in front of the brothel and strode away as though it wouldn't take much to change his mind or to alter his travel plans.

While she should feel somewhat victorious, she had to admit that she felt as unbalanced as a blindfolded child in a sack race.

How in creation was she ever going to pack for a trip like that in so little time?

Well, she couldn't very well stew about it a moment longer, so she hurried home as quickly as her skirts would allow. She did, however, stop briefly to let Ian Connor know that she'd be leaving town.

Ian, who'd been a dear friend and a colleague of her late father, had suffered an attack of apoplexy last year that left the right side of his body so weak that he'd had to retire from his law practice. He now lived with his widowed sister in a white clapboard house just down the lane from Katie.

As she'd expected, Ian greeted her with a warm smile. "Katie, my dear, it's always good to see you. Please come in."

"I'm afraid I don't have time to come inside. I just wanted to let you know I'll be leaving and will be away for a week or so."

Ian stroked his right arm and furrowed his brow. "Where are you going?"

"I'm taking Daisy Potts and Sarah Jane out of town."

Ian stiffened. "You're *what?*"

"I take it you heard about the attack. Poor Miss Potts was assaulted and nearly killed. I'm going to escort her and the child out of town."

"Yes, I heard about the attack—and her injuries. But why in the world are you getting involved in that?"

"You know me."

"Yes, I'm afraid I do." Ian blew out a weary sigh. "May I remind you that you're an unmarried woman, Katie? Traveling the country with a small child and a battered prostitute is dangerous and…well, it's uncalled-for. Think of your reputation."

"I'll have an escort—Mr. Tom McCain. So I'll be perfectly safe."

Ian clicked his tongue and shook his head. "Why are they leaving? Wouldn't it be best if Miss Potts stayed here in town until she recovered?"

Katie didn't dare mention the danger Daisy and Sarah Jane might be in, so she chose another reason for their hasty departure. "The town hasn't been kind to the child, and there's been talk of sending her to live in an orphanage."

The dear old man who, along with his sister, had become as close as family members to her, especially since her da's passing, blew out a weary sigh. "Sending that poor child away isn't necessarily a bad idea, Katie. People around here aren't likely to ever forget what her mother did for a living."

"I don't know much about her real mother, God rest her soul. Sarah Jane once mentioned that she used to work at a hotel."

"That's probably what the child considers the Gardener's House to be."

"You may be right, but a little girl shouldn't be punished for her mother's mistakes."

"I agree. However, that's the way of it, Katie. When are you going to learn there are some things you can't change or fix? I'd think that after getting arrested last November for creating a public disturbance at the town hall meeting you'd be smart enough to figure that out."

"First of all, I'm not the only woman in this community who spent time in jail for speaking her mind." Katie leaned against the doorjamb. "And secondly, I have given up. At least, here in Pleasant Valley."

"What do you mean by that?" Ian asked.

"I'm going to leave as soon as I return from escorting Miss Potts."

His face paled. "Where do you think you're going?"

She understood his concern. And the last thing she wanted to do was to hurt him or to cause him any undue worry. "I'm going to Wyoming. The school board in Granville is looking for a teacher."

"I thought you didn't like teaching and that you gave it up for good."

"Well, I've had a change of heart. Since I can't get

through to the adults in this community, I've decided to use another tactic. I'll begin by training the children when they're still able to see reason."

Ian blew out a weary sigh. "I told your father that I would be happy to oversee your trust fund, but he didn't take me up on the offer, giving you full control. If he'd known that you'd become so independent, he might have listened to me."

"Da always admired my independence."

"He wouldn't have in this instance."

Katie watched the emotions play across Ian's face, and she knew she was in for a battle. But try as he might, he wouldn't be able to change her plans.

"I can't allow you to go to Wyoming. Your father would roll over in the grave if I let you traipse across the country unescorted."

"I won't be alone, Ian. If things go as planned, I'll be traveling with Miss Potts and Sarah Jane."

"You're going to travel with a prostitute?" His voice rose an octave, and his face grew rosy and bright. "Have you lost your mind completely?" Ian slapped his good hand upon his hip. "Katie, listen to reason for once in your life. Women of virtue don't go to the Wyoming Territory, especially with soiled doves. They stay home and wait for a man to court them."

It was the same argument he'd used each time she showed her stubborn streak, so she wasn't surprised. Still, her answer was always the same. "That's not going to happen. Getting married would strip me of what few rights a woman has in this world."

"Well, it's probably just as well that you remain a spinster. You'd drive your first husband crazy and the second to drink."

"You may be right," Katie said with a chuckle. "But if I should suffer a blow to the head causing me to reconsider marriage, I'll look for a man as fair-minded as you or Da."

"Humph. Don't try to flatter me."

Katie stepped forward and wrapped the old man in a warm embrace. "I love you, Ian. You know that, don't you?"

The tension in his stance eased, and he hugged her back. "I love you, too, Katie. You've been the daughter I never had."

Ian would be as angry as a hornet in a bowl of honey if he knew all the details of her trip, of the possible danger, of her determination to adopt Sarah Jane in the end, but he'd settle down in a day or so. He always did when he realized her mind was made up. And it was.

Katie was going to take Sarah Jane to Wyoming, and nobody was going to stop her.

Needless to say, Katie had packed her clothing and toiletries into a valise as quickly as possible, then she'd hurried to the livery stable and rented a gentle roan mare. After mounting and adjusting her skirts, she rode to the Gardener's House to meet Mr. McCain.

Since she preferred not to butt heads with Sweet Heather again, she decided to wait outside. So she dismounted and tied her mare next to McCain's big bay gelding and the snorting team of horses harnessed to a buckboard.

Someone had already packed the wagon and lined the bed with several quilts. They'd also rigged a small canvas tarp over the top to provide the injured woman with a bit of shade. Katie wondered if one of the fallen women had thought of it—or if McCain had.

Before she could consider the thoughtful gesture, the brothel's front door swung open, and McCain stepped onto the porch with Daisy—or rather, Erin—in his arms. The injured woman wore a light blue dress—a plain and simple style with long sleeves and a delicate bow tied at the neckline. With her dark hair swept up into a modest topknot, she appeared to be as proper as any of the other ladies in town.

Katie thought it made a clever disguise, if one could call it that.

As McCain carried Erin down the porch steps, Katie caught a glimpse of the black eye and the nasty bruise that marred one side of her face, mocking the ladylike clothing. As they crossed the yard, Katie had a better view of her injuries and winced at the brutality of the attack.

She'd been so taken by the sight of the battered woman that she just now noticed Sarah Jane trailing behind. The child, her head downcast, wore a yellow calico dress and a small pair of moccasins on her feet.

Katie made her way to the little girl, then dropped to her knees and hugged her close. But instead of returning the embrace, Sarah Jane's arms hung loosely at her sides.

"Oh, honey," Katie said, hoping to infuse a little warmth and joy back into her. "I'm so glad to see you."

Katie's heart ached at the thought of what the child had witnessed, what she'd been through.

"Come on," McCain said. "We don't have time for idle chitchat. Let's get them in the wagon."

Katie didn't intend to dawdle. For goodness' sake, she wanted to get the child—and herself!—as far away from the brothel as they could. But she couldn't help being concerned about the girl and ignored the man long enough to satisfy her curiosity.

"Are you all right, honey?" Katie asked.

Sarah Jane nodded.

"Who hurt you?"

The child's gaze dropped to the small, beaded moccasins she wore.

Katie placed her fingertip under Sarah Jane's chin and lifted her face. "It's all right. I'm here now, and I'll protect you. You can tell me what happened."

"She can't talk," McCain said.

Katie knew she'd been traumatized, but she'd thought, well, hoped that her arrival, her presence and voice, might soothe the frightened girl, might comfort her.

Footsteps sounded behind her, and Katie turned to see a tall blonde carrying a large basket in the crook of her arm. A stocky brunette followed behind toting a white ceramic chamber pot.

"I've packed some vittles for you to take," the blonde said. "It'll be suppertime before you know it. And since Doc don't want Daisy to walk or move around very much, we thought it might be best if you took this pot along, too. That way she won't have to climb in and out of the wagon."

Katie knew Daisy had been injured, but she hadn't realized how laid up she'd be on the trip. But that didn't matter. Katie was prepared to take care of her, as well as Sarah Jane.

She'd nursed her da for several weeks before he passed, so she was used to tending the sick. And while being on the trail would be different from being at home, she was prepared to do whatever needed to be done.

According to McCain, the trip would take several days. Katie wondered what they would eat after they'd finished the food in the basket. She hated to think that they'd have to scavenge the countryside for berries, seeds and wild game. Surely someone had thought to pack more supplies. But if they hadn't? Well, she'd think of something. She always did.

Katie stood, shook the dust from her skirts and reached for Sarah Jane's hand. "Come on, honey. We're going on a grand adventure."

McCain, who'd helped the injured woman settle into the bed of the wagon, glanced her way and frowned.

Didn't he realize that Katie simply had been trying to reassure the child? She certainly wasn't looking forward to spending the next few days sleeping outdoors and eating whatever they managed to find, especially under his watch. Would she ever see his gaze untouched by judgment? A small part of her couldn't help wishing so.

"By the way," Katie said to McCain, deciding she deserved more information than he'd given her. "Do we have any pans for cooking? Or maybe a coffeepot?"

His scowl confirmed that he might have agreed to take her along, but he certainly wasn't the least bit happy about it. When he finally spoke, his words came out short and snappish. "This isn't a picnic, Miss O'Malley."

Under other circumstances, Katie might have let loose with an angry retort, but she bit her tongue, knowing it wouldn't do her any good to irritate him further, at least until they were too far along for him to change his mind and send her home.

"Tom," the blonde said, "I've got one more box to go on that wagon, and I'll need some help lifting it."

"There's not much room, Rose."

"It's not big, just a wee bit heavy."

McCain started toward the house, then paused when he reached Katie. "Help Sarah Jane into the wagon."

If Katie weren't so eager to get the child away from the brothel and this town, she'd remind him that she didn't take orders, and that a "please" and a little respect would go a long way. But she let it go this time and helped Sarah Jane settle into the back of the wagon, next to where Erin lay.

Once the child was seated, Katie leaned against the side of the buckboard, reached into the bed and placed her hand on the prostitute's arm. "Mr. McCain told me that your name is Erin, which is what I'll be calling you from now on."

Erin, her eyes a bit dazed, merely nodded.

"I'm sorry things aren't working out the way either of us intended," Katie added, "but don't worry. Once you're feeling better, we'll leave for Wyoming."

Erin merely closed her eyes and sighed.

Boot steps sounded on the porch, and Katie looked over her shoulder to see McCain approach the wagon carrying a small wooden crate. After he placed it under the wagon seat, he reached into his pocket and pulled out a gold watch.

He lifted the lid and glanced at the time. Then he circled the wagon and approached Katie. "I'll help you up."

"You don't need to," she told him. "I'm not as helpless or as troublesome as you think. I can do it myself."

In spite of what she'd told him, he slipped behind her and offered his assistance, gripping her elbow and reaching for her waist.

His hands were strong, his touch warm, his movements deft. Yet it was the scent of him, a manly combination of leather and soap that caused her breath to catch.

Hoping he hadn't noticed, she climbed up, settled onto the seat and adjusted her skirts.

She was just about to reach for the reins when Mc-Cain tied his horse to the back of the wagon, beside hers.

"What are you doing?" she asked. "I can drive a buckboard."

"We're all going to ride in the wagon. From a distance, maybe we'll look like a family."

Katie nearly snorted at the thought of her and McCain as husband and wife, but she kept her reaction to herself.

It was all part of the masquerade, part of the plan to get Sarah Jane to safety.

Yet as McCain climbed into the seat beside her, like a husband would do, her heart gave a funny little flutter.

"Everybody ready?" he asked the passengers in back.

"Are you sure we have everything we need?" Katie asked, hoping he'd thought of the things she might have included had he given her enough time to plan.

"It doesn't matter. We're going to make do with what we have. We're burning daylight as it is."

She wanted to object, but she had to admit that Mc-Cain was right.

The sooner they left Pleasant Valley, the better.

Traveling with two women and a child wasn't going to be easy, and Tom doubted he'd get much sleep over the next few days. If he'd had the luxury of waiting until tomorrow morning, he would have planned to set out before daylight.

The fewer people who saw them leaving, the less chance there was that the attacker would catch wind of it and follow them. Hopefully, the man had fled to parts unknown, but Tom wasn't taking any chances. According to Sheriff Droeger, they hadn't uncovered a motive for the assault—no robbery, at least, not that anyone knew. So was it personal? Had the man gone after Erin for some other reason? If so, that would give him reason to come back and finish the job.

Tom had purchased the wagon at the livery, and, fortunately, the old man who ran the place had been more interested in pocketing the cash than in asking questions.

So now here they were, about twenty miles outside of Pleasant Valley. Tom would have pushed harder so they could have traveled farther, but Dr. Hennessy had warned him not to jostle Erin too much. Of course, the doctor had also given her something to make her sleep, so she'd rested easily all afternoon.

They'd finally reached a good place to set up camp. Tom remembered this spot when he and Trapper had ridden through a few days earlier. With a creek nearby, its water clear and fresh, and the scattering of trees to hide them from the road, it was a good place to spend the night.

But he still wanted to scout the area and assure himself that the women and the child would be safe, even though he planned to watch over them while they slept.

So, after unhitching the horses, leading them to water and waiting for them to drink, he returned to the campsite and tethered them to a tree.

"I'm going to have a look around," he told Miss O'Malley. "Do you think you can handle things here?"

"Yes, of course. Should Sarah Jane and I gather some dried twigs for a fire?"

"Wait until I come back." He didn't want them to

wander too far or build a fire until he was sure they weren't being followed.

Fifteen minutes later, after taking care to hide their wagon tracks, he'd circled back to the campsite. All the while, he'd watched and listened for any sign that they weren't alone while keeping his right hand close to his holster.

When he'd convinced himself that they were safe, he headed back to camp. Not far from where they'd left the horses and wagon, while he was still near the stream, twigs snapped and skirts rustled.

Tom turned to the sound and spotted Miss O'Malley and Sarah Jane heading back to camp. They each carried a canteen, so he figured they'd been getting water. The woman also held a black valise.

He glanced at the setting sun. It would be dark soon. He was just about to call out, letting them know that he was nearby, but he stopped short when he saw Miss O'Malley drop to her knees and tend Sarah Jane with gentle hands and a soft voice.

Fascinated, he watched the attractive redhead gently run a silver-handled comb through the child's tangled locks.

"You have the prettiest hair," she told the girl. "Just like captured sunbeams."

Sarah Jane raised her eyebrows with a look of such obvious hope that Tom's heart melted. The poor kid had been through far more than was fair—the recent death of her mother, the assault of the woman who'd been caring for her.

Miss O'Malley reached for a white ribbon and handed it to Sarah Jane. "Hold this, honey." Deftly forming a long braid, she took the satin strip and tied a bow to hold her work together. "There you go."

Then the woman removed a small bottle from her bag, twisted the lid open and placed a dab of the contents behind each of her ears. All the while, the child watched with rapt attention.

And so did Tom.

"It's lilac water," Miss O'Malley said. "It's my favorite scent. Would you like some?"

When Sarah Jane nodded, the woman smiled and applied a bit behind the girl's ears, too, her movements slow and gentle.

It was nice to see a softer side to her. Apparently there was more to her than met the eye, although what met his eye was rather appealing. In fact, the sight was almost mesmerizing.

But Tom couldn't very well continue to gaze at her like an awestruck kid with a crush on the schoolmarm. What if she caught him doing it?

The last thing in the world he needed to do was to let down his guard with a woman as outspoken as Katie O'Malley, no matter how pretty she was, no matter how softhearted she might appear to be.

He'd seen the feisty side of her. And right now, he had enough trouble on his hands.

For a moment, his resolve waffled. If circumstances were different, if he were just passing through, he might have said or done something stupid. But he had a job to do, a child to protect. And there was another issue he couldn't ignore.

Katie O'Malley was also white.

And Tom McCain wasn't.

That might not make a difference to people like Hannah and Trapper Jack, but there were others who'd object. Others who'd made it more than clear that Tom wasn't to step foot on their ranch.

Tom had been about nine years old when he'd gone to the Lazy G to deliver a pair of moccasins his mother had made for Caroline. The girl hadn't been home because she'd gone into town with the housekeeper, but Randolph Haney, Harrison's friend and solicitor, had been there.

He'd responded to Tom's request to speak to Caroline with a shove that had knocked him to the ground.

"She doesn't need anything from the filthy likes of you. Get out of here. And don't ever come back." Then, for good measure, Haney had kicked him while he was down, splitting his head open with the toe of his boot.

Tom still bore a scar from the attack, a reminder to keep his distance from the Lazy G, which he'd made a point of doing. But nearly a year later, at the urging of his mother, he'd gone back with her one cold, rainy afternoon.

Haney had answered the door that day, too. His mother had begged him to let her talk to Harrison. Haney had left them outside and gone into the house. A few minutes later, when he returned, he'd pulled his gun and ordered her off the property.

And take your whelp with you.

It had been a hard lesson, a painful one—because Tom's mother had died several days later.

That was why Trapper had objected to Tom taking the job to find Caroline in the first place. But there were some things a boy didn't forget, some promises meant to be kept.

So after taking Sarah Jane back to the Lazy G, assuming Tom was convinced that she'd be treated as a rightful heir, he'd leave Stillwater for good. He had no need for Randolph Haney or Harrison Graves.

He didn't need Miss O'Malley, either—except for the next few days. After that, when he got to Hannah's place, he'd ask Trapper to escort the troublesome redhead back to Pleasant Valley. Then he'd be done with her for once and for all.

Yet he continued to watch her until she glanced up and spotted him. As their eyes met, their gazes locked.

He knew how she felt about women's equality. But how did she feel about equality for all people, even those with darker skin?

He supposed it really didn't matter.

Either way, he couldn't let her think that he was fawning over her. So he'd better put some distance between them. They might have to share a seat on the same wagon, but there were other ways to create distance. One way would be to let her know who was boss.

"It's time to eat," he said. "There are some supplies in the wooden box under the seat of the wagon, but Rose packed a basket of food for us to eat this evening. That's probably going to be the easiest and best-tasting meal we'll have for the next few days. So when you're finished with whatever you're doing here, you can start setting it out."

Miss O'Malley pondered his request for a moment, then she straightened, crossed her arms and tossed him a pretty smile. "I'll be a while yet. So if you're hungry, then maybe you ought to do it yourself."

It's not as if Tom had never set up camp before or fixed supper for himself and Trapper. But he wasn't about to let the schoolmarm order him around as though he were one of her students, and she may as well get that straight.

Of course, he wasn't about to have a showdown in front of the child.

"Sarah Jane," he said, reaching into his shirt pocket and withdrawing a small paper bag. "Go see about Erin and, if she's awake, offer her one of these. You can have some, too."

Without the least bit of reluctance, Sarah Jane pulled free of the woman's grip on her shoulders and approached Tom with an outstretched hand.

When she reached him, he handed her the bag. She peeked inside before heading back to the campsite.

"What did you give her?" the schoolmarm asked.

"Lemon drops."

When Sarah Jane was out of earshot, Tom crossed his own arms. "It seems that neither of us likes taking orders, but let's get one thing straight. I'll be making all the decisions on this trip. You'll do what I say—and when I say it."

"I don't mind yielding to you because of your experience and know-how, but I'm not going to take orders blindly, just because you're a man and I'm a woman."

"Like I said, you'll do as I say. And you won't question my reasons or motives. That means you'll handle the meals."

"Apparently you didn't hear me." The petite redhead stood firm. "I'll return to camp when I'm good and ready. And if you have a job for me to do, you'll ask me to do it, rather than tell me. You'll also use words like 'please' and 'thank you.'"

"Listen here, Miss O'Malley. You're not in charge. *I am*. And you're lucky I don't throw you on the back of that nag you call a horse, turn it around and slap its rump to send you back to town in a dead run."

"Are you trying to intimidate me?" she asked, her voice coming out a bit wobbly.

"Do you scare easily?" he asked.

"No, I don't."

He flashed a taunting smile. "I suppose you're too smart to be afraid."

"I'm bright," she admitted, "and better educated than most—male or female."

"That might be true, but driving a wagon and crossing rugged territory takes more knowledge than you can find in a book. It takes common sense, instinct and courage—things you can't learn in school."

"What I lack in experience, I make up for in determination."

"A determined fool won't last a day on the trail."

She clenched her fists at her side. "I'm no fool, and I have far more courage than you think."

While he'd like to believe her, especially when he wasn't sure what they might face down the road, he couldn't help thinking of her as a young, trigger-happy cowboy out to prove himself. But he doubted arguing with her would get either of them anywhere.

"I guess that's left to be seen," Tom said. "Now let's get out of here."

"All right."

Yet neither of them made a move.

"What are you waiting for?" she asked.

"For you to go first."

When she didn't move, he said, "Listen, Miss O'Malley, I can be your ally or your enemy. It's your choice."

"I choose my friends wisely, Mr. McCain." She

flashed an insincere smile then headed up the incline toward the wagon, passing him as she went and leaving a scent of lilac lingering in the air.

Tom raked a hand through his hair. He was going to need help with Erin and Sarah Jane over the next couple of days. And right now, the only human he had to rely on was a troublesome redhead who, given time, could surely provoke a gentle and pious preacher to spit and cuss.

Over the years, Tom had learned to trust God to see him through every difficult situation he had to face. The first time he'd called out to his father's God—he'd been a ten-year-old half-breed, cold, hungry and alone in a hostile white world.

Not ten minutes later, Trapper Jack had come along to change all that and to take him to live with Hannah McCain. She'd not only loved and cared for him, she'd shared her faith, and before long, Tom had become a believer himself.

Last night, Tom had prayed for guidance and help in protecting Sarah Jane and finding her a loving home. He knew God would answer that prayer. He surely did.

Trouble was, he feared that this time, instead of blessing him with a woman like Hannah, God had seen fit to punish him with Katie O'Malley.

Chapter Four

The next morning, as dawn broke over the eastern hills, Katie woke up stiff and sore. She'd no more than grimaced and tried to stretch out on the quilt-lined wagon bottom when she heard the sound and caught a whiff of coffee percolating on an open flame.

Apparently Mr. McCain had realized he shouldn't order her to cook all their meals. If so, why hadn't he backed down the day before? It would have saved them both some unnecessary trouble and anger.

Maybe he'd decided it was time for a truce. After all, they were stuck with each other for the next couple of days. Bickering wasn't going to do them any good. And it certainly wouldn't help Sarah Jane feel safe.

After biting back a groan, Katie rolled to her side and carefully climbed from the wagon, trying not to disturb the other woman and the child, both of whom still slept soundly. Then she made her way to the small campfire, where McCain sat upon a large rock, studying the flickering flame.

He hadn't shaved, and in the morning light, he appeared more rugged, more manly and even more handsome—dangerously so.

She lowered her sleep-hoarsened voice. "Good morning."

He glanced up for a moment, then gave her a cursory nod. "'Morning."

She bit down on her lower lip, unsure of how to broach an apology, then swallowed her pride and pressed on. "I'm sorry for being disagreeable yesterday. I'm afraid we both started off on the wrong foot, and I'd like to make amends. We have a common goal, and I think being at odds isn't going to help matters."

He seemed to ponder her words, then said, "You're right."

She let out the breath she'd been holding. "I think it's best if you call me Katie from now on. Miss O'Malley is too formal for this type of trip. Besides, if we're supposed to be traveling as—" she didn't dare say husband and wife "—as a family, then it's more believable, don't you think?"

Silence swirled around them like the steam from the coffee in his tin cup.

Finally she asked, "May I call you by your given name, as well?"

He reached into the wooden box that rested next to him and pulled out a second tin cup. "My name's Tom."

Another step in the right direction.

"I may not be one to take orders," she added. "But you'll find that I'm not afraid of hard work."

He filled the second cup with coffee. "I saw you tending Sarah Jane and Erin."

She waited for him to continue, for him to utter some kind of compliment or recognition of all she'd done to assist Erin yesterday and through the night by wiping the dust and perspiration from her brow, feeding her and changing the chamber pot.

When no other words followed, she supposed that was all he was going to grant her. She'd just have to be happy with that.

He handed the coffee to her, and she took the tin cup from him, being careful not to burn herself.

"Where do you plan to take Sarah Jane and Erin?" she asked.

"To stay with a woman named Hannah."

"Who is she?"

"A friend." A slow smile broke across his face, reaching his eyes and softening his expression. "She's a good woman, the finest one you'll ever meet. Sarah Jane and Erin will be safe there—and well cared for."

Katie's heart tumbled in her chest, although she wasn't sure why. Surprised by Tom's obvious respect and affection for the woman, she supposed. And curiosity, too.

Was he courting Hannah? Or was she merely a friend, as he'd said?

Katie took a sip of the hot, bitter coffee and bit back a grimace, wishing she had some cream and sugar to temper the taste. Yet she knew better than to voice a complaint. Instead, she relished the warmth it provided in the crisp morning hour as dawn broke over their campsite and accepted it as the first sign of their truce.

"How will Hannah feel about you bringing a couple of women with you and asking her to keep us until you return?" Katie asked.

"She's used to me bringing home strays."

Katie didn't like being referred to as a stray, and that's

certainly what Tom had implied. She hadn't led the same kind of life that Erin had, although smudged in dirt and covered in trail dust, they all seemed to be the same— except for the bumps and bruises Erin still bore.

Katie had half a notion to give Tom a piece of her mind for implying otherwise, but she wasn't about to hurt Erin's feelings, should she be awake and listening. Nor did she want their fragile truce to suffer a setback. So she kept her thoughts to herself.

Still, she didn't want to be a burden to a woman she'd never met, although she wouldn't mind a bit if Hannah got angry at Tom for bringing her a wagonload of trouble.

By the third day, the wind and sun had chapped and burned Katie's lips and cheeks. Sitting on the hard wooden slats had given her a backache and a crick in her neck, but she hadn't uttered a single complaint. The journey hadn't been easy on any of them, especially Erin, even though she'd managed to sleep through most of it, thanks to the medication Dr. Hennessy had told them to give her.

An hour ago, they'd stopped long enough to eat hard-tack, stale bread and apples for the noon meal, then they'd started out once again.

"How much farther until we reach Hannah's place?" Katie asked Tom.

"Late this afternoon or early evening."

Katie could hardly wait to be out of the wagon for good. She wondered if Tom was as eager to get there as she was. Most likely. He clearly cared about Hannah and undoubtedly missed her.

Again, she found herself curious about their relationship.

"I suppose Hannah will be happy to see you," she said.

As Tom flicked the reins along the backside of the team, the wagon swayed, causing his arm to brush against hers again, a warm touch she'd grown used to, an intimacy she'd actually found rather nice and comforting.

"Hannah will welcome me with open arms," he said.

Katie suspected as much and, if truth be told, she couldn't help feeling a bit apprehensive at meeting Tom's lady friend.

As the day wore on, her apprehension and discomfort grew steadily.

By the time the sun had lowered in the west, perspiration had dampened her collar and the fabric under her arms. Dust powdered her skin in spite of the long sleeves she wore, and the sun had no doubt burned her nose and cheeks.

She must be a sight. Yet, in spite of her reluctance to meet the woman herself, Katie looked forward to arriving at Hannah's house if it meant that she could stretch her legs and, hopefully, soak in a warm, soapy tub.

"How are our passengers faring?" Tom asked.

Katie glanced over her shoulder and spotted the child holding a rag doll while watching over a drowsy Erin, who'd had another dose of medication after they'd had their midday meal.

Sarah Jane turned, smiled softly and gave a little wave. What a sweet child. She seemed to like Tom, which was a bit surprising. Katie would think she'd find him intimidating. Of course, a six-year-old was easily swayed by lemon drops, handcrafted moccasins and the easy smiles that lit his eyes.

"They're both doing just fine," Katie said, as she scanned her surroundings.

It would be dark soon, which meant they were drawing near the end of their journey.

Up ahead, just beyond a small orchard chock-full of peaches to tempt hungry travelers, a white clapboard house sat surrounded by a whitewashed picket fence. Bright red geraniums blossomed in a planter beneath a single window in the front.

The two-story structure was clearly a home to someone, and it warmed Katie's heart to gaze upon it. She could easily imagine a loving wife, handsome husband and happy children living there. The vision was so clear, so strong, that she could almost feel it deep in her soul.

If she were to ever reconsider her decision never to marry, which she wouldn't do, she could imagine living in a home like that.

"That's a lovely little house and yard," she said. "Do you know who lives there?"

"Yes, I do. Hannah."

The woman's name rolled off his tongue simply, yet affectionately, and Katie's heart sank. She had to admit that she didn't like the idea of Hannah living in that particular house, although she couldn't say why.

Tom turned the team onto the property. When they reached the barn, he pulled the horses to a stop and surveyed the grounds, where a hen and several half-grown chicks pecked at a small patch of grass.

Four big pots of green plants and two flower boxes filled with pansies marked a walkway and graced the steps of a lovely little porch, where a roughly handcrafted bench and rocking chair beckoned anyone in need of peace and quiet. Yet in spite of the warm and colorful welcome of the house and yard, Katie felt uneasy about the type of reception they might receive.

Tom secured the reins and climbed down. Then he circled the wagon and reached up to help Katie. At one time she'd struggled with his assistance, but after traveling together the past few days, she found his help not only easier to accept but even comforting.

She took his arm and, as she lifted her foot to step over the side, he swung her to the ground, just as he'd done each day of their journey. But today, for some reason, her heart beat a little faster, her breath caught a little deeper.

As he released his hold on her, her legs wobbled a bit, and she reached for his forearm to steady herself, gripping the corded muscle, feeling his strength.

"Are you all right?" he asked.

"I will be."

"Good." He nodded toward the house. "If Hannah doesn't answer the door, take Sarah Jane inside. I'll get Erin out of the wagon and put her in the spare room. If you're hungry, you'll find cookies in a blue tin box in the kitchen."

Katie balked at his suggestion to just make herself at home. "I could never enter someone's house uninvited. If Hannah doesn't answer, Sarah Jane and I will wait on the porch."

"Suit yourself. Hannah usually keeps that tin full. I think Sarah Jane would like something sweet to eat."

The girl nodded and grinned, regaining a wee bit of the spark she'd had before the assault. She seemed to be healing—inside, as well as out. In fact, the bruising along her right arm had begun to yellow and fade.

Of course, the child who'd once been clean and dressed to perfection now had dirty hands and a black smudge across her nose.

"She needs a bath first," Katie said.

Tom chuckled, and his brown eyes sparked. "So do you."

He was teasing, of course, and probably didn't mean anything by it, but...

Katie ran her hands along the skirt of her soiled and wrinkled dress. She'd planned on bathing and changing into clean clothes, but to have Tom point it out left her uneasy and unbalanced.

As Tom untied the two horses from the back of the wagon and led them to the barn, she couldn't help but watch him go. He was an intriguing man and a formidable opponent. Yet she had to admit that she'd felt safe riding with him and knowing that he'd been watching over them.

As Tom entered the barn with the two saddle horses, Katie felt a tug at her skirts and glanced down at Sarah Jane, who pointed to the small outhouse in back.

"Good idea," Katie said with a smile. "And then we'll find the well and wash up outside. We don't want Hannah to think we're ragamuffins."

Again Katie worried about the impression her appearance might make, a concern she'd rarely had in the past.

What was the matter with her? She didn't care what others thought of her.

You're a lady, she reminded herself. Not a ragamuffin, a stray or a soiled dove. She was every bit as good and kindhearted as Hannah, no matter what she looked like on the outside.

Besides, Katie had no need of a life like Hannah's. She was going to Granville, where she would have a small but cozy home behind the school. She would be a fine teacher, an upstanding and respected woman in the community. A happy spinster. Life would be just as she'd always wanted.

So why did her tummy feel so fluttery?

Maybe she'd eaten something that hadn't sat very well.

After using the outhouse, she found the well and drew a bucket of water. Then she dampened her handkerchief and washed Sarah Jane's face and hands. When she finished cleaning the girl, she washed herself the best she could, then she led Sarah Jane back to the front porch and took a seat.

Katie chose the wooden bench, knowing Sarah Jane would prefer the rocker.

Moments later, Tom sauntered out of the house, where he must have taken Erin, and stepped onto the porch. Before Katie could question him, he headed for the buckboard, which he'd left near the barn. As he began to unhitch the team, a dog howled in the distance, catching his attention.

Katie turned to the sound and spotted a black buggy approaching the yard with a beast of a dog trotting beside it.

The driver, a stout, gray-haired woman, called out, "Lord be praised. You're home, Tom!"

Katie watched as the dog, which looked more like a wolf, barked and then raced toward the man.

Oh, dear. Should she grab Sarah Jane and run inside

for safety? Perhaps she didn't need to do anything yet. The house was still a good distance from the barn. And the creature didn't seem to notice anything other than Tom. So she and Sarah Jane were probably safe enough for now.

Tom laughed, the smooth, easy timbre calming her nerves. Then he started toward the road, bracing himself as the black wolf-dog leaped into his arms and gave him a slobbery lick across the face.

"Hey," he said to the creature. "How are you doing, boy? Is Hannah feeding you enough?"

The gray-haired woman pulled the buggy into the yard and halted the horse. "That dog eats better than you do, young man. It's good to have you home. I hope you'll be here longer than the last time you came."

"I can only stay for dinner. I need a good night's sleep, then I'm leaving in the morning." Tom set the wolf-dog down and ruffled its black woolly head before he strode to help Hannah down from the buggy. "Where's Trapper? He told me he was going to meet me here."

"He stopped by a couple days ago. I asked him to go with me when I called on the widow Johnson this afternoon. I took her some chicken stew and peach cobbler for her supper tonight, and he stayed at her place to do a few chores. But he should be back soon. He knew you'd be coming home any day."

"Good. I need to talk to him."

Hannah glanced at the buckboard, which the quilts still lined and the canvas tarp still shaded. "What's that? And where's your horse?"

"Caballo is in the barn. And that? Well, I suppose you could say that I brought you a surprise."

"Not another wolf puppy, I hope." She shook her gray head, chuckling.

"I think you'll like this one a lot better." He continued to talk to her, but he lowered his voice to the point it was impossible to hear from where Katie and Sarah Jane sat.

Hannah nodded, then spoke, too, her voice also a whisper.

When Tom pointed toward the porch, Katie got to her feet. While she was no longer concerned about meeting the woman she'd once thought Tom might be courting, she still wondered what kind of reception she would receive.

However, if Hannah held any ill feelings about Tom bringing three houseguests, she masked them with a warm smile on a rosy face.

Katie turned to the rocker, where Sarah Jane watched the homecoming. "Come on, honey. Tom has someone he wants us to meet."

The child's big blue eyes implored Katie to participate in the introductions without her.

"You can play on the rocker later." Katie held out a hand. "I promise."

Sarah Jane sighed, then stopped the swaying motion with little moccasin-clad feet and reached her small hand into Katie's.

As they approached Hannah and Tom, the big dog studied them intently. Too intently, Katie realized. She paused in midstep, determined to avoid a quick movement that might provoke the creature to pounce upon them with teeth bared. Katie waited, ready to jump in front of Sarah Jane as a shield, if need be.

"He won't hurt you." Tom stooped to one knee and

held out his hand to Sarah Jane. "Come here, sweetheart. I have a friend I want you to meet."

The child made her way to the man and dog, apparently not the least bit apprehensive.

"Sarah Jane, this is Lobo. He's part wolf, but don't let that scare you. I've had him since he was a puppy, and he's both loving and loyal." Tom placed a hand upon the animal's head. "Lobo, this is my friend. And now she's your friend, too."

The child warmed to the dog immediately. Judging by the way Hannah smiled warmly as she watched the little girl and the wolf-dog, Katie seemed to be the only one with any apprehension whatsoever.

"Sarah Jane," Tom said, "I also want to introduce you to a very special lady. Her name is Hannah McCain, and she used to be a schoolteacher."

Hannah *McCain?*

Was she his grandmother—or perhaps an aunt?

With a rather large nose, a wide mouth and a gap-toothed smile, Hannah wasn't much for looks. In fact, Katie doubted she'd been any more attractive in her youth, but her obvious pleasure at greeting Sarah Jane softened the harsh wrinkles etched on her face.

Hannah slowly lowered herself to her knees, grimacing as she went down, but she seemed to shake off any discomfort as she cupped Sarah Jane's face and smiled. "I have a cookie tin that never goes empty. And if you like storybooks, I have a shelf full of them. Reading is one of my favorite things to do."

Tom chuckled. "But watch out for the pianoforte in the parlor. Hannah thinks every child should learn to play as well as she does."

Books and a musical instrument? Hannah was certainly educated. But if Tom was calling her by her first name, then she wasn't his mother. Of course, there didn't appear to be a family resemblance, either.

Curiosity flared, and Katie was determined to learn more about Hannah McCain and how she and Tom had become so close.

The wolf-dog gave Sarah Jane's face a lick, which triggered one of the smiles Katie had been longing to see.

"Hannah," Tom said, "forgive me for skipping formalities, but now that Sarah Jane is at ease, I'd like to introduce you to Katie O'Malley."

The older woman returned to her feet and waddled to Katie, her pudgy hand outstretched. "How do you do, dear? It's nice to meet you."

Katie accepted the greeting. "I'm fine, thank you. Tom assured me that you wouldn't mind having us stay with you."

"I'm delighted to have you." Hannah turned to Tom. "Son, will you please put some water on to heat? These young ladies are going to need a bath. In the meantime, I'll get supper underway."

"I hate to be a bother," Katie said.

"It's no bother at all. Any friend of Tom's is a friend of mine."

Tom had said as much, but Katie suspected the kindly woman would have taken in anyone who'd needed a warm meal and a soft bed.

"We won't be staying with you very long," Katie told her. "Erin and I have plans to take Sarah Jane to Wyoming."

Tom's smile waned, and his expression grew stern. "I thought we had that settled."

"We *did* get that settled. You're going to Stillwater to check on a few details, and my plan to leave for Wyoming merely has been delayed until you get back."

Tom shot her a glance that suggested their truce might be short-lived, then he clucked his tongue and returned to the buckboard.

While the women went into the house, Tom unhitched the team and led them to the corral, where he could brush them down and give them some grain and water.

All the while, he grumbled under his breath. He'd lowered his guard when it came to dealing with Katie O'Malley, and now that they'd reached Hannah's house, she was back in rare form.

Where was Trapper when he needed another man to even things out?

He'd no more than wondered that question when Lobo's ears perked up and he barked.

A moment later, Tom heard it, too—the sound of a horse riding onto the property. As Lobo made a dash toward the road, Tom placed his right hand over the gun that rested in his holster.

He hadn't thought they'd been followed, but he couldn't be sure. A sense of uneasiness had dogged him from Pleasant Valley, and he hadn't been able to shake it.

Still, he was glad to spot Trapper riding up on his Appaloosa. He released the team of horses into the corral, then met his old friend in the yard.

As Trapper dismounted, he surveyed the buckboard and scrunched his face. "What's that contraption?"

Tom told him about the assault and why he'd brought Erin and Sarah Jane to Hannah.

Trapper, who'd gotten a shave and a haircut after his

return from Pleasant Valley, lifted his hat and mopped his brow. "Something just don't seem right."

"That's the conclusion I came to back in Pleasant Valley. We trailed Caroline from Casa de Los Angelitos in Mexico. And each time she'd settle down in a town and find a respectable job, she'd pack up and move a year or so later. But they stayed in Taylorsville nearly two years. So why didn't Erin stay put after Caroline died? Why would she take Sarah Jane to live at the Gardener's House? It doesn't make sense."

"You still think they was runnin' from someone or something?" Trapper asked.

"What else could it be? And you know how I felt about Caroline taking that tumble down the stairs."

"You had trouble believing it was an accident."

"The sheriff in Taylorsville hadn't found it suspicious, but something just didn't feel right about it to me."

"What did Erin have to say about that night?" Trapper asked.

"I hadn't gotten a chance to ask her before the attack. And those blows to her head really rattled her brains. Even if she wasn't so medicated and drowsy, her throat is so bruised that she doesn't have much of a voice now anyway. The doctor suggested we wait about a week for her brain and her throat to heal before we question her about anything."

"Maybe she'll tell you more then."

Maybe so, but Tom didn't have time to wait. He glanced down at his boots, then back at his friend, taking in the clean clothes, the haircut, the shave. "Well, now. Don't you look nice."

Trapper shrugged. "Did it for Hannah. Maybe one

of these days she'll agree to marry me. Then, whenever I'm passing through, I won't have to sleep in the barn."

Tom smiled. "Maybe she will if you ever get up the nerve to ask her."

The two were an odd match—the grizzled old trapper and the proper lady. But they were good friends who looked out for each other. Who knew what the future might bring?

"You going back to Stillwater?" Trapper asked.

"I'm leaving in the morning. I can't take Caroline back to the Lazy G now, but I can take word of her and the life she'd been living."

"You figure on takin' the little girl with you when you go?" Trapper asked.

"No, not until I'm sure of the welcome she'll receive."

"Good idea. I'll bet Hannah's thrilled to have another kid in the house. She loved being able to mother you. I'll bet she'll do the same thing with that little girl."

There was no doubt about that, assuming Katie O'Malley would let her.

Tom figured he might as well tell Trapper now, since he was going to find out soon enough. "By the way, Erin and Sarah Jane aren't the only women I brought home."

Trapper arched a woolly brow. "Who else came with you?"

"An outspoken ex-schoolmarm who'll likely be the death of me before this is all said and done."

"How'd *that* happen?"

"Don't ask." Tom scowled. "Come on. Help me with the team. Then we need to bring in the bathtub for Hannah and heat some water."

"I'll help you, but just hold on a minute. Does this ex-schoolmarm got a name?"

"Katie O'Malley. And while she may look like a lady, don't let that fool you. She's as stubborn as a mule. Hot tempered, too." Tom turned and lifted his finger at Trapper. "And no matter what you do, don't let her get it in her pretty head to try and take Sarah Jane anywhere. She's got some fool notion that the child is hers. And like it or not, Sarah Jane belongs to Graves."

Trapper crossed his arms and shifted his weight to one hip. "Belongs to him, huh? You make the poor kid sound like a stray pup. But don't worry. I ain't gonna let anyone take the little girl anywhere until you get back."

"Thank you. I'd appreciate that."

Trapper took a deep breath and sighed. "Kind of wish I wouldn't have gone in search of Caroline with you in the first place. I really missed Hannah this time."

Tom didn't doubt it. Hannah and Trapper provided each other with something they'd each wanted but never had—respectability for Trapper and a little romance for Hannah.

For years, Hannah had dreamed of being a wife and mother, but men hadn't found her the least bit attractive.

"Hannah might not be the prettiest woman in the world," Trapper added, "but she's the most loving one I've ever met. And each time I see her, I have a growing notion to settle down once and for all. You ought to try it sometime, kid. Find yourself a woman to love."

Tom scoffed. Yet for some reason, thoughts of feisty but pretty Katie O'Malley came to mind. When they did, he quickly brushed them aside. "I'm too much of a loner."

"That's what I thought before I met Hannah."

"Yeah, well, you and I aren't anything alike."

Trapper uncrossed his arms and wagged a finger at

him. "You could use a little of that kind of respectability yourself."

By respectability, Trapper meant love. And they'd had this talk before, back when Tom had though Sarah Jorgenson might make a good wife. But her father hadn't liked the idea of his fair-haired daughter being courted by a half-breed.

Tom remembered the man's claim to have his shotgun loaded and cocked if Tom should ever come calling.

"I don't need respectability—or matrimony," Tom told the old man.

"Humph." Trapper shoved his hands into his trousers' front pockets. "So when are you headin' out?"

"I didn't get much sleep over the last few days, so I'm going to turn in early—sharing the loft in the barn with you, I guess. I'll leave in the morning, but I spent nearly all my cash on supplies and a buckboard I'll never have any more use for. So I have to stop by Izzy Ballard's place on my way. He owes me some money, and I don't like the idea of riding into Stillwater with an empty pocket."

"That ain't as bad as ridin' into town with an empty gun."

True, but Tom wouldn't dwell on the danger. Instead he said, "Don't worry about me, Trapper. I wouldn't go to a church social unarmed."

Chapter Five

The inside of Hannah's house was no less inviting than the outside, especially with the scent of yeast and cinnamon filling the air.

In the parlor, a polished cherrywood bookcase holding a small library lined one wall and a stone fireplace adorned another.

Crocheted doilies that graced the backs of an overstuffed chair, a lovely brocade-upholstered settee and a colorful braided rug atop the hardwood floor added a cozy appeal, turning the little house into a home.

"I woke up this morning craving peach cobbler," Hannah said, "so I made two of them. I took one to Mary-Ellen Johnson, a widow who's been sickly, but there's one for our supper tonight. I also have a chicken stew on the stove."

"You have no idea how good that sounds," Katie said. "Our last meal was hardtack and beef jerky."

"Hopefully, we'll put those last few days of traveling behind you in good speed. Tom will have the bathwater ready before you know it. And since I need to put a few extra potatoes in the soup, we'll have time to bathe

Sarah Jane before supper. Then once we've all eaten our fill, you can have your turn in the tub."

A bath. Warm water, soap, lilac water…

Katie thought she might die of anticipation before her chance to bathe came.

"If you and Sarah Jane will wait a minute or two for me in the parlor," Hannah said, "I'll be right back."

Katie ushered the child to the settee and did as she was asked. Minutes later, Hannah returned and took a seat in front of an ornate, hand-carved pianoforte. Soon a medley of waltzes carried Katie's thoughts away to another time, another place.

Before long, Tom entered the room. He stood for a moment, waiting until the last song ended. Then he announced that the first bath was ready on the back porch.

Hannah graciously led Katie and a solemn Sarah Jane into the small enclosed area, where a metal tub full of water awaited.

"A warm bath will do us both good," Katie told the child. "After you're nice and clean, I'll braid your hair."

Hannah pulled a towel from a shelf. "Tom says Sarah Jane doesn't have any clean clothes, so I'll launder her dress tomorrow. In the meantime, I have a blouse she can wear. We can roll the sleeves and tie a satin ribbon at the waist. It won't be as pretty as the little dress I intend to cut out and stitch for her while she's here, but it will do for the time being."

"That's very kind of you." Katie lifted the soiled cotton dress over Sarah Jane's head and noticed a small leather bag hanging from around her neck. She lifted it. "What's this?"

Sarah Jane's only response was to hold the pouch close to her chest.

"You'll have to take that off while you bathe." Katie reached for the strap, but Sarah Jane shook her head and leaned back. Small fingers clutched the bag tightly.

"Well, I'll be." Hannah clicked her tongue and smiled. "A medicine bag, just like Tom's. He must have made it for her."

Had he made the moccasins, too?

He must have.

"What's a medicine bag?" Katie asked.

"A keepsake, I'd say. But powerful medicine, if you ask the Comanche, who are Tom's people."

There was a lot Katie didn't know about the man, and she found herself growing more and more curious about him and how he'd come to meet Hannah.

"What's inside the medicine bag?" she asked.

"Special things—healing plants, a magic feather, a bear claw. It's hard to say. Tom's had one for years. His mother made it for him. I don't have a clue what he keeps inside. It would be disrespectful to ask or to look."

Katie's curiosity about the contents of what Sarah Jane kept in her bag shifted to what Tom kept in his. She hadn't given him much thought before, other than his appearance, which she found most appealing. But she was going to make it a point to learn more about him.

As Katie helped Sarah Jane climb into the tub, the leather bag still in place, she said, "We'll try not to get it wet, honey."

Sarah Jane looked at the pouch. Pausing only slightly, she lifted the strap over her head and handed over the prized possession.

Katie placed it on the small table that held a cake of soap and a soft cloth for scrubbing. The little girl blessed her with a trusting grin.

"Katie," the older woman began, "you're welcome to stay with me as long as you like."

"Thank you." Katie immersed the washcloth into the warm water and reached for the soap. "I'd like to leave as soon as Tom returns."

She just prayed he wouldn't want to take Sarah Jane back to Stillwater with him. If he did, Katie fully intended to go, too, so she could meet these supposed relations. There was a reason her mother hadn't been close to them. What if they weren't good people? Or weren't kind to Sarah Jane?

What if they didn't want her?

Of course, if that were the case, and they were actually her relatives, perhaps they'd sign over guardianship to Katie. It would certainly make things simpler that way. She'd wait to see what Tom learned in Stillwater. And if he wanted to take Sarah Jane back, she'd insist upon going with them.

The women remained quiet for the rest of Sarah Jane's bath. By the time they helped her from the tub and dried her off, the aroma of chicken stew and biscuits filled the house.

"I'm sure you must be hungry," Hannah said. "I'll have food on the table in no time at all."

As they entered the parlor, Katie glanced out the open door, and her feet stilled as she spotted Tom standing near the barn with the wolf-dog.

"Maybe I'd better wait to call Tom to supper until he's finished talking to Lobo," Hannah said.

Katie turned to the elderly woman and cocked her head. "He's talking to the dog?"

"They have an unusual bond. Lobo won't be happy

about staying behind, but he'll look after Sarah Jane and me if Tom tells him to."

Katie scoffed. "If the dog doesn't tag after Tom, it's probably because he knows he has plenty to eat here."

Hannah touched Katie's arm. "You're wrong, dear. Tom and Lobo understand each other. Their loyalty is unbelievable."

Unbelievable was right. Katie had a pet once, a gray and yellow finch named Pretty Boy. The little bird chirped and sang to her every day. One afternoon, when she let it out of the cage to play, it flew away and never came back.

She glanced across the way at the man and beast. They certainly seemed to have a bond, an unusual friendship of sorts. They certainly had a closeness Tom and Katie didn't share.

They had reached a truce for the sake of Sarah Jane, but could they become friends? Could they form a relationship based upon mutual respect and trust?

They'd have to get to know each other first. And that meant setting their differences aside.

Katie was willing, but she wasn't so sure about Tom. He seemed too set in his ways to see reason. Of course, she was a bit stubborn, too. But she would try to talk to him as soon as she could get him alone.

But when an interesting old man entered the house, Katie feared that chance might never come.

"Miss Katie O'Malley," Hannah said by way of introduction, "this is our dear friend, Jack Cavendish."

The old man grinned, sporting yellowed teeth—one of them missing. "Pleased to meet you, Miss O'Malley. Tom told me about you, and while he said you were

pretty, I have to tell you, he didn't do you a bit of justice. No sirree."

Katie wasn't so sure Tom had said anything of the
sort, but she accepted the old man's compliment. "How
do you do, Mr. Cavendish."

"Call me Trapper—or just plain ol' Jack. No need
for us to be formal."

He smiled, his blue eyes glimmering like a child's
at Christmas, although she couldn't imagine what he
found so amusing.

Ten minutes later, after giving Erin her fill of chicken
stew, which was merely a few bites, they sat down to a
delicious meal, during which Trapper Jack chattered on
about one thing or another. When the dishes had been
washed, Katie excused herself to take her bath. It wasn't
until afterward that she thought she might have a chance
to catch Tom alone.

Since Hannah had taken Sarah Jane into the small
guest room to read a storybook, and Trapper had apparently gone into the barn, Katie used that opportunity to
search for Tom. She found him standing on the porch,
peering into the darkness, the wolf-dog resting on its
haunches beside him.

When she opened the screen door, he turned. For a
moment, as their gazes met, her breath caught.

What was it about the man that stirred her senses?

Unable to come up with an answer, she shook it off
and asked, "What time do you plan to leave tomorrow?
And when will you be back?"

"I'm leaving in the morning. If all goes well, I'll be
back in three days—more or less." Tom leaned back
against the porch railing and sighed before returning his

gaze to hers. "I just hope Harrison Graves is still alive when I get there."

Tom had mentioned that Sarah Jane was the old man's only heir. "If it's decided that she is his great-grand-daughter, who will care for her when he dies?"

"That's not my immediate concern."

A chill settled over Katie, leaving a trail of goose-flesh in its path. "Well, it certainly should be. What will become of her? Who will love her?"

"Harrison's housekeeper looked after Caroline when she was a girl, but let's take things one day at a time."

Patience had never been one of Katie's virtues. "But what if Sarah Jane isn't happy there? What if she isn't welcome? What if she isn't even the heir that dying cattleman is looking for?"

"Take it easy." Tom took a step forward and lifted his hand as if to...

As if to what? Reach for her cheek? Offer comfort?

She'd never know because he dropped his hand back to his side as quickly as he'd raised it and said, "Maybe he'll let you take her to Wyoming until she's of age. There are other, more immediate concerns. But keep in mind that I'm not taking Sarah Jane yet. I'm leaving her here, where she'll be safe."

"Safe? But what if the man who hurt Erin followed us here?"

"If I thought there was a good chance of that, I wouldn't leave. But just in case, Trapper will stay behind. And Hannah can handle a gun. Besides, you'll be here, too."

She lifted a brow. "Does that mean you trust me to look after her?"

"I'm not sure how successful you'd be, but you'd probably die trying." A smile tugged at his lips. "You're feisty, Katie. And I'd pity any man who tried to put you in your place."

Like Tom had once tried?

She returned his smile.

He studied her for a moment in the moonlight. It seemed that the truce they'd reached earlier might have grown a wee bit stronger.

"Just so you know," he said, "Hannah said that you, Erin and Sarah Jane are welcome to stay with her for as long as it takes."

"That's kind of her," Katie said. "But tell me something. I've been curious. How did you and Hannah meet?"

"Trapper brought me to stay with her when I was a kid. My mother had just died, and I didn't have anyone else in the world to look after me. Hannah took me in and raised me. And when I had trouble at school, she taught me at home."

"Did you struggle to learn?"

He stiffened. "I wasn't in need of tutoring, if that's what you mean. Apparently, some of the townspeople didn't like the idea of an Indian boy going to school with the white kids. They voiced their disapproval, and some of the boys thought they could take it out on me. I came home with several black eyes and split lips, but after a pretty serious beating, Hannah refused to send me back."

The children had singled him out, just like Silas and his friends had turned on Sarah Jane.

Katie's heart went out to the lonely boy Tom had once been, and she gained an even deeper respect for Hannah.

"I'm sorry you lost your mother," she said.

He gave a shrug. "It happens."

"I know. I lost my mother, too. When I was a baby. I suppose, in some ways, that's easier. But at least you have memories of yours. I don't have any."

Katie's father hadn't talked much about her, thinking it might be easier that way. So Katie had sometimes created memories in her mind of a woman who'd been too good to be true.

One day, when Katie had been about nine, the teacher had given the girls an assignment and asked them to write about their mothers. Katie had won a prize for having the best essay of all. She'd written about her imaginary mother, who wore yellow dresses, lilac water and a smile. A woman who baked cookies every day and kept a library of books that children would enjoy.

A kind, loving woman who could have been Hannah, only Katie had imagined her tall, slender and blonde.

Growing up without a mother had been very hard, which was why Katie was so determined to stand by Sarah Jane and provide her with a loving home. That's also why Katie wanted to know who'd be looking out for her, who'd be mothering her.

"Maybe I should go to Stillwater with you," she told Tom.

If truth be told, the words had surprised her as much as they surely surprised him, but if Sarah Jane had to live with strangers, Katie wanted to make sure they would treat her well.

"Don't be ridiculous."

"I'm serious." She placed her hand on his arm to convince him of her sincerity and felt the warmth of his skin under his shirtsleeve. Their gazes met again, and for a moment, the intimacy seemed to meld them together.

That is, until he drew back his arm and pulled away.

"You don't want anyone to see you travel alone with a man, especially a half-breed. It might ruin your chances of landing an upstanding husband."

If he thought she gave a hoot about what others thought of her, he was mistaken. In fact, after that unfortunate confrontation with Sweet Heather at the Gardener's House, he should know that about her by now.

She stood tall and crossed her arms. "I don't want an upstanding husband."

A slow smile stretched across his face, sparking a glimmer in his eyes. "What kind of husband *would* you like?"

"I don't want a husband at all."

"Why not?" He scanned the length of her, then let his gaze drift back to her face again as though assessing her. Had he somehow found her lacking?

The momentary insecurity took her aback, and she chided herself. His opinion didn't matter in the least.

"I don't intend to be some man's pretty little slave he refers to as a wife." She hadn't meant to say "pretty." It sounded so…well, so vain.

Katie never had placed much value on beauty or the lack of it. Her auburn hair always garnered a compliment or two, but not the freckles splattered across her nose. Nor her outspoken personality, for that matter.

"I don't think there's much chance you'll need to worry about that, Katie."

Heat rose to her cheeks. "What do you mean?"

His lighthearted smile faded, and a thought-provoking expression took its place. "You might be able to recite poetry or quote ancient philosophers, but I doubt you know enough to come in out of the rain. A man would have to be plain loco to consider asking for your hand. You'd be useless as a wife."

Katie stood tall. *Useless?* The word struck a hard blow. All her life she'd struggled to prove her worth, her value, her competence.

He took a step closer. "You'd argue even if obedience would save your own hide."

Katie's hands went to her hips. "And I suppose you think a woman would find *you* appealing?"

"*You* do."

The fact that he was right set her scampering to deny it, and she snorted, making a most unladylike noise. "When it rains lemon drops."

"Is that right?" His grin returned, blossoming into a full-blown smile. "Has anyone told you that the shade of your eyes darkens whenever you're not being completely honest?"

She let out another unladylike sound. "Are you insinuating that I'm lying?"

"Your eyes are usually the color of the summer sky. But when you're not being truthful, they turn a blue-gray."

If that were true, it wasn't dishonesty causing change. It was anger. And sheer disbelief. She shook her head. "It's too dark out here for you to even see the color of my eyes." Then she turned on her heel and returned to the house.

The sound of his low chuckle merely stirred the tempest within—and surely deepened the color of her eyes to a stormy gray.

The morning sun streamed through the crocheted curtains and cast a dappled light into Hannah's guest room, where Katie sat up amidst the rumpled sheets of the four-poster feather bed and rubbed her eyes. Sarah Jane had risen without waking her, and obviously so had Hannah, because the aroma of freshly ground coffee and fried bacon wafted through the air.

Her mouth watered, reminding her it was time to eat. She didn't need a clock on the bureau to tell her she'd slept later than usual, but that shouldn't be a surprise. After the past few days of eating dried beef and hardtack and sleeping in a wagon, it had been such a comfort to rest in a cozy, warm bed.

Rising quickly, she tidied up her room. Then, after combing her hair and dressing for the day, she headed for the kitchen, eager for a cup of coffee.

She'd written two letters last night, one to the Granville school board, explaining her situation and promising to arrive as soon as she could. The other had been to Ian Connor, letting him know she was safe and in good hands. She would ask Hannah to mail them for her, since she planned to leave the next day with Tom, although she expected him to fight her on it.

When she reached the kitchen, she found Hannah at the stove, frying bacon.

"Good morning," Katie said.

Hannah turned, and her smile made her almost look... Well, pretty wasn't the word, but there was something about her, a kindness, a warmth that Katie found appealing.

"Can I get you some coffee, dear?"

"Yes, please. That would be lovely."

Hannah poured a cup, then handed it to Katie. "Careful now. It's hot."

"Thank you."

"Cream and sugar is on the table."

Katie sweetened her coffee and added a drop of cream, then lifted the cup and blew across the rim to cool it. "I'm afraid I slept like a rock last night. How did Erin do?"

"She rested well. I offered her a little poached egg this morning. She ate nearly all of it. Then I gave her some medicine. She's sleeping again."

"That's good. Where's Sarah Jane?"

"Outside."

"Is she all right out there alone?"

"She's fine. Lobo is with her."

In spite of Hannah's attempts at reassurance, Katie scooted back her chair and carried her cup to the back door, where she peered outside to check on the child. She'd never been particularly fond of dogs, especially those that looked more like wolves.

It didn't take long for her to see that Hannah might be right, because Sarah Jane hooked her arm around the dog's woolly neck and cuddled against him.

About the time Katie was going to turn away, she spotted Trapper Jack coming out of the barn and heading for the house.

"Good mornin'," he said, his voice resonant and clear.

Katie greeted him, then stepped aside so he could enter the kitchen.

"I hope breakfast is ready," he said. "I'm hungry enough to eat a mule."

Hannah chuckled as she poured him a cup of coffee. "You're always hungry, old man. But now that you're here, I'll go outside and tell Sarah Jane that it's time to come inside for breakfast."

As the older woman made her way to the door, Katie took a sip of coffee, then asked Trapper, "Where's Tom?"

"He left a little bit ago."

"He *left?* Already?"

"Didn't get a chance to tell him goodbye, huh?"

"Well, no. But I'd actually hoped to go with him."

Trapper studied her for a moment, then stroked his chin. "Now that's a real shame that he left without you. As far as I'm concerned, it would have been best if you'd gone with him."

She wasn't used to men agreeing with her so readily. "Why do you say that? I mean, I have a good reason for going with him. I want to meet those people in Stillwater myself so that I can decide whether they're suitable to care for Sarah Jane."

"That's a good idea. Just 'cause folks have money don't mean that they're kind."

Katie blew out a sigh of relief, glad that Trapper understood her concern. "I couldn't agree more, and while that's been a real worry, it's too late for me to go now."

"I'm not so sure about that. Tom had a stop to make about three miles from here. The lonely old feller he went to see will probably talk his ear off, so we could catch up with him in no time at all."

"*We?* You mean you'd take me to meet him?"

Trapper stroked his chin again, as a slow grin stretched across his craggy face until it crinkled his eyes. "That fool kid would probably skin me alive for not stayin' put until he gets back, but how could he get mad at either of us when we're just lookin' out for that poor little girl?"

Katie figured Tom could get *plenty* mad at her, and

if truth be told, a part of her was tempted to stay here and wait with Erin and Sarah Jane. But Tom said he'd be back in a couple of days, which meant that Stillwater was probably only a day's ride—more or less. And while Tom would be upset, he'd probably get over it. Particularly since they both had Sarah Jane's well-being in mind.

"So what do you say?" Trapper asked.

"Well, for one thing," Katie said, "on the ride here, he complained about the horse I borrowed from the livery. He said she wasn't a trail horse. I'm afraid I'd never be able to keep up with him."

"You can ride Hannah's sorrel mare. Gully Washer is a bit testy, but strong and sturdy." Trapper's eyes fairly glimmered. "I'll have Hannah pack you some vittles while I saddle the horse."

He made it sound so easy, but Katie knew better than that. Still, she loved a debate and a challenge. And she'd have several hours to change Tom's mind—if not his mood. "Okay. I'll pack a few things for the ride. I just wish I would have brought some bloomers with me. They'd make riding a horse a lot easier."

In a fit of anger, her da had burned her only pair. She would have ordered another—or perhaps several—but he'd died shortly thereafter, and she hadn't felt nearly so rebellious when she'd been grieving his loss.

Still, a pair of bloomers would certainly come in handy now.

Trapper scrunched his face and shook his head. "I never did see any point in women wearing those fool things. You might as well wear men's britches."

"I would if I had a pair that fit."

"Hmm. Now, that's an idea. Hannah packed up all the

old clothes Tom outgrew and put them in the hayloft. I could find a pair that might fit you, but you'd probably look a sight."

"I don't care how I look. I mean to be comfortable and capable on the trail, and I want Tom to see me as an equal while we travel."

Trapper eyed her carefully, and a slow grin tickled his lips. "Those britches might be a bit snug, but I don't suppose they'd look too bad."

"As long as they fit and I can move around, I'll be happy."

The old man chuckled. "All righty. I'll get your traveling clothes while you pack. But be quick about it. If we don't catch Tom by the time he reaches the pass, it'll be too late."

Katie nodded and turned toward the house. Trapper had said to hurry, and she would. Still, she heard him chuckle and mutter, "The kid needs respectability more than he thinks."

She wondered what he meant by that, but it didn't matter. She was going to Stillwater with Tom McCain whether he liked it or not.

However, thirty minutes later, when Katie was packed and mounted on Hannah's sorrel mare, she was having second thoughts about leaving.

"You know, Trapper…" Katie paused, took a deep breath and slowly let it out. "I'm not so sure this is a good idea, after all."

"Why? This is the best idea I've ever had. Tom needs your help."

"He needs *my* help?"

Trapper nodded. "More than either of you know. Tom might be ornery at times and act as tough as nails, but inside, he's as soft as butter. And whether he's told you or not, he's downright worried about those folks in Stillwater, the ones that want the little girl."

Katie's senses reeled at the mention of Sarah Jane. "What's wrong with them?"

"Tom don't trust them to be good to her. But he's gonna make sure they ain't planning to make her sleep in the barn. And that they'll feed her at least once a day. Course, he ought to make sure they don't take too big of a stick to her when she don't get her chores done by nightfall."

Katie pointed her finger. "Believe me, Trapper. That child won't live with anyone who treats her as less than royalty."

"That's what I was hoping you'd say. Hannah's right attached to the little thing. She'll be glad to know you won't let those people be mean to her."

"Tom is in for a fight if he believes the only requirement of a good home is sleeping indoors and eating one meal a day. And I'll take a stick to anyone who even thinks to strike her." Katie clenched her firsts, her fingers tightening around the reins. "And if Tom disagrees, he'd better brace himself for a tangle with me."

"I figure there'll be a tussle between you. Course, I doubt Tom stands a chance." Trapper grinned from ear to ear. "And to tell you the truth, I'd like to see him get his comeuppance from a pretty little gal like you."

"If he tries to challenge me, he'll wish he hadn't."

"A tangle with you might be the best thing that ever happened to him. Might bring him some respectability."

Katie still didn't know what respectability had to do with anything, but she'd put a stop to any fool no-

tion Tom McCain had of leaving Sarah Jane in an un-
safe or unhappy situation, even if she had to fight him
tooth and nail.

Chapter Six

"This is where we part ways."

"Here?" On a trail surrounded by trees and brush? Katie didn't like the idea of being stranded in what appeared to be the wilderness.

Trapper removed his hat and mopped his brow. "Tom hasn't gotten this far yet. And you're downwind from him. He won't catch on before you spot him. And by then, it will be too late for him to send you back."

She wondered if she should reach for her derringer, something she'd purchased to protect herself after her father had died. For the first mile she'd ridden along with it tucked in her pocket, but with each swaying step of the sorrel mare, she'd worried the small gun would go off, wounding her in the leg. So she'd removed the loaded firearm and placed it in her saddlebag, where it was still within reach.

"Ride due south," Trapper instructed. "Wait near that patch of cottonwood trees growing along the stream. Tom should go that way."

He *should* go that way? "What if he doesn't?"

Trapper turned in his saddle, the leather creaking

with his movement. He scanned the rolling horizon and pointed at a small wooden structure. "See that cabin over yonder?"

Katie craned her neck and spotted the rustic log structure perched upon a grassy hillside. "Yes, it looks like it has a newly patched roof."

"It does." Trapper chuckled. "I fell clean through the old one last spring, trying to help Tom fix a rotten spot that leaked like old fury whenever it rained."

"Why were you two fixing the roof?"

"My friend and neighbor, Izzy Ballard, lives there. The old cuss and I go way back, and he owes me. I near broke my neck when I fell through and landed inside. Izzy will get you back to Hannah's place if Tom has already passed through."

"Are you sure he won't mind?"

"Not if he's still alive."

"Izzy might be *dead?*" Katie shuddered at the thought of walking into the cabin and finding a body.

Trapper laughed again. "Izzy's too stubborn to roll over and die. He'll be right flattered to be asked to help a pretty woman in distress."

Katie didn't like the idea of being pretty or in distress. But she liked being stranded even less.

Before she could give it much thought, Trapper said goodbye and headed back the way they'd come, leaving her on her own.

She wasn't sure how long she waited to catch sight of Tom or his horse. She supposed it had only been a few minutes, but she'd gotten so caught up trying to follow the trail that she'd nearly missed seeing him ride down the hillside, away from Izzy's cabin.

When he lifted his hat, adjusting it, a stray beam of

sunlight reflected off his coal-black hair, reminding her of an Indian brave, a warrior.

She meant to call out, to confront him with her plan, to insist he take her with him, but a second thought silenced her. In spite of what Trapper had said, she doubted Tom would be pleased to see her. And since they were only an hour's ride from Hannah's house, she realized he might send her back with Izzy. So she nudged her mount forward, keeping her eyes on the broad shoulders of the man she'd better keep up with.

The tight-fitting dungarees definitely made riding more comfortable, and Trapper had been right about Gully Washer. Hannah's sorrel mare certainly had more get-up-and-go than the old roan.

However, an hour later, Katie had nearly lost sight of Tom's gelding. She urged the mare along, worried she was too far from Izzy's cabin to find it again. She was just about to call out to Tom in spite of her reservations, knowing he'd hear her. But before she could do so, a rattle sounded from the brush, followed by the horse's whinny.

The mare reared. Katie grabbed for the pommel, but only caught a few strands of mane and fell to the ground with a thump.

As she struggled to catch her breath, her eyes locked on the largest snake she'd ever imagined let alone seen. A bloodcurdling scream seemed to come from someone else, as she froze in fear.

Gully Washer, on the other hand, had taken off like a rifle shot in the same direction as Tom, leaving her to stare at a coiled, black-and-brown diamondback that hissed and rattled in anger.

If Katie still carried the derringer in her pocket, she could have shot it, but the gun was stashed in the saddlebag strapped to the mare, so she had nothing to use in defense.

She ached in a hundred different spots, most notably her right ankle, which had taken the brunt of her fall on the hard dirt. But she didn't dare move. Instead, she sat quietly, waiting, hoping that the vile creature would just give up and go away when he realized she wasn't a threat to him. Either that, or that Tom would have heard her scream and come looking for a damsel in distress.

It seemed like ages, but it was probably only a matter of moments before the big, ugly snake finally slithered to the tall grass off to the side of the pathway. With her heart still pounding like a blacksmith's hammer, Katie reached for her right ankle, which throbbed something fierce.

Before she could even attempt to stand, a stranger's voice interrupted her efforts. "What do you know, Georgie. Look what we got us here. We done found us a woman."

Katie glanced over her shoulder, where two men atop their horses looked down at her. A short, stocky man did the talking. The other one appeared awestruck, his gaping smile revealing a mouthful of yellow teeth.

"Why, I ain't never had such luck before. She's a pretty one, even in britches." The stocky man spit a brown stream of spittle to the ground and wiped his mouth with the back of a beefy hand.

"Are we gonna keep her, Ned?" the one called Georgie asked.

Katie wondered if his wide-mouthed stare was due

to his reaction at seeing her or if his lips just couldn't close over his mouthful of teeth.

"Sure, we'll keep her. You don't expect us to just walk away from a gift that fell out of the sky, do you?"

They both seemed to find that funny, but the idea sickened Katie. She had no weapon. And even if the horse hadn't run off, she would've been hard-pressed to snatch the gun out of the saddlebag without them taking notice.

She wished she had something to fight them with— a hatpin, a rock, a stick. All she had was her wits, and something told her those might not be enough.

Where was Tom?

Surely he'd heard her scream and was on his way.

Or had he gone after Hannah's horse?

The short, stocky man named Ned stepped closer, a wicked gleam in his eyes. His belly hung over the straining waistband of his dirty gray britches. He reeked of month-old sweat and something else she couldn't be sure of—rancid grease, she suspected. And she cringed at the thought of him touching her.

She fought the physical reaction and struggled to gather her wits. "I do believe I'm the lucky one, gentlemen. I fell off my horse, and it ran off. I don't suppose I could talk either of you into running after it for me, could I?"

The man called Georgie stood ramrod straight and beamed. "I'll get it for you, ma'am." Then he turned to his stocky friend. "You don't care, do ya, Ned?"

"Go on. We'll have to take turns having a go with her anyway. And I aim to be first."

Katie's stomach reeled, but she pointed in the opposite direction of where the fool horse had run. "It's a sorrel mare."

"Don't use her all up," Georgie told his friend, before spurring his mount and riding off.

Taking advantage of the man's departure, Katie batted her eyes and smiled. "I don't suppose I could talk you into doing another favor for me, as well."

Ned eased closer. "After I'm done, maybe."

"Of all the luck," Katie said with a sigh. "It seems I lost my bag of gold coins."

At that, Ned slowed to a stop. "Did you say *gold?*"

"Yes, I had it in my hand, counting out the coins when the horse reared and threw me. The bag flew out of my hand and fell into that tall brush over there, and I heard them scatter."

Katie reached for her booted foot, stroking it carefully. "I'd get the bag and collect them all myself, but it seems I've twisted my ankle."

Ned strode to the edge of the road nearest Katie, bent and began to brush the grass aside with both hands. A rattle sounded too late for him to jerk back.

"Aagh! I been snake bit!"

Katie used the diversion to hobble to her feet, her ankle aching. "That's a real shame," she said. "You could surely die from that nasty bite."

Ned screamed again, this time louder. Then he fired his gun in the air. "Georgie! Git on over here. I need your help!"

Katie prayed that Tom had heard the commotion, because she could certainly use some help, too.

"I'm gonna die," Ned said. "For sure and certain."

"You need to see a doctor," Katie said. "So I suggest you ride to the nearest town. And fast."

Moments later, horses approached, their hooves crunching along the twigs and leaves. Katie watched as Tom rode his gelding and led Hannah's sorrel mare by the reins.

He looked fierce on that big gelding, his gun drawn, his eyes blazing. Katie never thought she'd be so happy to see anyone in her life, especially a man as frightfully angry as he appeared to be.

Ned strode forward, his wounded hand clutched tightly to his chest. "Help me, mister. I don't want to die. You've got some injun in you, don't ya? You gotta know all kinds of secret brews and remedies."

Tom looked at Katie, his face never so stoic, so unreadable. "What happened here?"

"He intended to hurt me. And that snakebite serves him right."

"You tricked me!" Ned, his hand clutched tightly to his chest, glared at Katie. "There weren't no bag of gold in them bushes. You knew that snake was there, and you wanted me to get bit."

"I didn't know that snake was still in those bushes. Not for sure. It could have slithered off for all I knew."

Tom dismounted and pulled a knife from his belt.

"What are you going to do with *that?*" Ned asked, his eyes growing even wider.

Did he actually fear a scalping? From the look on his face, she suspected he might.

"I'll help this time," Tom said, "but don't ever come near this woman—or any other woman—again."

"I didn't know she was *yours*," Ned said. "I thought she was free for the takin'."

"Free?" Tom snorted. "This woman is going to cost some man plenty."

Katie didn't know what he meant by that, but she was too relieved to see him to take any offense—and she wasn't at all ready to risk stirring things up any more than they already were.

Tom surveyed the area. "Where's his friend?"

"He went for Gully Washer, but I sent him in the wrong direction." Katie studied Tom, who wouldn't have fallen for her story about the bag of gold and who wouldn't have chased after a runaway horse without looking at the tracks first.

"Take off your shirt," Tom told Ned.

When the man complied, Tom ripped off a sleeve and used it to cinch the man's arm tight. Then taking his knife, he sliced into the darkening wound.

Ned cried out. "What are you doing? Don't cut my hand off."

Tom pulled him closer. "Suck the blood and spit it out. It'll help remove some of the poison."

Ned nodded, then did as he was told. Between spits and sputters, he looked up at Tom and asked, "Am I going to die?"

"Maybe. And maybe not. Either way, you'll probably get pretty sick. You'd better find a doctor fast."

When Georgie returned, Ned wasted no time in convincing him to hightail it back to town.

As Katie and Tom watched the two men ride off at breakneck speed, she returned her attention to the man who'd come to her rescue and had to admit that she was glad that he had. She might have outsmarted Ned and Georgie temporarily, but she wasn't sure how long she would have been able to keep them at bay.

But when she saw him slap his hands on his hips, she realized her moment of reckoning was at hand.

* * *

Tom studied the headstrong woman wearing one of his long-outgrown shirts. He would have recognized that blue-and-green-plaid material anywhere. Hannah had stitched it together one evening by candlelight, and he'd worn it with pride until it no longer had fit.

He assumed the pants and boots had once been his, too, and doubted that she'd found the old clothing on her own.

Trapper must have given them to her when he put her up to tagging along after him. Tom could see the old man's hand in all of this. He'd probably figured Tom would have to return her to Hannah's place and maybe give up his plan to go to Stillwater altogether. He never had liked the idea of Tom working for Harrison Graves. But it didn't matter. Tom's mind was set, and no one was going to change it.

"I suppose you want to know why I'm here," Katie said.

"For a start. I'd also like to know why you were riding Hannah's horse. You're lucky I spotted her running off—and that she came to me when I called. You were also lucky I heard that gunshot and Ned's holler."

"The poor horse was frightened by a rattlesnake and took off like a shot. Why did she go to you so easily?"

"I have a way with animals," he said.

"Apparently so." She tossed him an easy grin as if she could sweet-talk her way out of all the trouble she'd become. "I must say, Tom McCain, you're a sight for sore eyes—and an answer to a prayer. You came just in time." Her grin deepened into a pretty smile, as if that could make everything all right.

To be honest, it did help a little. When he'd realized

Ned and Georgie had planned to take advantage of her, he'd wanted to tear them limb from limb.

But that didn't mean Tom was no longer upset that Katie had followed him. Nor that he'd forgotten another time when a woman and a snake had gotten a man into trouble, taking all of mankind with them.

"What'd you do?" he asked. "Sweet-talk Trapper into helping you?"

"I really didn't have to." She brushed the dust from the denim jeans. "It was as much Trapper's idea as mine. He seemed to agree that I should accompany you to see Mr. Graves."

Tom didn't doubt that. And while he would have preferred to haul Katie back to Hannah's house, he couldn't afford to spend the additional time it would take to rid himself of her. So that meant that he was saddled with her for at least the next three days—long enough to go to the Lazy G Ranch, take care of business and then ride back to Hannah's.

Tom blew out a sigh. This wasn't the least bit funny, and once it was all said and done, he'd find a way to get back at Trapper for his shenanigans.

"Mount up," he told her. "We'll talk about it while we ride."

"I promise not to be any trouble."

Tom clicked his tongue. "You'd be a bushel of trouble if you were sound asleep."

She stood tall again and placed one hand on her hip. Her chin lifted, exposing an ivory-skinned neck, where her pulse fluttered.

When he faced her, close enough to breathe in her lilac scent, close enough to touch, he couldn't help but run his knuckles along her cheek. As he did, her breath caught, though she didn't draw back. She didn't smile, either. She just watched him with eyes as big and wide as the sky.

For a moment he forgot why he was here, why he was angry at her for tagging along, for slowing his pace.

But as reality set in, he slowly shook his head and said, "Let's go. I've wasted enough time already."

As she turned to take a step toward the mare, her right leg gave out. He reached out and caught her before she fell.

"What's wrong?"

"I twisted my ankle when I fell. If you'll just help me to my horse, I'll be fine."

He knew she wasn't the type of woman to ask for help, even if she were in a real fix. In fact, any other woman would have screamed and cried when the horse threw her. And then again when those ruffians found her.

Just thinking about what might have happened to her turned his stomach inside out. Ned and Georgie didn't seem to have a single brain between them, but that didn't mean they wouldn't have hurt her, given the chance.

Of course, Tom had to give her credit for outsmarting them, but what would have happened if that rattler hadn't been in those weeds?

And what if Tom hadn't recognized Hannah's mare? What if he hadn't heard all the commotion and come riding fast to see what was going on?

Katie might insist that she was fine, but he knew better than to believe her. So he scooped her into his arms, intent upon assessing her injury.

"You don't need to carry me. A shoulder to lean on would have been sufficient."

"It's easier this way."

He was surprised at how little effort it took to hold her—and amazed at the light scent of lilac that laced the smell of trail dust and leather.

In spite of the rugged denim she wore, she felt small in his arms—and soft. Yet he wouldn't underestimate her. He knew that he held a powerful pack of woman. And that it would take a special kind of man to tangle with a spitfire like her on a daily basis.

Tom might be stuck with her over the next couple of days, but once they returned from Stillwater and he sent her back to Pleasant Valley, he'd be through with her, and she'd be another man's problem.

He carried her to a good-size boulder and set her down on it. Then he reached for her right boot and gave it a gentle tug. She grimaced until it slipped off her foot.

Her ankle was bruised and swollen, although he didn't think that it was broken.

"Can you get that boot back on?" he asked.

"Yes."

After she'd done so, he lifted her into his arms again and carried her to Gully Washer.

It was easier that way, he told himself. It was nicer, too. He enjoyed the feel of her in his arms, the way she clung to him as if she needed him, as if they'd entered a dream world where their many differences no longer mattered.

But that world didn't exist.

After helping her mount, he said, "Let's go. We're burning daylight."

Then he climbed onto his gelding as if nothing had happened, as if he'd never held her in his arms.

As if he'd never imagined there could ever be anything more between them.

* * *

When Tom finally called a halt to eat the midday meal, it was already so late in the afternoon that Katie thought she'd ridden as far as she could go without collapsing from exhaustion and falling off her horse.

The dust alone made her clothing feel pounds heavier than when she'd started out this morning, and her stomach had growled and rumbled itself into a knot.

She licked her parched lips. What she wouldn't give for a cool glass of well water, a bowl of Hannah's chicken stew and a warm bath, but she'd die before admitting her discomfort. After all, she'd promised not to be any trouble, and she'd meant it.

Tom swung down from his mount and then surveyed the area he'd chosen for them to rest and eat. "There's a stream where you can wash up. I'll take care of the horses."

As much as she wanted to stretch her legs, she wasn't sure if she could dismount on her own.

Fortunately, Tom was by her side before she could try or ask for help. When he reached for her, she was tempted to object and claim she could do it on her own, but she feared she'd collapse into a heap if she didn't accept his assistance.

His arms were strong, his stance sturdy. So she leaned into him until he swung her from the horse. Yet he still held on to her.

"Can you stand on your own?" he asked.

"I'll try."

As he released her and took a step back, her right leg wobbled. Before she knew it, he wrapped his arms around her and drew her close. As her cheek rested against his shoulder, his scent, a swirl of musk, leather and soap, sent her senses reeling.

As if knowing that he'd somehow added to her unbalance, his eyes searched hers, holding her in some kind of silent dance—or maybe it was a duel. She couldn't be sure which.

"I'm fine," she said. "My ankle feels better now. It's just a little stiff and sore."

When he loosened his embrace and allowed her to stand on her own, a weakness settled over her. A weakness from the long, hard ride, no doubt.

But before she could gather her wits, a soft rattling sounded to the right of her. She stifled a scream, reached for him and held on tight. "Oh, no. It's another rattlesnake."

"It's cicadas."

"What's that?"

"A kind of locust."

"Are you sure it's not a rattlesnake?"

"I'd be in a real fix if I didn't know the difference between the two."

As she tried to take a step, her right ankle nearly gave out on her again, and she grimaced.

"Does it hurt that badly?" A hint of compassion softened his voice and warmed his gaze.

"No, not really."

"I don't believe you."

"All right, it does, but I'm not one to complain."

He lifted his brow as though challenging her honesty.

"I'm *not.*"

"Maybe not about pain, but you don't keep your complaints or objections to yourself. Not as a rule."

"I suppose you have a point."

A slow smile slid across his face. "That being agreed upon, I'm going to take you down to the stream that runs along here. I'll find a safe spot where you can rest. I think soaking your ankle will help relieve the pain. But the path may be a bit crooked and steep."

Then, in a move that was becoming all too familiar, he lifted her into his arms and carried her along a tree-lined path to the water's edge.

Katie held on to his shoulder with one hand and felt the corded muscles that lay hidden beneath his cotton shirt. At one time, she might have struggled with her vulnerability, but here, in the dappled sunlight with Tom McCain, she didn't feel the least bit helpless.

Why was that?

After he set her down on the sandy shoreline, he held her steady until she could balance herself—perhaps holding on a bit longer than necessary.

"Are you going to be all right alone?" he asked.

She nodded, not at all sure that she would be. Then she scanned the grassy brush that surrounded the creek. "You…uh…don't suppose there are any snakes around here, do you?"

"I'm afraid this is where they live, Katie."

She'd hoped to hold her reaction, but she feared her face had paled and her expression had given her away.

Thankfully, he seemed to take pity on her, because he said, "Just so you know, snakes don't attack. They only try to protect themselves. If you stay in the clearing, you should be safe."

Katie wanted to question him further, to insist that he stay nearby, just in case she needed help. But in her heart of hearts, she knew it was more than fear of snakes that had her wanting him to stay close.

The man held a dark and rugged appeal she was at a loss to explain, and she liked having him near.

But she couldn't very well admit to any of that, so she let him go, watching as he walked away and feeling more and more exposed with each step he took.

Chapter Seven

Tom watered the horses downstream, then he retrieved Katie's valise and returned to the spot where he'd left her to soak her ankle. He hoped her bag held everything she'd want or need. It was certainly bulky enough.

When he'd realized she'd been following him, he'd wanted to lash out at her for her rebellious nature, for her insistence upon going to Stillwater to meet Harrison Graves. He'd also wanted to throttle Trapper for setting up the fool travel plan.

But when Tom realized that Katie had been in danger and that she'd been injured, he'd softened to the point that he'd felt an overwhelming urge to protect her with his life. And then he'd wanted to lash out at himself.

What had he been thinking?

It must have been the scent of lilacs, the feel of her in his arms, the way she gazed at him as if he'd been some kind of hero, at least in her eyes.

For a moment, he'd even liked the thought of it.

How could he be the least bit tempted by a woman who'd surely be the death of him if he'd so much as consider her as a...

As a what?

A woman to court, to marry?

No, that was plum crazy, and he scoffed at the very idea.

When he neared the stream, his breath caught at the sight of her sitting on a rock. Even wearing boy's clothing, there was no mistaking her for anything but a woman through and through.

She'd rolled up her pant legs, and her bare feet hung in the cool water.

If he'd had all the time in the world, he might have remained in the shadows, watching her from several paces back. But he was determined to make it to the Lazy G before dark. And even if he hadn't had anything pressing to do, he wouldn't waste his time daydreaming about things that would never be.

"I brought your bag," he said. "I thought you might need it."

"Thank you."

He made his way toward the stream. "Does the cold water help?"

"Yes, my ankle feels much better now." She bit down on her lower lip, as if wanting to add something more but pondering the wisdom of it. She finally said, "I'm sorry for slowing your pace. I know you're in a hurry. I really didn't mean for this to happen."

A sharp retort would have come easy, but for some reason, he shrugged off his irritation. "I suppose we'll have to make the best of it."

At that point, he should have excused himself and left her alone, but he didn't. Instead, he studied the way she wiggled her toes in the water, the way she leaned forward, the way the sun highlighted the gold strands in her auburn locks.

She was an intriguing woman—not at all like the others he knew. She was pretty, to be sure. And as feisty as all get-out. Rebellious to a fault. She was also bright.

He really had to give her credit for outsmarting those ruffians who'd tried to take advantage of her. Another woman might have fallen apart at the seams, but she'd kept her composure.

Still, while he admired her wit, it was her outspoken nature he objected to.

"You must be a real challenge to the men in your life," he said.

She looked up and smiled. "That's true. My father valued education and taught me to read when I was very young. Once I mastered that, he taught me to debate. And I must admit, it frustrated him at times, but he appreciated a well-thought-out argument."

"I imagine you had some interesting conversations at the dinner table."

"We certainly did." Her smile drifted away. "But not everyone was as understanding. My teachers didn't like to be challenged. And the other children at school often avoided me for that reason. And for other reasons, as well. My childhood, while it seemed typical to me, was much different from the other girls."

"In what way?" he asked.

"I grew up with an imaginary mother instead of a real one—and a library of books instead of a playroom of dolls and toys."

Her candor surprised him.

"Children can be cruel," she added, "especially when they perceive another child to be different, which is why

I didn't put up with that kind of behavior in my classroom when I was a teacher."

Katie didn't have to tell Tom about how mean kids could be. At least the taunts she'd suffered hadn't led to fistfights, black eyes and bloody noses.

It was odd that they could be such opposites yet share some similarities. Of course, Katie could have saved herself a lot of trouble by keeping her mouth shut. And he couldn't do anything about the color of his skin or the Comanche blood that ran through his veins.

"Do you think you can walk?" he asked her.

"Yes, I'm sure I can." She removed her feet from the water, then reached into her valise and pulled out a handkerchief. After drying her feet, she put her boots back on, taking extra care with the right one.

He made his way to the rock where she sat, then reached for her hand and helped her stand. Before he could turn away, she swayed on her feet.

He grabbed her wrist and slipped an arm around her waist to hold her steady. "I thought you said you were all right."

"I was," she said. "I *am*."

As her gaze locked on his, the tint of her eyes took him aback, and as he watched, the hue deepened, darkened.

Her hand held his forearm, the warmth of her touch flaring from her fingertips. In spite of his better judgment and his resolve to keep his distance, he felt himself weaken.

Her lips, the color of wild strawberries, parted as if begging for a kiss.

He looked at her expression for disapproval, for a sign that he was about to overstep his boundaries, but as their gazes continued to hold firm, he was caught up in something too big to ignore.

He'd be sorry for this later, but he'd always been partial to strawberries.

As Tom leaned forward, as his lips met hers, Katie's heart skipped a beat. She probably should resist kissing him, but she was too taken by surprise, too swept up in the wonder of it all.

It started out sweet and innocent, like the time Orson Billings kissed her behind the mercantile when she'd been fifteen years old. But while that kiss had been a bit awkward but nice, this one was…oh, so much more.

The kiss deepened and, as she slipped her arms around him, she marveled at the scent of him, at the feel of his embrace, at the taste of his sweet kiss. Before she knew it, her knees nearly gave out, and she leaned into him for support.

The world tilted, and the sun spun round and round.

What was she thinking? What was she doing, kissing Tom McCain as if there were no tomorrow?

And there most certainly would be a tomorrow—in *Wyoming!*

She placed her hands on his chest, allowing them to linger just long enough to feel the steady beat of his heart pounding in time with hers. Then she pushed back and turned her head, pulling her lips from his and ending that mind-numbing kiss.

"I'm sorry," she said. "I don't know why I let you do that."

"You *let* me do that?" He chuckled.

Her cheeks warmed, and she knew they must be as red as new apples.

"You were every bit as willing as I was," he said. "And you liked it."

That was true. But she didn't dare admit it, so she let out a most unladylike huff. "No, not really."

"Oh, no? There's a telltale flush on your cheeks and throat, and your eyes have deepened to a lovely shade of liar blue."

Katie quickly glanced away, unwilling to allow his dark eyes to challenge hers any longer. She really wasn't lying.

All right, so she was, but she certainly didn't want Tom to know it. She started to walk away—and would have if he hadn't chosen that moment to chuckle again.

Childhood taunts in the schoolyard and the memory of all the snide male comments and laughter while she'd spoken on the dais in Pleasant Valley in support of women's suffrage hadn't prepared her for the sound of this particular man's ridicule. Without a conscious thought, her Irish temper flared, and she swung out her hand and slapped his cheek.

The sound, the sting, the jolt of her thoughtless re-action shocked her as much as it had him, because she froze in midmovement the moment it happened, wishing she could somehow take it all back—the kiss, the slap…

His laughter ceased, and he caught her wrist in an ironclad grip. "Don't ever strike me again." His dark eyes narrowed, and for a moment she witnessed a wounded look, a glimpse of something he usually kept locked deep inside.

"Then don't laugh at me," she said, her voice more a whisper of defense than a threat.

Without another word, he dropped her wrist, turned and walked away.

She wasn't sure what had just happened, but she sensed that they'd inadvertently shared an intimacy of sorts, a peek through cracks in the walls they'd both built around their hearts, allowing them each a glimpse inside the other.

A glimpse at something that went far beyond an earth-spinning kiss, a chuckle and a slap.

For once Tom's lack of conversation hadn't bothered Katie a bit. In fact, she considered it truly a blessing. She relished the time she had to sort through her reeling senses. If truth be told, her thoughts and feelings were all atumble.

He'd pointed out her lie, and he'd been right. She *had* wanted him to kiss her. And she'd liked it—a lot. She just hadn't been prepared to deal with the repercussions of it.

She still wasn't about to talk about the kiss, but after four hours on the trail with nary a word out of him, she'd grown tired of the silence.

"It's a lovely day," she said.

He merely gave a cursory scan of the horizon.

So much for an attempt to draw him into a conversation.

"Are we nearing Stillwater yet?" she asked.

No response.

Nevertheless, she asked, "How much farther do we have to go?"

This time, when he didn't reply, she lowered her voice and answered for him, deciding to carry on a conversation by herself. "Not much farther, Katie. It's been a long trip, hasn't it?"

"It certainly has," she said, returning to her own voice. "I'm just so grateful you were such a fine traveling companion. I don't know when I've ever had a more pleasant journey."

"Well, Katie," she answered, mocking him, "I must admit that I hate traveling alone. Thank you for joining me."

She cast a sideways glance, pleased to see the stubborn man had coked his head and caught her eye.

"You're not going *loco* on me, are you?" he asked.

She hadn't realized how much she'd missed his voice, especially with such a pleasant tone. *"Loco?"*

"That's Spanish for crazy."

She smiled. It wasn't her idea of a conversation, but it was a start. "I don't believe so, but how would one know for sure?"

"You probably wouldn't."

What did he mean by that? If she were crazy she wouldn't be aware of it? Or there wouldn't be any telltale difference in her behavior whether she was crazy or not?

She could have made an issue of his comment, but didn't. After six hours without any conversation at all, she was glad to have him talking again. And even happier to have that kiss behind them.

"How much farther do we need to go?" she asked, hoping this time to receive an answer.

"We've been on the outskirts of the Lazy G for the past hour, ever since we rode through that pass."

"The *outskirts* of the Lazy G?" Katie looked over her shoulder and scanned the sage-dotted landscape for a sign of habitation. "How large is the ranch?"

"Fifty thousand acres, more or less. The Lazy G was once a Spanish Land Grant."

"That's impressive. Mr. Graves must be very wealthy."

"He made most of his money growing fields of cotton

and raising longhorn cattle for hides and tallow. Just before the war, he began crossbreeding his herd. The last few years he's been running cattle drives and making a second fortune selling beef."

Katie could scarcely imagine the size of the ranch or the money it would take to control and run it. Her curiosity of Sarah Jane's family mounted. "Tell me about the people we'll meet."

She wondered if her question would anger him or if it would elicit more silence, but he responded as though they'd gone back to that truce they'd formed earlier.

"There's not much to tell. Harrison Graves is as rich as they come, at least around here. He has land, property, money and respect."

Katie had surmised that much. "But you said he was ill."

"Dying."

"What about his wife? What happened to her?"

"She passed away from a fever after giving birth to his only child, a son named Robert. Harrison was too busy running cattle and building a fortune to remarry."

Katie could hardly believe her ears. Tom was not only talking to her, he was actually relaying information. She'd have to remember that all it took to have him finally open up was a kiss, a slap and six hours of guilt-laden silence.

"You mentioned that Sarah Jane's mother was his only heir. I assume she was Robert's daughter, and that Robert passed away, too."

"He died in a stampede while on a cattle drive when Caroline was six."

"And Robert's wife?"

For a moment Tom seemed to withdraw from the

conversation. About the time Katie wondered if he'd ever speak again, he said, "Robert's wife, Juliana, was a blonde and frail woman from New England. I heard she couldn't take the heat or the separation from society as she knew it, so she returned to the East, taking baby Caroline with her. She caught a fever and died about two years later."

Now it began to make sense. "So Juliana took Caroline back East, and that's why Harrison was looking for her?"

"No." Tom stared straight ahead, his back ramrod straight. "Caroline was barely a year old when her mother left Texas, but Harrison went after the baby and brought her back."

"Juliana gave up her child?"

Tom turned in the saddle, and his dark eyes locked on hers. "You're the suffragist and the daughter of an attorney. You know how the law works. The child belonged to her father, and Juliana had no right to her. Harrison merely went after his granddaughter and brought her home to Texas."

"After Juliana died?"

"No, before she got sick."

A knot formed in Katie's stomach. Had Juliana really died of a fever? Or of a broken heart? And what about the baby? Had Harrison just taken her away from her mother?

No wonder there had been a family rift. The cattleman must not have a loving, paternal heart.

"I realize I've never met Harrison Graves," Katie said, "but I can tell you right now, I don't think I'm going to like him."

Tom shrugged. "You wouldn't be the only person who doesn't."

"So what happened to Caroline? When did she leave the ranch?"

"When she was sixteen, she and her grandfather had a falling-out, and she ran off."

"What did they argue about?" When Tom didn't answer, she prodded him. "You don't know?"

"For the most part, it's speculation on my part."

Katie waited for him to explain. When he didn't, she asked, "Where was she last seen?"

"When she was sixteen, a friend of the family took her to Casa de Los Angelitos in Mexico."

"I'm not familiar with that place. Is it a town or village?"

"It's a home for women who get themselves into trouble. Their families take them there before their neighbors realize they're pregnant. Then they leave the unwanted babies behind at a Mexican orphanage."

"Caroline was pregnant?"

"Harrison had hoped she would return home with her reputation still intact. He sent Jeremiah Haney, his solicitor's son, to pick her up when her confinement was up, but she was gone before he got there."

"And Sarah Jane? She was the baby?"

"Yes. Caroline refused to give up her daughter and return to the ranch."

"I can't blame her for that. So when Harrison Graves learned he was dying, he hired you to find Caroline?"

"Yes, but he never mentioned a thing about finding the baby."

Katie thought about that for a moment, realizing that was good news for her. If the man wasn't interested in an illegitimate heir, then maybe he'd be happy to sign over guardianship to her. If so, her plan to take Sarah Jane—and Erin, if she was willing to go with them—to Wyoming would come to pass.

They continued to ride, with Katie still trying to sort through all Tom had told her.

"So how does Erin fit into all of this?" Katie asked.

"She and Caroline met at Casa de Los Angelitos. And they both left together."

"Did Erin have a baby, too?"

"The nuns told me that Erin's child, a boy, was stillborn."

They rode in silence for a while, although Katie's thoughts remained on Caroline and the baby she'd refused to give up.

Had she remembered losing her mother at a young age? Is that what had compelled her to rebel against her grandfather and to face public scorn?

Or had her child been conceived in love?

"Do you know anything about Sarah Jane's father?" Katie asked.

"Just that he was one of Harrison's ranch hands."

"What happened to him? Where is he?"

"He quit working at the Lazy G before Harrison found out about the pregnancy, which was lucky for him. Otherwise, Harrison might have killed him. At first I thought Caroline had gone looking for him, but I learned that he died while working on another spread about fifty miles from here."

So Sarah Jane was all alone—other than for Katie. And Erin, of course.

"Do you think Harrison Graves would sign over guardianship to me?" Katie asked.

Instead of an answer, Tom lifted his arm and pointed. "Do you see that hacienda on the hill?"

"You mean that large house? It looks like a small town."

"Wait until you see it up close." Tom urged his mount on. "Come on. You're going to have your chance to meet Harrison Graves face-to-face. That is, if he's still alive."

As Tom and Katie rode up the dusty drive to the Lazy G, an old man wearing a white shirt, faded black pants and leather sandals knelt near an ornate iron gate, pruning flowers in one of several terra-cotta pots.

When he spotted riders, he shielded his eyes from the sun with a gnarly hand. It took a moment for recognition to dawn, but the old man got to his feet to greet Tom.

"Abel," Tom said. *"Cómo está?"*

"Bien, Lone Wolf. And you?"

Surprised that the groundskeeper had called him by his Indian name, Tom shook off the urge to glance at Katie so he could gauge her reaction.

Not that it mattered, he supposed.

"I'm fine, thank you. But Señor Graves. How's he doing? Is he still…?"

"Alive? Yes, but he's getting worse—weaker, sicker each day. And he's wearing a path in the floor, waiting for you to return." Abel glanced at Katie and smiled.

"This is Miss Katie O'Malley, Abel. She came along with me because she'd like to meet Mr. Graves."

Abel bowed graciously. *"Mucho gusto, señorita."*

"I see you're no longer working with the cattle," Tom said.

"Last winter, when I became too crippled to ride, Señor Graves let me work in the yard."

Tom hadn't expected the rigid cattleman, whose parents had been killed by renegades, to be so accommodating to an old employee, especially one who was of mixed blood—Comanche and Mexican.

"I'll go inside and tell Señor Graves that you're here," Abel said. "Then I'll see to your horses."

"Thank you." Tom dismounted, then went to help Katie down. He waited to see if her ankle would give out on her. It didn't, and he noted only a slight limp.

As Katie scanned the courtyard, Tom watched Abel shuffle away, his worn leather sandals sliding along as he walked. It must be difficult to get old, especially for a man who'd once been a legend. Tom had only been a little boy when his father had told him tales of Abel's valor and skillful horsemanship.

"It's beautiful," Katie said, breaking into Tom's thoughts.

He followed her gaze to the flower-adorned adobe walls, the tiled floor of the courtyard, the water fountain gracing the patio.

"I've never seen the like," she added. "It's rustic, yet charming."

The double door to the hacienda swung open, and Randolph Haney strode onto the patio, his countenance displaying obvious displeasure as he raked his eyes over Katie.

"She's not Caroline Graves, McCain. You're a fool to think you could pass her off as such."

Even if Tom and Haney hadn't had a history that dated back to the time Tom was only a boy, he wouldn't have liked the pompous solicitor. But before he could enlighten him, Katie moved forward as if she were wearing a ball gown instead of a flannel shirt and a pair of denim jeans. "My name is Kathryn O'Malley, and I've come to have a word with you, Mr. Graves."

The gray-haired lawyer, his stance as formal and overbearing as before, crossed his arms and frowned. "I'm not Mr. Graves."

"He's Randolph Haney," Tom said, "attorney-at-law."

Katie lifted her chin in that defiant way Tom found amusing at times and annoying at others. "How do you do, Mr. Haney. And as I said, I'd like a word with Mr. Graves, if that's possible."

"I'm afraid he's resting and not taking callers."

"I'll wait," she said. "I've come a great distance to speak to him, and since I heard that time was of the essence, I didn't dare waste an extra day to rent a carriage and hire a driver."

Haney softened only slightly. "Perhaps I can be of service."

"Perhaps. But it's ultimately Mr. Graves I must speak to."

He studied her a moment. "You do look a bit worn. Would you like a refreshment? Water perhaps?"

"That would be most kind. Thank you."

Tom crossed his arms and watched propriety take charge. Of course, he still doubted that Haney was any happier to see Katie than he was to see him.

"And you?" Haney turned to Tom. "Why are you here? Do you have any news?"

"My business is with Harrison, not you."

"He'll ask me to listen to anything you have to say."

Tom shrugged a single shoulder. "Maybe so, but that'll be his decision."

A rap-rap-rap sounded at one of the windows at the side of the house. All eyes turned to see Harrison Graves tapping a cane against the glass. He nodded to Abel, who stood at his side, and the gardener opened the window.

"Come inside," Harrison said.

Tom studied Haney out of the corner of his eye. The austere solicitor stepped back, hands to his side, lips tightening, and a muscle near his eye twitched as he allowed Tom and Katie to enter the house before him.

Katie's heart tightened as she stepped onto the Spanish-tiled entry of the hacienda and waited for Harrison Graves. Moments later, aided by a gold-handled cane, the white-haired gentleman entered the room.

She wasn't sure what she'd been expecting—someone sickly, of course, but powerful. And while both seemed to be true, the wealthy cattleman appeared to be broken, as well, although she couldn't say how.

Perhaps it was his rumpled appearance, and the fact that he'd hurried to meet them—or rather, Tom.

His thinning white hair stood on end, and in spite of having guests, he hadn't taken the time to comb it.

"Come with me," he said. Then he turned and headed down the hall, his pace slow and slightly unsteady. He led them into a sitting room, its walls white plaster, its ceiling open-beamed.

"Have you found Caroline?" he asked, his voice unable to mask a grandfather's hope.

"I think so." Tom nodded toward Mr. Haney. "But if you don't mind, I'd like to talk to you in private."

The gray-haired solicitor stepped forward. "That's not necessary, Harrison. Caroline was like a daughter to me. I'd like to hear what the bounty hunter has to say."

Was like a daughter? Katie stiffened. Did he already know she was dead?

"Mr. Graves," Tom said, "I won't discuss anything unless we're alone."

"Very well."

As Tom stepped behind the dying cattleman, Katie proceeded to follow, but Tom stopped abruptly and turned to her. "I said alone."

"But I—"

"You can discuss anything you'd like with Mr. Graves at another time. This conversation is private."

Katie watched as the two men, one old and dying, the other young and vibrant, walked across the Spanish-tiled floor and into the hall.

Moments later, they entered another room. When the door closed, she turned to the well-dressed lawyer, wondering if the exclusion bothered him more than it had her. A scowl on his face validated her suspicion.

With his lips pressed tightly together, the elderly gentleman made a sweeping assessment of her clothing, his cool gray eyes clearly finding her lacking.

"Why are you traveling with that breed?" he asked.

The jab of his question surprised her, irritated her. "I have something to discuss with Mr. Graves and needed an escort."

His narrowed eyes indicated his disapproval of both her quest and her appearance.

Undaunted in the least, Katie crossed her arms. "My father, God rest his soul, was an attorney in St. Louis before his passing, and I used to help him prepare for his trials. I'm well versed in the law, and while I might not appear to be much more than a backwards ragamuffin, I assure you that's not the case, Mr. Haney."

"You must have traveled a great distance."

She decided she'd given him enough information.

"So what do you think of Texas?" he asked, mellowing and offering her a bit of decorum.

But as far as she was concerned, it had come too late. He'd made assumptions based upon her appearance and her traveling companion.

"I'm afraid Texas—or rather Texans—aren't quite what I'd expected," she said.

Randolph glanced at the nail beds of his long, tapered fingers. "What did you expect?"

"That Texans had manners, and as far as some of the attorneys I've met, I've come to find that I was misinformed."

"Lemonade?" a woman asked from the doorway, her voice tinged with a Spanish accent, her arms holding a tray laden with glasses and a pitcher.

"Yes, please," Katie told the woman. "Thank you."

Then Katie turned to the attorney. "Manners are usually learned as a child, but perhaps, if you try very hard to observe those around you, you'll catch on."

"Touché, Miss O'Malley." Randolph Haney began to smile, then chuckled. "I apologize for being rude."

"Apology accepted," Katie said, although her heart hadn't quite meant it.

"Perhaps we Texans have more of a distrust of Indians than you're accustomed to. My brother lost his life in a massacre, and I've learned to be leery."

"Tom McCain has been a perfect gentleman," Katie said.

And while she'd had several occasions to be angry at the bounty hunter who'd seemed invincible on the trail, she felt the overwhelming urge to defend and protect him now.

Chapter Eight

Tom took a seat across the broad mahogany desk from Harrison Graves. The old man, who'd grown frailer in the past couple of months, grimaced as he settled into his cushioned chair.

"Did you find Caroline?" he asked.

"She's dead, sir."

Harrison's shoulders slumped, and the furrow in his craggy brow deepened. "Are you sure?"

"I'm afraid so."

"I had so much to…" He placed his bent elbows on the desk, then buried his face in his hands. "Oh, Lord. What'll I do now?"

Tom should have felt some sense of satisfaction at seeing the cattleman suffer. After all, if Harrison Graves had shown some compassion for a dying Comanche woman and her frightened son…

Yet the words Hannah had taught him, the scripture she'd shared with him over the years, came to mind instead. *And be ye kind one to another, tenderhearted, forgiving one another, even as God for Christ's sake hath forgiven you.*

"Are you all right?" Tom asked.

Harrison looked up, his eyes filled with tears. "I... I had so much to say to her. I wanted to tell her that I loved her, that I was sorry for being so stubborn. That I forgave her for the things she said to me when she left. I know she didn't mean them. She was just angry. And she had every right to be."

"I suppose you'll have to be content to tell God," Tom said. "It's His forgiveness that matters most."

"I have, although I must admit that I feel pretty unworthy of His forgiveness."

The man's humility took Tom aback.

"At one time, I was the master of my own universe. And now?" Harrison lifted a withered arm and slowly lowered it. "I'm broken and dying."

"In truth," Tom said, "we're all broken and dying."

Harrison seemed to ponder that a moment, then said, "The Reverend Mitchell has been coming out to the ranch lately. And he said as much. If he'd told me that five years ago, I would have run him off. Back then, I thought I was invincible, but you're right. I was broken and dying all along and just hadn't known it."

Tom studied the man a moment. Had he experienced a physical realization or a spiritual reckoning?

Either way, he supposed he deserved to know about Sarah Jane—if Jeremiah Haney, Randolph's son, hadn't told him already.

"Caroline had a daughter," Tom said, "but I suspect you know that."

Harrison stiffened, then raised his gray head. "I heard it was a boy. And that it died at birth."

If Sarah Jane hadn't favored her mother more than Erin, Tom might have questioned what he'd been told, too. He glanced at the large portrait that hung on the south wall of Harrison's study, at the lovely young blonde wearing a pale blue gown. Then he returned his gaze to Harrison.

"The child is a girl, and I've see her." Tom didn't mention her resemblance to Caroline as a child. Not when Harrison thought Tom's first and only introduction to Caroline had been the portrait he'd seen in this office just months ago.

"As much as I'd like to believe you," the cattleman said, "Jeremiah Haney, my solicitor's son, went to Casa de Los Angelitos to bring Caroline home six years ago. And the nuns told him Caroline's baby, a boy, had died at birth. They also told him that she'd left with another woman, a harlot who'd given birth to a girl. So you can understand my doubt."

Had one of the nuns been confused and given Haney's son details about Erin's baby, the one that had been still-born?

Tom didn't know Jeremiah, but he still sported a scar he'd received from the tip of the elder Haney's boot, a wound he'd received when his head had scarcely reached the top of the man's gold belt buckle.

"I'm not calling Jeremiah a liar," Tom said, "but you hired me to do a job, and I took my assignment seriously. While I was at Casa de Los Angelitos, I asked to see the baptismal records. And I assure you, Caroline Graves gave birth to a daughter who was born alive."

"Do you know where the child is now?" Harrison asked.

"Yes, I do."

"Then bring her back here. Let me see her for myself."

Tom couldn't bring Sarah Jane back. Not yet. He had to stall for time—time Harrison Graves might not have.

Should he explain why? Tell this grieving old man that someone had tried to murder the child's guardian? And that Tom also found her mother's untimely death a little suspicious?

He could, but he had nothing on which to base those suspicions, and something told him Harrison Graves wouldn't settle for a gut feeling.

Of course, bringing Sarah Jane to the Lazy G just might flush out the murderer—if Tom's suspicions had any merit. But that might also put her in jeopardy.

"If I bring the child here," Tom said, "and if you do see a resemblance to Caroline, what will happen then?"

"She'll become a very wealthy young lady. But I'll want proof that she's my great-granddaughter, and I'm not sure you can provide that."

Assuming Tom had both the time to get her here and that Harrison would accept her resemblance as proof, then what? After Harrison passed, who would take care of Sarah Jane?

If Tom could trust his gut—and he'd learned to do that years ago—Harrison Graves would undoubtedly leave custody of his great-granddaughter, as well as his holdings, to his old friend and solicitor. And while Sarah Jane deserved to inherit what should have gone to her mother, she didn't deserve to be raised by a man like Randolph Haney.

So how did Tom go about insuring that she receive all that was rightfully hers without falling prey to Haney's influence?

Harrison lowered his head again.

Years ago, Tom might have felt vindicated to see Harrison get what he deserved, to see him brought low by grief, as well as disease, but he didn't find any pleasure in knowing the old man would never receive Caroline's forgiveness—nor grant her his.

When Harrison looked up, his eyes red rimmed and filled with tears, he said, "I need some time to be alone. Will you ask Maria, my housekeeper, to come in? She can show you to a room. I'll talk more to you about this later."

"I'll do that. I've also brought along a woman who'd like to speak to you when you're feeling up to it."

"I'm afraid that will have to wait, as well. Other than having a moment with Maria, I don't want to talk to anyone else today. I just want to be left alone."

"I'll let Miss O'Malley know. And I'll send in Maria." Tom got to his feet. After softly closing the door to the man's study, he made his way down the hall and entered the sitting room, where he found an audience awaiting his return—the hopeful schoolmarm, the angry solicitor, the weary gardener and the worried housekeeper. They each watched him, waiting for him to speak.

Maria, who'd worked for Harrison as long as Tom could remember, had been the only woman in Caroline's life, as far as Tom knew. Her luminous brown eyes begged for news, but Tom wouldn't be the one to tell her. That was up to Harrison.

"Mr. Graves would like to see you," Tom told her.

When Tom shared the cattleman's request, Maria reached for a glass of lemonade and carried it down the hall.

Haney stood and grasped the lapels of his gray jacket with each hand. "So tell me. Did you find Caroline?"

Tom swiped a strand of hair from his brow, his thumb

grazing the narrow ridge of the scar he'd received from Haney's boot. "Mr. Graves will have to give you those details."

"I don't know why you're being so secretive. Harrison tells me everything."

"That's his choice, Mr. Haney. But I don't think he's going to tell you anything this afternoon. He asked to be left alone."

Katie stood. "When can I talk to him?"

"Later. Maybe tomorrow."

Maria returned to the sitting room, her face drawn, her eyes filled with tears. She managed a weak smile. "Señor Graves would like me to show you to a room, Señorita. I'll have one of the stable boys bring in a tub of warm water."

"Thank you," Katie said.

The housekeeper turned to Tom. "I'll be back to show you to your room, Mr. McCain."

"Don't worry about me," Tom said. "I'll bunk with Abel."

"All right, if that's what you'd rather do." Maria turned to Katie. "Please come with me."

Katie followed the housekeeper out of the sitting room and down a narrow hall.

"Señor Graves said that Señor McCain believes Caroline died," Maria said.

"From what I was told, she fell down a flight of stairs."

"She was very light on her feet," Maria said. "Her grandfather insisted that she be a lady, but she was more comfortable riding with the vaqueros. I always feared that she might have an accident while on horseback— like her father."

"I wish I could have met her," Katie said. "I'm sure I would have liked her."

"She was a wonderful young woman, so full of life. I can hardly believe she's gone. This house was never the same after she left." Maria's long braid swished along her back as she led the way down the hall. "Poor Señor Graves. All he thought about, all he prayed about, was for Caroline to return."

Katie continued to follow Maria until she stopped before a doorway.

Maria turned to Katie and attempted a smile. "This is Señorita Caroline's room. You may sleep here. The sheets are fresh. Señor Graves had wanted it ready for her."

"Perhaps he'd feel better if I slept elsewhere."

Maria opened the door anyway. "It is best that you stay in here. He should not spend so much time alone in her room. With a guest in here, he will have to stay away."

"If Mr. Graves feels the least bit uncomfortable with me staying in this room, I'd prefer to sleep elsewhere." She just hoped that "elsewhere" wouldn't be in the bunk-house with Abel and Tom.

"I have worked for Señor Graves for more than thirty years," Maria said. "Believe me. He doesn't come in here to spend time with her memory. He comes to pay penance with his guilt. And he's already paid plenty. It's good that he has a reason to stay away."

Katie wasn't so sure about that, but when Maria stepped into the large airy room, she followed.

Caroline's bedroom had the same brown-tiled floor,

white plaster walls and rough-beamed ceiling as the rest of the hacienda, but yards of lace and flounce made the setting decidedly feminine.

"Señorita Caroline didn't spend much time indoors." Maria gazed at the lace curtains. "But when she did, she liked pretty things."

"It's lovely." As Katie took in her surroundings, a small, wood-framed portrait on the wall near the window caught her eye. It was the painted image of a woman holding an infant.

Katie stepped closer, drawn to the willowy beauty who wore a faint smile.

"Who is this woman?" Katie asked.

"Señora Juliana." Maria smiled wistfully. "Caroline was a pretty baby, no?"

"No," Katie said. "I mean, yes. She's precious, but I wasn't talking about the baby. I was looking at the mother. She's hauntingly beautiful."

"Her unhappiness shows."

It did at that. Katie tried to spot a family resemblance, but couldn't say that she did. And the fair-haired baby, plump and sweet, could have grown up to be any blonde girl.

"I don't suppose you have a photograph of Caroline when she was a little older?" Katie asked the matronly woman.

"Yes, I do." Maria strode to the bureau where a brass-framed photograph rested upon a crocheted doily. She gazed wistfully upon the likeness prior to handing it to Katie.

A girl slightly older than Sarah Jane stood beside a potted fern and a wicker chair. Dressed in white lace, she held a porcelain doll in one hand and a flower in the other.

Katie studied the picture, praying she wouldn't spot a resemblance to the child she loved.

And dying a little on the inside when she did.

After he'd made sure the horses had been properly cared for, Tom went in search of Abel and found him dipping water from the well. The old gardener had been around for years, once riding the range, herding the stubborn longhorn and, later, managing fields of hay and cotton.

The old man looked up and brushed a dribble of water from his tanned, weathered chin. "I'm glad you came back."

"I said that I would." Tom scanned the courtyard. Abel had done wonders as a gardener. Red blossoms climbed a wooden trellis against the adobe wall. Plants, lush and green, hung from wrought-iron baskets throughout the patio. Colorful shocks of flowers grew abundantly in large clay pots.

Age might have reduced the old man's abilities while riding herd, but not his determination to see a job well done.

Abel crossed his thin arms, his wise old eyes crinkling. "There are some who hoped you would not return."

"That doesn't surprise me. I've never been welcome here."

"Other men would have stayed away."

"I'm not other men."

"No, you're more of a man than most. Your father would have been proud."

Tom didn't appreciate Abel's mention of his father. Not here. Not now.

"You don't favor him in looks," Abel said, not letting the subject die. "You're darker, taller. You also carry distrust in your heart. Your father wasn't so hard."

"He didn't have to be."

"No, but you always had a stubborn streak, like a wild horse unwilling to be broken. I'll never forget the day you tried to fight Haney." Abel chuckled and stroked his chin. "The man didn't expect a child to challenge him."

"He hurt my mother. I'm not one to forget cruelty to a woman."

"I can understand your anger at Señor Haney, as well as your sense of duty to Señor Graves."

"I don't owe loyalty to anyone. At least, not to anyone in Stillwater."

"Then you have come back for the reward?"

"I'm not after the money."

"Then what do you want?"

Tom's connection to the Lazy G had been a deep, dark secret even before his parents had died, leaving him orphaned and a thorn in the backside of Texas society.

"Respect maybe?" Abel asked.

That went without saying, but it was even more than that. Tom owed it to Caroline. On those rare occasions when they'd been allowed to play together, they'd formed a bond, a friendship. And if things had been different…

Abel studied Tom as though he knew what he was thinking, what he was feeling. Maybe he did.

Of all the people on the Lazy G, Abel was probably the one person Tom could trust. But he wasn't going to talk about it. And his lack of response didn't go unnoticed—or unacknowledged. And so that line of questioning was dropped.

"Did you find Caroline?" Abel asked.

"She died about six months ago."

The old man frowned. "Are you sure?"

"Yeah. I'm sure." He pondered whether he should mention Sarah Jane but held his tongue. "Caroline fell down a flight of stairs and broke her neck. She's buried in a town called Taylorsville."

Abel grimaced. "Does Señor Graves know?"

"I just told him."

"How is he taking it?"

"I'm not sure." Tom still wasn't convinced that Harrison was truly sorry, although he appeared grief stricken. Or was it more guilt and fear of meeting his maker?

"Your father would be proud of you," Abel said again.

"That's not why I'm here. And I'd appreciate it if you'd keep those thoughts to yourself."

"I've kept my mouth closed for more than twenty-five years and won't let my tongue run away from me now." Abel's brown eyes glistened, and a slow smile eased the harsh lines on his tired face. "Who's the woman you brought with you?"

"Her name is Katie O'Malley."

"Is she yours?"

His? The sharp-tongued woman with fiery hair and expressive blue eyes? For a fleeting moment he had a vision of her standing at his side, felt her reach for his hand, thread her fingers through his. But he shook off the image and scoffed. "No, she's not my woman."

"That's too bad. *Ella esta muy bonita.*"

Tom snorted. "There's more to a woman than her

beauty. Katie O'Malley wouldn't be happy unless she had a man on his knees and at her beck and call."

Abel laughed. "I might be old now, but there was a time I would have liked waiting on a pretty lady hand and foot."

"Not me. Once she started ordering me around, I'd send her on her way as soon as I could be rid of her." And that's exactly what Tom intended to do, once he returned with her to Hannah's. In fact, he might even offer someone a good week's pay just to drive her back to Pleasant Valley.

"She looks like the kind of woman a man ought to keep for himself," Abel said.

"Then *you* keep her," Tom said.

When Abel laughed as if he'd been let in on a secret Tom had yet to learn, Tom shook his head and strode away from the house, eager to put some distance between him and Abel.

And eager to squelch any thought of Katie O'Malley as anything other than a pain in his backside.

As the ornamental clock on the mantel struck ten, which was well past Randolph Haney's usual bedtime, Jeremiah Haney sat in his father's study and stretched out his long legs.

He didn't know why this conference couldn't have waited until morning, but he'd come when his father had summoned him—as he always did.

When he'd arrived, he'd found his father pacing like a cornered bobcat. His suit, usually neat and pressed, appeared to have been slept in.

"I've never seen you like this," Jeremiah said. "What's wrong?"

Randolph, his eyes bloodshot, stopped his pacing long enough to ask, "What do you think McCain told Harrison?"

Jeremiah reached for a cigar from the silver case that sat upon his father's desk and chose his words carefully. "I don't know what that half-breed told him. Maybe he's just trying to get into the man's good graces."

"For financial gain?" Randolph shook his head. "Not likely. Even in his befuddled mental state, Harrison wouldn't give a wooden nickel to a man like McCain. There's too much Indian running in his veins."

Jeremiah scoffed. "Who knows what a dying man would do? Harrison once rode the range like a king. Now he sits and mourns a woman who doesn't want to be found."

"Perhaps you're right. Harrison did, after all, cast Caroline out without a backward glance. And you've gone in search of her time and again—to no avail. And she certainly hasn't made any attempts to contact him."

None that Harrison knew about, anyway. Jeremiah studied the Cuban cigar he held in his hand, then reached for a match and leaned back in the brown tufted leather chair. "As long as Harrison doesn't change his will, his waning emotional state shouldn't bother us in the least."

"You're right, son. I wrote the will, and I'm not about to let Harrison talk me into changing it. Besides, Caroline is the sole heir, and if she insists upon staying away, as executor I have full control."

Jeremiah bit off the tip of the cigar and struck the match. "For what it's worth, I may have picked up her trail on my last search in a place called Taylorsville. I don't know for sure, but I think she may have suffered an unfortunate accident right before I arrived."

"What do you mean, you might have picked up her trail?"

"I was just piecing together some rumors. And if it was her, she was going by another name." Jeremiah lit the cigar, drawing on the end until the first wisps of sweet tobacco entered his mouth and filled his lungs. "Why do *you* suspect she's dead?"

"Caroline was always headstrong and impulsive, so I wasn't surprised that she ran off. But disappearing like a trail of smoke in the wind?" Randolph crossed his arms, resting them against the red silk vest that covered his distended belly. "She would have come home by now."

"If she's dead, then the only one left to inherit is you," Jeremiah said. *And, in due time, me.*

Randolph stood and walked toward the oak filing cabinet that held a cut crystal decanter of his favorite brandy. "The half-breed worries me, though."

Jeremiah found McCain a bit worrisome, too, although he kept that concern to himself. "So what do you want to do about him?"

"Nothing, but I want to know what he told Harrison. Or at least, what Harrison's thoughts are." Randolph poured two glasses, then handed one to Jeremiah. "And Harrison refused to talk to me until tomorrow, which is highly unusual. And *that* bothers me."

Jeremiah swirled the liquid in his glass. He'd prefer to savor his cigar rather than have a drink, especially when his father had clearly imbibed more than a fair amount already.

"There's a woman traveling with him," Randolph said. "Maybe she'll talk. Her name is Katie O'Malley."

"Why are you telling me this?" Jeremiah asked.

"I'm going to introduce the two of you. I want you

to do whatever you must do in order to find out what that breed knows."

"That shouldn't be a problem. I've always been able to charm the ladies."

Randolph clucked his tongue. "Don't remind me. Your charm nearly caused your father-in-law to disinherit you two years ago."

"My wife doesn't see to my needs."

"She has a wealthy father. That should fulfill a few of your needs."

"It does." Jeremiah inhaled deeply, then blew a large smoke ring. He watched it curl and twist above his head.

His father didn't need to worry about him. He'd had a rather indiscriminate beginning, but he'd learned to be discreet. And careful.

"So how would you like me to proceed with Miss O'Malley?" Jeremiah asked.

"First of all, we need to find out whether Caroline is alive or dead. Then we need to learn whether there's a child that may hold any claim to the estate. Surely you've thought about that."

Oh, Jeremiah had thought about it, all right. "I'll tell you what. The Cattleman's Ball is tomorrow night. Make sure Miss O'Malley is invited. I'll sweep her off her feet and find out all we need to know."

"It's not necessary for you to charm the pantaloons off her," Randolph said. "Just get her to talk."

"I'll have her talking her pretty head off before you can blink an eye." Jeremiah chuckled.

And if her pantaloons slipped off in the meantime? Then so be it.

Chapter Nine

Moonlight filtered through the lace curtains and danced upon the crisp white sheets, but Katie found sleep elusive.

She kicked the covers aside and climbed from bed. The cool tile floor chilled her bare feet. Had she been a guest in anyone else's home, she might have slipped into the study to find a book to read, something to lull her active mind to rest. But she didn't feel completely welcome at the Lazy G, so wandering through the house at this late hour wouldn't be polite or acceptable.

Instead, she strode toward the window, placed a palm against the rough-grained frame and looked out into the starry Texas sky. There was something mournful yet vital about this land, and she thought about the many people who had fought and died to hold on to it.

Outside, a shadowy figure moved, sending her heart thumping and her pulse racing—until she recognized him. Tall, broad shouldered. That solitary stance.

Tom McCain.

Without a conscious thought, she decided to join him—just for a moment—so she could talk to him about

Mr. Graves. She wanted to get an idea about what the man's decision would be when she broached him about her desire to adopt Sarah Jane.

She slipped into a robe Maria had set out for her, a garment that had once belonged to Caroline, and left the room, tiptoeing softly down the hall. In her haste, she neglected to look for slippers, but she continued anyway. If she took time to search for something to cover her feet, he might not be there any longer.

She saw him clearly in the moonlight. Never had she seen a full moon so large, so silvery.

Nor had she seen a man who seemed so alone.

Without shoes, her footsteps hardly sounded. She wondered if she would surprise him, but she shouldn't have considered it. The man turned sharply, as if he'd had the hearing of a wolf—a lone wolf, like the name Abel had called him when they'd arrived.

The name seemed to suit him.

In spite of her efforts to be quiet, he turned before she'd gotten within ten feet of him.

"What are you doing out here?" he asked.

Why did he have to sound so gruff? So threatening?

"I couldn't sleep, and when I saw you outside, I thought you might like some company."

Now who was she trying to fool? He'd never given her reason to believe he'd enjoyed having her company before.

"You shouldn't be outdoors," he said. "It isn't safe."

"Even with you?"

"Especially with me."

She fingered the lace-trimmed lapel of her robe.

"See what I mean?" he nodded at her hand. "I scare you."

She released her lapel and dropped her hand to her side. Then she lifted her chin and stood as tall as she could in her bare feet. "You most certainly do not. You'd never hurt me."

"Wouldn't I? Don't be so sure." He stepped forward in a move that ought to give her a start, then cupped her cheek in a large callused hand with a tenderness that surprised her. "I could tarnish your reputation if anyone saw me touch you."

Her breath caught, but she didn't step back.

His hand moved slightly, his fingers reaching into her hair, combing the strands. She reached for his wrist to pull his hand away, or so she thought. Instead, she found herself holding his hand in place.

"Go into the house," he said.

"All right." Yet she didn't move away. Something beyond her control rooted her in place.

He smelled of leather and soap, and his breath, which blew softly against her skin, held a hint of peppermint. "Go into the house before I forget myself."

"And kiss me again?"

"Yes, but this time, I don't want to get a slap for my effort."

"I didn't slap you for kissing me," she said. "I slapped you for laughing at me afterward."

In the moonlight, she watched him search her face. Had he realized she was inviting him to kiss her again?

That's not why she'd come out here, but if truth be told, she wouldn't mind sharing another embrace, another kiss.

"I promise not to slap you this time," she said softly. Then she reached up, slipped her hands behind his neck and drew his mouth to hers.

His lips were soft, warm, and as they moved against hers, the kiss deepened. She leaned into him, her arms holding him tighter.

She didn't dare open her eyes, but if she did, she imagined the stars would be spinning overhead. Her heart certainly was.

Before her conscience had a chance to speak up, Tom pulled away, breaking the kiss and putting the starry night back to rights again.

"Go inside," he said, his voice a bit huskier than she'd remembered. *"Now."*

"But—"

"But nothing. Being alone with me, especially here, isn't good. And it isn't right. You need to go back into the house. You've had your last kiss from me."

Then he turned and walked away. As his boot steps faded into the night, she pressed her fingers against her lips.

At the very thought that he might never hold her again, that she might never feel his lips on hers, a nagging sense of loss shuddered through her.

What was wrong with her? She couldn't afford to let anyone have that much power over her. Shaking off the crazy effect, she turned and padded back to the house.

Once inside Caroline's bedroom, she slipped off her robe and tossed it over the upholstered chair near the window. She told herself to forget Tom, to be glad he'd walked away, that he'd tried to talk some sense into her.

He'd been right. Kissing him out in the open, where anyone could see, wasn't proper. And in her nightgown and bare feet, of all things. Why, her da would be rolling over in his grave if he could see her unladylike behavior.

Still, against better judgment, she drew back the curtains and peered outside. Had Tom retired for the evening? Or had he remained outdoors, to commune with the moon and stars?

She spotted him near the fountain, where he continued to stand alone—a haunting figure who called to her heart.

Her heart?

No, that couldn't be. She knew herself too well. If she ever weakened to the point of considering courtship or marriage, she would choose another man, an intellectual, a moral equal. Someone who'd value a bright and capable wife.

Marriage to a man like Tom McCain would be just plain awful. She could envision them living in a sod house on the prairie, where she'd have to sweep dirt floors, wash laundry in a dirty creek, slop pigs and milk a goat. Why, she'd have to work herself to an early grave, no doubt.

Even if they were to have a home like Hannah's, she could still see him issuing orders and placing demands on her. Why, there'd never be a peaceful moment between the two. She'd have to fight for every ounce of respect she could get.

As she climbed into Caroline's soft, goose-down bed, she pulled the linen sheet to her chin and sighed. In spite of her best intentions to forget the man and the effect he had on her, she couldn't seem to put that knee-weakening, mind-spinning kiss out of her mind.

What kind of woman was she?

A brazen hussy, no doubt.

When he'd gazed into her eyes, she'd wanted him to kiss her more than anything. So she'd gone so far as to stroke his cheek, to bring his mouth to hers.

Could another man's kiss move her that much?

She certainly hoped so. Because if it couldn't, she'd be hard-pressed to ever forget Tom McCain.

And then where would she be?

Katie slept much better than she might have guessed she would in a strange bed, but she'd dreamed of Tom McCain all night long and woke with her arms wrapped around her pillow.

After freshening herself, she donned one of the dresses she'd packed, a light yellow-and-white floral print. Then she took a quick glance in the mirror to make sure she looked presentable, if not a bit wrinkled no matter how carefully she'd packed the frock in her valise.

As she made her way out of the bedroom, the aroma of fresh-brewed coffee drew her to the kitchen. She expected to find Maria bustling about, preparing breakfast. What she hadn't expected was to see Maria gone and Randolph Haney seated at the head of a long, rectangular table.

He stood and bowed his gray head in greeting. "Good day, Miss O'Malley."

"Good morning. You're here early. Or did you stay the night?"

Randolph laughed as though he found her witty. "No, but I do spend a lot of time here. Harrison is my friend, and I know he would be supportive of me in my last days."

The image of a vulture wearing a suit and tie came to mind as Katie scanned the kitchen. "Where's Maria?"

"She took breakfast to Harrison." Randolph got to his feet, strode toward Katie and took her hand with his. "I'd like to apologize for my rudeness yesterday. It was uncalled-for."

He was right, of course. And perhaps she'd been too hard on him, as well. She didn't appreciate his distrust of Tom merely because his mother had been an Indian, but she really couldn't fault the lawyer for trying to protect his old friend and client from being taken advantage of by strangers. Besides, it wouldn't do to upset the man who might ultimately have some say over where Sarah Jane might live.

"I accept your apology. We were all on edge yesterday, Mr. Haney."

He smiled broadly and pulled out a chair, the legs scraping across the tile floor. "Call me Randolph, and please sit down."

"Thank you." Katie withdrew her hand from his, then took a seat.

"I don't know how long you intend to stay, but the Cattleman's Ball is tonight. It's a yearly event—and more like a community dance than a formal cotillion—but I'd like you to go with my son and me. I think you'd enjoy it."

Katie wasn't sure that she would, but it wouldn't hurt to get to know the people in Stillwater. "I'll give it some thought, although I really don't have anything suitable to wear."

"My dear, a pretty woman like you would look lovely in a grain sack."

Katie tried not to roll her eyes. She wasn't susceptible to flattery and didn't appreciate his attempt. Still it was an olive branch, she supposed, so she accepted it and thanked him.

Moments later, Maria swept into the room, her colorful skirts skimming the floor. "*Buenos días,* Señorita O'Malley. Did you sleep well?"

"Yes, thank you." Katie couldn't help thinking of the man and the kiss she'd dreamed about and glanced out the large kitchen window.

"If you're looking for Señor McCain," Maria said, "he and Abel were up early this morning, but I don't think they left the yard."

"I wasn't looking for him," she lied.

Maria poured a cup of coffee, then handed it to Katie. "Can I fix you some breakfast?"

"Yes, please. That would be nice."

"I'd like fried eggs and ham," Randolph said. "And make sure the yolks are runny this time. You know I don't like them overcooked."

A shadow moved outside, and Katie craned her neck. As she suspected, Tom and Abel were in the yard.

"Excuse me," she said. "I'll be back in a few minutes."

"Where are you going?" Randolph asked.

"For a walk."

His forehead furrowed, but she reached for the brass doorknob and continued outside, her skirts rustling with each step. She'd intended to speak to Tom about Mr. Graves last night, but the conversation…well, needless to say, it had taken an unexpected turn and had ended before she'd had a chance to steer it back on course.

As she made her way to the place she'd seen Tom, memories of the kiss dogged her, but she shook them off. She had a perfectly good reason to come out here bright and early this morning. And fawning after Tom McCain wasn't it.

Baritone whispers stilled when she neared the fountain where Abel and Tom stood.

Tom wore denim jeans today and a white shirt unbuttoned at the collar. He didn't wear a hat, and the sun glistened on the black strands of his hair.

Both men turned at her approach.

"I'd like to speak to Mr. Graves as soon as possible," she said.

Tom crossed his arms. "What's your hurry?"

She sighed, then glanced at Abel, unsure of whether she should speak in front of the gardener.

"Abel knows how to hold his tongue," Tom said.

"All right then," Katie said. "I think Sarah Jane is his great-granddaughter. And when he sees her, he's going to believe it, too."

"I agree," Tom said.

"Does that mean you're going to bring her here?"

"Not until I'm sure she'll live to see her seventh birthday."

Katie's stomach clenched. "If you don't think she'll be safe, then you shouldn't bring her back here at all."

"That's still left to be seen."

"What are you waiting for?" she asked.

"There's a man I want to talk to."

"Who?"

Tom paused, as if he wasn't sure if he trusted her with the information. "Jeremiah Haney."

"Is he related to Randolph?"

"They're father and son."

"Then I'll look forward to meeting him."

Tom grasped her arm, his fingers tightening into her flesh, and his eyes narrowed. "Stay away from him. I don't want you getting involved in this."

Katie lifted her chin. "I'm already involved. In fact,

Randolph Haney has invited me to attend the Cattleman's Ball with him and Jeremiah tonight."

Tom's gaze locked on hers. "You're a stubborn woman, but you'd better not cross me on this."

"I told you before, obedience doesn't sit well with me."

"It had better when the order is mine."

Katie tried to twist and pull her arm free of his grip, but her efforts didn't succeed. When she stopped struggling, he finally released her.

"Don't try to bully me."

"Then don't cross me."

She folded her arms, facing off with him. "Or what will happen?"

"I'll haul you back to Hannah's—*pronto.* And I'm not opposed to binding your hands and feet and throwing you over my shoulder."

"That sounds rather savage," she said.

His expression hardened. "Consider it this warrior's attempt to be civilized."

Abel shuffled his feet as a slow grin formed on his wrinkled face. "Don't worry, *señorita.* He only jokes with you. Lone Wolf doesn't mean it."

Tom turned to the old man. "You might not think I'm serious, Abel, but if she doesn't watch her step, she'll be riding over the rump of a mare all the way back to Pleasant Valley."

Katie unfolded her arms and slapped her hands on her hips. "The only steps I intend to watch are the ones that lead me within an arm's reach of Mr. *Lone Wolf.*"

Tom's dark eyes narrowed as he returned his attention to Katie, making her wonder if she might have gone a bit too far. She hadn't meant to mock his Indian roots, but she sometimes didn't temper her words when angered.

Nevertheless, she turned on her heel and marched off. But instead of heading for the kitchen, where Randolph Haney was sure to say something to catch her off guard, she rounded the house and went to the courtyard, using the main entrance instead.

As she headed for the hallway toward the bedroom she'd been assigned, Harrison Graves shuffled out of one of the rooms.

His surprise at running into her rivaled her own at seeing him.

Did she dare speak to him now?

She might have, had her tongue not suffered momentary paralysis.

"Good morning," he said, his gaze never leaving her eyes.

Unable to waste time with formalities, she took a deep breath, then pressed on. "Mr. Graves, we haven't been formally introduced, but I'm Katie O'Malley."

"Yesterday wasn't a good day."

"I don't suppose it was, but I've come a long way to speak to you. Would now be a good time to talk?"

"I suppose so. I'm not sure how many more days I can prolong anything. Let's go into my study."

Katie followed the elderly man down the hall and into an open doorway. With one liver-spotted hand upon his cane for balance, he used the other to motion toward the chair in front of his desk. "Have a seat, Miss O'Malley."

"Please call me Katie."

When she realized he continued to stand on wobbly feet, awaiting her compliance, she quickly pulled out a chair and sat down.

"What is it you have to say?" he asked, as he took his own seat.

"I have reason to believe your great-granddaughter is a little girl named Sarah Jane."

"Is that what Caroline named her? Sarah Jane?"

"Yes. I've grown to love her and would like your permission to adopt her."

Mr. Graves appeared to rally and gain both strength and control. "First of all, I haven't yet met this child. Secondly, I'm not sure she really is my great-granddaughter. And thirdly, I don't know you from Florinda Grimwood."

"Florinda Grimwood?" Katie arched a brow. "I'm afraid I'm not familiar with her."

"Neither am I." His smile began to loosen Katie's taut nerves.

At least Harrison Graves had a sense of humor.

"Let me explain, Mr. Graves. I've been offered a teaching position in the Wyoming Territory, where women have the right to vote."

"You're a suffragist?"

"Yes. I believe women are the intellectual equals to men. I also believe that Sarah Jane has great potential. I promise to love her and educate her and allow her the freedom to nurture her own strengths and dreams."

He seemed to think about that for a moment, although he didn't argue. That was a good sign, wasn't it?

"My solicitor worries that a charlatan might try to take advantage of my imminent death." Mr. Graves glanced out the study window and into the garden. "It's no secret that my holdings are vast and that the cattle industry is booming. My only heir, assuming it is the child in question, would be a very wealthy young lady—as would her guardian."

"I don't intend to live in Texas, nor do I want control of your estate. Perhaps you could place it in trust for Sarah Jane until she reaches adulthood."

Harrison leaned his head against the back of his chair and crossed his arms. "The money doesn't interest you?"

"Not at all. My father had a respectable law practice and holdings of his own, which I inherited. I'm not rich, but I'm quite comfortable. And although I have no intention of living in splendor, we won't live in squalor, either. I'll see to it that Sarah Jane will have plenty to keep her happy."

He studied her for a moment, then said, "Randolph Haney insists I'm losing my mind, but I assure you, Miss O'Malley, I'm in full control of my faculties."

"I don't doubt that for a moment, sir. Place everything you want Sarah Jane to have into a trust until she comes of age. I don't want a thing."

"Thank you for your confidence, but I'm not about to give a child I've never met a penny. I've asked McCain to bring her to me. If there's a resemblance, I'll see it for myself."

"And if you do see it?"

"I might allow you to live here and care for her."

"Mr. Graves, that's not at all what I had in mind."

"I'm sure it isn't."

Katie took a deep breath. "Then I'll just hope and pray that you don't see any resemblance to my little girl. I'm not going to give her up."

"Why do you call her your little girl?"

"Until today, I was the only one in the world who

could offer her a proper home and stability, along with love."

"You're a stubborn woman, Miss O'Malley."

"So I've been told."

A slow smile warmed his wrinkled face. "Then I suppose we'll continue this conversation when my alleged great-granddaughter arrives."

It wasn't quite what Katie had been hoping for—but it was certainly a start.

Chapter Ten

Katie hadn't been in the house long before Abel began to chuckle.

"What's so funny?" Tom asked.

"You are, *mijo.* Your fight isn't with *la señorita,* it's with yourself."

"What are you talking about?"

The old man merely smiled. "Feelings like anger and love can be very strong. Sometimes it's difficult to tell the two apart."

"You're *loco.* I have no feelings for her at all—other than pure exasperation."

Abel laughed again. "Maybe you should kiss her and see if that clears things up."

He *had* kissed her—twice. And each time it had only made things worse. In fact, last night, as she'd pulled him close, cloaking him in lilacs and lace, he'd nearly lost his head.

She'd certainly lost hers. Hadn't she realized the risk she'd taken in kissing him? Thank goodness, he'd come to his senses and sent her back to the house.

"Señor McCain?" Maria asked from the wrought-iron gate.

Tom turned to the sound of her voice. "Yes?"

"Señor Graves would like to see you. He was having breakfast in his room when I left him, but he asked me to find you and have you meet him in his study."

After asking Abel to excuse him, Tom followed Maria into the house. When she turned toward the kitchen, he made his way to the hall that led to Harrison's study.

The door was closed, so he knocked.

"I'll be with you in a minute," Harrison said from behind the closed door.

"Take your time." Tom shoved his hands in his pockets, then paced along the hall. His steps slowed near an oil painting of Robert Graves that hung over a small mahogany table.

Robert, who'd been fair-haired like Caroline, had been in his early twenties when that portrait had been painted. He'd been a good man, a kind soul. But he'd never stood up to his father. If he had, things might have been different.

He might have married Runs With Horses, the Indian woman he'd fallen in love with when he'd been nineteen. And if he had, Tom would have been legitimate— whether Harrison accepted him or not.

Several moments later, the door to the study opened and closed. Tom turned and watched Katie exit.

Well, what do you know? She'd wanted to talk to Harrison and had sought him out.

Their eyes met, but only for a moment. Unwilling to make a scene, Tom shook his head, then turned his back to her, refocusing his gaze on Robert's portrait. Yet he couldn't shake the urge to stomp after Katie and…

And what?

Give her another piece of his mind?

Kiss her into submission?

As her footsteps disappeared down the hall, Harrison's voice sounded from behind. "I wasn't a good father to him."

Tom turned and watched as the old man shuffled through the doorway and into the hall, his cane tapping along with his steps.

"Robert died before I ever told him I was proud of him." After a pause, Harrison added, "Or that I loved him."

"I'm sure he knew," Tom said, although he had no idea why he'd made such a claim. As far as Harrison Graves knew, Tom "Lone Wolf" McCain had never stepped foot on the Lazy G until he'd been summoned here just a couple months before.

Harrison shook his head. "No, I'm not sure that he did."

Tom figured the old man wanted to talk, not necessarily converse, which was just as well. He'd waited a long time to hear what the old man had to say, even if the words were only addressed to the bounty hunter he'd hired and not to the boy he'd run off the Lazy G years ago.

"Would you like to go back to your study?" Tom asked.

"That's probably a good idea. I'm not as strong these days, and I tire easily."

As Tom followed the old man through the open doorway, Harrison added, "Funny thing about life. You spend each day as though it's your last. Then one day you wake up and learn that it just might be. And you realize that you never got the chance to do half of the things you should have done."

"What would you have done differently?" Tom asked.

"I would have taken my son to the swimming hole, tied a rope on an oversize branch, watched him swing and drop into the cool water. I would have taken my lovely granddaughter to town, proudly displayed her on my arm for all the world to see what a delightful young lady she'd become, what a quick wit and bubbly laugh she had."

And now it was clearly too late to do any of that.

Harrison took a deep breath, then slowly let it out. "Do you believe in God, McCain?"

The question took Tom aback, but he answered, "Yes, I do."

Harrison eased himself into the leather chair behind his desk. "Glad to hear it. You'll find yourself standing in front of Him before you know it. And that's a frightening thought for a man like me."

"Why is that?"

"Every person God placed in my life, I either browbeat, took advantage of or abandoned."

Sadly, the old man probably didn't even know half of all the pain he'd caused, all the people he'd hurt—like Tom and his mother.

Harrison pointed to a shelf on the wall. "See that crude wood carving, next to the cigar box?"

Tom couldn't make out what it was. "Yes, I see it."

"Robert gave it to me for my birthday. He must have been about eight years old back then. Made it himself."

It was nice to think that Harrison had given the carving a place of honor.

"I found it in his bottom drawer after he died," Harrison added.

"But I thought you said it was a gift."

"Oh, he gave it to me. I tossed the creation into the fireplace—or so I thought. The boy must have retrieved it afterward and kept it."

Tom sat quietly, allowing the man to talk, to confess his guilt.

Harrison nodded toward a Saratoga trunk in the corner, a few feet from the bookshelf. "Do you see that?"

Tom nodded.

"I kept Caroline's photographs hidden in a drawer for nearly six years. Didn't want to see them. One evening after I drank myself into a senseless rage, I nearly burned them. Maria threw such a fit that I locked them up in that chest instead. But now I cherish her memory."

"You told me that you'd show those pictures to me," Tom said.

Harrison nodded. "So you could see if the child looks like Caroline."

Tom didn't need to see them, though. He'd never forget what Caroline had looked like as a child. And Sarah Jane favored her.

"You didn't tell me the girl's name was Sarah Jane," Harrison said.

"Didn't I?"

"No, your friend Katie O'Malley did."

Tom hadn't intentionally kept the news. "What does her name have to do with it?"

"My mother's name was Sarah Jane."

Tom hadn't known that, but then, how would he? He'd never been privy to any of the Graves family stories. At least, not very many of them.

"Tell me about the girl," Harrison said, his eyes hopeful yet leery.

Tom wasn't sure what to tell him, other than to offer a physical description. "She's six years old, blonde and has large, expressive eyes."

"What color are they?"

"Blue."

"Like Caroline's." Harrison faced him, his gaze searching Tom's. "Tell me about her heart, about her spirit. Did she get Caroline's zest for life—or my stubborn streak?"

"She's a beautiful child, inside and out."

"I want to see her for myself. And I don't have much time left. How long will it take for you to bring her back?"

"That's the problem, Mr. Graves. I'm not sure if she'll be safe in Stillwater."

Harrison lifted a white eyebrow. "Why not?"

"She witnessed an assault back in Pleasant Valley. And the man tried to silence her." He still didn't want to mention that he also thought Caroline's death was a little suspicious, especially when he didn't have anything to base it on except a feeling.

"Surely you don't think the girl would be less than safe here," Harrison said. "I can close this place up like a fortress. No one can get to her."

Tom was really stepping out on a limb, but he couldn't help saying, "I haven't ruled out the idea that it might actually be someone from Stillwater."

"Who? And why?" Harrison's brow knit, and he cocked his head. "You're not suggesting Caroline's death wasn't an accident, are you?"

"I think a fall down the stairs is a little suspicious. I also know that she moved to several different towns over the last six years. She might have been running from someone."

"I'll double your pay if you find whoever may have killed her."

"If her fall wasn't an accident, I'll find her killer—eventually."

Harrison, who'd seemed frail just moments ago, steeled himself. "I may not be around long enough to see the culprit come to justice, but my solicitor will see that you get paid."

"I'm not doing it for the money, so don't worry about paying me. And I'd rather you didn't mention anything to Mr. Haney."

"Why is that?"

Tom and Harrison might have struck the first chords of respect and friendship, but he wasn't ready to tell the man that his primary suspect was the man Harrison trusted most in this world.

"I'd like to keep my suspicions to myself for now," Tom said. "So please keep our conversation between the two of us. I'll notify Mr. Haney when the time is right."

"All right." Harrison pushed back his chair and got to his feet, signaling that their conversation had ended. "By the way, Randolph invited Miss O'Malley to the Cattleman's Ball tonight with him and Jeremiah. I think it's a good idea if you go along with them."

So did Tom.

Because the thought of Katie on the arm of either of those scoundrels was as welcome as a poke in the eye or a punch in the nose.

* * *

In the solitude of Caroline's bedroom, Katie stood before the full-length mirror and studied her reflection.

Earlier today, Maria had set out one of Caroline's gowns for Katie to wear to the ball, going so far as to alter it to fit. She'd also insisted upon fixing Katie's hair, painstakingly weaving the red tendrils into a fashionable coiffure while leaving soft wisps of curls to frame her face.

Katie tugged at the purple satin zinnias that trimmed the neckline of the gown, hoping to cover more of her cleavage. She felt uncomfortable with that much exposure.

Still, the lavender gown was lovely. Maria had done an exceptional job making it fit as though it had been made for Katie alone. Caroline had stood taller and had larger feet. The matching doeskin slippers Maria had set out nearly fit. Katie just hoped she could get through the evening without tripping or slipping out of them. She was nervous enough as it was. In a few minutes, she would be meeting Jeremiah Haney, Randolph's son and the man Tom intended to meet—the man he hadn't wanted Katie to speak to.

Tom should have realized Katie O'Malley didn't obey anyone unless she wanted to. Just because he didn't consider her especially competent on the trail didn't mean she wasn't bright enough to judge a man's character and do a bit of investigating on her own. If Sarah Jane wasn't safe in Stillwater, Katie would determine that for herself.

"Randolph and Jeremiah are here," Maria said from the doorway. When Katie turned, the woman's face broke into a radiant smile. She clasped her hands together and brought them to her heart. "How beautiful you are."

"I have you to thank. You're a talented seamstress."

Maria shook her head. "Oh, no. God blessed you with beauty. The gown only frames His handiwork."

Katie's cheeks warmed. Never having primped and preened over herself, the compliment unbalanced her. She stole a quick glance in the mirror to see whether her cheeks were flushed and she winced when she saw that they were. But there wasn't much she could do about it. She'd always blushed easily.

"I'd better go," she said. "I don't want to keep the gentlemen waiting."

"For you, they will wait." Maria winked. As she stepped aside, Katie lifted her hem and strode out the door.

In the sitting room, the men stood beside the settee speaking in low voices. When Katie entered, they paused and turned.

Surprise flooded Randolph's face. "Miss O'Malley, you look absolutely stunning. Allow me to introduce my son, Jeremiah."

Dignified, and dressed to perfection in a black suit and crisp white shirt, the younger Haney reached out his hand and greeted Katie with a warm, engaging smile.

He was older than her by close to twenty years, but the well-dressed gentleman was rather handsome, with a distinctive mole on a strong chin that made him quite memorable.

Jeremiah brought her hand to his lips. "It's a pleasure to meet you, Miss O'Malley."

"Thank you."

"My father says you're from Missouri."

"Yes, I am."

"I was in St. Louis last summer. It's a bustling city—and impressive."

Randolph placed his hand on Katie's arm. "Our carriage is ready, my dear. Shall we go?"

"Yes, of course."

Twenty minutes later, they arrived at the Cattleman's Ball, which was held in the well-lit and gaily decorated town hall.

With Jeremiah at his side, Randolph introduced Katie to several of the Stillwater residents. As far as she could tell, they all seemed to be decent people, friendly, welcoming and courteous.

"Katie, would you like a glass of punch?" Randolph asked.

"I'm sure she would," Jeremiah said. "Why don't you bring her one?"

When the elder Haney strode toward the refreshment table, Katie looked at the dignified escort at her side.

"Have you always live in Stillwater?" she asked.

"Yes, I have."

"Then you knew Caroline Graves."

"Our fathers were very close, so Caroline and I grew up together, so to speak. I was older than she. Ten years to be exact. I looked at her as a little sister and assumed the role of a big brother."

"I wish I could have met her," Katie said.

"I'm not sure you would have liked her. She had a wild side."

Katie wondered if people often said that about her.

"You may find this odd, Mr. Haney, but I might have admired that about Caroline."

Rather than quiz her about that, he asked, "So where did you meet McCain?"

"In Pleasant Valley."

"I see."

She wasn't sure what he thought he *saw* or why he was interested in how she knew Tom. But she had a few questions for him, too.

"I hear Harrison sent you in search of Caroline when she ran off," Katie said. "And that you weren't able to find her."

"Actually, I found her—several times."

Katie couldn't hide her amazement. For at least the past six months, and maybe even the past few years, Harrison had desperately wanted to find Caroline. And his friend's son had known of her whereabouts all along? "Then why didn't you tell Mr. Graves?"

"I couldn't. It would have crushed him."

"I'm not sure that I understand."

"If it would have actually helped Harrison to know the truth of her occupation, I would have told him." His brown eyes searched hers, as if he'd just given her some kind of cryptic message he hoped she'd understand.

Katie lowered her voice to a whisper, even though the music was so loud it really wasn't necessary. "Her *occupation?* You mean…she and Daisy were both…?"

"Oh. So you knew Miss Potts." Jeremiah lifted a single brow. "In Taylorsville she went by the name of Erin Kelly. And they were friends, weren't they?"

Katie didn't know what to say, what to think. She'd been told that Caroline and Erin had respectable jobs in Taylorsville.

"You thought Harrison would hold her…occupation against her?" she asked.

"I'd hoped that, in time, Caroline would have come to her senses and seen the error of her ways. And that I'd be able to talk her into coming home of her own accord."

"But that didn't happen?"

"Time ran out."

"I still think Harrison deserved to know," Katie said. "He might have been more forgiving than you thought."

"The real problem wasn't one of Caroline's sinful life. She hated her grandfather with a passion. I couldn't bring myself to tell the poor old man she wouldn't ever return. Knowing how she felt about him would have killed him faster than the disease that's eating away at him now. My father and I love Harrison. His death will be a cruel blow, even though we know it's coming. But I don't want to see it happen any sooner than need be."

Katie still believed that Harrison had deserved to know the truth. Perhaps if he had known sooner, he could have gone to see Caroline, spoken to her face-to-face, met Sarah Jane.

"Come, my dear." Jeremiah took her arm. "Let's drop this horrid subject before I embarrass myself with tears. Dance with me."

As the musicians played fiddles, banjos and a slightly off-key piano, Jeremiah swept Katie into his arms and onto the dance floor before she had a chance to object. And she soon found her steps matching his.

She had to admit that Jeremiah Haney was an exquisite dancer. And a kindhearted human being, it seemed.

Each time he spun her to the right, she spotted Tom McCain standing near the refreshment table.

He appeared rather dapper himself tonight, in a pair of dark slacks and a white shirt.

Yet a scowl on his face spoke volumes, all of it directed at her.

As Katie and Jeremiah graced the dance floor, Tom stood beside the refreshment table, a glass of punch in his hand and a knot in his gut.

Katie appeared utterly captivated by the scoundrel who held her in his arms. And right now Tom wanted to pry the starry-eyed redhead from his grip, then knock the arrogant Haney on his backside.

Anger flared, and Tom did his best to tamp it down. But he wasn't the only one in the room who resented what might be considered an uncivilized presence.

A few haughty glances and condescending looks told him half of the people in this room didn't appreciate a half-breed being here. And the only thing keeping the town fathers from asking him to leave was the fact that Tom had a business arrangement with Harrison Graves, which meant he had the cattleman's approval.

When Katie smiled up at Haney, Tom fought the need to protect her as well as give her a piece of his mind. She had no way of knowing why he despised and distrusted both Randolph and his son, but as far as Tom was concerned, Katie O'Malley had just entered the enemy camp—with a pretty smile and of her own accord.

Her soft auburn locks, swept up in a riot of curls, exposed that slender neck. The lavender gown she wore was more than becoming. It actually suited her. Tom could almost smell her lilac scent, and a sense of ownership flooded over him.

As he emptied his punch in one quick gulp, his eyes

followed her every move, and he wished he could hear
the conversation she was having with Jeremiah Haney.

"Would you like some fresh air?" Jeremiah asked
Katie. "There's a beautiful courtyard outside. The townspeople hired a custom craftsman to build it. The fountain
alone took over six months to complete."

His brown eyes beseeched her to agree.

The privacy would give Katie a chance to question
him further, get to know him better, to decide for herself whether he could be trusted or not.

"All right," she said.

As the fiddlers stepped forward, the Virginia reel
was announced. Applause, laughter and gaiety broke
out in the crowd. The other men scampered for a partner, while Jeremiah escorted Katie off the dance floor
and out the side door.

The moon was no longer as big or silvery as it had
been on the night she'd joined Tom outside, the night he'd
kissed her, but the air was cool and calming.

Jeremiah tucked her hand in the warm crook of his
arm. "You look lovely."

"Thank you." Compliments didn't often affect Katie,
but she felt especially pretty tonight. It must have been
the lavender gown. Or perhaps the atmosphere that made
her feel special. Either way, his words touched her.

Jeremiah looked impressive, as well, but she didn't
say so. Some women fussed over men, but Katie had
never been one of them.

"Miss O'Malley, I've always appreciated a woman
with a compassionate heart. However, I've never had
the pleasure of meeting one that also looked like a god-

dess." Jeremiah patted the top of her hand as it rested on his forearm.

Katie laughed. "A goddess? Now I doubt your sincerity."

Jeremiah touched her chin with the tip of a long, tapered finger and drew her gaze to his. "You'll never find a man more sincere than I."

Katie's cheeks warmed, and she hoped the lack of lighting hid her flush. She wondered if anyone could see them but decided she and her escort had wandered a bit too far from the gathering. They probably should turn back, but she was enjoying the company and the night air.

"I'm thoroughly taken with you, Miss O'Malley. I enjoy your bright mind."

At that she broke into a warm smile. "Now, that's a compliment I'll thank you for."

Festive lanterns around the community hall cast a faint light, enabling Katie to catch the intensity in his gaze. She felt oddly flattered yet embarrassed at the same time.

She wiggled her toes inside the loose-fitting doeskin slippers.

He tilted her chin with his finger again, and when she looked up, his mouth lowered toward hers.

He was going to kiss her.

For a moment, she wondered if another man's kiss would be as moving as Tom's, if it would have the same effect on her. But there was something unsettling about kissing another man, especially this one, so she placed her hands on his chest to push him away.

Another man might have realized that she wasn't in

agreement, but Jeremiah pressed his lips against hers anyway.

She pushed against his chest, trying to free herself, but he didn't let go. So twisted her head, breaking the unbidden kiss and intending to slap him senseless.

That is, until a familiar voice cut in. "Good evening, folks."

Jeremiah released her, and Katie glanced over her shoulder, although she didn't need to see who'd joined them.

Tom glared at Jeremiah as though he wanted to throttle him with his bare hands.

And had she not been so embarrassed and guilt riddled for agreeing to go outside in the first place and to wander so far from the festivities, Katie might have helped him do just that.

Chapter Eleven

"What are you doing here?" Jeremiah asked, his tone crisp and cool.

Tom smiled, but not with his eyes. "I'm worried about the lady's safety. She's new around here."

"She's in good hands," Jeremiah said. "Go back inside."

The men stood eye to eye, and although they'd said very little, Katie sensed their hatred and distrust of each other. And for once, she found herself on Tom's side, although she didn't want to admit her foolishness—or the uneasiness she'd felt with the man she'd been warned about.

"If you don't mind," she told Jeremiah, "I'd like to speak to Mr. McCain."

"You don't need to address an Indian as *mister*," Jeremiah said. "Not around here."

Katie's stomach knotted. "Then, if you don't mind, I'd like to speak to Tom."

"Now *I'm* the one who's worried." Jeremiah put an arm around her. "You shouldn't be alone with him, especially outside in the dark."

She placed her hand on Jeremiah's chest, felt his heart pound beneath his jacket and gave him a push toward the dance. "I'm perfectly all right. Please leave us alone. I'll be inside soon."

Jeremiah hesitated but turned to go. Pausing, he glared over his shoulder. "If you so much as treat her with an ounce of disrespect, you'll deal with me, boy."

Tom stood silent, his eyes boring into Jeremiah.

"I'll be *fine*," Katie repeated. "Please go inside. *Now*."

She waited for Jeremiah to leave. When he finally reached the lighted building, she turned to Tom.

He crossed his arms and scowled. "What are you doing out here?"

She wished he hadn't witnessed the brief but intimate exchange, but she didn't want him to know she had any regrets. Or that Jeremiah had actually frightened her, that he hadn't stopped when she'd tried to push him away. She'd felt so out of control that a sense of relief had surged through her when Tom had arrived, in spite of her embarrassment at being caught.

"I wasn't doing anything out here. Not really."

"You *kissed* him."

No, she hadn't, but telling Tom that Jeremiah had been so bold, so forceful, would only make things worse between the men. And a physical altercation at this point wouldn't help their investigation.

"You don't have any claims on me," she said.

"No, I don't. But I suspect Haney's wife wouldn't appreciate you kissing her husband."

"His *wife?*" Katie's jaw dropped, and she took a step back. "Jeremiah's married?"

"I take it he didn't tell you."

"Why, no." Katie hoped it wasn't true. She might not

intend to marry anyone, but that didn't mean she didn't value the institution of matrimony. Had she known, she wouldn't have allowed the man to walk her outside alone.

Maybe Tom was mistaken. "Why would Jeremiah come to the dance alone if he had a wife? Why isn't she here?"

"She's at home. From what I understand, she's sick and bedridden."

Katie dropped her hands from her hips, momentarily taken aback. Why hadn't Jeremiah mentioned something as important as that? And why on earth had he tried to kiss her?

"Would it have made a difference?" Tom asked.

"Of course, it would have." Katie's temper flared, and with Jeremiah out of range, she focused all of it on Tom. "What kind of woman do you think I am?"

"I'm not sure."

Katie raised her hand to slap him, and he caught her wrist in a hard grip. "I told you once before, don't ever strike me again."

Katie truly wasn't prone to violence, but Tom Mc-Cain seemed to bring out the worst in her. "You're the only man I've ever wanted to strike."

Of course, that wasn't true. Right now she wanted to pummel Jeremiah Haney.

With her arm still raised, Tom's hand holding hers at bay, Katie knew she'd never overpower him. But then, she really didn't want to. She'd had no business coming outside with Jeremiah in the first place. Tom had warned her about him, and she hadn't paid him any mind.

When she relaxed her pose, Tom released her wrist.

"Coming out here with him was a bad idea," she admitted.

"Then why did you do it?"

"To talk to him. And to see the fountain." Katie scanned the grounds, just now realizing there was no fountain in sight.

"If you're looking for the courtyard, it's on the other side of the building." Tom glared at her. "You came out here to kiss him."

Katie tapped his broad chest with a pointed finger. "Not intentionally. And to be honest, we didn't actually kiss, although he tried to force himself on me. However, you can be sure that I won't ever go off with him alone again."

Tom removed her tapping finger from his chest, his hand encompassing hers. *"Good."*

"Don't tell me you're jealous." Katie hoped her words might embarrass him, cause him to back down and leave her be.

Or maybe she wanted him to admit that he didn't like the thought of her kissing another man.

"I'm not jealous," he said, pulling her close.

She ought to fight the intimacy, but his touch and his scent caused her thoughts to jumble, her knees to weaken.

Yet no matter how badly she might be tempted to lose herself in Tom's embrace, they had no future together. After all, they were an ill-suited pair. Tom insisted upon obedience, and Katie wouldn't give up her independence for anyone.

"Go inside," he told her. "Tell Jeremiah that you have a headache or that you've suffered an attack of the vapors. Use whatever excuse you women make. I want you to return to the ranch."

Katie fought the urge to challenge him, but for the

first time in her life she actually wanted to retreat. And even more distressing and unusual, she felt foolish for not listening to Tom in the first place. He'd been right, and she'd been wrong.

Jeremiah Haney couldn't be trusted. He'd lied, first about the courtyard, but more importantly by omitting the fact that he had a wife.

Why had he escorted her to the one side of the building that would hold little interest to the others in attendance?

Had he wanted to speak to her privately, the kiss being entirely unexpected? Or had he wanted her away from the crowd for something more clandestine?

Something nagged at her in addition to the cloying scent of his tobacco-laced breath. Something that told her to respect the niggle of fear she'd felt when he'd disregarded her wishes and tried to force a kiss she hadn't wanted.

Eager to escape the accusations in Tom's eyes, she turned on her heel and strode toward the community hall in a most unladylike fashion, her temper barely in control.

In her haste to make her way back to the festivities, her foot lifted out of her shoe, leaving one foot bare and a lavender slipper along the pathway. She turned to retrieve the oversize dancing shoe, stepping on a stone in the process. "Ouch," she mumbled under her breath.

"Did you throw a shoe?" Tom asked.

Katie glanced up awkwardly, the wry grin on his handsome face only serving to escalate her humiliation and fuel her anger. How dare he tease her? Did he actually mean to refer to her as a horse?

Katie reached for the doeskin slipper, tempted to sling it at him.

He stood still, arms crossed. "Planning to throw it at me?"

"How did you know?"

"Lucky guess."

"I'd rather wait until I'm wearing a boot or something that's a lot heavier and would inflict more damage." She bent and hobbled while placing the slipper back onto her foot.

She could imagine him chuckling behind her back, but she ignored her annoyance as she returned to the community hall.

Once inside, she forced a smile, trying to appear unruffled, even though hiding her emotions had never been easy.

Moments later, Jeremiah was at her side, handsome, gallant and—*married.* If she'd worn sturdier shoes, she might have kicked *him* in the shins.

"Are you all right?" he asked.

"Yes, I'm fine. Please tell your father I'm ready to go." She didn't have a headache and had never had an attack of the vapors in her life. She wanted to leave, and that's all there was to it. No excuses or explanations needed.

"I'm ready to go, too," Jeremiah said. "But first, I want to tell you something."

"What's that?" Katie expected to hear a long overdue confession of his marital status. She crossed her arms and would have tapped her foot if the instep wasn't so tender.

"Please be careful what you say to McCain."

Katie stiffened. The man who'd taken her to see a nonexistent fountain and had neglected to tell her he had a wife at home was offering her a piece of "trusted" advice?

"What do you mean?" Katie asked.

"I think he intends to blackmail Harrison."

His words caught her off guard. "Why would he do that?"

"Since he followed Caroline's trail, he knows what she was up to the past six years. And some people have no conscience, especially where money is concerned." Jeremiah took her arm and led her toward the door. He motioned to Randolph, alerting the older man of their impending departure.

"Tom doesn't seem to be the type to be impressed with money," Katie said.

"My dear, *everyone* has a price."

Perhaps they did. Her mind whirled with facts that didn't quite add up.

Something told her there would come a day when she'd have to place her trust, maybe even her very life, in someone's hands.

She just hoped and prayed that when that day came, she would make the right choice.

The next morning, while Katie sat at Caroline's dressing table, brushing her hair, Maria pulled a dress from the closet.

"Did you have fun at the dance?" Maria asked, a wistful smile crossing her face.

Katie didn't have the heart to tell her no. "It was a pleasant evening. But I'm curious about something. What do you know about Jeremiah's wife?"

Maria clucked her tongue. "*Que lastima.* Such an unhappy woman."

"Why do you say that?"

"Martha Haney lost her mind. Her husband had to hire a nurse to look after her. *La medicina* helps. She does not rave and cry as much as before."

"What's wrong with her?"

"Jeremiah said it happened slowly over time, but I think it was sudden."

"Sudden? What do you mean?"

"She stopped by here about six months ago and spoke to Señor Graves alone in his study. She left with a paper in her hand. She mumbled something about hiring a detective. I thought that was odd." Maria shook her head. "That is the last I saw of her. She seemed *inojada,* angry. But she did not seem *loca.*"

"How long after that did she become ill?"

"Three weeks? Maybe more. Maybe less. The doctor confined her to bed."

"Has anyone gone to see her?"

"No. Señor Jeremiah does not allow visitors, but the woman who takes care of her is my friend."

"What does your friend have to say?"

"Only that Martha sleeps most of the time, which is a blessing because she cries without the medicine."

"And when she raves? What does she say?" Katie couldn't believe she was questioning the words of a crazy woman, but quite frankly, she found it all very odd.

"My friend speaks only Spanish, so she doesn't understand very much, but she told me Martha cries for her father and for Señor Graves."

"Where does Jeremiah live?" Katie asked. "I'd like to meet his wife."

"Oh, no. That is not possible. Señor Haney told my

friend that she would lose her job if she couldn't keep his wife quiet or if she ever let anyone into his house when he isn't home." Maria frowned, large brown eyes watering. "*Por favor, señorita.* My friend is a widow. She needs the money to feed her children."

Katie placed a hand on Maria's shoulder. "I won't do anything to put your friend's job at risk."

But thoughts of Martha Haney tugged at her heart.

Something didn't seem right, and she didn't mean Martha Haney's illness.

Jeremiah had told an entirely different story about Caroline than Tom had, and neither man trusted the other. Quite frankly, after last night, Katie didn't trust Jeremiah. And while Katie might have plenty of reason to resent Tom's attitude toward women—or, at least, his attitude toward her most of the time—he'd never lied to her.

"Maria," Katie said, "do you know where I can find Tom?"

"He rode off early this morning, but I saw him come back about an hour ago."

"Thank you. I need to speak to him. Will you excuse me?"

"Yes, of course."

Moments later, Katie found Tom at one of the corrals near the barn, cooling down his gelding.

"I'd like a word with you," she said.

He turned, his expression unreadable. "What's on your mind?"

"What do you know about Martha Haney?"

"Are you wondering if she's likely to pass on and leave the dashing Jeremiah Haney a widower?"

Katie blew out a ragged sigh. "That was uncalled-for."

"I'm sorry. Sometimes the uncivilized savage comes out in me."

Is that what had set him on edge? The fact that he felt he had to prove to her and everyone else that he wasn't tainted by his Indian blood? That he was just as worthy as any other person on the ranch or in town?

Did he think that she felt the same way as the Haneys? If so, he didn't know her very well.

"I learned the hard way that Jeremiah Haney can't be trusted," she admitted. "And I've come to believe that you and I need to join forces and work as a team if we're going to protect Sarah Jane."

When he didn't object, she uncrossed her arms and leaned against the corral. "I'm not sure what you know, but Maria told me that Martha Haney lost her mind."

"I'd heard that."

Katie lifted her hand, shielding her eyes from the glare of the morning sun. "I was told she's on medication to keep her quiet."

Tom stepped to the right, blocking the sun's glare for her, a thoughtful move that took her by surprise.

"I'm not sure about her condition or the treatment," he said.

She bit down on her lip, unsure how much she should share of the information she'd gathered. Finally, she opted to trust him with all of it. "Did you know that Martha came to see Harrison a few weeks before she became ill?"

"The families have been friends for a long time."

"I know that, but Maria said that Martha left with a piece of paper."

"I'm sure there wasn't anything unusual about Martha asking Harrison for advice or information."

"Aren't you curious?"

"Yes, and I'm glad you told me, but don't get any wild ideas about investigating."

"Why not?"

"I told you that I don't trust that man or his father."

"But you never told me why."

"I shouldn't have to."

"If you want me to follow your orders and instructions, you'll need to give me reason to."

He seemed to ponder her words for a moment, then said, "Years ago, Randolph Haney used to be a cruel man, and I have no reason to believe he's changed."

"You used to know him?"

"Yes, I spent a lot of time in Stillwater when I was a kid. But he knew me as Lone Wolf back then, and I've changed."

He'd grown up, of course. And he'd apparently taken Hannah McCain's name. "What makes you say that Randolph was cruel? What did he do?"

"A lot of it was hearsay. But I can tell you for a fact that he hated Indians. He threw my mother off the Lazy G twice, the last time when she was dying and begging for help."

"Why did he do that?"

"He said he was doing Harrison's bidding." Tom lifted his hand and fingered his forehead, where a scar marred his brow.

"Does Harrison know who you are?" she asked.

"No, he hired me to find Caroline because of my reputation as a bounty hunter."

"And you took the job in spite of the bad blood between you and Haney—and Harrison, as well?"

Tom tensed. "Yes, I took the job."

"I don't understand. Why would you do that? If someone hadn't shown my dying mother any kindness, I wouldn't have given them the time of day."

"I had my reasons, but I'd rather not talk about that now."

While curious and tempted to prod him, Jeremiah's words came to mind. *Everyone has a price.*

Had Tom hired on for more than the money he'd been promised in payment?

Had Katie been wrong about him?

They stood like that for a moment, lost in the silence, lost in their thoughts.

Did she dare tell Tom the other piece of information Jeremiah had told her?

Did she dare not?

"Jeremiah knew where Caroline was all along. He told me that she'd been living a sinful life, just as Erin had been in Pleasant Valley. And that she hated her grandfather and didn't ever want to go back to the ranch. He never told Harrison because the news would have broken his heart."

"He's lying. I had a feeling he'd been the one who'd been following her. Erin may have had a shady past, and I grant you that she wasn't living a respectable life at the Gardener's House. But that's not true about Caroline. She was never a prostitute. And while she might have been angry with Harrison, she would have come home if she'd known he was dying, especially if she knew he wanted to make amends."

"How do you know that?"

"I just do. Caroline might have been quick to anger, but she had a kind and loving nature."

"You knew her personally?"

"Only when we were children."

Again came the silence, the drifting thoughts. Katie suspected Tom was remembering Caroline, until he said, "Tell me something."

"What's that?"

"You kissed Jeremiah Haney last night. Why?"

Her cheeks flushed, and her heart thumped. Her first impulse was to lie or downplay what had actually happened when Jeremiah had taken her outside. After all, she wasn't sure if she could trust Tom with her heartfelt revelations—or her uneasiness.

But she knew without a doubt that Jeremiah Haney was a scoundrel. And that was something upon which they both could agree.

"I'll admit that I momentarily considered kissing him," she said.

"To see how it compared?"

Her cheeks burned with the shame of it, but she pressed on. "I was curious, yes. But only for the briefest of moments. I wouldn't have gone through with it. But when I told him no and tried to push him away, he persisted. I may have snapped at you last night after your arrival, but I was actually relieved to see you. Then, when I found out that he was married… Well, he's not an honorable man."

"Stay away from him, Katie."

That was one order she intended to keep, but she'd rather wrestle a pig in a mud puddle than admit it. "I'm going to return to the kitchen before my coffee gets cold," she said. "So if you'll excuse me?"

"Did you *hear* me?" he asked.

"I heard. And I think it was wise advice. I think

I'll probably heed it." Then she turned on her heel and headed for the house.

As she approached the kitchen, she heard the low mutters of whispered voices.

Her steps slowed, more to avoid interrupting than to eavesdrop. Still, she couldn't help hearing Maria speak, her words a mixture of English and Spanish.

"That boy and his mother came here years ago— that last time—asking to speak to Señor Graves. *Por que,* Abel?"

"I do not know."

"*Sí, tu sabes.* Tell me the truth."

"I cannot. I made a promise many years ago. I will not break my word unless Lone Wolf asks me to."

"I have known you for many years. *Somos como familia.* You can tell me. I can keep a secret."

"No," Abel said, determination in his voice. "If a man's word means nothing, he is worth nothing."

"Caroline spoke of him once."

"Que dijo, la señorita?" Abel asked.

"She said that she had met her Indian brother."

Katie's breath caught. Caroline had an Indian brother? Surely that wasn't possible. Even if she'd wanted to back away from the voices, she couldn't. Her feet wouldn't move.

"Caroline was just a child," Abel said, dismissing Maria's claim. "Who knows what she meant by that."

"*Sí.* You are right. She was only six years old at the time."

"Children have big imaginations," he added.

"Sometimes. *Pero quién sabe?*"

"Did you question her at the time?"

"No," Maria said, "I thought she was…*como se dice?*"

"Dreaming?"

"*Si.*"

"*Es possible.* Why do you care now?"

"Because if she was talking about Lone Wolf, I believe he has come back. And I do not know why he would, not after he was sent away so cruelly, especially that last time." Maria sighed heavily. "Did she speak the truth, old man?"

"How would I know? You will have to ask the boy."

"He is a man now," Maria said, "but I will ask him."

Katie cleared her throat to announce her entrance as she stepped into the warm kitchen. The aroma of spicy beef and eggs sizzling on a cast-iron skillet filled the air.

"Something smells delicious," Katie said, her mind on anything but food.

There were more than a few secrets at the Lazy G, and Katie planned to uncover them all, beginning with Tom "Lone Wolf" McCain.

Chapter Twelve

Tom had planned to leave early in the morning to get Sarah Jane, but this new piece of information Katie had provided needed further investigation.

He wanted to know why Martha Haney had visited Harrison Graves and what she took with her when she left. And only one person could give him that answer.

So he knocked lightly on Harrison's study door, hoping the man was awake, alone and ready for an unexpected visitor.

"Come in," the cattleman called from within.

Tom turned the brass knob, stepped inside and closed the door behind him.

Harrison sat at his desk, shrunken—now just a temporary fixture in the office he once ruled. Sunlight streamed through the window behind him, giving him a heavenly glow and reminding Tom of how little time the man had left.

"I'm leaving for the girl," Tom said. "But I'd like to ask you a few questions before I go."

Harrison motioned toward the leather chair in front

of the large desk, then studied him momentarily. "Have a seat. What do you want to know?"

"I heard Martha Haney came by to visit you about six months ago." Tom pulled out the chair and sat. "Do you mind if I ask what she wanted?"

The question seemed to take Harrison by surprise, but he held a blank expression as he studied Tom warily. "She wanted the name of a detective I'd used in the past."

"And you gave it to her?"

Harrison nodded. "I probably would have been more inquisitive, but I felt faint and wanted to get rid of her before I keeled over and embarrassed myself."

"Did Mrs. Haney mention why she wanted an investigator?"

"No, but about that same time, someone had broken into the Haney house and stolen some heirloom jewelry. I assumed it had something to do with following an old employee."

"Why didn't Jeremiah approach you?" Tom asked.

"He was out of town at the time."

"It seems he's away from home a lot." Tom watched Harrison carefully, trying to gauge what the old man thought.

Harrison leaned back in his chair and placed his elbows on the armrest. "He has a lot of business to take care of."

"Maybe Martha was suspicious of her husband."

"Of Jeremiah?" Harrison snorted. "I wouldn't doubt it. The man played around more than most men would. I suppose he still does."

Tom bit back his opinion. He didn't trust a man who was unfaithful to his wife. Sure, some men thought it was part of their nature to exercise their prowess, but if a man couldn't hold himself to a marital vow, Tom found little to admire or to trust in him. People were either loyal and honest or they weren't.

"Did Martha mention anything about Jeremiah?" he asked.

"If she actually wanted to have him followed, I don't think she'd tell me. She would have been worried that I would have tried to talk her out of it. Or that I would have told Randolph. But like I said, I was in no mood to quiz her, and she didn't explain." Harrison crossed his arms. "For the most part, I tried to appease her. Jeremiah had confided in me that the woman was acting very strange."

"Was she?"

Harrison threw his hands up. "She's a woman. They all act a bit strange, if you ask me."

"I suppose they do," Tom said, thinking of Katie and cracking a slight smile. "Who did you suggest she contact?"

"Cord Rainville. I'd gotten his name from a friend of mine. I'd heard he was a good man—smart, trustworthy, discreet. He lost his wife and child in a fire a couple of years ago and took it hard. I was told that he tends to drink to forget, but that he's good at what he does and will get the job done."

That struck Tom as odd. "Why didn't you ask him to look for Caroline? Why did you hire me?"

"Actually, I tried. Cord had a job out of state, and my schedule didn't fit his. I hear he might be back now."

"Where can I find him?"

"Rio Seco."

That was a three-to-four-hour ride from Stillwater.

"Do you know whether Martha Haney ever contacted him?" Tom asked.

"No, I don't. What's on your mind?"

"Just a hunch." Tom didn't know if he dared to share his suspicions.

Harrison eyed him critically. "You don't think it had anything to do with Caroline, do you?"

"I have a bad feeling about all of this, sir."

"You said that before, but I'm sure you understand my reluctance to believe it."

Tom had meant to spare Harrison as much of the ugliness as possible, but the man had to face the truth. "Caroline's daughter witnessed an attack on the woman Caroline met at Casa de Los Angelitos. The trauma left the child mute."

"Just exactly where is the girl now?"

"She's safe. But it wasn't that difficult for me to find Caroline, even though she moved several times—once in the dead of night. I think she was running from someone. And Jeremiah Haney traveled a lot. I also have reason to believe that he's known where Caroline was all along."

Harrison's lips tightened. "Don't let your thoughts wander in that direction. Jeremiah loved Caroline. She was like a sister to him."

Tom could taste the bitterness that rose in his throat. "But he *wasn't* her brother."

"No, but as children, they—"

"No, sir." Tom shook his head. "Jeremiah was more than ten years older than Caroline. He never thought of her as a sister."

Harrison frowned. "How would you know how he felt about her?"

Because a brother would look out for his sister. He

would have done anything he could to help her, to find her, to bring her home.

"It's just a gut feeling," Tom said.

"You seem to have a lot of those."

"I haven't been wrong very often."

"You're wrong this time." Harrison slowly scooted his chair from the desk.

"I hope so." But as Tom stood, he knew his intuition was too strong to discredit any longer.

"When will you leave for Sarah Jane? I don't have to tell you how anxious I am to meet her. Your horse should be rested by now."

"Soon," Tom said, implying he would go immediately after Sarah Jane, but that wasn't his intent. First he would go to Rio Seco.

"Will you take Miss O'Malley?"

"No, I'll leave her here. I think it might be a good idea if you took the time to get to know her."

"She asked if she could raise the child." Harrison's tired blue eyes searched Tom's as though he wanted his opinion.

"She'd be a good mother," Tom said.

Now, if he could only convince himself the child would live to adulthood, everything would work out fine.

Just after breakfast, while Katie read a book in Caroline's room, a horse whinnied, drawing her attention. She might have ignored the sound, but curiosity got the better of her, and she padded to the window. After drawing the curtains aside, she peered out and spotted Tom leading one of the ranch horses from the stable, a saddlebag draped over his shoulder.

Where in the world was he going? And why wasn't he taking his own horse, Caballo?

If he thought he would sneak off without telling her what he was up to, he was horribly mistaken. She dashed out of the house and entered the yard, just as he was about to mount a dun gelding.

"Are *we* going somewhere?" Katie asked, while catching her breath. She batted a loose strand of hair from her eye.

He turned slowly, then looked her up and down. "*I'm* going somewhere for a while."

"Without telling me?"

His eyes swept over her again, this time granting her an appreciative smile. "I didn't think I needed to."

Katie stood tall and crossed her arms. "Under the circumstances, we're partners of a sort. And you at least owe me the courtesy of telling me where you're going. Or giving me the opportunity to go with you."

"I'm going to speak to a man named Cord Rainville. Martha Haney had asked Harrison to refer her to a private investigator, and I'd like to know why. And since I need to be back late tonight, I'll be riding fast and hard. So I'm going alone."

"What's wrong with Caballo?" she asked.

"Nothing's wrong with him. I'm leaving for Sarah Jane tomorrow before dawn, and I want my horse to be fresh."

Katie still didn't like the idea of being left behind.

"How do I know you'll be back tonight?" she asked.

"Because I told you I would." He touched her chin with the tip of a finger, the smile leaving his face. The intensity of his gaze took the fight from her. "Have I ever lied to you?"

"No," she answered again, realizing he hadn't. At least, not that she knew of.

He dropped his hand to his side, but his eyes remained on hers, unwavering. "May I suggest that you start considering the type of people you put your faith in? There are those who lie and those you don't. There are some who can be trusted, some who can't. Think long and hard about it, Katie. Your life, and the lives of those around you, could depend upon your ability to tell the difference."

"I will, but you have to admit, you don't say much to me at all. A person can lie by omitting the truth."

He shrugged, then turned toward the gelding.

Katie grabbed him by the arm, amazed at the swirl of goose bumps that fluttered over her whenever she and Tom touched. Did he feel it, too?

"Tom," she said softly, drawing his attention.

He turned warily, but his gaze fixed on hers.

"If there was something I should know, would you tell me?"

"Yes." His eyes grazed hers. "But the real question is, would you listen?"

Katie smiled. "I'd certainly give it a great deal of thought."

A grin brushed his lips as humor sparked in the depths of his eyes. Something else sparked, too. Something she didn't recognize.

Her stomach turned topsy-turvy. What was happening here? Had they reached a different level of familiarity? An intimacy?

Affection, maybe?

Katie almost preferred to get angry at the man rather than cope with this rush of uncomfortable and enigmatic emotions. She took a deep breath, wanting to broach an-other subject. "I overheard Maria talking to Abel ear-lier. I didn't mean to eavesdrop, but she asked him if you were Caroline's brother."

Tom stiffened, then scanned the empty yard. "What did Abel say?"

"He didn't answer."

Tom didn't respond, either.

"Is it true?" she prodded. "*Are* you Caroline's brother?"

"Let it go, Katie. Some things are better left alone."

She suspected, that if the answer had been no, he would have come out and said so. And her heart ached for the boy he'd been, for the hurt he must have suffered when he'd been cast out by the family who should have nurtured him.

Yet here he was, determined to protect Caroline's daughter, as well as her memory.

Katie reached out and touched his cheek, her fingers in plain contrast to his copper-colored skin. "What was your mother's name?"

"What does it matter?"

"It matters to me."

He studied her as if trying to decide if she was sin-cere or not. Apparently he decided she was. "Her name was Runs With Horses."

Katie smiled. "I wish I could have met her."

"Why?"

"So I could tell her that she had a brave and loyal son. And that she could be proud of the man he grew up to be."

Tom placed his callused hand over hers and brushed his thumb over her knuckles. "I don't like leaving you here, but knowing you'll stay on the ranch and keep away from the Haneys would make me feel a lot better about it."

Katie's heart fluttered like a swarm of honeybees soaring over a meadow of wildflowers.

Would he kiss her again?

He'd said he wouldn't, but suddenly she wanted his arms around her, his lips on hers. And while her pride begged her to pretend that she couldn't care less whether he did or didn't, her heart leaped when he dropped the saddlebag to the ground, then wrapped his arms around her waist and drew her lips to his.

Tom knew he'd be sorry for this later, but he couldn't help himself. His mouth came down on Katie's, as if making a claim on her, as if making some kind of promise.

Yet something deep within him called out for reason, and he sobered.

What was he doing? He was yearning for a woman that would never be his, dreaming of a life that he could never have.

This madness had to stop, and it certainly looked as though Katie wasn't going to do anything to help him. So he pulled his lips from hers, took a step back and dropped his arms to his sides.

"Is something wrong?" she asked.

Yes, something was terribly wrong. "This isn't a game. We can't keep doing things like this."

"Like kissing each other?" She cocked her head. "Why not? It's becoming rather enjoyable."

"In case you've forgotten, I'm a half-breed. We also fight like cats and dogs. We're like oil and water. We don't mix. Neither one of us wants marriage, at least, not to each other. It would never work out between the two of us. We're too different."

"Who said anything about marriage?" she asked.

"You can't keep kissing me like that and not expect things to progress in a serious direction."

"When you put it that way…"

"We can talk about this later. Right now, I need to go. The sooner I leave, the sooner I'll get back."

"If it makes you feel better," she said, her voice husky, "I promise not to be with Jeremiah alone."

He ran his knuckles along her cheek. "That does make me feel better, but I don't think Jeremiah will be around here very long."

"Where's he going?"

"He's going to follow me."

She placed her hand on his arm, and worry filled her eyes. "Be careful, Tom."

He could tell that she meant it, that the games and contests of wits and wills they each had been trying to win had ended, at least for the time being. And that touched him.

"Don't worry about me. Jeremiah Haney couldn't track a fat old cow in a snowdrift." Then he picked up his saddlebag, slung it over the back of the saddle and mounted the gelding.

Considering the fact that she always had an opinion or a comment to make, her silence surprised him. And it pleased him.

He glanced down at her. In the morning breeze, loose strands of auburn hair whipped across her face, and she brushed them aside from her pensive eyes.

"Be careful," she said again, this time in a near whisper.

Her concern sent a warm rush through his chest. "I'm always careful."

Then he urged the gelding onward, prepared to bring Jeremiah Haney to his knees.

Katie's heart tightened as she watched Tom ride away, handsome, solemn and gallant.

She still didn't know nearly as much about Tom "Lone Wolf" McCain as she wanted to, but as sure as the sun rose in the east and set in the west, the brooding loner had found a place in her heart. She cared for him deeply.

Could it be love?

Perhaps, but if that were the case, what was she willing to do about it?

Dreams and plans, once carefully structured, tumbled in her mind. Questions, too.

She could pray about it and ask for divine guidance. But ever since her very first run-in with Reverend Codwell back in Pleasant Valley, she'd found herself uneasy in church.

The pompous and self-righteous minister had called her a rebellious woman so often that she'd found more and more reasons not to attend.

And ultimately, she'd turned away from God, too. Not that she didn't believe in Him. But He'd… Well, He'd come to seem so distant and not at all like the benevolent Father or the comforting friend she'd once considered Him to be.

A sense of loneliness cloaked her shoulders as she watched Tom ride away, and for the first time since meeting him, she feared for his safety.

Please, Dear God, watch over him, protect him.
And bring him back to me....

She continued to watch Tom ride until she could no longer see him. Then she slowly made her way back to the house.

She entered the vast kitchen, breathing in the scents of beans simmering on the stove and yeast and cinnamon baking in the oven.

Maria stood over the table, skillfully patting balls of dough into round, flat pancakelike circles and humming a tune Katie had never heard before.

The older woman smiled, a smudge of flour on her cheek. *"Buenos días."*

"Good morning." How could she resort to tact and grace when she had only one thought on her mind?

"I have a question, Maria. I'm not sure if you remember this, but years ago, a young Indian woman named Runs With Horses came by here with her son, Lone Wolf. Do you know why she came and why she was sent away?"

Maria sighed and shook her head. "That was a long time ago. She and her boy were hungry. She wanted work and asked if there was anything she could do. The old caretaker, the man who worked in the yard and garden before Abel, felt sorry for them. So did I, but we knew how Señor Graves felt about Indians. His parents had been killed by renegades when he was a child."

"How long did the woman and boy stay?"

"Señor Graves was not home, so were going to feed them and let them spend the night. But Señor Haney arrived. When he saw them here, he chased them off. He had a walking stick, and he struck the woman with it. She fell down, and that little boy ran at him, swinging his fists. Señor Haney pushed the boy down, then kicked him." Maria lifted her hand and touched her brow. "His boot cut that boy's head, and all Señor Haney worried about was the blood on his pants."

"Did they leave?"

"Yes, but I went in the house and got some clean rags and warm water. Then I snuck it out the back door and took it to the woman. I helped her clean the boy's wound. It was very deep. But he did not cry. He was very brave."

"What did Mr. Haney do?"

"He went into the house and fixed himself a glass of whiskey. The caretaker felt so bad about it, he didn't eat or sleep for days."

"Which Haney did that?" Katie asked, not sure Jeremiah would have been old enough. Of course, how much brute strength and courage did it take to run off a woman and her small child?

"Señor Randolph." Maria itched the tip of her nose with the back of a flour-covered hand. "He dresses in fine clothes and acts like a gentleman, but he is not a kind man."

Katie didn't doubt it. She wondered just how cruel he and his son could be, especially if Jeremiah found out what she intended to do while he was gone.

"I want to talk to Martha Haney," Katie said.

"Oh, no, you must not do that." Maria continued her rhythmic hand motions. "Jeremiah will not allow it."

"Then I'll wait until he leaves town."

"You cannot go alone. My friend does not speak English."

"Are you willing to go with me?"

Maria sighed, her face grim. "Only if Jeremiah is far away."

"We'll wait until he's gone," Katie said. "I think he intends to follow Tom."

"Why would he follow Senor McCain?"

"I'm really not sure. It's just a hunch."

After a four-hour ride, Tom arrived in Rio Seco. As was his habit, he stopped first at the sheriff's office and asked where he could find Cord Rainville.

"Look in the Silver Buckle," Tom was told. "The man hasn't left the saloon in days."

Tom strode through the swinging doors and scanned the nearly empty room. Hazy sunlight filtered through dirty windows, and specks of dust floated in the stale air. In the far corner, a grizzled older man sat hunched over a table.

"Cord Rainville?" Tom asked.

The man looked up, steel-gray eyes drilling into his. A pink, ragged scar ran down the length of a bristled cheek. He had a hardness about him and a haunting pain in his eyes that whiskey apparently hadn't stilled.

"Yeah," he said, his voice raspy from either lack of use, too much tobacco or drink. "What do you want?"

A Colt .45 sat on the table beside a half bottle of whiskey. Tom didn't see a glass.

"Can I buy you a cup of coffee?" Tom asked.

Rainville began to chuckle, then broke into a booming laugh. "You gonna try and sober me up?"

"I thought it might be a good idea before hiring you." Tom didn't smile. "Otherwise, I'll try my luck and see how loose your tongue is."

Rainville studied him like a man facing a growling dog, sizing him up quickly. Apparently he chose to wait it out instead of drawing a gun or retreating.

Those cold eyes held a wariness, but Tom figured the man might talk—some.

"What's your name?" Rainville asked.

"Tom McCain."

"I don't know you."

"No, but you've probably heard of my employer, Harrison Graves." Tom hadn't meant to drop the old man's name so quickly, but he hadn't anticipated the suspicion behind those reddened eyes.

"Well, order that coffee and sit down. I don't like talking up to a man."

Tom called to the apron-clad Mexican bartender sweeping the floor. *"Dos cafés, señor."* Then he pulled out a chair and took a seat.

Rainville had that fermented smell of dust, sweat and stale liquor. Still, he didn't appear to be too inebriated to talk.

Of course, Tom had a feeling Rainville wouldn't disclose anything he didn't want to say in the light of day or in the dark of night—drunk, sober or with a noose around his neck and a gun to his head.

Tom liked that in a man.

The bartender brought two cups of steaming hot coffee. His hands trembled slightly as he set them down.

"Gracias," Tom said.

The man nodded and quickly returned to his broom.

Tom focused on Rainville. "I'd like to hire you to complete the job you started for Martha Haney."

"I finished that job."

"Then I'll pay you to extend the work."

Rainville leaned back in his chair and pushed the bottle away. "All right. You got yourself a deal. Tell me what you want me to do."

Chapter Thirteen

The Haney house loomed before them, dark and vacant like a forgotten crypt. Katie shivered as she helped Maria climb from the buckboard.

"I think it is best if we go to the back door," Maria whispered. She pulled a rusty lantern from the wagon. "Come this way."

The flame cast an eerie glow as the two women made their way around to the rear entrance of the two-story house. Maria opened a side gate and waddled past a large oleander bush.

A branch whipped back and scratched Katie's arm, but she didn't cry out.

When a coyote howled in the distance, Katie envisioned a vicious wolf bounding at them, teeth bared. "They don't have a dog, do they?"

"Not that I remember. Watch your step."

After making their way to the back porch, Katie rapped lightly at the door. "Should I knock louder?"

"No, Olivia sleeps in the bedroom just off the kitchen. She should hear us, even if we are quiet."

"*Quién es?*" a voice asked.

"Olivia, soy Maria."

The door creaked open, revealing a woman wearing a pale blue robe and holding a flickering candle.

When Maria explained in Spanish why they'd come, the woman's dark eyes widened. She clutched at her robe and stepped back. *"No, el señor dice nadie puede vistar."*

Maria turned to Katie. "Olivia says that Señora Haney is not allowed visitors."

"Tell her we won't stay long, and that we won't tell anyone she let us inside."

Maria nodded, then interpreted for Katie.

As Olivia stepped aside, Katie and Maria entered the house. Maria introduced the women, and Katie attempted a sincere smile. Still, the hired nurse didn't appear to appreciate their presence.

They followed Olivia up the stairs. A loose step creaked under Katie's foot, causing her to jump and her heart to beat wildly. She reached for the banister and continued to climb.

At the landing, Olivia paused, whispering a few words in Spanish to Maria, who then turned to Katie. "She is worried she will lose her job."

"Tell her I have money. I'll hire her myself." The words rolled out of Katie's mouth without any forethought, but she wasn't lying. She had some money put aside for unexpected emergencies, and if need be, she could assist the family until other employment was found.

Maria addressed her friend, and a look of relief crossed Olivia's matronly face before she opened the door.

Without warning, a musty, medicinal smell assaulted

Katie, making her gag. She wanted to open every single upstairs window to air out the room at once but held her tongue.

Light from the hallway illuminated their way until Olivia could strike a match and build a flame in the small hurricane lamp on the bedside table.

Katie stepped closer, watching Martha Haney's chest rise and fall. The woman was stout, with dark hair, her coloring pale and ghostlike.

Taking a chair beside the bed, Katie reached for the woman's hand. "Martha, wake up."

"Dios mío," Maria uttered, crossing herself.

Heavy lids blinked once, then opened. "Who are you?" the woman asked in a soft, gravelly voice.

She might be as crazy as a loon, or perhaps wildly dangerous, but Katie believed everyone was entitled to courtesy, so she stroked the top of her hand. "I'm a friend of Harrison Graves. My name is Katie."

The woman sighed then closed her eyes.

"Martha, please wake up. I'm here to help you."

The eyelids lifted again, and she blinked several times. Finally, she whispered, "Need…help."

"I'll do whatever I can. Can you answer a few questions for me?"

Martha Haney shook her head slowly. "Sleepy."

"I know. You're taking strong medication."

Martha didn't respond.

"Are you in pain? Do you need the medicine?"

Martha's eyes flickered open momentarily. "No. Yes. I…don't know."

"I'm going to ask your nurse not to medicate you. Can you hear me, Martha?"

The woman nodded, but her eyes didn't reopen.

"When you cry out, it frightens Olivia. She doesn't speak English." Katie placed a hand on Martha Haney's brow. "I'll return tomorrow. Try to be patient. I need to talk to you. I want to hear what you have to say. It's very important that you not take the medicine."

"Uh-huh," the woman mumbled, as her head rolled to the side.

Katie realized that would be her last chance to speak to Martha Haney tonight.

"Maria, tell Olivia to soothe Martha if she cries, but not to give her the medication as long as she stays calm." Katie pulled a gold coin from her purse and handed it to Olivia. "I'll bring her more money tomorrow."

Maria smiled and nodded, then directed her words to her Spanish-speaking friend.

Olivia responded.

"What did she say?" Katie asked.

"She will try."

"I can't ask for more than that." Katie made her way to the door. "Let's go. It's late, and there's not much more we can do here. Tell Olivia to call on us if Martha gets wild and out of hand. I have a feeling she'll be as eager to speak to me as I am to speak to her."

"She did *what?*" Tom slammed down his fist on the scarred oak table near Abel's bed.

"She went to speak to Martha Haney." Abel, who'd been sound asleep in the adobe bunkhouse when Tom had returned to the Lazy G late that night, scratched his head and yawned. "She took Maria with her."

Tom rolled his eyes. "Why in the world did she do that?"

Abel shrugged. "The nurse does not speak English."

"I mean, why did she go at all?" Tom raked his fingers through his hair.

All he'd wanted Katie to do was to stay out of trouble, but apparently, the only thing she knew how to do was to chase after it.

"Why didn't you try to talk her out of a fool notion like that?" he asked Abel.

"For one thing, I told Randolph Haney that you'd gone to Pleasant Valley after the little girl, just like you asked me to. And you were right, Jeremiah suddenly had business to attend to and left town right after that. So when Katie heard he was gone, she went to his house."

"Didn't you try to talk her out of that?"

"Yes, but her mind was set. Did you ever try to talk a woman out of something she was determined to do?"

Not *that* woman. Tom shook his head and scowled. There was no telling what mischief Katie would manage to get into if he left her on the ranch for a couple of days.

"I'm sorry," Abel said.

"I can't leave her here when I go after Caroline's daughter. It's too risky—there's no telling what she might do. Now I have no other choice but to take her with me."

"What did Señor Rainville have to say?" Abel asked.

"Among other things, Jeremiah had been visiting Caroline for years, yet he always told people in Stillwater he hadn't found her. When Martha had him followed, she found out about Sarah Jane. She was absolutely convinced that Jeremiah had fathered Caroline's baby and was furious with him."

Abel blew out a long, slow whistle. "Did she get crazy mad?"

"I don't think so. Maybe she just got angry enough

to need quieting, because Jeremiah clearly didn't want anyone to know where Caroline was—or that she'd kept her daughter."

"Is Jeremiah the girl's father?" Abel asked.

"I don't think so, but he had some reason for wanting to keep Caroline and Sarah Jane away." Tom patted the old man on the back. "I'll fill you in on the rest of what Rainville told me after I inform Katie that she's going with me."

Abel nodded, and Tom strode to the house. When he reached the bedroom in which Katie was sleeping, he opened the door without knocking. He intended to wake her and didn't care how polite he was in the process.

"Get up," he told her sleeping form.

Clearly startled, she bolted upright in bed, clutching the blanket to her chest, her eyes open wide. "What are you doing here?"

"I came to take you with me. Get out of bed."

"Where are we going?"

"To get Sarah Jane. But let's get something straight. I don't like the idea of taking you, but you've left me no choice. I can't trust you to keep your nose out of things that don't concern you."

"As a matter of fact, Martha Haney does concern me."

Tom slapped his hands on his hips and sighed. "You don't even *know* the woman."

"She asked for my help."

"She'll have to wait for your help. Abel's saddling Gully Washer as we speak. So get dressed. I suggest you wear those old clothes of mine, if they're clean. It'll be easier to keep a faster pace that way. And be outside in ten minutes."

"That's not enough time."

"Nevertheless, that's all the time you'll get."

Katie crossed her arms, the blanket dropping to her lap. "We'll have to stop at the Haney place. I told Martha I'd be back. I don't want her to think I don't keep my word."

"You're not in charge—no matter what you might think."

"I *promised*," Katie stated simply. "And I *never* break a promise."

Tom wanted to plow his fist through the wall. Instead, he turned and strode toward the door. "If you want to make a quick stop by the Haney's house, you'll need to be outside in *five* minutes."

"I'll do my best."

"Don't lollygag. If you're not outside and ready to go by the time the horses are saddled, I'll…"

"You'll what?"

Instead of an answer, he pulled out his gold pocket watch and made a note of the time. Then he spun around and closed the bedroom door.

Katie surprised Tom by coming outside—and wearing his old clothes—just as he was about to go in looking for her.

So after they mounted the horses, he kept up his part of the bargain.

Twenty minutes later, they reached the Haney residence, just as the sun peeked above the horizon.

The white two-story house stood alone, far from town. Weeds had overtaken a struggling garden, hinting that Jeremiah Haney hadn't concerned himself with day-to-day chores since his wife had taken ill.

A thin wisp of smoke rose from the chimney, snaking up into the dawn sky.

Someone was awake.

Tom didn't expect Jeremiah to be home, but he figured he'd better have an excuse for coming here without an invitation. Yet, other than the truth, he couldn't think of anything else a reasonable man would believe.

Katie swung down from the mare, the denim fabric stretching to accommodate her movements and revealing each feminine curve. Tom heaved a frustrated sigh, wondering if it might have been wiser if he hadn't insisted she wear his old clothes.

She tucked a loose tendril behind her ear. "Let's go around to the back. I'll show you the way."

"I knock at a man's front door," Tom said.

She gave an exasperated sigh. "But Olivia's room is in the back. She may not hear us if we're in the front."

Tom strode up the front steps, leaving Katie standing in the yard with her hands on her hips.

Shortly after he knocked, a Mexican woman answered the door, her eyes leery. When Tom introduced himself in Spanish, she nodded, then smiled shyly.

Katie, who'd relented and climbed the porch steps, reached into the front pocket of her pants and handed Olivia a ten-dollar gold coin piece.

"What are you doing?" Tom asked.

"I'm her new employer."

"It looks like a bribe to me," he said, somewhat surprised at her resourcefulness.

"Oh, no. It's not a bribe. Maria told me she has to support three young children, and she's afraid she'll lose her job. So I guaranteed her employment."

While her compassionate foresight surprised him—pleasantly so—he still resented her insistence upon making this stop, so he merely shook his head. "Come on. Let's make this quick."

Tom and Katie followed Olivia into the house and up the stairs.

When they reached the darkened bedroom, Katie strode inside as if she were a delegate of the Ladies' Aid Society and took a seat next to the bed. "I'm back, Martha."

As she stroked Mrs. Haney's arm, the woman's eyes shot open. "Daddy? Where's my daddy?"

"It's me, Katie. I came back, just as I said I would. How are you feeling this morning?"

Mrs. Haney's eyes were glassy, but when her gaze caught Tom's, she paled. A look of fear crossed her face.

"I'm Tom McCain," he told her. "I've just come from talking to Cord Rainville."

She swallowed hard and made an attempt to lift her head.

"Don't try to talk, Mrs. Haney. I want to help you. Jeremiah is more cunning than you think."

She nodded weakly, then covered her eyes and began to weep until she cried out with long, sobbing breaths.

"Dele la medicina," Tom told Olivia.

The nurse rushed to the bureau, grabbed a spoon and uncorked an amber bottle.

"No," Katie said. "Don't give her medicine. She needs to be lucid if she's going to talk to us."

"You can't just take her off the laudanum. She's been on it for close to four months, as far as I can figure." Tom turned to Olivia. *"Es importante que tome la medicina, pero reduzca la dosis."*

The woman nodded, then questioned him in Spanish, and he responded.

"What did you tell her?"

"To decrease the dosage slowly."

"Why? She seems to be taking too much. She doesn't make much sense."

"Laudanum is a form of opium," Tom said. "If she suddenly stops taking it, she'll get very sick."

"Do you think the medication is making her ill?"

"I'd bet on it. Jeremiah is no fool. He had to know what laudanum would do to his wife. The question is, why did he give it to her? And why did he instruct Maria to continue giving it to her?"

"To keep her quiet?" Katie asked.

"That's one way to ensure her silence and cooperation."

Fortunately, Katie held her tongue while Martha Haney took her medicine. He hoped that meant she understood what he'd been talking about, which he found surprising. Up until now, she'd fought him every step of the way.

They both watched as Martha closed her eyes and slowly relaxed into a state of slumber.

"She asked for her daddy," Katie whispered. "I hope that's not a sign of her mental state. I'd feel horrible if she was being drugged for good reason."

"I think she's mentally sound, if that makes you feel better. And I think she'd be happy to have her father come take her home. I'll tell Olivia to have Maria send word to him. In the meantime, let's get out of here. There's a storm brewing in the wind, and I want to be well on our way when it hits."

Katie took him at his word, and moments later they were mounted and on their way.

They rode for an hour, yet the sky never lost the gray of dawn, and coal-colored clouds enveloped the sun.

"You said you wouldn't bring Sarah Jane to the Lazy G unless you were sure she'd be safe." Katie tucked a strand of hair behind her ear. "Will she? Be safe?"

"I have a gun, and I'll use it if necessary." He slowed his horse to let Katie ride up beside him, and looked her in the eye. "I won't let anything happen to her. She's Caroline's child, and I'll protect her with my life if I have to."

She had no doubt that he would, and the thought of his loyalty, his vow to protect Sarah Jane, warmed her heart. Yet it struck fear in her, too. She'd just begun to see an unexpected side to Tom McCain, and she didn't want anything to happen to him.

A flash of lightning cracked across the Texas sky, followed by a rumble of thunder.

Katie shivered, but more from the intensity in Tom's gaze than from the chill in the air.

He urged his mount forward before she could respond, and she followed his lead.

Within minutes, the rain began to fall, first in sprinkles, then in sheets. Lightning cracked and ripped across the sky in jagged streaks. Thunder, deep and ominous, rumbled and roared, causing the horses to become fretful and agitated. Still, Tom seemed to ride harder, faster.

"Where are we going?" she asked, her voice straining to be heard over the sound of pelting rain, creaking leather and her pounding heart.

"To find cover," he called over his shoulder. "Can you keep up?"

"I'll try." Katie hoped he knew where he was going,

because the horses weren't the only ones uncomfortable and skittish.

"There's a cave not far from here."

Katie envisioned a long, narrow tunnel—cold, dank and dark, with bats clinging upside down from a craggy ceiling. "I think I'd rather get wet than go into a cave."

"We'll be fine. It's more of a hollowed-out spot under a rock ledge."

"How do you know about it?"

"My mother and I once stayed there for a few days." He urged his horse forward, and Katie did the same.

With the wind and the rain in her face, Katie tried to keep her eyes on his back. She certainly hated to lose sight of him now. When Tom pulled up, she stopped beside him.

He nodded toward a dark space in the rocky hillside. "That's it. We'll wait out the storm in there."

Katie nodded, only too happy to dismount and escape the drenching rain. When they reached the small shelter, she climbed from the mare. "What will we do with the horses?"

"I'll take care of them." He handed her his bedroll and saddlebag. "Take these, then go inside and change into some dry clothes."

Shivering, Katie nodded and surveyed her newfound shelter. They might stay dry in here, but they certainly wouldn't have any privacy.

She called to Tom's back. "There's no door. How will you knock before coming in?"

"Make it quick and you won't have to worry about me interrupting you."

Katie ducked her head as she stepped under the ledge, her arms laden with her bag, as well as his bedroll that was protected by an oiled-canvas cover and the wet saddlebag. She set them just inside the opening. Peeking over her shoulder, she saw Tom tethering the horses outside, his back to the open entrance. She doubted he'd stay out in the rain any longer than necessary and decided to hurry.

Her fingers fumbled with the metal buttons. She struggled to peel away the wet denim clinging to her skin and change into something dry. She wouldn't bother with underclothes, or with tucking in the tails of a red flannel shirt.

Once in dry clothing, she scanned the three-sided shelter protected by rock walls and tried to imagine a mother making a home here for her son. Had they camped here to hide? Or had they stayed here after they'd been told to leave the Lazy G?

Sighing, Katie opened a bedroll and made a place to sit and wait out the storm.

"Will you hand me my bag?" Tom asked from the entrance.

Katie tossed him the saddlebag and watched him withdraw a change of clothing.

"Turn around," he said.

Katie did as she was told. She listened to the sound of the rain pelting the ground and ignored the sounds of him changing his clothing.

When it was clear that he'd finished, she asked, "Now what do we do?"

"Wait."

"Then sit by me." Katie patted a spot beside her on the blanket. "There's no need to stand for the next few hours."

He ambled toward her, although she sensed reluctance in his steps. Still, he took a seat beside her.

"Tell me about your mother," she said, hoping to learn more about him.

He furrowed his brow. "Why?"

"Just curiosity. I'd like to know more about her."

He glanced outside, watching the rain splash off the gray ledge. "She was a pretty woman who worked long and hard. Sometimes she sang in the Comanche dialect, but usually she spoke Spanish. It was the language my parents had in common."

"Tell me about your father." Katie wondered if he would mention him by name. Would he admit to being Harrison's grandson, and Caroline's brother?

"We didn't see him often. My mother and I lived in a small cabin near the Lazy G. My father would visit us at times, but for the most part, we only had each other."

Katie couldn't imagine having no one to talk to as a child. "It sounds like a lonely life."

"Sometimes it was. It was also tough. Yet, as mean as some people could be to her when she'd go into town for supplies, she never complained about the life she was forced to lead."

His answer brought only more questions to mind, but Katie didn't want to ask too many at once. She preferred to quiz him gently. "How old were you when she died?"

"Ten."

"Losing both parents while you were so young must have been difficult," she said.

"It was." His jaw tensed. "I think it was hardest on her, though. She knew she was leaving me alone, with no one to look after me."

"So she knew that she was dying?"

"I think so. When she took me to the Lazy G and they ran us off, she tried to take me to her people. On the way, we camped here."

"Did she suffer?" Katie hoped that she hadn't.

"Some, but I think she suffered more from the rejection of my father's people than from her illness. They hated her for being an Indian and blamed her for loving a white man and having his illegitimate child."

Katie saw the pain in his eyes as he continued to stare out into the rain. It gripped her heart. "Were you with her when she died?"

"Yes, and I did my best to bury her deep enough so the wild animals wouldn't disturb her bones." He grew quiet, pensive.

Katie grieved for the small boy who had lost his mother. Longing to take Tom into her arms and console him, she reached for his hand.

At her touch, he turned to face her. When she looked into his eyes, she saw his pain, felt his need for love and affection. And maybe even more than that, his need for acceptance.

She couldn't think of anything to say that would sufficiently convey her sympathy or her desire to make things right.

"I'm sorry," she said again, knowing it wasn't nearly enough.

"It was a long time ago."

Tom turned his head, facing the gray wall of the cave, shutting her out of the memories he'd only begun to share. Out of his life, so it seemed.

Well, Katie wouldn't let it be that easy. Even though they fought like a stray hound and a wayward tabby, there were things she respected him for, things she admired.

And whether either of them liked it or not, she'd fallen in love with Tom McCain.

Chapter Fourteen

Katie and Tom remained in the cave until the rain let up, then they proceeded to ride until they reached Hannah's house.

Lobo heard their approach first and ran out of the barn. When he spotted Tom, he barked then raced toward him like a long-lost friend—or maybe a brother.

Next came Trapper, who limped out of the barn much slower. When he realized Tom and Katie were back, he called out, "Hannah! Come on outside. Tom's home."

The old man tried to pick up his pace, then reached for his right knee, his efforts to hurry clearly causing him pain.

The front door swung open as Hannah came out of the house. She wiped her hands on the dish towel she carried. Then she tossed it over her left shoulder and cupped her hands around her mouth. "Sarah Jane! Look who's here!"

Lobo stopped about six feet short of Tom's horse, turned his woolly head back to Sarah Jane, who'd just ventured out from the barn, as well, then he looked at Tom and barked several times.

"It's okay," Tom said. "I understand."

Lobo then trotted back to the child.

It was amazing, Katie thought. She wouldn't have believed it if she hadn't seen it for herself. Tom and the dog seemed to have communicated, just as Hannah had said they could.

Tom had told Lobo to look after Sarah Jane, and the dog had understood the order. Even now, he seemed to be questioning whether that order still stood.

When Katie and Tom reached the yard, they dismounted. Katie had no more than turned around when Hannah greeted her with a warm hug. "It's good to have you back."

"It's nice to be back. How's Erin doing?"

"Better," Hannah said. "The bruises are fading, and she's getting up a little more each day. I had Dr. Crandall come out to check on her yesterday, and he said that her larynx was injured when the man tried to strangle her, so it's difficult for her to talk. He says it will heal, but he wants her to rest her voice."

"I'm glad to hear that. I'd like to talk to her when she's able."

"The doctor seemed to think that would be in a week or so."

"How about Sarah Jane?" Katie asked. "Is she talking yet?"

"Not a single word. Dr. Crandall said to give her time—and plenty of love, which is easy to do. She's a real sweetheart."

As Sarah Jane approached the adults, the wolf-dog at her side, Katie offered her a smile. "I hope you had fun with Lobo, Hannah and Trapper while I was gone."

Sarah Jane nodded.

"Did you miss me?" Katie asked the girl.

Sarah Jane smiled and, again, she nodded.

"I'm glad, honey. I missed you something fierce. Do you have a hug for me?" Katie dropped to her knees and held out her arms. When Sarah Jane stepped into her embrace and squeezed her back, Katie's heart soared, and she offered a prayer of thanksgiving.

"How'd it go?" Trapper asked Tom.

"Not bad."

For a moment Katie's eyes sought Tom's. She saw a flash of sentiment, but for the life of her, she couldn't quite peg what it was—pain? Regret? Tenderness?

"We can talk while you help me cool down the horses," Tom told Trapper.

"Come on inside," Hannah said to Katie. "You, too, Sarah Jane. I'll fix us all something to eat."

As hungry as she was, Katie would have preferred to stay with the men and listen to what Tom had to say, but she followed Hannah into the house.

Once inside the kitchen she washed her hands in the tub of water in the sink. Then she watched the older woman move effortlessly about, removing plates, slicing bread and meat.

"Can I help?" Katie asked.

"Absolutely not. You sit down and rest."

When Katie complied, Hannah turned to Sarah Jane. "I have some cookies I'd like you to take to Erin."

"I'd be happy to take them to her," Katie said.

"Are you sure?"

"Yes, of course." Maybe Katie would get a chance to ask her a couple of questions. Erin might not be able to talk, but there were other ways to give a yes or no response—like nodding her head or squeezing her hand.

After Hannah filled a plate, Katie carried the cookies into the bedroom that had been assigned to Erin. Although the door was open, Katie remained in the hallway and said, "Good afternoon. How are you feeling?"

The brunette turned to the doorway and gave a little shrug.

"You certainly look better than you did when we first brought you here."

Again, Erin gave a slight shrug of the shoulder.

Katie carried the cookies into the room and set them on the table near the bed, where a piece of paper and a pencil sat next to a Bible. Apparently, Hannah had found a way for Erin to communicate, which was good.

"Would you like a cookie?" Katie asked.

Erin shook her head no.

"I'm not sure if Hannah told you, but Tom and I went to Stillwater to meet with Harrison Graves. Did Caroline ever mention her grandfather?"

Erin nodded.

"Did she like him?"

Erin reached for the paper and pencil. After a few minutes, she handed it back to Katie.

He was stubborn and hateful. They fought a lot. He sent her away and cut her out of his will.

"That's not true," Katie said. "I mean, he didn't cut her out of his will."

Erin bit down on her bottom lip, then reached for the paper and wrote again.

A man used to visit Caroline sometimes. He said her grandfather hated her for disobeying him and never wanted to see her again.

"Her grandfather had been looking for her. I'm not

sure for how long. Maybe not for six years. But recently he hired Tom McCain to find her."

Erin's brow furrowed as if she was trying to make sense of that information.

"Who told Caroline about the will?" Katie asked.

Again, Erin wrote out her answer. *Jeremiah Haney.*

Just as she suspected. Katie blew out a sigh. What would provoke Jeremiah to tell Caroline that her grandfather hated her and that he'd disinherited her? Had Harrison really threatened to cut her out of the will? Or had Jeremiah wanted to keep her away from the Lazy G?

And if he'd wanted to keep her away, how far would he have gone to keep her away permanently?

"Okay, now you can tell me how things went in Stillwater," Trapper said, as he and Tom led the horses to the barn. "What did Harrison Graves have to say?"

"He believes that I was able to find Caroline's trail— and that she's dead." Tom removed the saddle and blanket from Caballo and draped them over the top rung of the corral. "But he stopped short of believing me when I told him not to trust Jeremiah Haney."

"Who's that? Randolph's son?"

"Yes. And I think he's somehow responsible for Caroline's death. If I can prove it, I'm going to make sure justice is served."

"They got a sheriff in Stillwater. That's what he's paid to do. I don't know why you have to make it your business."

"You know why."

Trapper sighed. "So in the meantime, what are you going to do with Sarah Jane? She's a pretty little thing.

And she don't make no trouble. Hannah would love to keep her here."

"I'd feel good about her staying here, too," Tom said, "but that would deprive her of the ranch and estate that are rightfully hers."

Trapper kicked at the ground with the toe of a scuffed boot. "I suppose you figured out a way to take her to Stillwater and to keep her safe."

"Yes. I just hope my plan works."

Trapper crossed his arms and eyed Tom carefully. "And if it doesn't work?"

"Then I'll bring Sarah Jane back here."

Trapper began to brush Gully Washer. "I really like that little moppet. And Hannah near glows when she's fussin' over her. That wolf-dog likes her, too."

That was good because Tom planned to take Lobo back to Stillwater with them. Sarah Jane needed the extra protection the dog would provide.

Trapper grinned, his eyes crinkling. "Did you know that little girl snuck Lobo into her room last night after she thought Hannah went to sleep?"

"Does Hannah know?" Tom didn't think so. Hannah had always been pretty fussy about animals sleeping in the house. It had taken him a long time and a lot of coaxing to talk her into just letting Lobo come inside on occasion.

Trapper chuckled. "Yep, only a blind woman would miss seein' the dog hair on the sheets. But Hannah didn't say nothing about it at all for fear Sarah Jane would run off and sleep in the barn with him and me."

Tom couldn't help but smile. "It sounds like Sarah Jane is starting to feel at home here."

"I think so, too. And I gotta tell you, I hope your plan don't work out and she comes back with you."

"Don't hope too hard, old man. If my plan doesn't work, there's a good chance none of us will come back."

Bright and early the next morning, with a knife in his boot, a gun on his hip and a Winchester rifle attached to his saddle, Tom got ready to return to the Lazy G.

Hannah had tried to hide her tears while fussing over Sarah Jane. It tore at Tom to see her fretful and sad. He would have given anything to let Sarah Jane stay, but there was no other way.

Besides, he'd promised Harrison he'd bring her back. And the Lazy G belonged to Sarah Jane—not to Randolph Haney.

As he adjusted the saddle on Gully Washer, he heard footsteps and glanced up. Katie, again dressed in denim and flannel, approached. She appeared comfortable in his outgrown clothing, filling it out in a way that made him struggle not to gawk at her.

She tucked her thumbs in the back pocket of her jeans. "Can I talk to you before we leave?"

"Sure," he said.

"There's something I have to tell you, something I think you should know."

"What's that?"

She paused, as if she'd come to confess something that was sure to ruin his entire day, maybe something that would ruin his entire life.

And knowing Katie O'Malley as he'd come to know her, he didn't doubt it for a moment. She was as unpredictable as she was lovely.

"Spit it out."

She stood tall, and as was her habit, she lifted her chin. "I'm not sure what will happen when we return to the Lazy G, but I want you to know…"

He'd never seen her at a loss for words, which ought to worry him. "What did you do?"

The question seemed to take her aback. "I didn't *do* anything. It's just that I… Well, I've come to admire and respect you."

Was there a "But" coming from her?

"I care for you, Tom McCain."

The muscles in his cheeks tightened, and the proverbial cat not only caught his tongue but ran off with it.

Of all the things she could have told him, of all the things she could have said to put his life on edge, to set him off balance, he'd never expected that. She admired and respected him? And she cared about him?

Where had a confession like that come from? And why had she felt the need to tell him now?

And what in the world did she expect him to do with it? Admit that he was feeling something for her, too?

Well, maybe he was, but nothing could come of it. Loving Katie O'Malley would be the death of him.

What did she expect him to do now? Weaken and say something soft and sentimental?

He thought back to the first kiss they'd shared. She'd wanted it as badly as he had. And just like *that,* she'd slapped him.

"Don't say things like that, Katie."

She crossed her arms. "Don't you care for me at all?"

Care for her? Yes, but did he dare admit that kind of vulnerability to a woman like her, a woman who had the power to break his heart when she came to her senses?

"I care for you," he admitted. "But if you're suggesting anything more than friendship, you're overlooking the obvious."

"What's that?"

"The difference in our skin color."

"I don't give a fig about that."

Knowing Katie, she probably didn't. But that's not where the problem lay, and she ought to be bright enough to figure that out.

"Not all people are as broad-minded as you are," he said.

She sighed, then offered him an impish grin. "You do have a point, I suppose. I've been cursed with skin that sunburns easily and freckles beyond compare. I've learned to live with it, in spite of all the taunts I had in the schoolyard. I'm just surprised that you're allowing it to bother you."

"Don't make light of this, Katie. Do you have any idea how difficult life would be if you and I were to start courting?"

"I couldn't care less."

"Well, I care a great deal. I've seen how cruel some people can be. And I won't allow them to hurt you the way they've hurt me."

"People have said a lot of cruel things to me over the years, and I've learned to overlook them."

That might be true, but she brought on a lot of her trouble just by speaking her mind. A little common sense and tact would make her life much easier. She had no idea how difficult things would be if the two of them even considered something romantic—no matter how appealing the thought might be to either of them.

But if they were to succumb to temptation and marry,

what about a child they might conceive? Would their son or daughter grow up to have a happy, charmed life?

That was highly unlikely. Besides, Tom had given up the thought of fathering a child a long time ago. He wouldn't risk putting a kid through something like that.

So he decided to diffuse her romantic thoughts, even if it set her off again.

"The last thing either of us needs to do is to act on any feelings we might have for each other," he said.

"Why?"

"When I fall in love, it'll be for keeps. My wife will have to promise to love me—and to *obey* me. And you'd be hard-pressed to make a vow like that, let alone keep it."

"If I ever marry anyone, he would have to agree upon our marriage being a partnership."

"Something tells me that a partnership with a woman like you wouldn't be good enough. You'd want to wear the pants in the family." He glanced down at the outfit she wore, the britches that had once been his.

He hadn't been trying to make a point, it just seemed to…jump out at him.

"*You* told me to wear your pants to make traveling easier," she said. "Tom McCain, you are the most exasperating…" She lifted her hand as if she were going to shake her finger at him—or maybe even let him have it. Then she lowered it almost as quickly, turned on her heel and marched away.

As Tom watched her stride from the barn, he told himself how much better off they both were now that she'd gotten any foolish romantic notions out of her head.

Of course, they might be better off, but the ride to

Stillwater was going to be one of the longest trips he'd
ever had to make—even if it was only ten hours.

As they prepared to leave, Katie berated her foolishness. Why had she thought telling Tom how she'd come
to feel about him would make things better, easier?

Thank goodness she'd never mentioned love, because
just admitting that she'd come to care about him hadn't
gone over as she'd hoped it would.

She'd hoped it would make them a better team, a
stronger team. And she'd hoped that he would have...

What? Told her he was falling in love with her, too?

She grabbed the reins and placed a foot in the stirrup,
the leather groaning as she swung herself up on Gully
Washer. She'd almost bared her soul to Tom, revealing
feelings too new and too vulnerable to be exposed. Instead she'd only tiptoed around it.

Tom placed Sarah Jane behind the saddle of his gelding, then mounted. And without a backward glance, they
were off.

Every once in a while, Katie ventured a surreptitious
glance at him, hoping to catch a glimpse of emotion, an
indication that he struggled with his feelings, too. Instead, she saw a stoic profile.

So be it. She'd just have to put it all behind her, too.
She cleared her throat and spoke to Sarah Jane. "How
are you doing, honey?"

The little girl smiled and pointed to the big dog trotting alongside the gelding.

"You're happy Lobo gets to come along?"

Sarah Jane nodded, eyes glimmering. It was good to
see a spark of life returning to her. Katie had worried

more than she let on that Sarah Jane might not fully recover. Maybe the child's voice would return soon.

Tom turned in the saddle, giving Sarah Jane a warm smile. "Let me know if you need to stop, sweetheart."

Katie adjusted the old gray felt hat she wore, tilting the floppy brim to block the sun, as well as Tom's profile.

She wished she could block out her disappointment and the ache in her heart just as easily.

Chapter Fifteen

When Jeremiah heard McCain had gone to Pleasant Valley to get Caroline's daughter, he'd tried his best to pick up the half-breed's trail, but he hadn't had any luck at all. Fearing that he might lose track of McCain altogether, he'd chosen another tactic and had gone back to the Lazy G, hoping to catch him on the way back.

If McCain planned to bring the kid to the ranch, they'd have to ride through the pass, so Jeremiah would wait on the bluff, with the sun on his back, and pick them off like tin cans on a fence post.

Then, finally, the killing could stop.

Every now and again he had a pang of conscience, but he wasn't a real murderer. If he was, he wouldn't have spared Martha's life when she accused him of fathering Caroline's baby and threatened to tell Harrison the wild story she'd dreamed up.

Jeremiah wasn't the father of Caroline's brat, but he had gone to great lengths to make sure Harrison didn't know the kid even existed.

And what about Caroline? Her death had been an accident, really. Her own fault, not his.

If she'd only kept her mouth shut, if she hadn't tried to run, she'd be alive today. But no, she had to threaten to tell the Taylorsville sheriff that Jeremiah had taken advantage of her. And he'd done no such thing. He'd offered to pay her for her favors.

Sure, she'd sniffled and cried after, but the tears had been for effect, to make him feel guilty. But Caroline had wanted him as badly as he'd wanted her. Women just didn't find it easy to come out and admit it. It was a game they all played.

Besides, she'd been born a harlot. Oh, she'd looked pure, even as a child, but she wasn't. She might have fooled Harrison, but she'd never fooled Jeremiah.

That's why she'd always avoided being alone with him whenever he'd visited the ranch.

Overhead, a flock of sparrows took flight. No use dawdling. He may as well get himself ready and in place.

Jeremiah stroked the butt of the rifle strapped to the side of his horse. Then he placed a booted toe in the stirrup and swung a leg over the saddle. He clicked his tongue. "Come on, boy. We're going to wait them out in the perfect spot."

But three hours later, in that prime location, as the sun burned high overhead, Jeremiah lowered the spyglass and cursed.

He could have sworn they'd come this way. Getting rid of them would be easier away from the ranch. He reached into his saddlebag, pulled an apple from his dwindling supplies and buffed it against the sleeve of his shirt before taking a bite.

It was hot today, and he was getting anxious to sleep in his feather bed instead of on the hard ground. He seated himself on the flat side of a big gray rock, drew up a knee and tilted his hat. He'd wait one more day before going back, but not with his tail between his legs. Of course, he had a secondary plan. A wise man always did. But he preferred to do it this way. Fewer questions asked, fewer answers needed.

When he bit into the apple, a burst of sweetness filled his mouth. A dribble of juice spilled between his lips and ran down his chin. He caught it with a shirtsleeve.

He liked apples. Fresh off the tree, stewed or baked in a pie. Martha used to make the best apple cobbler. That was one of the things he missed most. That and the lively tunes she played on the fancy piano he'd bought her.

He shook his head. He could live without cobbler and music. And had Martha carried out her threat to tell Harrison Graves what that private investigator had told her, he stood to give up a lot more than that. All Jeremiah had to do was to keep Martha quiet until after Harrison died. With Caroline gone—and no kid in sight—the estate would pass to Jeremiah's father and ultimately to him.

Martha's father might be angry if she ran home to him in tears, but her daddy's ranch paled in comparison to the Lazy G. Besides, Martha would come to her senses in time.

Jeremiah reached for the spyglass and placed it to his eye. "Well, what do you know? McCain chose this route after all."

And Katie O'Malley rode with them.

Jeremiah had thought she was just a nosy do-gooder, but he'd underestimated her. Apparently, she had plans of her own to lay claim to the Lazy G. What a pity. He'd hoped she might prove to be a willing lover during her brief visit. Now her visit would have to be cut short.

He slipped the rifle from the pouch, raised the weapon, adjusted the scope and aimed carefully.

Just a little bit closer. Then it would all be over.

The killing would stop.

It was nearing the end of the trail. As much as Katie would have willed it otherwise, she and Tom had yet to strike up a friendly conversation since she'd opened her heart to him in Hannah's barn.

Instead, he'd pushed hard for them to return to the Lazy G by nightfall.

Katie rode Gully Washer, Hannah's mare, while Sarah Jane rode with Tom on Caballo and Lobo trotted along beside them.

The blazing sun had finally lowered into the west, but the air was still too warm for comfort. What little breeze came their way only served to chap her lips and parch her throat.

Katie wiped the perspiration from her brow. She figured they must be getting close to the ranch. The land looked vaguely familiar.

"How much longer will it take to get there?" she asked.

"About an hour's ride once we enter the pass. It's just up ahead." Tom scanned the rocky horizon.

She'd noticed that his vigilance had increased the longer they rode and the closer they got to the Lazy G. If there was something she'd learned in the past few days, it was to trust his instincts.

But she didn't want Sarah Jane to sense her apprehension, so she said, "I'm looking forward to arriving back in civilization."

Tom stopped abruptly, the gelding sidestepping, snorting and throwing its head. "Hold up."

Katie pulled back on the reins. "What is it?"

"Up there. Near the top of the ledge." He didn't point. He merely nodded to the west. "Do you see the glare of sunlight reflecting off something?"

She placed a hand over her brow and searched, her eyes catching a glimmer of light. "Yes. What is it?"

"My guess is a gun barrel. Come on, we've got to make sure we're out of range. Then we'll take an alternate route."

He reached for Sarah Jane's hands, making sure they were snug around his waist. "You'll need to hold on really tight, sweetheart. We're going to ride hard and fast."

The child nodded, her eyes bright and trusting.

"Good girl," he told her.

As they turned, a shot ricocheted off a rock near the horses' hooves.

Tom cursed under his breath. "Hang on, Sarah Jane. Let's go."

Another shot rang out, this one grazing Katie's head. Afraid to take time to assess the damage, she ignored the sting of her brow and urged the mare to follow Tom and Sarah Jane. Several more shots followed, but she doubted they remained within the rifleman's range.

Something warm eased onto her eyelid, and she quickly swiped a hand across her face to clear her vision. Her fingers felt damp and sticky, yet she didn't dare look at them. She didn't have to. She'd been shot.

Afraid to do anything but follow Tom's lead, ride fast and hold on for her life, Katie looped the excess rein around the saddle horn and gripped it tightly. At first, she worried that Lobo had taken a bullet, or that he wouldn't keep up, but he ran to the side of them, his strides even, his tongue hanging from his mouth.

Then, as the thundering hooves plowed on, she worried about her own ability to keep up. Tom had slowed the pace, but still they all rode hard. Her head hurt and a wave of dizziness made it difficult to focus, but she didn't dare complain.

When Tom glanced over his shoulder, perhaps to see if she still followed behind, his expression grew solemn and he halted the ride.

"You've been shot," he said. "Why didn't you say something?"

Katie tried to read his expression, but his features all blurred together.

"You didn't ask," she said, her words ringing and spinning and echoing in her ears.

She clutched at the pommel with clammy, tingling hands. She probably looked a fright, and she hoped the sight of blood wouldn't upset Sarah Jane.

"I'm all right," she told the child. "Don't worry about me, honey."

But as she tried to manage a smile to reinforce the assurance, the world began to spin all around, and darkness enveloped her.

She was going to collapse, and there wasn't a single thing she could do about it except hope and pray Tom wouldn't leave her in the dirt.

Katie awoke in one of the guest rooms at the Lazy G Ranch, but she wasn't alone.

Tom sat beside the bed, watching over her, his eyes darting across her face, his hand holding hers.

"How are you feeling?" he asked.

"My head hurts, but I'm…all right."

He gave her hand a gentle squeeze, and when she gazed into his whiskey-brown eyes, when she saw the compassion brewing deep inside, the worry and vulnerability etched upon his handsome face, she realized she was seeing a different man than the one she'd thought she'd known before.

"Where's Sarah Jane?" she asked. "Is she all right?"

"She's taking a bath in Caroline's room, and she's in awe. Maria is filling her head with stories about her mother as a little girl."

"Good. Does Mr. Graves know she's here?"

"Not yet. Maria said he had a severe spell early this afternoon. He hadn't wanted to take the medicine the doctor left for him, but she finally insisted he do so. He'll have to wait until tomorrow morning to meet Sarah Jane."

"He'll be disappointed."

"That's why he resisted taking the medication—until he couldn't stand the pain any longer."

"I suppose that's just as well." Katie had wanted to be present when the introductions were made. "Is Sarah Jane nervous about meeting him?"

"She's still not talking, but you should have seen her brighten at the sight of Caroline's bedroom. She stood before the large portrait, then studied each small photograph for the longest time. The only way Maria could talk her into taking a bath was to promise to brush and curl her hair the same way she used to fix her mother's."

Katie smiled wistfully. She knew Sarah Jane would find comfort in these surroundings. And Maria would appreciate telling Sarah Jane stories of Caroline as a child. Katie almost wished she could be there with them, that she could listen to those memories unfold, too. But even if she were physically able, she didn't want to intrude upon a special moment she had no right to witness.

"And what about Lobo?" she asked. "Where is he? Vanquished to the barn?"

"Actually, he's overseeing Sarah Jane's bath. It took some convincing on my part, but Maria finally agreed to let him remain with her."

Katie smiled, then began to sit up, but Tom gently placed a hand on her shoulder and pushed her back onto the white cotton sheets of the feather bed. "The bullet only grazed your scalp, but you lost a lot of blood. I don't want you passing out again."

"I'm all right." She touched her forehead and fingered the gauze bandage.

"I believe you, but I'd feel better if you took it easy."

He'd feel better? Something hadn't just changed about him. Something had changed about...them.

"Why would you feel better?" she asked.

"I should have been more careful. I didn't figure he could reach us that far away, but he had a scope."

Katie had been prying and prodding Tom into revealing his feelings, but when he reminded her of the danger, of the man who'd tried to ambush them, her focus changed to one that was more immediate. "Who shot at us?"

He didn't answer, but she assumed he had a suspect. She had one in mind, too. "Do you think it was Jeremiah?"

Tom's eyes, once compassionate and loving, grew hard. "I'm going after him before he hurts either of you."

His resolve surprised her—not so much because he meant to protect Sarah Jane, but because he included her in his vow. She chuckled softly while searching his face, hoping to see a revelation of his feelings. Did she dare hope to see love in his eyes?

"What's so funny?" he asked.

"I would have thought that you might have been relieved to be rid of me."

"Katie," he said, his voice soft and husky. "I'm beginning to think that I'm going to be burdened with you for the rest of my life."

"Burdened?" she asked. "And maybe just a wee bit blessed?"

He smiled. "That's left to be seen."

She glanced down at their hands, which were still clasped together. He might be fighting what he was feeling, just as she had fought it since the first time she laid eyes on him on the street in Pleasant Valley, but it was there—plain as day. She wasn't sure how she knew what he was feeling—or why. She just did.

"Don't you think you could care for me?" she asked, hoping he'd admit it. "Just a little?"

He sighed, closed his eyes momentarily then opened them again. "I do, Katie. But love isn't enough for what we'd have to face."

Katie's heart fluttered. "Your love would be enough for me."

He shook his head. "Maybe right now, but not as the days passed."

She squeezed his hand. "God seems to have brought us this far. Let's see where He leads us next."

"Fair enough." Tom lifted their hands to his lips, his breath warm, vibrant and promising. Then he placed a kiss on her fingers.

She opened her heart again, hoping this time he would

accept her gift and not toss it back at her feet. "I love you, Tom McCain."

"Don't say that." His voice came out soft and gruff at the same time.

"I'll say it as often as it comes to mind, so you'd better get used to hearing it."

He glanced away, as though struggling with himself somewhere deep inside.

"You said that you cared for me," she continued. "Did you mean it?"

"Yes. And I care for you enough to walk away rather than ruin your life." He ran his knuckles lightly along her cheek, setting off a rush of warmth to her very core.

"I won't let you walk away," she said.

He reached for a strand of her hair, letting it curl around his finger. "I can't see this working out between us."

"It will work, Tom. And someday you'll thank me for being so insistent."

"We'll see about that. But just so you know, I do love you, Katie O'Malley. More than I should."

"No, never more than you should. Kiss me, Tom."

Good man that he was, he did just as she asked.

The morning sunlight danced upon the west wall of Harrison's study as Tom paced the tiled floor and awaited the old cattleman's entrance.

Katie, her skirts fanned upon the brocade divan near the bookshelf, fiddled with a crocheted handkerchief. She looked every bit the lady as she faced the unknown.

Tom knew relinquishing Sarah Jane to Harrison's custody would be difficult for her, but it had to be done. Caroline's daughter belonged to the land, and so did her descendants, who would live in the adobe-walled hacienda, ride the vast range and raise strong, healthy sons and daughters.

Dwarfed by the tufted leather chair on which she sat, Sarah Jane swung her feet and tapped her fingers on the hand-carved mahogany armrests.

Tom thought of her mother. Like Harrison, there were things he wished he could say to her, too. *I brought your little girl home, Caroline. I only wish I could have brought you, as well.*

As the door opened, everyone turned and watched Harrison enter the room.

The old man shuffled inside, but as he spotted Sarah Jane, he stopped to study her. After a moment, a slow smile crossed his face. "You do, indeed, favor your mother, young lady."

Sarah Jane perused the old man just as intently as he studied her, then returned his smile.

That said and done, Harrison slowly took a seat behind the large, mahogany desk. He'd no more than set his cane aside when the little girl got to her feet, crossed the room and approached his desk. Then she reached behind her neck and removed the leather medicine bag Tom had given her.

The silence of the room was palpable as Sarah Jane loosened the leather drawstrings and pulled out a small, gold locket.

"What do you have there?" Harrison asked, leaning forward and arching a gray brow.

Katie opened her mouth as if she intended to answer for the child but, appearing to have second thoughts, remained silent.

Tom sat beside her and took her hand in his. She

smiled at him, her bottom lip quivering, then gave his fingers a gentle squeeze. They both watched intently as Sarah Jane offered the locket to her great-grandfather.

Harrison fingered it before springing the tiny clasp. When he peered inside, his mouth dropped open.

"This is me," he said, as tears filled his eyes. "Where did you get it, child?"

Sarah Jane pointed to the portrait of Caroline hanging on the wall.

"Was that woman your mother?" he asked gently.

She nodded.

He took a deep breath and sighed. "About eight years ago, I took your mother to Dallas. She insisted I have my photograph taken. We argued about it for two days, but I gave in—that time. I should have given in more often, but I was a stubborn old man. I can't tell her how very sorry I am, but I'll tell you now. Will you forgive me for not being a better grandfather to your mother, and for not being a part of your life until now?"

Sarah Jane nodded, then reached out small, thin arms to hug him. Harrison embraced her, and his shoulders shook as he wept.

Moisture filled Tom's eyes. Unwilling to let anyone see it, he turned and glanced out the window.

He'd wanted to meet his father's people. To learn what kind of blood he carried in his veins. And he'd wanted the satisfaction of seeing Harrison Graves apologize for not helping him and his mother years ago.

Never had he entertained even a brief hope that Harrison would accept him as the grandson he never knew he had, nor had he thought to find peace with the stubborn old man. He still didn't. But this poignant display of love and acceptance for Sarah Jane would be enough. And it would last a lifetime.

Harrison Graves had redeemed himself in Tom's eyes.

"Sarah Jane," Harrison said, "I'll have Maria get your mother's dollhouse out of storage. She used to play with it for hours. I think you'll like it."

"I'd like to see it, too," Katie said. "Perhaps we can play together later. I never had a dollhouse of my own."

Sarah Jane broke into the liveliest smile Tom had seen since Erin's assault, and it seemed as if her healing might truly take place on the Lazy G.

"You'll both enjoy playing with this dollhouse," Harrison said. "It cost me a small fortune to have it made years ago. Perhaps you ladies can make new curtains— or whatever else you think it might need."

Katie smiled. "We'll have to ask Maria for help. I'm not much of a seamstress."

"I'm sure she'd be delighted to be included." Harrison patted the top of Sarah Jane's head, his fingers lighting upon the long strands as though they were spun gold. "Katie, would you mind taking Sarah Jane to find Maria and asking her to get the dollhouse?"

Tom expected an objection of one kind or another, but Katie surprised him by getting to her feet, striding toward Harrison's desk and reaching out her hand to Sarah Jane. "Certainly. Let's go, honey."

When they'd left the room, Harrison turned to Tom. "Now that we're alone, I'd like to have a word with you."

"What's on your mind?"

Harrison took a deep breath, as though unsure of whether he should share his thoughts. "I saw Jeremiah Haney early this morning."

"Where?"

"In my kitchen. He said he was coming to check on me, but I found him rummaging in a drawer. He had a candle beside him because the sun had yet to rise."

Tom clenched his fists, and fought off a curse word. "Do you really think he came to check on you?"

"I'd like to think so." Harrison leaned back in his chair and closed his eyes, but Tom wasn't fooled. The old man, his complexion pale, was in pain. And the meeting with Sarah Jane had weakened him. "But to tell you the truth, I didn't like the uneasiness I felt when I looked into his eyes."

"Then maybe you're ready for the truth."

Harrison gazed steadily at Tom. "I'm always ready for the truth. What's on your mind?"

"A couple of days ago, I rode to Rio Seco."

Harrison arched a gray brow. "Why?"

"To find Cord Rainville and ask why Martha Haney hired him to follow Jeremiah."

"And?"

"He followed Haney to Taylorsville, where Caroline and Sarah Jane lived. Rainville told Martha that Jeremiah had been visiting Caroline off and on for years."

Harrison paled, and his jaw tensed. "He'd better have a good reason for not telling me he knew where to find her."

"I'm sure he had a good reason, but one that only suited him."

"What do you mean by that?"

"It wasn't long after Rainville reported back to Mrs. Haney that word got out in the community that poor Martha Haney had lost her mind. Jeremiah hired a Spanish-speaking nurse to continue to medicate her with laudanum."

"What are you speculating?"

"My guess is that he wanted to insure her silence and cooperation."

Harrison leaned his head back in the seat. "Suspecting my friend's son of wrongdoing doesn't sit well with me."

"I don't suppose it does. Murder is a very serious charge."

Harrison shook his head. "I can't believe he'd go to that extreme."

"Then I suggest you speak to Rainville yourself. I asked him to meet me here."

Harrison studied Tom intently. "I'm not admitting I agree with you, but tell me something. Why have you gone to the trouble of trying to solve the mystery of this crime?"

Because Caroline had meant more to him than Harrison would ever know, but Tom didn't think the old man would care to know why.

Then again, maybe he feared that none of it would even matter. So instead, he said, "Caroline was a loving, goodhearted woman. And I don't believe she stayed away from you because she was angry. I think she would have come home years ago if she hadn't been convinced that you'd disowned her."

"I threatened to disown her," Harrison said, voice rising. "But I never followed through. I never would have. I had a terrible temper, and so did she. Our arguments were loud and furious, but they rarely lasted more than a day or two. Until that last one."

"Someone, other than you or Caroline, created the estrangement, Harrison."

"How do you know?"

"Caroline suggested as much to a friend." Tom sauntered toward the door, his steps slow and methodical. He paused at the doorway and looked over his shoulder. "I also think Sarah Jane's life is in danger. Someone tried to ambush us when we rode to the Lazy G. So I asked Cord Rainville to hire on for a few days. I want that little girl watched at all times."

"I told you before that I could lock this place up tighter than a fortress. I'll have guards posted. No one will get to her except by our invitation."

"Good. Why don't you invite Jeremiah and Randolph to come for dinner this evening. I think it's time to confront them both."

Harrison cocked his head. "What are you planning?"

"Let's watch Sarah Jane's reaction when she meets him."

"You expect her to recognize him?" Harrison asked.

"I think she'll expose him as the one who assaulted her mother's friend, and possibly as the man who shoved her mother down the stairs."

"I hope you're wrong."

"I'm sure you do."

As Tom opened the door, Harrison spoke to his back. "Were you in love with my granddaughter?"

Tom turned his head, his response slow and deliberate. "No, sir. I thought of her as a sister."

Harrison nodded, then locked his eyes on Tom's. "She would have been lucky to have a brother like you. I only wish you would have found her sooner."

"So do I." Tom stepped from the room and closed the door.

He hadn't been able to save Caroline. But, God willing, he'd lay down his own life to save her daughter.

Chapter Sixteen

❧

Katie sat with Maria, watching Sarah Jane arrange small furniture inside a little, open-sided, blue-and-white house.

While growing up, Katie didn't have dolls or toys like other little girls had. She really hadn't known what she'd been missing since her love of reading had provided her and her father with so many hours of conversation and debate.

Yet living in a world of adults or literary characters had put her at a disadvantage when it came to conversing with the other children at school, most of whom struggled to comprehend the stories in their McGuffey Readers.

Looking back, she supposed that was one reason the other girls excluded her so often. She hadn't minded being left alone to read under the shade of a tree, but it would have been nice to have been included in games of tag sometimes. Or to have been defended when one of the boys had pulled her braids or called her names.

"I remember one Christmas," Maria said, drawing on yet another memory to share with Sarah Jane. "Your mother decorated that little dollhouse with sprigs of pine needles and red ribbon. Then the following spring, she went out into the meadow beyond the adobe walls and picked the colorful wildflowers that grew near the cottonwood trees. Then she made tiny bouquets and placed them in each of the rooms."

Sarah Jane looked up from her play and smiled, her eyes brighter than Katie had ever seen them before. She really was thriving at the Lazy G. The memories of her mother were helping to make her whole again.

Harrison had been right. The child would undoubtedly enjoy playing with her mother's dollhouse for hours.

Boot steps sounded, and Katie glanced up to see Tom enter the sitting room. Lobo, who was lying contentedly upon a gray-and-black woven rug in front of the fireplace, wagged his tail and whimpered a greeting.

"Katie," he said, "will you come out into the courtyard with me?"

"Yes, of course."

After asking Maria to excuse them, Katie followed Tom outside.

He lifted his hat and adjusted it on his head. "I'm going to ride into Stillwater to see the sheriff."

"What about?"

"I'd like to set up a meeting between Jeremiah and Sarah Jane. I think she'll be able to identify him as the man who assaulted Erin in Pleasant Valley. And after those shots were fired at us when we arrived today, we should have enough evidence for an attempted murder investigation—on you, as well as Caroline, especially if Erin has anything to add."

Katie reached for Tom's arm. "Please be careful. He might have been gunning for you."

"I'll be all right. If everything goes according to plan, I'll be back in an hour or two. But before I leave, Harrison wants me to have a couple of his men guard the house and yard."

"Do you think Jeremiah will come looking for Sarah Jane here?"

"I doubt that he'd be that daring. But just to be on the safe side, keep Sarah Jane in the house until I return with the sheriff."

"I'll look after her," Katie said. "And we'll both stay in the house. I promise."

Tom stroked her cheek, his gaze locking on to hers. "Watch yourself, too."

"I will. And just so you know, I may not follow orders, but I always keep my promises."

"So you told me."

She thought he might kiss her before he left, but he merely smiled then walked away.

Still, they were a team. And she'd never been more committed, more determined to follow one of his orders, than she was today. She would stay inside the house. And she'd guard that child with her life.

After Katie returned to the sitting room, Maria rose from the chair on which she'd been seated. "I'm going to find some old toys and some scraps of cloth and ribbons for Sarah Jane to use to decorate the little house. Do you want to help me?"

Katie glanced at the child and saw her playing happily, the dog resting beside her. Knowing that guards were being placed outside the house, she felt comfortable leaving the room.

"Sure." Katie followed the housekeeper down the hall,

around the corner and into one of the guest rooms at the back side of the hacienda.

"We do not use this room much anymore," Maria said, as she opened the door of an ornate mahogany wardrobe. "Just for storage."

She pushed aside a stack of blankets on one of the bottom shelves, then pulled out a basket filled with small pieces of fabric and doodads.

"I thought these scraps would come in handy one day," Maria said.

After she set the basket on the table, they began to sort through the ribbons, lace and pieces of cotton and flannel. Next they searched the wardrobe for other odds and ends Sarah Jane might find useful.

When Katie and Maria finally returned to the sitting room, carrying a doll, a wooden horse, a stuffed dog, the basket of fabric scraps and a box of buttons, they spotted the dollhouse in the middle of the floor but no little girl playing beside it.

"Sarah Jane?" Katie called. "Where are you, honey?"

She placed the basket on the settee. Where had she gone?

"Perhaps she went to the kitchen," Maria suggested.

Katie hoped so, but an uneasiness settled around her. She'd promised Tom that she would look after the girl, but now she didn't have any idea where she was. At least the dog was with her.

"She has not been gone long," Maria said. "Maybe she wanted another cookie. Or some milk."

"Maybe, but I'm not going to be happy until I know where she is. I'd better look for her."

"I will start in the kitchen," Maria said. "Then I will check the rest of the house."

"I'll go outside." Again, Katie reminded herself that Lobo was with the child, and that Tom had instructed the dog to protect her.

Fortunately, two cowboys now stood at the edge of the courtyard. She assumed they were the men Tom had asked to guard the house, and she felt instant relief.

"Excuse me," she said. "I'm looking for Sarah Jane. She was supposed to be in the sitting room, but she's not there."

"We just took up our post," the taller man said. "But we haven't seen her. Maybe she's in the outhouse."

"I'll check."

But Sarah Jane wasn't there, either. She hadn't been gone long enough to go very far. Still, Katie couldn't shake a growing sense of dread.

When she returned to the courtyard, she checked inside the house. Maria hadn't found her yet.

Back outside, one of the guards in front said he'd check the barn and the gardens while the other had to remain at his post. "If I don't find her, I'll gather up some of the men to go in search of her."

"Yes, please have the men look for her," Katie said. "In the meantime, I'll check outside the perimeter of the courtyard."

There was still no sign of the dog or the child.

Katie searched the horizon. To the east lay a grassy meadow, and farther ahead, a thick copse of cottonwoods.

Oh, dear. Had the girl gone in search of flowers to decorate her dollhouse, just as her mother had?

Had she left before Tom had sent the men to guard the courtyard entrance?

She spotted Abel heading for the barn, obviously

searching for her there. And several men were striding toward the outbuildings.

Katie cupped her hands to her lips and called out as loud as she could. "Sarah Jane!"

No answer.

Well, for goodness' sake. What did she expect? The poor child couldn't speak.

Again, Katie looked ahead, hoping to see the black-haired dog or the blue color of the gingham dress Sarah Jane wore. But she feared Sarah Jane's blond head would blend with the high, wheat-colored grasses swaying in the breeze.

Where in the world could she be?

When Katie had been that same age, she'd wandered off at least five times and had been brought home by the sheriff on one occasion. But then, Katie had always been a rebellious and adventurous child. On the other hand, Sarah Jane seemed quieter, more eager to please.

Picking up her skirts, Katie rushed forward, scanning the grassy areas while keeping her eyes on the trees ahead. Surely, her imagination had begun to play tricks on her, frightening her and goading her into over-reacting.

Why, Sarah Jane might be at home this very moment, sitting safely in the kitchen, munching on oatmeal cookies and drinking a large glass of frothy milk. And here Katie was, gathering thistles and foxtails in her stockings and along the hem of her skirt. Perhaps they would all laugh about it later, about how Katie had come back looking like a frazzled wild woman.

Still, Katie couldn't settle the knot in her stomach, the ache in her heart. Nor could she fight back the sting of tears in her eyes. After all, Maria would have called her back to the house if she'd found her, wouldn't she?

Unseen insects, buzzing and chirping along the way, reminded Katie of the nasty rattlesnake she'd frightened nearly a week ago, with its ugly head raised, rattles shaking, eyes staring her down.

She blinked back the memory, fought the bone-chilling fear and took care in watching her steps while looking for the child.

Dear Lord, she prayed, *I know it's been a while since You and I have talked. And that's my fault. I've drawn away from You—out of pride, stubbornness and just plain foolishness. I'm sorry for that. It's just that I've always tried to do things on my own before, but I'm finally beginning to realize how much I need You. And how much I need others—like Tom and Sarah Jane. So please forgive me. I need You, Lord. Especially now.*

"Help me find Sarah Jane," she said aloud, raising her eyes heavenward. *"You know where she is. Be with her and protect her. Be with me, too. And guide my steps."*

Well, would you look at that? Jeremiah was in luck.

About a hundred yards from the hacienda, just inside the copse of trees where he hid, Sarah Jane peered to her right and then her left, as if she was searching for something.

"Lobo?" she whispered. "Come back, Lobo. Where did you go?"

When she turned her back, Jeremiah stole away from his hiding spot and grabbed her from behind. Then he clamped his hand around her mouth before she could scream.

"So we meet again," he told her.

His arm circled her tightly. He could feel her little heart pounding like a runaway locomotive.

"I told you I'd be back. Remember what I said I'd do if I caught you talking about me? And what I'd do if you told anyone you'd seen me?"

Her head nodded.

"I ought to strangle you here and now, then leave your body for the wild animals to find."

Her heart beat all the faster, as if she knew the danger she was in. But he continued to hold her mouth shut, keeping her quiet until he could insure her silence for once and for all. "There's a ravine not far from here. It would be a shame if you wandered off that way and fell to the rocks below. What a terrible accident. It would be even more tragic than your mother's unexpected tumble down a flight of stairs, don't you think?"

As he started across the grassy meadow toward the ravine, his grip loosened on her mouth. He started to adjust his hand, but before he could do so, she bit down on his finger as hard as she could.

Jeremiah swore, then struck her face, jarring her silly. The brat was as feisty as her mother, but he'd deal with them both in the same way.

He'd no more than taken two steps when he heard a bark. He looked to the sound and spotted a wolf racing toward him, eyes blazing, teeth bared.

Again he swore, then he drew his gun and shot the animal, dropping it in its tracks.

The kid let out a bloodcurdling scream. "No!"

"Shut up," he said. "I've got another bullet just for you."

"I hate you," she cried. "You killed my mother, and you killed my dog."

"Well, now. That surely hurts my feelings. Yes, it does." Then he slapped his hand across her mouth again, quieting her, and headed for the ravine, where he would rid himself of her for good.

As Katie continued through the meadow, following what appeared to be bent and broken blades and stems of grass, she spotted a mashed spot up ahead that had been trampled down.

Was it fresh? Could Sarah Jane and Lobo have passed this way and stopped to play here?

She wished Tom was here to read the tracks, to relieve her fears, to hold her hand.

But he wasn't, and Katie was all Sarah Jane had.

A gunshot sounded from where the cottonwoods grew in a thick cluster. Before Katie could consider her next move, she gathered her skirts and darted toward the trees.

"Sarah Jane," she called, realizing the foolishness of charging head-on into gunfire.

She slowed her steps as she reached the trees, all the while looking for a sign of Sarah Jane—a footstep, a hair ribbon, something that would convince her to continue into the shadows.

A whimper sounded to her left. When she turned toward the noise, her heart turned inside out. For there, in the grass, lay Lobo, his head and shoulders bloodied.

"Oh, dear God," Katie muttered. All her fear came rushing forth. If she had a gun, she would put the poor animal out of its misery, but she didn't have a weapon.

No weapon....

What was she to do now?

She'd been so intent upon finding Sarah Jane that she'd marched forward without forethought and had fallen into a trap.

Lobo raised his head and slowly hobbled to his feet. The poor dog. Katie wished she could take the time to help him, comfort him, but as it was, she feared she might not find Sarah Jane in time.

She hadn't gone far when a twig snapped under her foot, and she nearly jumped out of her skin. "Well, now," a male voice drawled. "You have someone to keep you company, kid."

Katie turned slowly, her eyes lighting upon the narrowed brown eyes belonging to Jeremiah Haney.

"Let her go," Katie said, hoping her voice didn't betray her fear.

Jeremiah cocked the hammer of his pistol. "Put your hands in the air."

Katie lifted her arms slowly, her mind reeling at how to save Sarah Jane. She'd worry about her own life later. "Take me and do as you will, but let Sarah Jane go. She can't talk, so she can't possibly hurt you."

He laughed, the tone hollow. "Oh, no? She didn't have a problem telling me she hated me just minutes ago." He glanced at the child he still held, his hand pressed against her mouth. "Isn't that right, kid?"

Sarah Jane didn't respond, but she didn't have to. Her face, which had lost all color, and her eyes, as wide as those of a cornered wild animal, said it all.

Katie didn't challenge the comment, either. She just watched Jeremiah warily, her heart pounding to beat the band.

Jeremiah chuckled. "The kid used to jabber all the

time, just like a mockingbird. How Caroline could stand it, I'll never know."

"What are you going to do with us?" Katie asked, ignoring the issue of Sarah Jane's speech and hoping to gain some time, time for someone to come to their aid.

"I can't let you go. Start walking," he said, nodding his head deeper into the grove. "I've got to get out of here before someone figures out where that gunshot came from."

Katie had no alternative but to advance in the direction he indicated, hoping and praying someone found them in time.

With each step through the trees, Katie's fears intensified. She had to think of something to distract Jeremiah, to slow him down. If she could buy some time, someone might find them before he killed her and Sarah Jane. For she had no doubt that was exactly what he intended to do.

"Why did you murder Caroline?" she asked.

Her question seemed to take Jeremiah aback. He slowed his steps but continued to point the gun at Sarah Jane's head. "I didn't. She fell down the stairs."

Katie decided to take another line of questioning. "Why are you keeping Martha medicated?"

At that he stopped. "What are you talking about?"

"I was at your house. I saw your wife, and I spoke to Olivia."

She had his attention now, because he stopped walking altogether. And her only hope was to stall for time until someone found them.

"Martha isn't sick," Katie said. "And she isn't crazy. Why did you imprison her in the house like that?"

"Because she accused me of marital infidelity. She would have gone to her father, who's been holding her inheritance over my head, even though he had his own share of indiscretions. And I need to keep her quiet, at least for a while longer."

Apparently, Jeremiah hadn't gone home yet. So he didn't know that his wife had left with her father. Either way, Katie had to keep him talking. "Martha accused you of having an affair with Caroline?"

"Oh, I was willing. I'd always had my eye on her, but she went out of her way to avoid being alone with me. I'm not really sure what kind of game she was playing."

"Perhaps she wasn't interested in you."

Jeremiah's eyes narrowed as though he could see something Katie couldn't. "She was a natural-born harlot. She wore those britches by day and low-cut gowns at night. So one day, when I caught her in the hayloft with one of the cowboys, I ran the guy off. Then, when she and I were alone, I had my chance. She struggled some and pretended she didn't want it. But I knew that she did. And when it was over, I wiped her tears and told her it would be better next time."

"You forced yourself upon her," Katie said, her fists clenching at her sides.

"Like I said, she only pretended not to want it. Besides, I wasn't her first. When Harrison had caught her and that no-account cowboy kissing, he'd threatened to kill the kid if he ever caught them together again. So I told Caroline that I would tell her grandfather I found them both in the hayloft."

"That kept Caroline quiet?" Katie asked, not sure why the young woman wouldn't have approached her grandfather first and simply told him what Jeremiah had done to her.

"Before that preacher started coming around here, talking about love and forgiveness, Harrison had a fierce temper. He would have shot that kid before Caroline could blink an eye and she knew it. And she would have done anything to protect him."

"How old was Caroline when all of this happened?"

"Old enough to bear a child." Jeremiah glared at Sarah Jane, then chuffed.

"So when Martha hired that investigator and found out about Caroline's baby, she thought the child was mine. But look at her. Anyone can tell she's not. She's too pale and scrawny. She doesn't look at all like me."

Katie swallowed back the bile that had risen in her throat, trying hard not to imagine the painful thoughts going through Sarah Jane's mind. But before she could speak, the little girl turned her head, freeing her mouth from Jeremiah's grip.

"My daddy's name was Davie. And he was strong and brave. Mama never would have loved a man like you. My daddy was good and kind."

Jeremiah glared at her, "Oh, yeah? Well, your good 'daddy' left her when he found out about you."

"That's not true," Sarah Jane said, lip quivering slightly.

"What would you know? You're just a couple years out of a diaper."

"I know a lot," Sarah Jane said, small chin lifting. "I know my mama hated you, and I know why she fell down the stairs. She was trying to get away from you, and you pushed her."

"Yeah, I pushed her all right," Jeremiah said, all signs of humor leaving him. "And I'm going to give you and your pretty friend a push, too."

* * *

Tom hadn't ridden as far from the ranch as he'd hoped when he'd heard a gunshot and a child's scream. He didn't know how or why—just that the unthinkable had happened.

The thought that Katie hadn't kept her word hadn't crossed his mind. She'd promised not to leave the house, and he believed her. It was as simple as that.

He rode as fast as he could, following the sound toward a field of wildflowers before reaching a thick grove of cottonwoods.

As his eyes landed upon a patch of dried leaves soaked in blood, Tom stopped abruptly, his heart pounding.

No body, but a trail of crimson drops led deeper into the trees. If Jeremiah had hurt either Katie or Sarah Jane, Tom would make sure justice was served if he had to join the posse that went after him.

Walking lightly, he followed the blood trail. At first he thought he might only have imagined Katie's voice, but as he moved closer, she spoke again. His movements stilled as his senses keened.

"What do you think you're going to do after you've killed us? Tom will come looking for you."

Jeremiah gave Sarah Jane a push, then stepped closer to Katie and nudged her with the barrel of his gun. "I'd just as soon shoot that Indian as look at him. And nobody will care about the death of a half-breed. That's the way of it in these parts."

"Then I suggest you watch your back," Tom said, his gun already drawn.

Jeremiah grabbed Katie, jerked her close and pointed his own gun to her temple. "Drop it, McCain, or I'll shoot."

If he'd held another hostage, anyone except Katie, Tom might have refused to lower his gun, might have tried to call his bluff. But he couldn't risk the life of the woman he loved more than he dared to admit.

As Tom lowered his gun, he spotted Lobo, creeping along on his haunches, bloodied and battered, his dark eyes on Haney. As the Colt .45 dropped to the ground, Lobo jumped toward Jeremiah's leg, grabbing his thigh.

"Aah!" Jeremiah loosened his hold on Katie, but before he could aim the gun at Lobo, Tom lunged forward, knocking both the dog and the man off balance.

With one hand gripping the wrist that held the six-shooter, Tom landed on top of Jeremiah. He swung his fist, striking the man squarely in the jaw.

"Back off, Lobo," Tom called.

The wolf-dog growled and snapped one last time before obeying the command.

A crack sounded as Tom's fist connected with Jeremiah's nose. Slamming the hand that gripped the weapon to the ground, Tom managed to jar the pistol free. Then he snatched the gun and aimed the barrel at Haney.

His finger strained against the trigger. So intense was his anger at the man who'd surely murdered Caroline and would have killed Katie and Sarah Jane that, for a moment, Tom didn't know whether he'd fire or not.

"They'll hang you for shooting me, half-breed," Jeremiah said, his eyes wild with fear. "That's the way it is around here."

Haney was right. And nothing would ever change that. Tom could rid the world of a cruel, evil man, and then he would be punished for the deed—all because of the blood that ran in his veins.

But more than that, there was God's law to worry about. And it wasn't up to Tom to judge the man.

Letting Haney live would be more of a punishment because Jeremiah Haney, a pillar of the Stillwater community, would be tried, convicted and executed for what he'd done to Caroline.

At that point, several of Harrison's men arrived, with guns drawn.

"Can one of you get a wagon?" Tom asked. "I'd like to haul my dog back to the house. He was injured trying to protect Harrison's great-granddaughter."

Katie, who'd knelt to comfort Sarah Jane, slowly rose, lifting the whimpering child, who clutched her with a grip not likely to loosen anytime soon. "It's over, sweetheart. You don't have to be afraid any longer. Tom will see to it that you and I are safe—now and forever." Then she turned to Tom and smiled. "I knew, if I kept him talking long enough, you would come to find us."

"I'd hoped your clever wit would come in handy. It looks like we've both found some things we admire about each other."

"I agree."

"We can talk about this later, but maybe we ought to consider forming a permanent partnership."

"I'd like that." Katie tossed him a smile, then gently placed Sarah Jane onto the ground, took her by the hand, and led her back to the house.

Chapter Seventeen

❧

Back at the Lazy G, Sarah Jane stood watch as Katie and Maria tended Lobo's wounds and refused to leave her heroic friend's side until she was sure he would live. The bullet had cut a deep gash across the dog's head, nearly taking off his ear before striking his shoulder.

Katie worried that someone might suggest putting him out of his misery, especially in front of Sarah Jane, but she hadn't needed to be concerned about that. Tom had insisted they treat the animal as if he were human, and she had no objections whatsoever.

A couple of Harrison's men had summoned the sheriff, and when he arrived, he found Jeremiah under armed guard, his hands and feet bound. Before taking him into custody, the sheriff took statements from both Tom and Katie.

"If you don't mind," Sheriff Tipton said, "I'd like to question the little girl."

"She's been traumatized," Katie said. "Please don't press her too hard."

"I'll go easy on her, ma'am. I have a couple of little

ones of my own. But she's a witness to more than just this incident."

Katie nodded, then followed him into the hacienda and to the sitting room, where Sarah Jane sat beside a sleeping Lobo, stroking his fur. The dollhouse, now forgotten, rested just a few feet away.

"That's a fine family of dolls you have," Sheriff Tipton said.

Sarah Jane nodded. "They belonged to my mama."

"Did they now." The sheriff took a seat in the chair closest to her, removed his hat and learned forward, resting his forearms on his knees. "Miss O'Malley tells me you were playing with these dolls earlier today, before all the trouble began."

Sarah Jane nodded. "I wanted to find some wildflowers to decorate the rooms, just like my mama used to do. So me and Lobo went outside for a walk in the meadow where they grow. And that's when Mr. Haney came and got us. Lobo tried to help me, and Mr. Haney shot him."

"You have a very brave dog."

She nodded. "He's the *best* dog in the *whole* world."

"That he is."

Sarah Jane gave Lobo a soft and gentle hug.

"Is this the first time you saw Mr. Haney?" the sheriff asked.

Sarah Jane slowly shook her head. "He's the man who hurt Erin when we were going to the mercantile. He wanted us to go with him that day, and she told him no because she didn't like him. Mama didn't like him, either. But he kept telling me and Erin that we had to go with him or else."

"Or else what?" the sheriff asked.

"I don't know. Something bad would happen, I think.

She told him to turn her loose, and then he hit her really hard. And he kept hitting her. I cried for help, and when Blossom came running, he grabbed my arm really hard and pulled me with him. I thought he was going to take me away, but I kicked him and bit him, and he let go. Then I ran as fast as I could."

"You're a smart girl. And very brave. Did you tell the sheriff who hurt you and Erin?"

"I was *afraid* to tell. Because when we were in Taylorsville, Mr. Haney told me that if I ever told anyone about him, he'd push me down the stairs, too."

At that, Tom eased closer to the child. "He'd push you down the stairs, *too?*"

Sarah Jane nodded, the tears welling in her eyes. "Just like Mama."

"I knew it," Tom said. "That fall wasn't an accident."

"Tell me about the day your mama fell down the stairs," the sheriff asked. "Who was at home?"

"It was almost dinnertime, and Erin went to see Mrs. Phillips about a job because they didn't need her to work at the restaurant anymore. Mama was in the kitchen."

"Was Mr. Haney there?"

"Yes. Mama never liked it when he came. When he left, she always cried. But this time, it was different. Their voices were loud. I heard them go upstairs. She told him to leave, but he wouldn't."

"Where were you?" the sheriff asked.

"Downstairs, in Erin's room playing with my doll. But I opened the door and came out."

"What were your mother and Mr. Haney doing?"

"He was all red in the face and angry. And Mama was crying. She told me to go back into the room, so I did. But then I heard her scream. I thought someone really big ran down the stairs really fast. When I came to see what happened, Mama was lying on the floor. And there was blood."

"Where was Mr. Haney?"

"Upstairs. He came down and looked at Mama. Her neck was crooked. And she wasn't moving or talking. She just laid there with her eyes open. Then he looked at me and said, 'I'm leaving now. But if you tell anyone you saw me here, I'll come back and push you down the stairs, too.' Then he left, but not out the front door. He went back upstairs to Mama's bedroom. I think he must have climbed out a window."

"Then what happened?"

"I knelt down by Mama, but she just laid there for the longest time, making funny noises. When Erin came home, she called the doctor. But Mama never woke up again."

Tom cleared his throat and said, "They told me in Taylorsville that Caroline broke her neck. She lived for a few hours, but never regained consciousness."

"Sarah Jane," the sheriff asked, "did you tell the sheriff what you saw and heard?"

She shook her head no. "I was scared. I thought he would come back and hurt me."

"And you didn't tell Erin, either?"

"No. Am I in trouble?"

"Of course not. Jeremiah Haney is the one who's in trouble. He's a bad man. And he'll be punished for what he did."

"Sarah Jane," Tom said, "I have a question you might not be able to answer. But I'm going to ask it anyway. Why did you and Erin move from Taylorsville? I thought you might have left because you were both afraid of Jeremiah."

"We left because someone took all the money Mama had been saving. And Erin couldn't pay the rent. After Mama died, Erin looked for it in Mama's bedroom, but it wasn't there."

Had Jeremiah stolen it? Is that what they'd fought about?

Either way, the child's account of her mother's death was enough evidence to charge him with murder.

After the sheriff and his deputy took Jeremiah back to town, Sarah Jane finally collapsed into tears.

Nearly an hour later, Katie still held her while she wept. The poor little girl's grief tore at Katie's heart until she wondered if the tears would ever stop. She glanced around the sitting room at Tom, Harrison, Abel and Maria, noting her concern was mirrored by them all.

Finally, Tom got to his feet and strode across the tiled floor. "Can't you do something? It's killing me to see her cry like that."

Katie continued to hold the girl, rocking her gently and stroking her back as she sobbed. "I think it's best if we allow her to grieve."

Maria nodded in agreement. "*Sí,* she has kept too much inside for too long."

She was right. The self-imposed silence had surely taken a toll on the child. Tom sighed and looked to Harrison as if hoping for a suggestion.

The old cattleman sat stoically in a chair next to Abel, his face pale, his jaw taut. Finally, he got to his feet, too. Then he shuffled forward, placing a frail hand upon Sarah Jane's head. "Sweetheart, I swear to you, Jeremiah Haney will pay for what he did to your mother."

Sarah Jane continued to cry as though her great-grandfather's words held no comfort whatsoever.

Katie knew she had to soothe the child for the sake of the adults who suffered along with her, all of them wanting to help but unable to ease her pain. "I know you miss your mother something awful. But I want you to know something. She's in Heaven with the angels now," Katie said.

Sarah Jane's cries began to abate just a bit, and Katie knew she was listening.

"You can't see her, but I know she was there with you today. She watched over you until we found you."

The little girl took a deep breath, shuddering as the racking cries began to subside little by little.

"Now that your mama has angel wings, she'll continue to be with you, even though you can't see her. She'll watch out for you always."

"But," Sarah Jane began, lip quivering and words coming slowly. "I can't…ever hug…her again. I…can't…tell her…that I love her."

"No," Katie said. "You can't hug her here on earth, but I think there will be times she'll be so close that you'll feel warm and loved and safe. And you'll be able to hug her again someday in Heaven."

"I miss her."

"I know you do, honey." Katie brushed a strand of hair from her wet cheek. "But there's something important she wants you to do."

Sarah Jane sniffled. "What's that?"

"Your mama wants you to enjoy all the earthly things she can no longer experience."

"How can I do that?"

Katie smiled warmly. "Well, you can take an extra

sniff of a lilac. You can enjoy the warmth of the sun on your face for just a moment longer. And you can walk barefoot in the wet sand along a creek bed a few more steps."

"How do you know that?"

"Because that's what I've done since my mother went to Heaven."

Sarah Jane looked at Katie, eyes red rimmed and puffy, nose runny. She sniffled again. "Do you think our mamas have met?"

"Absolutely," Katie told her. "And they're both smiling right now, knowing that we have each other. I can feel it. Can't you? Just a little?"

Sarah Jane wiped her nose on her sleeve. "Maybe. Does that mean you'll stay with me and take care of me, just like a mother?"

"Yes," Katie answered, her heart nearly ready to burst.

How she would have liked to have had a loving woman hold her, just like a mother. Someone who smelled of lilac and who always had time for a hug or a kiss.

A daddy might be special in his own right, but he wasn't a mama.

"What about Wyoming?" Sarah Jane asked. "Will you take me with you?"

"No, honey," Katie said, her decision already made. Sarah Jane belonged in Texas, at least while Harrison was still alive, and Katie wouldn't leave the child, not now, not ever. "I'm afraid the people of Granville will have to find another teacher."

Katie doubted Harrison would turn down her offer to raise Sarah Jane, especially after today, but she would just have to trust God that the details would work themselves out.

Sarah Jane turned to Harrison. "Can we live here?"

Relief flooded the old man's face and he broke into a broad grin, eyes twinkling. "Until long after your children have great-grandchildren."

For the first time in hours, Sarah Jane began to smile. She glanced at Tom. "And will you live with us, too? You and Lobo?"

A hard smile formed on Tom's face. "I can't live here, but Lobo can. I'll come by every once in a while to visit, though."

Katie's heart sank. She glanced first at Harrison, then to Tom and back to Harrison. Surely Tom understood she couldn't leave Sarah Jane. Not now, and probably not ever. The grief-filled little girl needed her.

Maria stepped forward. "I have prepared a bath for you, *mija.* Come with me to your mother's room."

When Sarah Jane and Maria left the room, Katie turned to face Tom. "Surely, you can stay for a while."

His features were cool and unreadable. "Just for a few days."

"But what about Sarah Jane?" Katie asked hopefully. "She needs to feel some stability right now."

And what about me? she wondered.

Tom scanned the faces in the room. "She'll have everything she needs right here. This is her home. It's where she belongs."

Katie's heart ached, torn between a man and a child. She doubted she was the first woman to feel that way, but it hurt. And right this moment, life seemed anything but fair.

At that point, Abel got to his feet, faced Tom and

lifted a gnarled finger. "Tell Señor Harrison who you are."

Tom didn't answer.

"If you don't want to admit it, then why don't you tell him what time it is. Pull out that pocket watch you carry, the one your father gave you."

Harrison cocked his head and looked at Tom. "What's he talking about?"

Tom still didn't respond.

Katie wanted to throttle him for not speaking up.

Harrison stepped closer to Tom. "Let me see the watch."

Slowly, Tom reached into his pocket. He withdrew the round, gold timepiece and handed it to Harrison.

The old man's jaw dropped and his eyes widened. "This is Robert's watch. I gave it to him. It was meant to be an heirloom. Where did you get it?"

Tom took a deep breath then averted his eyes. "My father gave it to me."

"Your father?" Harrison asked, his demeanor ramrod straight, focused.

"My father told me to bring it to you if I ever needed anything, if I ever wanted to convince you of my parentage."

Harrison stepped closer, taking in every feature of Tom's face. "You're Robert's son? My grandson?"

Tom appeared to lean back. "I don't need anything from you, and I won't be staying."

Harrison opened his arms, reaching out to embrace Tom. At first Katie thought Tom might pull away from the old man, refuse his offer of love. But as Harrison wrapped his arms around the younger man, he seemed to pull Tom right into his heart and family.

Katie could only hope the man she loved would find peace for the rejected little boy he had once been.

Quietly, she turned and left the room. Abel followed her out, granting grandfather and grandson a moment of privacy, such a precious gift in the short time they had left.

Katie sat upon the settee in the sitting room, staring in her lap at an unopened book. She almost wished for Sarah Jane's company, but the poor child had nearly collapsed in exhaustion after her bath. Even Maria had retired early, completely drained from the emotional turmoil following Jeremiah's arrest.

Fingering the gold lettering of the title on the dark blue cover, she glanced at the closed doorway to Harrison's study. Tom and Harrison had slipped in there an hour ago and had yet to emerge.

An ornate clock upon the mantel slowly ticked away the time. Reading was out of the question. Whenever Katie tried to focus on a passage, her mind raged with curiosity about the conversation taking place on the other side of the closed double doors.

She hoped the words that passed between the men would change Tom's mind about leaving. Sarah Jane wasn't the only one who belonged at the Lazy G. As Harrison's grandson, Tom was an heir, also.

Could the two of them work things out? She said a prayer, leaving it in God's hands.

Footsteps clicked upon the tile floor, and Katie turned toward the kitchen.

Abel walked into the room with a linen-covered tray. "I brought you some cookies and milk."

"Why, thank you." Katie hoped his company would divert her thoughts.

When a sharp rap sounded at the front door, Katie nearly jumped from her seat, jostling the book on her lap. She snatched one side of the cover to keep it from falling to the floor. The frightening ordeal with Jeremiah certainly had set her nerves on end.

After placing the tray upon a small, hand-carved table, Abel answered the door.

An older gentleman of medium height and build entered the room. He removed his hat.

"Come in, Señor Wellman," Abel said. "I will let Señor Graves know you are here."

The man wasn't at all handsome, but a fine linen suit and a crisp white shirt gave him a distinguished look. Katie didn't remember meeting him at the Cattleman's Ball. She wondered if he might be a neighbor.

"Thank you." Mr. Wellman's eyes met Abel's. "I'm actually looking for Jeremiah. Have you seen him?"

"Yes, but he is no longer here," Abel said.

The man narrowed his eyes. "Where did he go?"

"To jail," Abel answered.

The man scowled. "What's the charge? I have a few of my own to add."

"Murder," Abel said. "He killed Caroline Graves."

The man paled then mumbled something under his breath. He glanced at Katie. "I'm Martin Wellman. My daughter is married to Jeremiah, although she won't be much longer."

Katie set the book aside and stood. Walking toward Martha Haney's father, she extended a hand. "I'm Katie O'Malley. I met your daughter a couple of days ago."

Mr. Wellman's expression softened. "Martha told me about you. You saved her life."

Katie shrugged her shoulders. "I'm not sure if that's the case, but I believe Jeremiah had been drugging her for months."

Mr. Wellman snorted. "Drugged? According to the doctor, he nearly killed her. It's going to be a long and difficult recovery for her, but Martha is determined to regain her health."

Katie sighed in relief. "I'm so glad. He kept her a prisoner in that darkened upstairs bedroom."

Wellman shook his head. "A prisoner usually has his wits about him. Haney nearly drove my little girl mad. I'd ring his neck if he were here right now. As it is, I'll see she gets an immediate divorce."

"Let me get you a cup of coffee," Katie said. "I'm sure Harrison will want to speak to you."

Katie was right. After Abel left to announce Mr. Wellman's arrival, the study door opened and Tom and Harrison entered the sitting room. Her heart filled with expectation, but she held her questions.

Tom appeared relaxed, yet he didn't smile or offer a clue to his mood or whether he'd made a change of plans.

"Martin," Harrison said, his voice warm, his expression sober. "What brings you all the way out here at this hour?"

"I came looking for Jeremiah. I hear he's in jail."

Harrison nodded slowly. "He is. And my only regret is that I may not live to see him hang."

"I never did trust him," Mr. Wellman began.

"How is your daughter?" Tom asked the man.

The older gentleman looked at Tom, his eyebrows furrowed. "Who are you?"

Tom stiffened, but before he could answer, Harrison spoke up. "This is Tom McCain, Robert's son and my grandson. He'll be running the Lazy G from now on. Everything I own will be his. I expect you'll help me introduce him to the community, especially since he was instrumental in freeing Martha."

Wellman reached for Tom's hand. "It's a pleasure meeting you. I've got a spread about forty miles from here. It's not as big as yours, but it's a nice size."

Katie held her breath, waiting for Tom to take the man's hand, hoping he would confirm Harrison's statement—not just about his relationship with the cattleman, but his agreement to stay in Stillwater.

Tom shook Wellman's hand and thanked him. Then, turning to Katie, he smiled. "I assume you've met Miss O'Malley. If she'll agree to be my wife, we'll be inviting you to a wedding soon."

Katie nearly collapsed in a dead faint. "You're going to stay?" she asked Tom.

Harrison interrupted. "Of course, he's going to stay. He's a Graves, and this is his land."

Tom winked at Katie, and a slow smile stretched across his face. "You will marry me, won't you, Katie?"

She was in his arms before she could answer. She had no idea what problems life might present them, but their love would see them through. Of that she was certain.

Tom caressed her back. "I take it this means you've agreed."

"Yes, I'll marry you," Katie said. Then she cocked her head, staring into his warm, bright eyes, and grinned. "That is, under one condition."

"What's that?"

"About the vows…you really don't expect me to promise to obey, do you?"

He laughed, and the rich, baritone sound filled her heart. "I doubt you have an obedient bone in your body, but I love you, and I'll do my best to make you happy."

"Just promise to love me," Katie said, lifting her lips to his.

"Forever," he whispered softly, sealing his vow with a kiss.

Epilogue

The wedding day dawned bright and clear, not a cloud marring the Texas sky. The courtyard, festively decorated with flowers and lace, had an aura of happiness in the floral-scented air.

Tom would have married Katie the day he asked her to be his wife, but Harrison had insisted it would take at least a week to plan a proper marriage ceremony. The dying cattleman wanted to present his heirs to the community in grand style.

It was just as well. Hannah would have been hurt if she hadn't been included with the planning of the festivities. She and Trapper, along with a much-improved Erin, had arrived two days ago, Hannah and Trapper both grinning from ear to ear and proud as prize peacocks.

The trip had been difficult on Erin, so she'd been relegated to rest until the ceremony, but Hannah had been treated as a queen from the moment she stepped into the hacienda. Katie and Maria included her in every decision, both large and small. It warmed Tom's heart to see her so happy.

Erin had been included, too, although she stood on

the outside looking in most of the time. In some ways, Tom understood how she felt. Long after he'd moved in with Hannah, he'd felt out of place, too.

Being warmly accepted into a family had seemed too good to be true, but slowly and surely, Hannah's love had chipped away at Tom's hardened heart, finding the frightened boy inside. And he had no doubt that the same would happen with Erin, who'd already agreed to stay with Hannah indefinitely, helping her with the house and gardening.

Tom fingered the starched collar of the white shirt he wore under a new store-bought suit. He stood with Harrison, greeting each of the wedding guests as they arrived at the hacienda. Harrison introduced him as his grandson and made a point of telling everyone Tom was now the owner of the Lazy G.

As the chairs slowly filled with smiling friends and neighbors, Tom's thoughts turned to Katie. He hadn't seen her since the day before yesterday, thanks to Hannah and some silly old custom. Denying himself the sight of his bride-to-be, the lilt of her voice and the warmth of her embrace had begun to fray his nerves. But Tom only had a few more minutes to wait, then she would be his wife. He couldn't believe his good fortune, and, as Harrison had said, God had surely blessed them all.

With Harrison's overwhelming approval and the legal paperwork filed by an attorney in Rio Seco, Tom's acceptance in the community was all but set in stone. Katie would soon be his wife, and Sarah Jane would have both a mother and father to love and care for her the rest of her life.

Harrison nodded toward a distinguished, gray-haired

man who arrived in the back of a black carriage. "I believe Ian Connor is here. He's the only one I don't know."

Katie had sent a telegram, hoping Ian could make it in time. He'd responded, saying he would hire a coach, but that his sister was ill and unable to attend.

Tom strode out to greet the man who'd been like family to Katie. "Mr. Connor?"

"Yes," Ian said, as the driver helped him from the carriage and handed him his cane.

"I'm Tom McCain."

Ian extended his weak hand, a smile breaking out on his face. "I'm pleased to meet you, son."

"Thank you, sir."

"Call me Ian."

"I may not be the man you expected Katie to marry," Tom said, "but I want you to know that I love her, and I'll do my best to make her happy."

Ian straightened his tie. "I must confess that I never took the time to imagine who Katie might marry or what he might look like."

"Why is that?"

Ian laughed. "Quite frankly, I didn't expect to live long enough to see Katie's wedding day. She has a stubborn spirit, and not many men can handle her."

Tom grinned. "I think it would be best if another man didn't try."

Ian patted Tom on the back and laughed. "Son, I wish you a lifetime of happiness along with all the challenges Katie will undoubtedly present."

"I'll admit we've encountered a few disagreements along the way," Tom said with a chuckle, "but I'm looking forward to living the rest of my life with her."

Ian laughed. "You have no idea how glad I am to see you take on that responsibility."

"It's my pleasure," Tom said as he spotted Harrison making his way toward them.

Harrison sported a broad smile on his pale and wrinkled face. The event had undoubtedly placed a strain on him, but the tough old cattleman was determined to remain as strong as his frail body would allow.

"I hope I'm not interrupting anything," Harrison said.

"Not at all."

When Tom introduced the men, Ian stretched out a hand in greeting. "I'll be giving away the bride."

"And a beautiful bride she is," Harrison said. "I can assure you, she's getting a fine man in my grandson."

"Katie may have a stubborn streak and a quick temper, but her heart has always been warm and true. If she tells me she loves him, and that he's a good man, that's all the impressing I need."

In the far corner of the courtyard, a lone cowboy dressed in his Sunday finest began to pluck a melody on his guitar.

"It's time to take our places," Harrison said. "Come along, Ian. I'll show you where to find Katie."

Tom watched the men go, feeling a warmth like no other he'd ever known. His eyes sought Trapper, the man who'd become both a father and friend to an orphaned boy. It was time for the groom and his best man to stand before the minister.

Within minutes the murmurs of the wedding guests had stilled and everyone had taken their places. As Tom waited for his bride to walk down the aisle, he thought about the changes that were about to take place. He would become a husband, father and cattleman all in one fell swoop. And he vowed not to fail any of the people depending on him.

He scanned the guests seated on benches and chairs throughout the courtyard. Martin Wellman and Martha Haney sat near the front. Tom gave a slight nod to the gentleman and his daughter, acknowledging their support and presence.

Not everyone in Stillwater had come to the wedding, but then again, not everyone had been invited. Randolph Haney for one.

Shocked and embarrassed by his son's arrest, Randolph had apologized before packing his belongings and heading for parts unknown. All that remained of his law practice was a for-sale sign hanging on the front door.

The women in the crowd oohed and aahed as a happy Sarah Jane walked down the aisle, blushing and beaming.

Tom winked at her as she approached. No longer just his niece, but now his daughter, she took her position at the side of the table that served as an altar.

Next came Erin, her cheeks flushed, her eyes darting to the right and left, as if not sure she deserved to be a guest at the wedding, let alone Katie's maid of honor. There might be some in the community who wouldn't approve—if they'd known of Erin's past. But Katie believed Erin should continue to be a part of Sarah Jane's life, and Tom agreed.

As Erin stood beside the minister, the cowboy changed chords on his guitar, indicating that the bride would soon enter the courtyard.

Tom's heart nearly burst with love and pride when he saw Katie upon Ian's arm. Beautiful Katie, soon to be his wife.

Dressed in white organza, she'd never looked lovelier—or happier. God had truly blessed them this day.

Ian placed Katie's hand in the crook of Tom's arm, handing the bride over to her husband's keeping. He quickly swiped at an eye before taking his seat.

"I love you," Katie whispered to Tom.

"I love you, too."

Then they both turned to the minister, ready to vow before God and man to love, to honor and to cherish each other from this day on.

Tom had figured they may as well leave *obey* off the list, since Katie told him she'd promise to try, but he'd need to exercise patience with her.

And that was all right with him. Where there was love and respect, everything else would all fall nicely into place—now and forever.

* * * * *

SPECIAL EXCERPT FROM

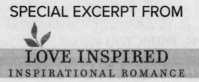

LOVE INSPIRED
INSPIRATIONAL ROMANCE

*When a young Amish woman returns home
with a baby in tow, will sparks fly with her
handsome—and unusual—neighbor?*

Read on for a sneak preview of
The Baby Next Door
by Vannetta Chapman.

Grace found Nicole had pulled herself up to the front door
and was high-fiving none other than Adrian Schrock.
He'd squatted down to her level. Nicole was having a fine
old time.

Grace picked up her *doschder* and pushed open the
door, causing Adrian to jump up, then step back toward
the porch steps. It was, indeed, a fine spring day. The sun
shone brightly across the Indiana fields. Flowers colored
yellow, red, lavender and orange had begun popping
through the soil that surrounded the porch. Birds were
even chirping merrily.

Somehow, all those things did little to elevate Grace's
mood. Neither did the sight of her neighbor.

Adrian resettled his straw hat on his head and smiled.
"Gudemariye."

"Your llama has escaped again."

"Kendrick? *Ya.* I've come to fetch him. He seems to
like your place more than mine."

"I don't want that animal over here, Adrian. He spits.
And your peacock was here at daybreak, crying like a
child."

Adrian laughed. "When you moved back home, I guess you didn't expect to live next to a Plain & Simple Exotic Animal Farm."

Adrian wiggled his eyebrows at Nicole when he seemed to realize that Grace wasn't amused.

"I think of your place as Adrian's Zoo."

"Not a bad name, but it doesn't highlight our Amish heritage enough."

"The point is that I feel like we're living next door to a menagerie of animals."

"Up, Aden. Up."

Adrian scooped Nicole from Grace's hold, held her high above his head, then nuzzled her neck. Adrian was comfortable with everyone and everything.

"Do you think she'll ever learn to say my name right?"

"Possibly. Can you please catch Kendrick and take him back to your place?"

"Of course. That's why I came over. I guess I must have left the gate open again." He kissed Nicole's cheek, then popped her back into Grace's arms. "You should bring her over to see the turtles."

As he walked away, Grace wondered for the hundredth time why he wasn't married. It was true that he'd picked a strange profession. What other Amish man raised exotic animals? No, Adrian wouldn't be considered excellent marrying material by most young Amish women.

Don't miss
The Baby Next Door *by Vannetta Chapman,*
available April 2021 wherever
Love Inspired books and ebooks are sold.

LoveInspired.com

LIEXP0321

LOVE INSPIRED

INSPIRATIONAL ROMANCE

UPLIFTING STORIES OF FAITH, FORGIVENESS AND HOPE.

Join our social communities to connect with other readers who share your love!

Sign up for the Love Inspired newsletter at **LoveInspired.com** to be the first to find out about upcoming titles, special promotions and exclusive content.

CONNECT WITH US AT:

Facebook.com/LoveInspiredBooks

Twitter.com/LoveInspiredBks

Facebook.com/groups/HarlequinConnection